Dragonstorm

Graham Edwards was born in Shepton Mallett, Somerset, in 1965, and brought up in Bournemouth. He attended art school in London and now works as a design studio manager. He lives in Nottingham with his wife Helen and their two children. *Dragonstorm* is his second novel.

'A story about dragons, with an unusual twist in that it's written entirely from the dragons' point of view . . . a novel with a difference. The characterization is excellent . . . *Dragoncharm* is a strangely compelling story and a must for all dragon fans.'   *Starburst* on *Dragoncharm*

Voyager

GRAHAM EDWARDS

Dragonstorm

HarperCollins*Publishers*

Voyager
An Imprint of HarperCollins*Publishers*
77–85 Fulham Palace Road,
Hammersmith, London W6 8JB

A Paperback Original 1996
3 5 7 9 8 6 4 2

Copyright © Graham Edwards 1996

The Author asserts the moral right to
be identified as the author of this work

A catalogue record for this book
is available from the British Library

ISBN 0 000 648022 5

Set in Meridien by
Rowland Phototypesetting Ltd,
Bury St Edmunds, Suffolk

Printed in Great Britain by
Caledonian International
Book Manufacturer Ltd, Glasgow

For P.D.E.

PROLOGUE

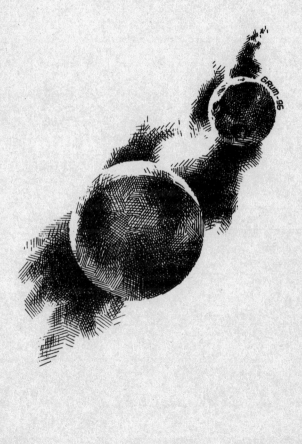

THE BASILISK RAISED A CLAW and the world vanished.

Silver eyes reflected space. Stars turned past and were caught in their deadly shine. With its stare the basilisk drank the blackness of the cosmos and contemplated the world it had just obliterated. The turned world.

It lowered its claw and the world reappeared.

So small, that with a single gesture I might blot it out.

The basilisk was far away, far enough to be able to hide the smooth arc of the world behind that single upraised claw. This it did over and over, first lifting its arm to conceal the distant globe then lowering it to reveal the view again. The basilisk had to admit that of all the vistas over which it had gazed in its infinite life, this was the only one of which it had never grown tired. The view was ... magnificent!

A black disc against a spectacular shower of distant stars, its upper edge blazing orange and white with the scattered light of the rising sun. The sun soaring up from behind a glowing crescent, throwing filaments of light across the upper atmosphere and revealing the essential solidity of the planet, its rays snaking out, touching cloud and filling out the flatness of the eclipse. Dawn charging over the world, bringing it life and warmth and hope.

Hope? For the basilisk?

It floated nearer, this ancient creature, this being which bore the greatest of curses. As it approached, the basilisk moved up over the swell of the planet until it looked directly down upon the sunlit face. Oceans sparkled; lands pressed up against broken cloud. The world shone, it sang, it *lived*.

I am older than this world will ever be, yet I can never shine as this world does now. Though I exist, I will never live as it does. This is the curse from which there is no release. The curse of immortality.

Suddenly sickened by the beauty of the planet, the basilisk turned away from the light and rolled nightwards until it fell into shadow. Here the world was flat and dark, the sun eclipsed again. Lightning flashed in the night, silent explosions of energy flickering like sparks in some great, black eye. Here the basilisk found its vision of the present blurring with visions of the past, many of them. Other darknesses loomed, other storms surged, other worlds turned . . .

So many memories.

The basilisk had used countless tricks to try to suppress the massive reservoir of memories which had built up relentlessly over the ages, but none had met with any success. Nothing, not even the strongest charm, could dull the cacophony inside its mind. An immortal mind brought infinite memory, and brought its bearer many times to the brink of insanity by the sheer weight of recollection.

Such a curse this state of being, its torture even worse now than when first the basilisks had been created. Then immortality had seemed a boon and the infinity of memory they already possessed a treasury which might be plundered over and over without ever depleting its vast store of wonders.

Created? Yes, there was a point in time when the six basilisks were created, but as they themselves knew so well, this did not mean that before that event they had not existed. No paradox this, for at the instant they came to be so their past came to be too, and it was a past in which they had always lived. Immortal; sexless; infinitely old. The six basilisks.

The Deathless.

As they had always done the memories seethed in the basilisk's mind. Lives and deaths, and none of the deaths that death for which it yearned – its own; creatures forming, creatures evolving, creatures falling from existence; worlds rising, turning, falling; charm, and its fall. So many moments were stored here now that it could see none of them clearly,

4

and this was in many ways its greatest agony; they blurred like single droplets of water lost in the immensity of the ocean. Or such had been the case up until now . . .

Controlling the self-loathing, drifting slowly through the darkness in the lee of the world, this deathless creature pondered the events of the Turning which had brought at least a little clarity to the turmoil of its senses.

And perhaps, somewhere near what passed for its heart, a little hope?

The dragons had come to the Plated Mountain. That in itself had been of little consequence, but when they had started to involve themselves in the events leading up to the Turning and finally even influenced those events, then the basilisk had been forced to wake from its long sleep and take note. As these curious, resilient dragons had moved through the world so the world had turned, and in the death throes of charm the Maze of Covamere itself had been destroyed, the very Maze which had held this world and others in the mesh of magic which had also been the fabric of the cosmos. Now new forces were taking over, and a new fabric. Natural forces. Gone was charm, and gone was the Maze.

Gone, but not forgotten.

The basilisk had been there at the end. The Maze had become a pathetic, shrunken thing, spinning in the void it had left in its place, its tattered web contracting towards oblivion. Knowing of no way to save it, nor of any reason to try, feeling like nothing but a predatory beast, the basilisk had opened its jaws and consumed those sad remains with a single, titanic gulp. A curious supper, even for one of the Deathless.

And the result? At first the basilisk had been horrified, for the Maze held a store of memories rich enough to rival its own. But gradually the truth of what had happened dawned on it, for now there was a new light in its mind which shone out bright and clear, separating certain of those memories from the dull melange of the rest. The residue of the Maze acted like a beacon, illuminating moments which had been lost to the basilisk for millennia.

Not least of these was the revelation of its name. The

return of that simple knowledge – long since lost – swept through it like an icy flood, bringing with it echoes of old emotions, old ambitions, and for the first time in an age of ages the ability to think of itself as more than just an ancient, deathless husk with no task in the world but to sleep and sleep until time itself had come to an end.

Ocher! My name is Ocher!

It remembered its name, and of all the things it remembered now and later, it was that sudden recollection which it would come to regard as the starting point of all that was to follow.

In fact, it all seemed to come down to names in the end, for as well as its own the basilisk found itself able to remember those of its erstwhile companions – the other five of the Deathless. It clung to their resurrected images with a fanaticism it was powerless to quell. *The others: Bacht. Mediel. Veil. Tellere. Geiss.*

These basilisk names echoed through its mind like a continual call to action. At first Ocher felt no desire to respond to their urging, but gradually the coldness of space soothed its anger at having lived through yet another Turning, at having passed up a possible chance to end its own existence. It decided not to return to sleep. As it reflected on those recent events, it was forced to conclude that even had it tipped the Turning out of true, still it would in all likelihood have survived whatever cataclysm might have resulted. The realization was a bitter fruit, for it was yet another reminder of the infinite future which leered at it through the mists of time. And it was that more than anything which urged it to seek the one thing which had so far eluded it: death. Escape. An end to the eternity.

Bacht. Mediel. Veil. Tellere. Geiss.

Could they help? *Would* they help?

Can they help me to die? Can it be that we might all *die together, reunited at last, at the end?*

Perhaps. The more Ocher pondered, and especially now as it circled the planet, casting its silver gaze down across the continents, the more it believed that the escape it sought so desperately could come only from basilisk claws. The world could not bring it; not even the power of a Turning could bring it. And the dragons could surely never bring it. But the Deathless could.

Here, at this thought, Ocher did something it rarely did: it shuddered. The urging of the basilisk names was strong, but there was something else which had given it an even greater motive to enter oblivion, and if possible to take the other basilisks with it. Something to do with these dragons. And it too had a name: *bringer-of-shadow*.

Wraith it had been who had so nearly unleashed that hideous power. The Black Dragon, one of the more memorable of those flimsy creatures who roamed the skies and dug into the rock. Old powers of charm, old legends had locked themselves around Ocher and Wraith, drawing them together until their bodies had fused into a single organism.

Almost.

Revolted by its own subjugation, horrified at the prospect of the awesome powers of charm this monstrous hybrid *bringer-of-shadow* would have had at its disposal, the basilisk had resisted the final, total absorption with all its strength. In the end Wraith had perished and Ocher had been flung clear, living still and shaken to the core by what had so nearly happened to it.

Bringer-of-Shadow. Power, certainly, but power so great as to be all-consuming. If *bringer-of-shadow* were ever to be made then it would destroy all it found without consideration. World, cosmos, creation would be swallowed in a single, evil gulp and all that would be left would be *bringer-of-shadow* itself, insane and alone. And still immortal.

Eternity was a hell, but eternity trapped inside a monster was an ordeal to which Ocher would subject neither itself nor any of its kin. But as long as dragons remained in the world the possibility remained that *bringer-of-shadow* would come. That the world would almost inevitably be annihilated in its creation was of little concern to Ocher, but for one of the Deathless to be . . . to be *used* in such a way was utterly intolerable.

Bringer-of-shadow *will not be. Other Wraiths may rise but the Deathless will not be around to meet them. We will be no more.*

* * *

The world turned through the black sky. A rain of dust struck the air and ignited, sending a shower of sparks deep into the twilight as the crescent of dawn raced towards it. A lesser disc rose from behind the brightening globe: the moon, riding high above its parent and gleaming cold and grey in the hard light of the sun.

Many worlds, thought Ocher. *Many hiding places. But I will find them. Soon we shall be Deathless no more.*

Spinning, patterns of light and dark chasing over its skin like duellists locked in eternal combat, the world rolled. Around it rolled the moon, while beyond and beyond turned the stars in their constant dance of light. The moon alone occupied its orbit now; no creature floated in the void. Ocher had gone.

The Gathering had begun.

PART ONE

OUT OF THE EYE

CHAPTER 1

After the Turning

The sea wind was warm and full of salt. Fortune squinted into the driving spray as it crashed against his face, scoring the sensitive skin around his eyes with a thousand tiny abrasions. A scant wing's width beneath him the waves licked hungrily, reaching up towards his speeding body as though trying to drag him under. He laughed, long and loud, lost to all but the moment which surrounded him. Ahead loomed land and the return of all his cares but for now, for just this one instant, he was free.

With a flick of his tawny wingtips, he dragged himself clear of the treacherous waves and climbed briefly towards the open sky. Here the wind still blew hard but the flying was a little easier. As he levelled out again he saw dragons ahead and below, mere dots against infinite shades of blue and green but instantly recognizable nonetheless.

The white dragon was Velvet, her long wings beating hesitantly yet bearing her on through the difficult air with more efficiency than their erratic rhythm suggested. Still awkward and jumpy on the ground, she exhibited a certain quirky elegance in the air, and in flight was now more than a match for most of the other dragons of Haven. She flew low and straight, close to the waves yet above the worst of the spray, leaving the third dragon to dart to and fro above them both, occasionally diving down towards the sea to herd in wayward strands of the shoal, troubleshooting. He was Thaw.

As Fortune watched, Thaw jerked suddenly, opening yellow and black striped wings wide and flat against the warm wind so that his speed dropped almost to nothing. Stalling and twisting, he spun over and tumbled down and back towards where Fortune flew. With a rush of air he was past, his keen smile sharp and hungry as it entered Fortune's vision then vanished again as quickly. He plummeted away, accelerating in sure, controlled tacks until at the last possible breath he pulled his wings in tight and flattened out, skimming the waves and leaving a trail of foam behind him where his tail sliced through the crests. He weaved once, to the left, then soared up again to resume his former position high above his companions.

'Show-off,' muttered Fortune with grudging admiration. Thaw's military background was evident in everything he did and made him a most impressive dragon; when he had been Charmed he must have been formidable indeed. But now he was a Natural.

Now they were all Naturals.

'Fortune! Get ready!' Velvet's cry filtered up through the crash of the surf. Their goal was in sight.

They were already upon the reef, but in these outlying parts it was hidden below the waves. Ahead it broke the surface to form a ragged, circular ring of brilliant coral, and it was towards this ring that the three dragons were speeding with a single, common purpose: food.

The fish which predominated here were large and brightly-coloured, and within a moon of their arrival on the island the dragons of Haven had refined a highly efficient system of fishing. The technique was simple enough and relied on the fact that these fish were particularly sensitive to the light. Any shadow falling across them would cause them to turn away and flee towards lighter waters. Thus a shoal could be herded by any small group of airborne dragons adept enough to keep them moving, and such was their fear of the darkness that even when they reached shallow water the fish did not stop, nor even slow down. If they could be driven fast enough, they would beach themselves in their hundreds, giving the dragons just enough time to swoop in and drag them further inland before they were able to flip themselves back into the sea.

But it only worked in the vicinity of the reef. In the open sea the fish would simply break to the side or turn back on themselves, leading the dragons in a fruitless dance across the water. Near the reef however were many coral channels whose tips just pierced the wave tops. Once herded into one of these channels, the fish had no option but to accelerate through its confines in the hope of escape at the far end. If the dragons had chosen well, the fish would end up wriggling helplessly on a shallow shelf of coral and drowning in the open air.

Rather different to hunting rabbits at South Point, thought Fortune as he raced through the thumping air. Rather different indeed; this was exhilarating!

The waves roared on the coral beach ahead. Velvet flew on low and steady, the broad shadow of her wings keeping the main body of the shoal moving at the necessary speed. Fortune hung back, his own shadow standing guard at the rear to prevent a sudden about-turn, while Thaw ducked and swooped, cutting the shoal off at the occasional breaks in the channel through which they might otherwise have swerved off course and out into open water.

Fortune loitered, judging the distance to the approaching reef, but already he could feel his elation beginning to ebb like an unwelcome tide. As the ring of coral rushed towards him he sensed the approach of other things, of other cares and concerns. Until this instant he had not realized how much he relied upon the sheer physical release of flight to keep himself sane.

Not sane, he thought suddenly. *Awake. Living on Haven is like living in a dream!*

Six moons earlier he had entered that dream; six moons since the dragons had arrived on Haven. Since the turning of the world.

At first all had been relief and rejoicing. Most of the dragons who escaped the war were battle-hardened, strengthened by the terrible experiences they had undergone on the Plated Mountain both before and during its final, cataclysmic eruption. The dragons who landed on the large, golden-beached mass of land which was to become Haven Island, though of all ages and from richly varied backgrounds, were survivors all, yearning for peace and hopeful of a new life in a calmer world. At least, so it was at first . . .

The initial celebrations swiftly gave way to a more sombre mood as dragons realized the magnitude of the devastation which they had so narrowly escaped. Their mourning was not just for friends they had lost but for the thousands of dragons taken both by the war and the Turning itself. Barely one hundred were they now, for all they knew the only survivors of an entire race. Was the world really turning away from dragons; would they yet be wiped from its skin? For many days few dragons moved from the shallow scrapes they had made in which to sleep when they had first arrived, and the cloud which hung over them all was black.

By and by this melancholy mood lifted and it seemed to dragons that the skies were brightening again. Exploratory flights were made out around the island chain, and although in the end it was decided that this first island was by far the most suitable for settling, these early sorties did much to create a new sense of purpose among the colonists. That they would settle here was never in any real doubt: with its warm breezes, golden sands and lush inland vegetation, the Haven archipelago was exactly that – a haven, a tropical world hidden beyond the darkness from which they had so recently emerged.

Haven Island itself was a long oval with a ragged coastline which boasted countless coves and beaches, each as beautiful as its neighbour. The land rose towards the middle of the island but not to any great height, so that most of the land was rich in palms and ferns. Springs abounded, running cool, fresh water out to the sea, filling secret pools and fuelling waterfalls. Food was plentiful, from the fish which were caught out at sea to the shore crabs and the lizards and rodents which lived inland. Each exploratory flight was a revelation, each new discovery a joy, and it was no wonder that no dragon, having arrived here, wanted to leave.

Soon proper nests were made and food caches constructed, and then the first and most important collective decision was made: Haven would have no leader. Too much of what had gone wrong in the past, so dragons now considered, was directly attributable to corrupt leaders, and so instead a leaderless and democratic council was voted in to settle general community affairs and mediate in any disputes. This decision above all, dragons prayed, would surely help to build a more peaceful settlement than many of those which they had left behind. Neither a Wraith nor a Shatter would be tolerated in Haven; here was a chance to begin again, to get it right. Fortune was elected to the council, and Cumber – indeed, they were the first to be chosen, by virtue of their heroic status following the Turning – as well as the impressive Thaw and three others – Quill, Ledra and Rangle. Within nine days of the dragons' arrival at Haven the nascent democracy was firmly in place. By chance, the councillors were split equally between Naturals and ex-Charmed – a happy coincidence.

A warm wind began to blow from the south, banishing the last chill of winter and dragons dared to hope.

But even then all was not well.

When the world had turned, at the instant when charm had left the cosmos, all charmed creatures had been compelled to surrender their magic to the void. No, not even compelled: the magic had been *snatched* from them as winter snatches the life from the trees. Thaw, himself an ex-Charmed, likened it to having all his claws and all his teeth drawn out in a single, agonizing wrench. No natural dragon could ever imagine the trauma of such an experience – all they could offer was sympathy and assistance in coming to terms with a new role in a natural world. They were now counsellors, necessary guides on the journey every ex-Charmed had been forced to take.

And that, for the once-charmed dragons, was hard to accept. Every single ex-Charmed was now, by all the laws by which he or she had ever lived, a cripple, unable to wield magic, unable even to draw fire. The Realm, that distant other-world from which fire charm had originated, had been annihilated by the awesome events of the Turning; even basic earth charms were now almost impossible to manufacture. A little magic remained to be sure, gathered here and there in random pools of energy, but it was hard to find and even harder to wield; this abandoned charm was of little use to dragons more familiar with fire and the spells of the sky. In their old settlements they would have been outcasts, and the last thing many of them needed was the sympathy – however well-meaning – of what they saw as brutish Naturals who were traditionally their inferiors.

Many of them made valiant efforts to come to terms with their losses and cast off their prejudices, and not without success. Councillor Quill was an ex-Charmed and she spoke passionately about the importance of accepting their fate and not dwelling on the past. But Quill was more mature than most, past her middle-years and used to making hard decisions, having presided over Covamere's centre of healing for many years. Despite her prickly exterior she cared deeply about any dragon put in her care; now that included every dragon who lived on Haven. She knew that most of the ex-Charmed would take many years to get over the trauma – if indeed they ever would – and that while many seemed prepared to put their hardships to the backs of their minds and get on with life as best they could, just as many had become bitter. Tensions were growing.

The resulting division was distressing enough to the more peaceable dragons of Haven such as Quill, but at least it was acknowledged. Dragons argued – and occasionally fought – over old prejudices and new agonies, but there was an honesty about the feelings which was somehow good. Arguments were, for the most part, settled by confrontation and angry air was swiftly cleared.

But beneath the choppy surface waters of the infant colony was a far more treacherous current, an undertow which all dragons recognized but none dared speak of. An unspoken fear so profound that it had so far remained unshared.

When the dragons arrived together on Haven, there was among them a single female bearing a fertile egg, although none but she suspected it at the time. That female was Gossamer, and from the egg hatched Aria, her daughter by Fortune. Aria became a symbol of hope, although by the time of her hatching the other colonists had put a great deal of effort into bringing forth any number of eggs which might hatch into a future race of dragons. There was a veritable storm of love-making shortly after the first day of landfall, due partly to the enormous sense of release which all the dragons felt, but also to an unspoken desperation. *We must not be the last of the dragons*, seemed to be the hidden dialogue in many of those passionate, often frantic congresses. *There must be generations beyond ours.*

The passion prevailed for several moons, during which time only Aria was born, and gradually dragons began to suspect that all was not well. The suspicion was so shocking that none even talked of it, save perhaps to a loved one or close friend, nor was the subject raised at any public meeting, large or small. So great was their fear that, although all dragons felt its claws, all kept it hidden deep inside themselves.

The unspoken fear was simply this: that the dragons of Haven were sterile. Hope was fading now that – other than that which had borne Aria – a fertile egg would ever be brought forth again by any dragon. Here, on Haven, unless some new magic could be found, their race would end and dragons would be no more.

And Fortune himself? All these concerns he shared. Yet beneath them all there was another fear. It lurked beneath the busy surface of his mind like the reef beneath the waves.

It's coming back, he would think in the depths of the night, when he could not tell whether he was awake or asleep. *The storm!*

'Now!' bellowed Thaw.

With a tremendous hiss and the rich crackle of scale and surf upon coral, the shoal of fish crashed clear of the sea and slithered up the gently sloping beach. The three dragons descended upon the writhing, silvery mass and pushed and clawed and bullied the doomed creatures further inland. The shoal was enormous, the catch great; even though several hundred fish made it back to safety, still there must have been over a thousand which did not. The noon sun sparkled off their shiny bodies as the dragons, puffing and gasping, alighted next to their prize catch.

'We'll be eating well until the moon turns again, that's for certain,' exclaimed Velvet.

'Aye, that's a fact,' agreed Thaw in his clipped, military way. 'Successful flight, Fortune, you'll agree.'

Fortune nodded, savouring the pressure of the blood in

17

his veins, the pounding of his heart in his ears, the heat in his wings. He clung to the sensations with something akin to desperation, for he knew that as they faded so duller matters would begin to press themselves into his mind; he clung to the *reality*.

'If we can keep them fresh,' he commented, the statement serving only to remind him of the mundane world which awaited him back on Haven Island. Salting the food, storage, suitable rations . . . and of course the next council meeting. Worries.

As if reading his thoughts, Thaw said solemnly, 'There's much to be said at the meeting tonight, Fortune. I hope dragons have thought about what should be done.'

Fortune nodded absently, unaware of what Thaw was driving at, largely because he was still distracted by his own thoughts. He flexed his wings and turned into the brisk, warm wind.

'I'll bring the fetching party,' he began, only to be cut short by Thaw.

'You stay here, Fortune,' said the big ex-Charmed. 'You look all in. I daresay you've a lot on your mind. You and Velvet just make sure these fish don't take off again!'

As Fortune thanked him Thaw struck out across the reef to gather up a group of dragons big enough to carry the mountain of fish back to Haven Island. He watched the big dragon's sure, steady wingbeats and was reminded of Tallow. As soon as he had gone, Velvet turned to Fortune and said,

'Are you all right? You haven't seemed yourself lately, you know, and Cumber's a bit worried about you, too. Is it Hesper and his crowd? Because if it is then don't forget you've got any number of friends ready to stand by you when the time comes, that's for sure.'

When he did not reply, she snuggled up against him, smiling with wide, open eyes and shielding him from the wind.

'Oh, Fortune,' she laughed, 'you spend so much time worrying about the rest of us dragons that I swear you don't have any time for yourself!'

Fortune smiled then, a wry smile, as he scolded himself.

'You're right, Velvet, of course,' he sighed, 'but then you're always right. I shouldn't take it all so seriously, I know.' He hugged her. 'Just keep talking to me like that.'

'You're the first dragon who's ever told me to keep talking!' cried Velvet with glee. 'Not even Cumber says that to me, Fortune; do you really know what you're letting yourself in for? I mean to say, are you sure you want me on at you day and night, never taking breath, not letting you get in a word, not even . . .'

'All right, all right!' laughed Fortune. 'I surrender!'

He looked down at this small, slender female dragon and remarked on how she had matured since they arrived here. Her pairing with Cumber had brought her confidence and while retaining her open innocence she had developed a formidable wit. The youngest of all the dragons of Haven – except Aria of course – she was rapidly becoming one of the most valued, at least in Fortune's eyes.

'Cumber's a lucky dragon,' he chuckled, nudging her wing. 'Come on, let's make a start on these fish.'

The sun was balanced on the clean, western horizon by the time all the fish were gathered and sent to the salting cache. Still the south wind blew, growing humid and sultry now as the evening closed in; the wind threatened bad weather as it had threatened it constantly for ten days now, but still no storm came.

Fortune hovered on its cloying breath, high above Haven Island. He gazed out over the turquoise sea, seeking out the source of the gale.

The storm, he thought presently. *It's coming back.*

CHAPTER 2

Fears Confessed

'Another fish?' giggled Velvet, flapping one of the rainbow-hued creatures right in front of Cumber's upturned snout. For several breaths he managed to keep his composure, but then he could stand her teasing no longer and leaped up, batting her down on to the sand and knocking the fish from her grasp.

'I've eaten far too many fish since we arrived here, as well you know, Velvet,' he growled. 'What are you trying to do – make it even harder for me to fly? I mean to say, what is a dragon supposed to do with wings like these, hmm, tell me that if you please?'

So saying, he stood back and unwrapped his long, white wings from where they had been folded against his flank.

'Well, Fortune,' he sniffed, 'what do you have to say on the matter?'

Fortune relaxed comfortably into Gossamer's embrace and appraised his friend. Once a Charmed, Cumber was now quite definitely a natural dragon. Having spent more time among Naturals than the average charmed dragon, he had actually made a reasonably good job of restructuring his body, especially considering the fact that an erupting volcano had been trying to knock him from the sky at the time, and that the magic had been dying even as he had been wielding it.

Some features he had retained: he was still white – as were Gossamer and Velvet – having taken on the colour as camouflage on the snow-covered mountain. He also still had four legs where all true natural dragons possessed only two, so that his long, tapering wings sprouted from his back rather than being formed from his actual forelimbs; this reluctance to relinquish those extra limbs was common to most of the ex-Charmed of Haven and was the most obvious way to differentiate them from their Natural cousins. His wings had enlarged enormously, for now they were required to act as proper engines of flight rather than just the decorative aids they had been before, and so he had needed to grow large muscles behind his shoulders to work them properly. When Fortune had first met him his scales had been golden and his wings comically small, mere fins on his back, accessories of magic. Now even without charm he was almost as adept as Fortune himself, who along with Velvet was considered to be one of the finest fliers in the air above Haven.

But despite these changes, in all other respects he was still Cumber: his face was the same, his eyes were still sharp and intelligent, his movements still staccato, and his words still tumbled out of his mouth as though they would never stop. Yes, though he was white, even though he was no longer charmed, and even though his scrawny frame was actually beginning to show signs of thickening around the middle, despite all these things he was still Cumber.

'I think,' yawned Fortune lazily, catching Gossamer's eye and smiling, 'that if you ate a few less fish and exercised those wings a bit more often then we might just make a flier out of you yet.'

'The cheek of it!' exclaimed Cumber, lobbing a fish in Fortune's direction. 'Is no one on my side? Gossamer? What about you?'

'I think you should all keep your voices down,' she replied tartly. Abashed, the other three dragons looked past her outstretched wings to the small, folded bundle which lay on the sand between her and Fortune: Aria, sleeping soundly.

'Oops,' whispered Cumber in a voice barely audible. 'Sorry, Gossamer, although I have to say that she'll need to be moved quite soon if none of us is to be late for the council meeting, unless of course you plan to stay here for the rest of the night, or perhaps you're planning on asking the rest of the colony to convene here? Of course, if you really wanted to . . .'

21

Gossamer interrupted him with a light chuckle.

'Oh really, Cumber. For one thing you don't need to whisper – just try not to disturb her – and for another I have no intention of missing the meeting. None of us should, not tonight, isn't that right, Fortune?'

Fortune sighed. The uppermost arc of the sun was still just visible above the glowing horizon, turning the gold of the sand into a broken mosaic in which every grain cast its own long, pale shadow towards them. Here on the northwest of the island they were sheltered from the constant wind, but he was suddenly reminded of its presence. Would it ever blow itself out?

'Gossamer's right.' He got up, taking care not to disturb his daughter, and ambled down towards the shore where the waves were breaking gently on the shallow slope of sand. 'Which brings us back to where we started, doesn't it?'

It had really started several nights before. Gossamer had woken suddenly, her eyes filled with tears. Although the nest she shared with Fortune was built in the lee of a palm-rich patch of hillside, the wind seemed to have pierced the fronds and was gusting against her face with unwelcome ferocity.

'Too long!' she wailed, still half in her dream. 'We've forgotten them for too long!'

Fortune woke then and tried to comfort her, but she would not be consoled. He knew instantly the source of her distress, for these particular tears came regularly, but this time it was different: this time, he recognized, they would have to tackle the problem once and for all.

'Next meeting,' she said the following morning. 'It must be decided then. I have to know what's happened to them.'

'We all do,' reassured Fortune, but the tears in her eyes and the ache in his heart told him that it was for her alone, in the end, that he would do what needed to be done. That same day they talked with Cumber and Velvet and agreed without question that the time had come to search for Brace.

Gossamer's younger brother had left Haven not long after the Turning, taking with him a small group of dragons as he set out on his quest. Scoff had been the only ex-Charmed among them; dear, brave Scoff who had somehow managed to retain his fabulously coloured wings during his enforced transformation from charmed to natural dragon. Tallow, navigator extraordinary, and his lifelong friend Volley had gone too, and the fifth dragon had been Werth, who had introduced them all to the Flight, the core of natural dragons who had subverted Shatter's army shortly before the cataclysm of the Turning. Five dragons on a rescue mission, one with little chance of success but on which many hopes rested, now even more so.

The rescue of the dragons of Aether's Cross.

Those wretched dragons had been imprisoned for well over a moon by the time Brace led his party from Haven back over the sea towards the Heartland. Wraith it was, the Black Dragon, who had purged Aether's Cross of its Natural population, forbidding their slaughter but commanding instead that they be incarcerated deep in the tunnels behind the canyon walls. Despite his many evils, Wraith had retained a certain nobility of purpose until very near the end: he had wished simply to rule, and what use was a ruler without subjects?

'I do not kill,' he had said often. 'I prevail.'

But the canyon collapsed, sealing the prisoners underground, and Brace – himself a native of the Cross – swore an oath that he would return someday and free them, for among those dragons were his and Gossamer's own parents, and indeed all the dragons he had known and loved up until that fateful moment. That oath he swore, and through all the trials which followed he never forgot it. Then at last, with the world turned, he took up its challenge and set out again with his companions across the Heartland.

Six times the moon had turned full since then and still Brace had not returned. Even if he had failed in his quest he surely would have sent word by now.

'Are we decided then?'

Fortune's question floated on the evening air. The others murmured their agreement.

'I hope the council agrees,' said Velvet uncertainly.

23

'Well,' sighed Fortune, 'I'll go anyway, but there's no reason why they shouldn't endorse the decision. I'm sure Thaw will be behind us and we all know Quill's view on the matter.'

'What about the others?'

'Rangle will probably back it,' interjected Cumber with a shrug. 'I'm not sure about Ledra – you can never quite predict what she's going to do next at the best of times, let alone at a council meeting.'

'They'll be outvoted anyway,' said Gossamer sharply. 'Four against two.'

'All that's left is to decide who else is to go,' concluded Fortune. 'I have my own ideas but . . . I think that's best left for the council proper to decide.' He gave Gossamer a hopeful smile. 'Happy now?' he asked.

'I will be,' she replied in a quiet voice. 'When they're found.'

'Does anyone want this last fish?' announced Cumber suddenly, to Velvet's exasperation.

'Really, Cumber!' she exclaimed, slapping him on the flank with the tip of her wing. 'This is no time to be thinking about your stomach. I've half a mind to tell you just what to do with that fish!' She stopped abruptly, suddenly aware that Gossamer was laughing.

'It's all right,' she chuckled, gathering Aria up on to her back. She nudged the infant half-awake as she did so, just enough to prompt her to grip her dorsal scales with tiny claws. 'Come on, let's get going – it's nearly time.'

'You know,' mused Cumber as they ambled off up the beach. 'Of all the charms I used to wield, I think it's only the cooking I really miss. What I wouldn't give for a good fire and fish that's roasted instead of raw!'

'Maybe there's a way to make fire without charm,' suggested Velvet, pressing close against the dragon she loved as they walked together into the shade of the palms. 'You know, like lightning does sometimes.'

'Don't be silly,' scoffed Cumber. 'Fire without charm? It's impossible.'

*   *   *

The council platform was situated at the centre of Haven Island. Here a rising dome of land emerged from the palm fringe, its steep slopes overgrown with spare moorland grass almost as far as its flattened peak, whereupon the hard rock of which it was built finally punched through the soil to form a parade of ridges and boulders which ran from north to south like a crest across a dragon's head.

Ever had rocky places been centres for gathering dragons. From formations such as the Sink, the meeting place of ill-fated South Point, to the very caverns of the Charmed themselves, those deep, underground chambers long devoted to wisdom and parliament – and unfortunately, in the end, to madness – such places had always been held in high regard by dragons the world over. The very solidity of the rock, its permanence in a shifting world, brought necessary weight to both council meeting and common debate in almost every dragon settlement. Haven was no exception.

The sky floated behind a close, purple haze. The last red of the sunset cast a fading glow across the backs of the dragons congregating at the top of the hill. They jostled and laughed, flurrying from one rock outcrop to the next as they gradually met up with friends and settled themselves into familiar groups, until slowly the rippling sea of horns and wings and flicking tails quietened to become a lake as still as night. The conversation continued, but muted now and a trifle uneasy, as though spirits initially high had sunk along with the vanished sun.

First on to the broad plate of rock which was the council dais were Quill and Thaw. Both ex-Charmed, they ascended the rough steps to their appointed places with the same easy grace. Thaw stood courteously, his striped wings neatly folded, while orange-scaled Quill settled herself at the far end of the dais, then he too lay comfortably on the smooth rock platform to await the others. As they waited they smiled and nodded to faces they recognized in the crowd, and occasionally exchanged a whispered word between themselves.

Ledra came next, flying in from her nest on the east side of the island and landing with a flurry on the platform. Designed for maximum effect, her arrival impressed at least the small group of young dragons who pressed at the front of the crowd, gazing up adoringly at her as she preened and acknowledged their presence with a demure smile. Rolling her tightly muscled Natural shoulders with deliberate sensuality she lounged down next to Thaw, who murmured something unheard to Quill.

'Am I late?' the crowd heard her ask, her voice deep and rich.

'You are not,' responded Thaw coolly.

'Makes a change,' muttered Quill.

Ledra looked disappointed. She preferred to be last on the platform: it allowed her to make more of an entrance. She inspected her claws petulantly, glancing up only occasionally to smile graciously at one of her fans.

The restless buzz of the crowd grew louder for a while, then suddenly quietened as two more dragon shapes appeared in the sky behind the dais. They grew larger, stroking the dusk with long and easy wings, and as Velvet and Gossamer squeezed their way towards the front of the crowd so Fortune and Cumber flew in to take up their places on the dragon council of Haven.

As the two friends coasted in to land, many of the watching dragons hissed appreciatively, a quiet signal that they had not forgotten the heroism which these dragons had displayed during the terrible days of the Turning. Some even saluted with upraised wings, although not nearly as many as had done so during the early days. It was not without some pleasure that Fortune noted this latter fact: these days he found the pressures of his council duties almost overwhelming, especially when what he most wanted to do was be with his beloved Gossamer and little Aria, and it was encouraging to see that the adulation with which many dragons had showered him to begin with was at last wearing off. Perhaps soon he would get some time to himself. Everything seemed such a blur these days . . .

Cumber for his part quite enjoyed the attention, and grinned and nodded as he tucked his wings away. But Fortune had only ever found it embarrassing to be thus hailed, so hard was it for him to accept this role of hero; as far as he was concerned, the sooner they all forgot, the better. After all, was he not still just a dragon?

As he thought this he caught Gossamer's eye and knew that she understood his discomfort. She flashed him a sympathetic smile.

Let them love you, it seemed to say, *at least for a little while longer. The novelty will wear off soon enough, and then you can get on with being an ordinary dragon again.*

Such words she had spoken to him on many a night of anguish, when he had ranted about the pressures he felt to be pulling him apart.

'This is a beginning,' she would soothe him, 'it is bound to be hard. But we have to get it right this time, so that future generations will not suffer what we have had to suffer.' And so saying she would point to their daughter. 'Do it for these dragons who still love you so much,' she would conclude, 'but do it for us too. For Aria. *She* is the future.'

He nodded to her now, letting her know that he had heard her unspoken words. She bent her head forward, just a little, so that he could see Aria, still fast asleep on her back. He felt at least some of the weight shift aside. The crowd buzzed again, then relaxed into silence as finally he stood forward from his four companions and opened his mouth to speak.

'May I . . .' he began, but he got no further. In the crowd behind Gossamer a pair of rough, tan-coloured wings bustled dragons aside and a hoarse voice cried,

'Let me through, please, I'm a councillor! Let me through there! Thank you. Oops, excuse me. Yes, thank you . . .'

'In your own time, Rangle,' sighed Fortune as this scruffy Natural clambered up the steep side of the dais, stepping on the wings and tails of several dragons as he did so, and threw himself, apparently exhausted, to the ground beside Cumber.

'Sorry I'm late,' he coughed. 'But you see . . .'

'Thank you, Rangle,' hissed Quill. 'Fortune?'

'Yes, thank you, Rangle,' Fortune continued. 'Now, where was I?'

The early part of the meeting consisted largely of formalities: those present on the council were named and welcomed, and the decisions made at the previous meeting were restated and seconded. The only outstanding item of significance concerned an argument between two dragons over territorial rights to a particularly splendid stretch of beach, but the individuals concerned had since managed to reach an amicable agreement without the help of the council.

The sky had turned deathly black by the time Fortune stood and called for new items of business. As he stood back again to wait, the warm wind which had blown through Haven for the past ten days found its way to the hilltop and whipped the palms into life. Several dragons flinched, as though an uninvited stranger had descended into their midst. Fortune glanced at Cumber, who shrugged and whispered, 'You might as well start, Fortune.'

Fortune nodded. 'I would like to raise the first item myself,' he said. As he spoke, the audience tensed, catching its collective breath. There was an unmistakable air of anticipation. What was making them so restless? 'As you know, six moons ago a small group of our comrades set out for the Heartland. They have not returned. I wish to propose that we assemble a search party and go after them, and if necessary, complete their mission. I welcome any discussion on the matter.'

He sat down and cast his eyes across the crowd. They were visibly disappointed, as though this was not the issue they had expected him to raise. A few of them exchanged puzzled glances and whispered words, but before any of the dragons in the audience could reply, Thaw rose to speak. Silence awaited his words. It was Haven's large contingent of ex-Charmed warrior dragons had voted Thaw to council. One of Wraith's more senior commanders, Thaw had broken from his legion early on in the battle and led a small platoon up the mountainside to safety. Strong and reliable, with a fearsome intellect, he was greatly respected by all those who followed him, and indeed by many of those who did not.

'Thank you, Fortune, for reminding us of this matter, which too many of us have allowed to slip to the backs of our minds. I for my part welcome the idea of preparing a rescue for Brace and his companions, although we must first consider carefully how many dragons we can spare from our small community. After all, what are we to do if this rescue party does not return either?'

There were murmurs of agreement in the congregation and all eyes turned back to Fortune. But before he could speak Ledra stood dramatically, tossing her head and half-spreading her pale green wings.

'I am sure I speak for many dragons here,' she proclaimed, throwing her words to the back of the crowd but reserving her gaze for her eager followers, 'when I say this is a foolish notion. I suppose a dragon such as Fortune might want to go on such a hopeless journey, but I fail to see why any of us others should be dragged along. We are united now, and must not be divided again.' As she concluded her impassioned plea, she flashed a seductive smile at the current favourite among her crop of devotees.

'And we all know what "united" means,' muttered Quill in a voice just loud enough to raise a few chuckles from the dragons in the front row of the crowd. Ledra scowled at the older female dragon and sat down smartly in her place. The laughter released some of the tension in the audience and a few voices started to call out from the ranks.

'It's a praiseworthy idea, but Thaw's right – we can't spare enough dragons to go.'

'We're few enough as it is without losing any more.'

'It's such a long way from here, and they're probably dead anyway.'

At this last call Fortune lunged forward again. He could clearly see the hurt in Gossamer's face and resolved that if he achieved nothing else tonight he would get this proposal accepted. He prowled the dais, his voice thundering out across the sea of faces with unexpected anger. Dragons flinched, surprised at his vehemence.

'Yes, there are few of us now, and that is exactly why we *must* go! Think about it, all you dragons, think about it for more than just a breath and you will see that I am right!' He paused, frowning. 'It seems to me that we have all been anticipating a difficult meeting tonight, but for different reasons. For my part, I confess that this matter of Brace's absence is burning brightest in my mind, but . . . am I right in thinking there is something else which burns even brighter for most of you?' Here he caught Thaw's eye, remembering something the big warrior had said earlier . . .

There's much to be said at the meeting tonight, Fortune. I hope dragons have thought about what should be done.

. . . and then it was that he realized what Thaw had meant. It came to him with blinding insight and for a moment he could not catch his breath.

'I'm sorry,' he gulped. 'I know many of you don't want to hear about Brace and Aether's Cross but believe me when I say that you cannot separate the two issues: my fear for the trapped dragons, and the other fear – the fear we all share.' He took another deep breath. 'The fear that we as a race are sterile!'

The crowd hissed again, this time with surprise. Heated discussions and protests broke out at once, heads were raised, dragons jumped and opened eyes wide. At last a dragon had dared to speak the horrifying words in public: the prospect of an end to the dragon race here on Haven. That, old and infertile, they would be the last of the dragons!

Fortune waited for the hubbub to die down again, absorbing the unexpected strength of the reaction, the emotional rush of the moment. Clearly the time had come to bring this fear out into the open.

'Listen to me please, and trust me in what I am about to say,' he continued, his anger quite gone now, replaced by an urgent desire to communicate the argument he felt building itself in his head. 'Admitting our fear is only the first stroke of the wing on an even more difficult flight. It is extinction that we fear, that and simple loss of honour; we fear that our race will have no inheritance, no future. The time has come to talk about it, but before we do we must all understand that the fate of Brace and his company is bound up with this terror which we all share yet which until now none of us has dared to express.

'Let me explain, and to begin with let us be hopeful. We have no evidence that the infertility is permanent. It may be a phase, a kind of aftershock following the Turning. Time may reveal things to us which we cannot yet imagine. And there is Aria – she at least is proof that not all hope is lost. Hope! Yes, we are only one hundred dragons and, yes, we cannot see a future for our race, but if it is hope that we seek then what better place to look than Aether's Cross? There the Black Dragon imprisoned an entire dragon community, perhaps five hundred dragons in all. If they can be freed then what new hope would that be for us? Our numbers would swell fivefold. *And those dragons may not be sterile!*

'Think about it, dragons, I beg you. I freely admit that Brace and his mission are especially near to my own heart. But these dragons of Aether's Cross, should they not be close to *all* our hearts? Should we not try every means at our disposal to give them their liberty? They are our fellows; they are *dragons*! They deserve our help.'

Stars bristled across the rich ebony of the sky and the wind whistled through the palm leaves. All else was still. Fortune waited, breathing hard in anticipation of the crowd's reaction to his words.

The furthest ranks of the assembly suddenly shook. Dragons parted clumsily, cursing and throwing their wings out for balance. Fortune and the other council members stretched their necks in an attempt to see what was causing the commotion, although they all had a good idea what it was. A split opened up in the audience as a group of some fifteen dragons shouldered their way through and marched towards the dais, at their head a thick-set individual with a low, horny brow and a tail fully as thick as Fortune's body.

'Fine words, little dragon!' he boomed as he barged his way through the protesting congregation. 'But not much use when the dragons you speak of are more than likely dead, eh?'

'Oh no,' groaned Cumber, 'it's Hesper.'

CHAPTER 3

Council

He seemed to sway a little, his thick body off-balance as though he had eaten some intoxicating leaf, which he probably had. Ex-Charmed like all his followers, Hesper had retained much of the body armour which his position in Wraith's army had required him to bear, despite the disadvantage the extra weight gave him now he was effectively a Natural. Grey spikes and plates still sprang from his back and sides; of all the dragons of Haven he was the most warlike. Despite his aggressive appearance however, few dragons seemed actually to fear Hesper, regarding him more as a nuisance than as a threat. Just as few realized how much this infuriated him.

Hesper bore a grudge. Though he had dreamed of glory and valour he had never received a posting more noteworthy than mere sentry at one of the lesser gateways into Covamere. Twenty years in the same lowly rank had seen him grow jealous of his more capable comrades and his mind, always angry with a world which he saw as his enemy, had twisted into a cast of envy and bitterness. By virtue of his physical bulk and a tendency to bully, he was able to dominate certain of his subordinates, but in this dragon's head it was ever himself against the world. The elections on Haven had done nothing to change this.

Several dragons had stood for election to the council and failed to gain enough votes; of these, most had withdrawn gracefully. Most. However, one in particular had never been content with the rejection he had suffered: Hesper.

He could not believe some of the decisions. Ledra, for example – a controversial choice if ever there was one. In general she was not well-liked; however, by the time of the election she had managed to gather around her a group of followers large enough to provide her with the requisite number of votes. Elegant and alluring, she appealed to the young dragons – both Natural and ex-Charmed – who had loitered at the periphery of the battle and found themselves swept up the mountain more by luck than bravery. Still a little lost and afraid, these dragons needed a charismatic role-model to look up to; Ledra, to Hesper's dismay, was it.

And then there was Rangle. He was old and scatter-brained, although possessed of a remarkable ability to see through to the heart of a problem where other dragons could see only confusion. Many laughed at his crotchety temper and his shaking wings, but he was valued nonetheless, especially when there were difficult issues to be resolved. For him, Hesper felt nothing but scorn.

One vote alone had separated Hesper from Rangle, the least popular by vote of the chosen six. One vote, one dragon's choice had denied Hesper what he felt to be rightfully his. Like Ledra, he had his own tightly-knit band of followers who would, he was confident, support him in any way he asked, but their numbers had not been quite sufficient.

So Hesper was not chosen; he was forced to find another way.

'So,' he drawled, his voice surprisingly high-pitched for so large a dragon, 'you've made all your decisions without me then, as usual?'

'We have made no decisions, Hesper,' snapped Thaw. 'And your voice is as welcome here as any.'

'So kind. If only I believed you.' Hesper smiled suddenly, displaying a row of chipped teeth. 'Do I gather that we are concerned about eggs here? About barren females? About finding a way to drag our race back up from the point of extinction?'

'You would do well to consider that a male dragon may be just as barren as a female,' growled Quill, her dislike for Hesper quite apparent. The crowd murmured its approval of this rebuke and Hesper conceded the point by bowing his head.

'A subject for future debate, perhaps,' he acknowledged. 'So, what does our learned council suggest we do about the problem?'

'I am afraid there is little we can do,' answered Fortune, speaking as much to the crowd as to Hesper. He was angry at this disruption of what could become a crucial discussion and determined that Hesper should not bring his own agenda to the meeting. 'But I suppose your opinion is as welcome as any dragon's, if you wish to speak it.'

Hesper swayed to the left, his eyes clouding, then recovered himself and sneered.

'Oh yes,' he cried, his voice suddenly loud. 'Very gracious of Fortune to allow me to speak, very gracious indeed! Free to speak, am I? Then speak I will, and you'd better all listen well!'

Some of the dragons in the crowd began to mutter among themselves, clearly unimpressed with Hesper's swagger and increasingly irritated by his presence here at all. As Fortune looked on, heads turned away from the dais to face this unwelcome intruder; the open space in which Hesper and his gang stood began to shrink as dragons closed in. The gang members huddled together, whispering to each other and casting eyes greedy for action into the approaching throng. All of a sudden a confrontation was looming and the air thickened with the prospect of violence.

'Stop!' Fortune shouted. He exchanged a glance with Thaw and they leaped side by side into the clearing, sweeping their wings around wide so as to force the crowd back. Reluctantly the dragons retreated and the gang members relaxed a little. Hesper met Fortune's eye and smiled.

'So kind,' he said with a parody of a bow. 'Please carry on with your meeting; I have no wish to interrupt.' So saying he gestured his followers to settle down close to him in the centre of the crowd.

The debate restarted and dragons began to discuss their mortality. Passions suppressed for too long released themselves that night as dragons spilt their fears into the darkness. Many wept as they spoke of the futility they felt to have descended upon them all. Ex-Charmed mourned the loss of magic, while Naturals mourned simply for the infants they felt they would never have. The councillors listened gravely and noted each point as it was made, until finally Fortune was called upon to speak again. The crescent moon lifted over the palms and brought a silvery glow to the hilltop, and as he spoke the wind swirled up from the southern slopes and whistled behind his voice like an idiot echo.

'It is clear,' he began, 'that none of us has a solution for this problem – if it is indeed a problem and does not resolve itself of its own accord. Let us at least be glad that we can speak of it at last; if nothing else, tonight has allowed us to do that. As for policy, the council will now decide on the practicality of the proposed rescue mission, which may or may not have bearing on our greater needs. I for one believe it does.'

Here the wind gusted afresh and cut through his words like spread claws. The moonlight glinted off the distant ocean, its faint glow catching the underside of a great mass of cloud which was slowly stacking itself on the horizon.

'You see, there may not be much time,' he went on, the suddenly dreamy tone of his voice causing several dragons to exchange quizzical glances. 'This wind,' and as he spoke now he paced restlessly up and down the platform, 'it doesn't seem right to me. I am afraid of many things, but most of all I am afraid that it isn't over yet.'

'Go on, Fortune,' rumbled Thaw before the crowd's obvious confusion distracted the young Natural. 'Tell us what you fear. You are among friends.'

Fortune looked down at Gossamer. Her slim face was barely visible to him in the dim light yet he saw her love for him blazing out from it like a sun, and it was that alone which brought the words for which he searched.

'Many of us have said that the Turning was like a storm,' he continued, 'the greatest storm the world has ever seen. We all survived that storm and for that we must give thanks to whatever power it is that moves such things.

'But it wasn't just a storm, was it? It was a hurricane! It wiped out thousands of dragons; it destroyed the land; it killed charm. It swept across the world, picked us up in its frenzy and deposited us here. Here at the eye of the hurricane, where all is quiet, all is peaceful until . . . until the eye passes and the hurricane returns.

'It's coming back, dragons. The storm is returning.'

There was a hush then as dragons tried to understand what he was saying, until suddenly an unexpected voice rang out in agreement. 'Quite right!' exclaimed Hesper. 'That's the first intelligent thing you've said since you got here, dragon!'

He was shouted down almost at once but Fortune protested reluctantly that Hesper be permitted to speak, which the truculent dragon duly did.

'The eye of the hurricane,' Hesper mused, rolling the words around his mouth as though tasting some exotic food. 'Well, yes, I believe our young friend has got it right for once. And shall I tell you why? I shall: I have evidence that it's not all over, and that more than just a storm is on its way back again. Oh yes, much more than that.'

Hesper's voice boomed out and he began to swagger and sway again. Clearly revelling in his oration he licked his lips and pressed on with renewed gusto. 'But before I tell you about that, my fine dragons, let me share a little secret with you. You see, very soon this splendid council of dragons will be no more. Democracy is all very well, votes are all very well, but how can dragons ever get anything done if everything must go to a committee? Isn't it better to elect a leader, like dragons did in the old days? Give him advisors if you must, but just give one dragon the power to rule. Do it . . . or else. Oh, don't take this as a threat, I beg you, rather take it as . . . a prediction. It is simply the way of things. The future's going to be grim for any dragon who doesn't make the right choices now about who he's going to follow, or what he really believes.

'What's Hesper going on about? you may ask. And what's this evidence he promised? Well may you ask, dragons. I'll tell – no, better still, I'll *show* you. I'll demonstrate to you here and now that it's not just the Turning, not just a storm or what dear dragon Fortune so whimsically chooses to call a hurricane that's descending on us again. Oh no, it's much more than that.

'It's the magic – the *charm* is coming back!'

Hesper grew more and more agitated as he spoke. Dragons were pulling away from him in fear that he might actually lash out and injure them. As he ended with a great flourish of his grey wings he looked around to find himself again in the middle of a space in the crowd.

'Perfect!' he cheered, and into the air he sprang.

Wings billowing, breath steaming, he opened his mouth wide and belched a long jet of orange flame straight down on to the patch of earth where he had just been standing. The nearest dragons swore and scrambled back in panic as Hesper's fire lit up the hillside with its fierce glow. At the same time a gasp of awe rose from the ranks of the ex-Charmed, rapidly followed by a mounting excitement. Here again was the fire charm they thought they had lost! Several dragons surged forward against their retreating neighbours and a few minor scuffles broke out. Over the din Fortune, Thaw, Cumber and Quill cried out, trying to calm the crowd, but to little avail.

The air crackled with light as jagged filaments of charm lanced between Hesper's body and the ground, but before long the magic was spent and he dropped to earth again, panting. The more attentive of those who were watching noted that it was sheer muscle-power that had held him in the air during his display: he might have rediscovered the magic of fire but evidently the miracle of effortless flight still eluded him.

'Well, dragons?' Hesper gasped, eager to sustain the momentum he had generated. 'Do you want the fire or not? The charm is there for any dragon to take; just ask me and I'll show you how.'

His words were clearly directed only at the ex-Charmed among the crowd, and it was this more than anything that enraged Cumber to the point that he marched to the front of the council dais and shouted,

'Don't listen to him, any of you dragons! He hasn't found any secret fire and the charm isn't going to come back. Any one of us could use some pool of abandoned charm to produce a few sparks, just to impress the gullible. But that's no more real charm than a drop of dew is an ocean. And we all know who Hesper would see elected as leader, don't we? Hesper! In charge of dragons? It's a joke, nothing more, just like the fire is a joke.'

'Cumber's right,' Fortune went on smoothly before his friend got too beside himself. His anger was useful – indeed, many of the ex-Charmed whose eyes had lit up at the sight of the fire charm were now nodding in grudging agreement with his words – but Hesper needed to be embarrassed, not attacked. 'Hesper is perhaps well-meaning but surely misguided. Charm *has* left the world – Mantle would confirm that were he here, as would great Halcyon, the last years of whose life were devoted to finding a way to ease its departure. As for your notions of government, Hesper, your proposal is noted. If the council votes in favour of such a motion, rest assured that you will be the first to know.'

The snub was elegant and effective, and Hesper recoiled with an angry hiss. He whirled round, staring wildly into the crowd, but saw only hostile or disinterested faces gazing back at him. The support he had hoped to raise had failed to materialize and even his own mob was stirring restlessly, keen to be gone from this hostile assembly. Kicking furiously at the scorched earth beneath his claws he marched up to the foot of the dais and glared straight at Fortune.

'Don't think you've beaten me, young Natural,' he spat. 'The charm may be scattered but it's still there all right, and I know ways of hunting it down just like you hunt your precious fish. Take heed of your own warnings, because the storm is coming again, oh yes, and it'll blow you and your council to the crest of the world before it rips you into pieces. It's *my* storm, dragon. Remember that!'

With that, Hesper rallied his gang around him and together they flew off into the night. They were visible for some time, a pattern of dark dragon shapes against the starlit sky, heading north and entirely away from Haven Island. They slipped in front of the slender moon, tracking a course across the darkness until finally they flew low behind the reaching palms and were gone.

It was Rangle who stood forward and called the broken meeting back to order, old, wrinkled Rangle, who had said nothing during Hesper's exhibition – who had so far contributed nothing at all to the assembly. He lurched forward on trembling wings and cleared his throat.

'There is business to be concluded here, dragons,' he croaked, 'and we should not lose sight of that. I do not believe my colleagues will contradict me when I say that an expedition *shall* go in pursuit of Brace. All that remains is to decide which dragons are to go, which I suggest we discuss immediately, before anything else happens to disrupt our council!'

He finished with a dry chuckle and motioned Fortune forward again. The young dragon nodded his appreciation of his elder's brief but well-judged intercession and took the dais once more. As he did so it seemed to him that his body and voice were operating automatically and that his heart had abandoned the discussions altogether. It was settled; the rest of it was just formality. Yet again he caught Gossamer's eye and saw a tear shining there in the pale moonlight, while on her back Aria breathed softly, oblivious to all that was going on around her. In that instant he decided that he would not go.

It had always been an unspoken assumption between himself and Gossamer that he would be the one to lead the search party, whether it went with or without the blessing of the council. After all, he knew Brace, he knew the terrain, and he was surely too involved not to go. But now that the moment had come he found that he did not want to leave Haven. Though part of him yearned to be free of responsibility again, to abandon this dreamlike place and fly out on some new adventure, yet a greater part could not bear the thought of leaving Gossamer again, nor Aria at all.

Haven is about starting afresh, about building the world we truly want to live in, so should that not be true of me as well?

But if not him, then who?

'We could debate long over the wisdom of sending a councillor on such a mission,' rumbled Thaw, taking over from Fortune as his young colleague faltered, 'but I feel I must take the lead here. This journey is likely to present unlooked-for hazards. That none of Brace's party has returned suggests that there may be great danger in the Heartland or in the mountains beyond. Tonight's discussion has reminded me for one of our mortality . . . and so I put up my own name to lead the expedition. Are there any objections?'

Despite a few gasps and muttered protests, no dragon actually spoke out against this proposal. The council retired briefly to confer and returned having agreed unanimously that Thaw would indeed head the group, which would consist of himself and four other dragons, to match the number of Brace's original party. When volunteers were called for, several of Thaw's own band of followers stepped forward, and from their ranks he chose one, a massive ex-Charmed called Ratchet, who had served Thaw loyally for many years when they had both been in the ranks of Wraith's army. His recruitment was immediately accepted by the council, for they all knew that these two together would make a formidable team.

Other dragons called to be taken on, and of them one was selected, a Natural female dragon called Smoke, known for her skill in pathfinding. Herself a native of the central Heartland across which they planned to journey, her familiarity with the land and her tracking skills would be invaluable. In addition, it would be of no small benefit that she too was muscular and battle-trained, having fought long and hard during the battle of Covamere before, at the last, joining the Flight.

All through the selection process Fortune kept quiet the turmoil inside his heart, for as each place was taken he felt bound to cry out, 'I'll go!' But each time he forced himself to look down upon his mate and their daughter, and his mouth clamped shut of its own accord. He hung back on the dais, letting Thaw organize the planning, relieved that he was not forced to participate. As he loitered Cumber nudged him and whispered,

'Don't feel guilty about it, old fellow, because I understand entirely the conflict you're going through. No, don't argue with me,' he went on as Fortune tried to protest, 'just listen: I remember I didn't want to leave Ordinal at South Point, although I knew I had to, just as you feel you can't leave Gossamer and Aria now. But you don't have to!'

'I don't?'

'No,' Cumber was triumphant now, his whisper raising to a cry, 'because I'm going instead!' With that, he bounded forward to stand beside Thaw. 'You see, I was there,' he explained to the wary crowd. 'It's vital a dragon goes who was there, and that means either me or Fortune or Gossamer. Obviously neither of them can go, so that leaves me!'

There was some uncertainty at this, largely because such a decision would leave the council short of two of its members, but again Rangle stepped in with a few calming words.

'Despite the obvious arguments against such a decision, I believe Cumber to be right,' he proclaimed. 'We can operate a reduced council for a short while – after all, the duties are light and our population shows little sign of expansion in the near future.'

There were a few bitter laughs at this last remark, and it was eventually agreed that Cumber would indeed go. Thaw himself suggested that if they did not return within two moons, then they would be judged to have forfeited their places on the council and new members would be duly elected.

'Still it may be a good thing,' he added, 'to have councillors abroad, for we may also on this mission be ambassadors to foreign lands; the dragons of Aether's Cross may not be the only dragons left who need to be saved.'

As Cumber's name was added to the others, Fortune felt a great pressure release itself from around his heart. Though a part of him still felt guilty that he was simply abandoning Brace and the others to whatever fate had befallen them, he felt mostly at peace with his choice.

I am torn so many ways already, he thought sadly. *It would not do to add yet another.*

'I will be travelling with you, my friend, in my heart,' he whispered to Cumber as the young ex-Charmed rejoined him at the rear of the platform. 'Find him, please. Find them all.'

'Or you'll come looking for me, I suppose?' smiled Cumber.

'You can rely on it.'

The final place was not so easily filled. Thaw could not

decide between a young male Natural who was greatly skilled in flight but something of a loner, and an older dragon who claimed actually to have lived at Aether's Cross for a while. But as he consulted with Quill and Rangle, a voice suddenly broke into their huddle, and laughter rang out through the crowd. Fortune stretched his neck to see what the commotion was about and was curiously touched to see genuine amusement on the faces of most of the dragons spread out before him. So far the meeting had seemed full of doom, and so it was wonderful to see such a lightness of spirit reassert itself in the crowd. He followed their collective gaze up into the sky, where a pair of white wings cycled against the stars and a strong, female voice echoed down on to the platform, and at last he understood the laughter, and joined with it himself. It was Velvet, and she was determined not to be left behind.

'If you think you can fly off on another of your adventures and forget about me, Cumber, then you've got another think coming, because let me tell you, you wouldn't get far without me! And as for you, Thaw, if you're looking for a flier then look no further. What other dragon can do this?'

So saying, she pulled her wings hard to the left and arrowed towards the clump of palm trees which sprang up immediately behind the raised rock dais. Spiralling sideways, she rolled straight through the middle of the thicket, missing trunks and leaves with a claw's width to spare in every direction. It was not an especially dangerous manoeuvre, but the skill it required was not lost on any of those dragons watching. As she resumed her station above the councillors, Thaw called up to her with a wry smile.

'I suppose you would have us believe that all of Cumber's council decisions are made by you anyway, young Velvet?'

'Well, we all know that's true!' cried some wit from the middle of the assembly. 'Let her go – he'll be no good without her!'

Again there was laughter, and all of a sudden it seemed that a great cloud had lifted itself from over the gathering. Though the meeting had begun in twilight and descended swiftly into darkness, yet a warm light seemed now to cover the hilltop. Velvet swooped down to land in unprecedented style on the council dais and embrace her mate, at which a hearty cheer erupted from the watching dragons and for a time it might have been not midnight but midday for despair had departed and determination and optimism had taken its place. Again dragons were remembering that Haven was a place of new beginnings, and what was this journey but another new beginning?

Taking advantage of the temporary confusion as dragons chattered and chuckled, Fortune slipped down from the platform to hug Gossamer.

'You're not ashamed of me?' he asked nervously.

'Oh no!' she answered at once, her eyes shining. 'Oh, Fortune, don't you know that this is what I want: you and me and Aria together?'

'And Brace.'

'Of course. But . . . but if that isn't to be then it isn't to be, and I don't want to lose you in the process of finding that out. I've lost too much already – we've both lost too much – ever to be able to bear that.'

Fortune listened quietly, for this was the first time he had heard her admit the possibility that Brace might not return at all. Somehow, with the decision finally made that her brother would at least be searched for, Gossamer was able to release that final fear, and he was glad.

'They'll find him,' he said, holding her close. 'If any dragons can, they can.'

'I know,' she replied softly. 'But I'm glad you're staying, all the same. Now, get back up there before you're missed. You'll have to work even harder once Thaw and Cumber are gone so you might as well start now!'

Thaw had just called the other dragons who had been selected for the rescue party up on to the platform so that all could see them. As the other two – Ratchet and Smoke – lined up with Cumber and Velvet, Fortune found himself thinking again of Hesper, and of what he would make of this latest decision of the council of Haven.

He will think us weakened, he mused, *with only four of us left. That is, if he ever troubles us again.*

But he could not keep his thoughts long with that thug of a dragon and soon found himself drawn into the party which was developing on the hilltop. More and more dragons were clambering up the rough sides of the council dais and all of the councillors except Ledra – who watched this unheard-of breakdown of etiquette with a haughty sneer – welcomed the informality. Over the growing din, Thaw announced that Fortune's proposal was passed and that the expedition would set out in two days. Few dragons heard him actually draw the meeting to a close, so rowdy had the proceedings become.

Though on the face of it there was little actually to celebrate, celebrations there were. Some dragons rejoiced in relief that their greatest fear had been expressed and shared; others recalled Hesper's humiliation with glee, mocking his clumsy ambitions and empty threats, while still more were glad simply that something was being *done* at last. Many dragons were reminded that the idyll of Haven, while undeniably a splendid place to live, was not everything. Haven was only a tiny part of a great world which still demanded that dragons journey across it to meet with the dangers it presented. And only by doing so could they hope to contend with any of the problems they now faced.

So perhaps above all it was the future that was celebrated that night, and many times before the sun rose again on a group of exhausted, strangely contented dragons Fortune's words were repeated among friends and comrades:

Here at the eye, all is peaceful until . . . until the eye passes and the hurricane returns.

For, threatening though those words had been when Fortune had spoken them, to many now they seemed inspiring, and if some new storm was indeed about to fall upon them, then at least they would be ready for it with a storm of their own. A storm of hope.

CHAPTER 4

Goodbyes

On the morning of the rescue expedition's departure, Fortune flew up to the council hill to be alone for a while. He was tired, having not slept at all since the night of the meeting, and the thought of facing the crowd which was gathering down on the great east shore was too much for him just yet. He shut his eyes and slipped into a shallow doze, not really sleeping, just drifting. Palm leaves sighed in the humid air and beneath his wings the rock baked.

He still felt a little guilty about not going with the others, but Gossamer had reassured him over and over that his decision to stay was the right one, and at last he was beginning to believe her. And as he rested here on the empty hilltop, he found himself smiling at the course of his own thoughts, for was this not a perfect opportunity for him to face up to his new responsibilities? With Thaw and Cumber gone the council work would be more difficult, especially with the unpredictable Ledra now carrying a quarter of the votes. He had flown up here daunted by the prospect but a small smile broke across his face as he realized that he was actually beginning to warm to the challenge.

'Well, Fortune,' he said to the open air, 'perhaps it's time you rose to the occasion.'

'And what occasion would that be, dragon?'

Fortune was so shocked by the intrusion of another voice that he leaped halfway into the air before recovering himself. He whirled round, still blinking in surprise, to see none other than Ledra perched delicately on the edge of the rock dais. He stared at her open-mouthed for a breath or two, amazed that she should be here with him and doubly amazed that she had arrived at the very instant his thoughts had been turned towards her.

'Don't worry, Fortune,' she laughed, evidently pleased with the effect she had on him. 'I won't bite!'

'Ledra! You startled me!'

'Obviously.'

She lay back on the flat rock and preened her lustrous wings, luxuriating in the heat of the early sun. Far below them the east beach was a broad band of gold dotted with black specks: dragons, preparing a send-off for the adventurers. Hot wind wafted up the southern slopes of the hill but here they were mostly sheltered from it; all was peaceful.

'You know,' said Ledra presently, 'I wondered why you didn't volunteer, Fortune. You would have been the obvious one to go.'

'Well, some dragon has to keep an eye on you, Ledra,' replied Fortune with an easy grin. Unfortunately the humour in his response was quite lost on the reclining Ledra and she pulled herself up haughtily, glaring at him through half-closed lids. Then, as quickly as it had come, her anger was gone again and she drew herself nearer to her fellow councillor.

'Yes, maybe you should keep a close eye on me, Fortune,' she cooed, pressing her flank against his. 'A very close eye.'

Fortune swallowed hard. Ledra was undeniably an attractive dragon, with slender, well-muscled wings and a long, elegant neck. Her eyes were deep and her voice low, but it was her body, with its sinuous grace and warm curves, which promised seduction.

'How close did you have in mind, Ledra?' he breathed, gazing into her rich, green eyes. Her response was to inhale sharply, filling her breast with the morning air and then breathing it out, warm and damp, across Fortune's neck.

'We could make a great team, Fortune, you and me,' she whispered. 'Two young dragons with power to share. What could we not do together?'

'Two is only half of four,' Fortune replied, closing his eyes as she rubbed her short, blunt horns against his neck.

'Rangle is old,' was her immediate answer. 'Soon he might

no longer be with us. Soon there might just be you, and me, and the old crone.'

'Quill is hardly a crone.'

'You and me, Fortune, you and me.'

Nuzzling the sensitive skin beneath his jaw, she pulled away slowly, her wings opened wide and her sinuous tail draped down over the surrounding rocks.

'You and me,' she repeated in a whisper. 'Here. Now.'

'Now?' mused Fortune.

Without warning, he unfurled his own wings and sprang behind her so that she was forced to look up into the sun to see his face. She squinted at him, her expression folding into one of confusion.

'The only "now" you and I are going to experience is a now in which we are utterly opposed!' Fortune exploded. 'How dare you do this, Ledra? Even if I didn't have a mate and an infant daughter, probably even if you were the last dragon alive in the world, I wouldn't share anything of my life with you. I accept that you were elected as fairly as any of us, but if you ever try anything like this again, I swear I'll have you struck from the council! Now go away and leave me in peace!'

A little shocked by the depth of his own wrath, Fortune jumped on to one of the adjoining boulders and turned his back on Ledra. He sat there, staring westwards out to sea and trembling slightly.

Why did I react so violently? he wondered to himself. *Was I actually tempted by her?*

He heard nothing for a few breaths, then felt a brush of air as Ledra swooped down in front of him. He stared into wild, green eyes.

'Oh, you'll regret this, Fortune,' she crooned. 'You all think I'm stupid, just because I like to have a good time, but just you watch your flank from now on, dragon. I hold power here and I have no intention of losing it, not for you, not for any dragon.' She looked him up and down for a long, drawn-out moment. 'You wouldn't be worth it anyway,' she commented finally, 'and I doubt Aria's yours either!'

'Just go away, Ledra,' said Fortune wearily. 'Save your make-believe for the fools who follow you around.'

Hissing at this final rebuff, Ledra slipped into the air with light strokes of her pale green wings, stood poised on the updraught from the hillside then turned and was gone into the morning sun, leaving Fortune breathing hard with suppressed anger.

Why does she get to me so? he wondered.

But as Ledra vanished into the haze he felt his anger fade too. Faint sounds drifted up from the shore now and he coasted down on the back of the breeze towards the sand, wondering how any dragon could fail to be happy on such a beautiful morning as this.

Cumber and Velvet were easy to spot among the milling dragons, since their white scales shone brilliantly in the sunlight. Fortune made his way over to where they stood deep in conversation with a small group of eager young Naturals who had evidently asked Cumber about Aether's Cross. Cumber must have been speaking for some considerable time on the subject, for the dragons were looking around restlessly, desperate for some diversion by which they might make their escape.

'. . . but above all they were resourceful . . .' Cumber was saying. 'Oh, hello, Fortune. I was just trying to impress on these dragons how resourceful the Cross dragons were. After all, they must have been to have lived actually on the walls of the canyon like that, don't you think?'

'Of course,' agreed Fortune, watching Cumber's audience disappear gratefully into the crowd. Velvet peered round her mate's wing and grinned at their visitor.

'Hello, Fortune!' she beamed. 'Come to see us off?'

'Oh, how I'll miss you!' Fortune's response was to hug her so hard that he almost lifted her off the ground. 'You both keep me laughing, you know. I don't know what I'll do without you.'

'You'll fall to pieces, just you see,' came Cumber's dry response.

'Probably. When do you fly?'

'Just about now, I think,' said Velvet, craning her neck over Fortune's head to look down the beach. Near the shoreline Thaw stood with Ratchet and Smoke; all three were looking eastwards, out to sea, and from the set of their wings it was plain that they were more than ready to leave.

'How's Aria?' asked Cumber.

'Getting better.' The infant dragon had been violently sick the previous night and Gossamer had not wanted to move her from their nest, nor even wanted Fortune around, claiming that he would only get in the way. Cumber and Velvet had both stopped by briefly that morning to say their farewells and they had been touched by Gossamer's concern for the infant.

'Take care of each other,' she had said, her voice shaking. 'And find my Brace, please.'

'I think the occasion's a bit too much for her,' Fortune suggested for the benefit of Cumber and Velvet – unnecessarily, for his two friends were quite aware of how deep Gossamer's emotions ran. 'She loves her brother.'

'She loves them all,' corrected Velvet. 'Brace and Scoff, Tallow and Volley. Even Werth.'

'We all do,' agreed Fortune.

And there seemed little more to be said. The dragons around them were moving over to where Thaw and the others were waiting, leaving the three friends alone on the broad reach of the sand. Wordlessly they embraced one last time, and then Fortune watched as Cumber and Velvet made their way to the shoreline.

All the speeches that were needed had already been made and so it was without word or ceremony that the five adventurers took to the air. The watching dragons cheered them into the sky but the cheer was muted, as though the seriousness of the expedition had suddenly become a tangible presence on the beach. Waves hissed on the fine, golden sand, flattening the sound of the air as it rushed from beneath five pairs of beating wings, cleansing the shore of the clawmarks which the hovering dragons had made there. One by one they turned to the east, striking out confidently and climbing high as they flew, up towards the sun and into the stronger currents of air which were already pulling white clouds towards the distant, invisible mainland. As they dwindled so the clouds overtook the sun and the day grew dull, as if the dragons were taking the light on their journey with them. Soon they were gone.

Take it if you must, Fortune called silently to the departing dragons. *Leave us in darkness if that is the only way for your mission to succeed. We will wait for you, whatever happens.*

A dragon detached itself from the crowd and ambled up the shallow slope of the beach to where Fortune stood; it was old Rangle, his wing membranes thin and almost transparent against the greying sky. Everything about him seemed grey, from the chipped scales along his back to the dusty wrinkles which surrounded his eyes. Nevertheless those eyes were bright and blue and, Fortune noticed for the first time, not without kindness.

'A big day for us all,' Rangle commented, twitching his head at the gathering behind him.

Fortune smiled and nodded. 'A lot of hopes have flown with those dragons,' he agreed. 'More than many would care to admit, I think.'

'You are perceptive for so young a dragon, Fortune. May I offer you a word of advice, however?' Again Fortune nodded, although he wondered what might be coming. 'Always remember that it is harder to be left behind than to go. It is a truth often felt but seldom spoken; we should remember it now, for we are the ones who will find it hard from now on. Is that not right?'

'Yes,' whispered Fortune. 'Yes, it is right.'

'And one other thing,' added the wizened old dragon as he turned to leave. 'Watch out for Ledra – if she hasn't tried to seduce you already she soon will. Goodbye, Fortune.'

Momentarily dumbfounded, Fortune had to smile as Rangle departed. Fortune could think of no dragon less like Ledra than Rangle, nor was he in any doubt which of the two he would rather share the council dais with.

Two odd meetings in a single morning, he mused. *Now – what about Quill? Where does she really stand in all of this?*

He could see the imposing figure of the ex-Charmed dragon in the midst of the throng down on the shore, but for the moment he had no desire to go and speak to her. All he wanted now was to return home. The Haven dragons would probably rest for a while after the flurry of excitement following the last council meeting and no agenda, nor even a day, had been set for the next meeting, so he intended to make full use of however much free time was now available to him.

His mood was still buoyant as he flew back inland, but whichever way he twisted in the air the wind blew ever hotter, as though despite taking the light of the sun away the adventurers had somehow left its heat behind. The palms swayed uncertainly, their broad leaves nervous, while above him the sky was turning to pale metal as a skin of cloud drew itself tight over the islands with the relentless speed of a rising tide. To the north the sky was dark.

The air felt heavy despite a strong wind from the sea and Gossamer wandered out on to the cliff to clear her head. Her senses tingled with long-forgotten responses as she opened herself to the world for the first time in what seemed to her an age.

She loved this place so much. When Fortune had brought them to Haven she had been overwhelmed by the perfection of its setting in the turquoise sea, and much of what she had so far experienced here had been joyful. Everything about Haven made her want to smile: the complex geometry of the central reef, the clean sea air, the hugeness of the sky, the richness of the food . . . everything. It was an idyll, strangely unreal.

They'd built their nest on the sheltered north-east corner of the island, halfway down the slope of a gentle hill. Tall palms arched over the bowl they had carved in the loose soil, and the broad leaves which they shed Gossamer laid across the ground to create a warm and comfortable floor. The nest was wide and welcoming and its position both kept it free of the ever-present south wind and gave it an imposing view of the ocean to the north.

Apart from the immediate surroundings, which boasted a sizeable thicket of palms and much spiky undergrowth, the hillside itself was fairly barren, steepening as it did towards a cliff edge some way further downslope. Whether consciously or not, the two young dragons had chosen a spot which reminded each of them of their own home, for in this place were reflected both the cliffs of South Point and the canyon walls of Aether's Cross. And it was secure, for no dragon could approach from upslope without crashing through the trees and vegetation nor from downslope without being seen in the air. Somewhat remote from the more heavily populated southern valleys, this was their own, private haven.

Then there was the greatest joy of all: Aria. After the excitement of the hatching Gossamer stayed mostly around the nest, busying herself with her new daughter. Most of the food they needed Fortune brought to them, and visitors stopped by so frequently that she hardly needed to go anywhere herself. She – or more particularly Aria – was quite a centre of attention during those early moons, and she revelled in the tranquillity of her new life, especially when recalling the hard times through which she and Fortune had just passed.

But suddenly it seemed to her that the visits by other dragons, except for Cumber and Velvet, had grown less frequent. She supposed that the novelty was wearing off, but suspected too that it had more than a little to do with this dreadful fear of infertility, now unmasked; perhaps to some she and Aria were all at once a painful reminder of what they themselves might never have. She wondered whether or not to tell Fortune about this idea, but decided not to for the time being: he had enough on his mind without worrying about jealous females threatening her when he was elsewhere.

Would it come to that? she wondered, thinking inevitably of Ledra, who of all the females on Haven was surely the most spiteful. As she flexed her wings in the strange heat of the wind, Gossamer felt that the time had come to busy herself again. A brief flight this afternoon had stretched muscles long unused and the feeling that had left her with was a good one, even wonderful. The wind blew past her, carrying away with it her recent desire for solitude. She felt exhilarated.

Fortune glided in for a swift landing only to find his mate standing alert on the pale curve of the clifftop. He held his breath as he coasted down towards her, for as ever when he saw her slender, white form set against the light grey rock he was reminded of how beautiful she was. Raising an infant had only made her more lovely, for now she carried herself with a new confidence which shone from the set of her wings and the grace of her neck and head. As he drank in the sight of her she glanced up and rewarded him with a dazzling smile.

'You look gorgeous!' he exclaimed as he dropped to the ground beside her. 'How's Aria?'

'I've left her sleeping. She needs to catch up after being so sick. I flew for a while.'

Fortune nodded and inhaled deeply. The sea air was refreshingly cool and salty and as invigorating as a draught of clear spring water. 'They went off all right, anyway,' he said presently. 'Not much ceremony in the end; I think everyone was worn out.' He looked up into the sky. 'I think the weather might be turning, too.'

'Your storm?' Gossamer hunched close against him, tucking her wing beneath his as though seeking protection.

'Maybe. I noticed on the way back how dark the sky was getting, particularly . . .'

He stopped suddenly, his eyes drawn again to the north. Gossamer pressed closer. 'What is it, Fortune?'

Feeling the echo of his own heartbeat in the contact with Gossamer's body – as though it alone were beating for both of them – Fortune peered into the distance in an attempt to make out what he thought he saw there. 'I don't know,' he replied. 'Can you see it?'

Together they looked out towards the only other land mass visible from Haven Island itself: Sharp Island, the next north in the chain. It was called Sharp because that was exactly what it was. Shaped like a pair of curving claws, it held a long lagoon between its pincers, and only along the shore of that lagoon did any vegetation grow. The main bulk of the island rose steeply from sea level in a series of precipitous terraces too sheer to be settled on; it had never been considered as a place to be colonized.

From their clifftop, Sharp was usually visible as a thin, grey wedge resting just below the horizon. On a clear day a dragon could make out the contours of its low and ragged mountains; if there was the slightest haze it was reduced to a mere blur. Today the sky had started off clear enough but now the cloud was thickening rapidly and the greyness of the light made Sharp difficult to see properly. Nevertheless, there was something odd about it.

'I can see . . . something,' ventured Gossamer hesitantly. 'It looks like a shadow in the sky above the island, or a dark cloud of some kind.'

'You're right,' agreed Fortune grimly. 'And I have a nasty suspicion I know what's causing it: smoke.'

'Fire?'

'Just that. I rather think our friend Hesper hasn't gone as far away as we might have hoped. I'd wager anything that's him out there, making fire and working charm.'

'Well,' sighed Gossamer, 'let's hope he stays there. He's never really scared me – after the Black Dragon a simple thug like Hesper is nothing – but there's something detestable about him all the same. You're not worried about him, are you?'

'No,' sighed Fortune after a breath's consideration. 'No, he likes to make trouble, that's for certain, but I think dragons here have got the measure of him.' They contemplated the far-off smoke for a few moments more, then he concluded, 'Well, I'm certainly not flying all the way out there just to confront him – he's as free to do what he likes as the rest of us. Are you hungry?'

'Ravenous! We've a lot of those giant nuts left – care to indulge?'

'I'll indulge you in anything you like, my dear – just lead me on.'

And so, giggling like the pair of young lovers that they were, the two dragons raced back up the slope towards their home, while above them the sky turned to iron and a pall of black smoke stained the distant horizon.

CHAPTER 5

The Place of Rocks

Had it chosen, Ocher could have made the lengthy journey to its destination in the merest blink of a dragon's eye. Why it elected to linger on the way it was not certain. Perhaps it had something to do with the sudden clarity of its memories, for in the vast store-place of its mind the vestiges of the Maze still shone with a hard and revealing light. Whatever the reason, the basilisk found itself loitering far from the world yet still short of its final goal. It was in the place of rocks.

Many aeons past – indeed many Turnings past – the basilisks built for themselves a gigantic stronghold floating in the heights of the sky. Here they resided, building out and out from a central nugget of rock with the brute power of raw charm. In those times charm was a mighty force indeed, and the feats they achieved by its power were prodigious. Old though they were then (but had they not always been old?), it seemed to Ocher now that those were young times, times of energy and bravado, of endless and intense competition. The citadel they constructed soared through the heavens, an ever-expanding monument to magic and the might of the Deathless.

But the basilisks grew bored, and in the end they shattered the palace. For years debris rained from the heavens and where it fell the land of the world was broken and blighted. The basilisks scattered, each fleeing alone into the cosmos, each on an individual quest . . . in yet another futile attempt to fill the vacuum of immortality. Only later, as this never-ending, never-starting cycle of congress and exodus repeated itself over and over, did the basilisks reconvene to make their next citadel, this one earthbound and beautiful where its sky-borne counterpart had been rough and cruel. Here they gathered again during a time of gentle reflection . . . but that time did not last either and again they parted, this time into what was planned to be final and eternal sleep.

The cycle will end, thought Ocher savagely as it lingered in the place of rocks. *The Deathless shall gather again, and this time will be the last!*

All around it tumbled the craggy and pitted boulders which were the ruins of the sky citadel. By far the greater part of the incredible structure of the palace had not fallen to earth but had remained in the heavens, fragmenting to form a chain of wreckage strewn across the skies. In earlier times, shortly after the citadel's destruction, the cosmos had been small and the crushed rocks had clung to its boundary. But it had grown since then . . .

The most recent Turning had caused the cosmos to expand, suddenly and violently. Ocher launched senses out in pursuit of its receding perimeter, but its velocity was too great. Shaken by the sheer magnitude of what the universe was becoming, the basilisk pulled back its probes with sudden fear, but not without a certain hope.

The sky is expanding into something far greater than it has ever been before! Surely in so mighty a firmament there exists the means to end eternity?

Swiftly narrowing its attention back into the cloud of rocks through which it flew, Ocher cast a sensory net over its more immediate surroundings. Some of these rocks, rich in metal and dark against the background of space, had once comprised part of the inner core of the citadel. Other rocks were darker still, like charcoal. These were the remains of the charm-rich skeins of fire which had held the entire citadel together; now the fire had guttered and its unnatural flames had condensed to stone. Still more rocks were bright and free of metal while yet more were twisted almost beyond recognition; yet the basilisk knew them all as old friends. In its mind it reassembled the citadel from these tattered remnants, uncertain of whether or not it mourned its passing.

Beyond the belt of rocks, the worlds swam as they always

had, but now they moved through a far greater ocean. Were it not now committed to ending its own wretched existence, Ocher might have considered the depths of that ocean worthy of exploration. But something compelled it to look back, pulling an image of the world close despite the colossal distance which separated them.

The Gathering will be greedy. Power will be needed if we are to render ourselves mortal at last. As the last magic is drained from the world, so life shall drain from the Deathless. It is the power of the abandoned charm we need.

As if in response to Ocher's thoughts the world shuddered. Charm was indeed in motion, working spells beneath its skin. The southern pole glowed as scattered pools of charm flowed together, joining. Gathering.

The magic moved, and with it the land began to move, too. Not slowly, as it always had in the past, but with sudden, blinding speed. Subterranean realms rode up over mountain slopes, tasting air for the first time in aeons; oceans spilled across deserts; continents warped and stretched, some fusing into unfamiliar lands, others breaking apart and sinking beneath the swell of the moving seas. Never had the basilisk seen the world so agitated. It looked on with wide, silver eyes as the icebound polar continent hunched like a crouching dragon, pushing new mountain peaks up from its depths. So far the changes were confined to the lower part of the southern hemisphere, but gradually the charm's influence was extending north. Soon it would encompass the entire world.

Such power! thought Ocher with mounting excitement. *Surely now the power is there for the Deathless to command! Surely now our time has come!*

Further resolved, it cast itself free of the ruins among which it had delayed for too long and sped towards its destination. Behind it the place of rocks settled like a veil between it and the world, while all around creation swelled as its borders sprinted into the endless night.

Ahead, the Red Planet grew large in its gaze.

CHAPTER 6

Falling Stars

The Plated Mountain sprawled beneath shifting layers of vapour, dead and broken and covered with a skin of colourless ash. What had once been a towering cone of black rock was a grey and shattered ghost. Split into two fractured halves, it lay empty as though it had been consumed from within and left as a mere husk, unable any longer to support its own tremendous bulk. The crooked space left between the halves was dark and ominous, as though it led to places deeper even than the deepest parts of the world – as once, of course, it had. But no more.

'Come,' said Thaw, his dark yellow face pointed with shadows in the hard, noon light. 'I would like to see Covamere again, just once.'

But the brief flight to Covamere ended in disappointment, for Covamere was no longer there; it had simply vanished. The once-mighty settlement had been utterly consumed by the ash which had rained down from the sky in the long days following the eruption of the mountain. In its place was an immense grey plain from which protruded a few lonely spikes and spars – scant fragments, pieces of towers and the tops of sentry-ways, piercing the dusty fluid which had poured on to the claw-shaped valley. These alone showed where an entire dragon city had existed. The watching, mourning dragons could only guess at how many corpses lay entombed beneath the surface of the ocean of ash and it was not long before they moved on, their mood sombre, their pace swift as they betrayed their eagerness to leave this morbid place behind.

They did not speak for some time, not until they landed

to rest in the middle of the afternoon. The landscape had flattened gradually as they had flown north, broken mountain slopes giving way to crumpled foothills which soon began to bleed into the grey desert which awaited them. They alighted at the summit of a gentle knoll which overlooked the first stretches of sand, spreading themselves out on the rough grass that clung to the thin volcanic soil.

Cumber remembered this territory from his flight south from Aether's Cross all those moons before, and he remembered it with some discomfort. He shivered as he recalled the trauma of Realmshock which had whipped through him during those dreadful days. Seeing his distress, Velvet snuggled close to him and whispered,

'What is it, my love?'

Cumber sighed, and for a breath or two was not sure what to say. So much had changed now . . .

'It's this place,' he explained heavily, 'the Heartland. Once magic was so powerful here that it shone from the air. When Fortune and I and the others travelled through here its strength was greatly diminished, already, but still the land was *alive* somehow, if you can understand that. Not now, of course.'

'But you don't really miss it, do you, Cumber?' Velvet reminded him gently. 'You've never mourned it like the others.'

Cumber mused. 'Well no, not really – except sometimes, like when I'm aching for the taste of smoked meat!' He smiled, but it was a fleeting smile, quickly replaced by an expression of gloomy introspection. 'But no, Velvet, my dear, you're right of course. Earth charm was always gentle, and I liked that well enough, but the fire charm was terrible, and the Realm where it came from was a place of evil. Dragons died as a result of me using fire charm at Aether's Cross. Scoff helped me get over the shock, and so did Fortune of course, although he didn't realize it, but I've never forgotten the dying, Velvet, never. Miss the charm? No, I can't honestly say I do, my dear, not really. Dragons abused its power more than any others, and I think that the world will be a better place without it, because you see nature is . . . simpler, somehow.'

'Dragons still die,' suggested Velvet, 'whether by charm or by nature; death is always with us, no matter what we do. It is the one thing all creatures can be sure of – we're none of us immortal.'

Cumber nodded at this, but she could see that he remained restless. She hugged him close and they lay together like that for some time, resting quietly together as the sun slipped gradually lower in the clear, acidic sky.

They ended up staying the night there, for the demanding flight across the sea to the mainland had greatly tired them all, even ex-Charmed warriors Thaw and Ratchet. That, coupled with the emotional return to Covamere, had served to bring them all to the point of exhaustion, and so it was without much discussion that they agreed to begin the main part of their journey the following day.

'Seven more days should see us safely to Aether's Cross,' predicted Smoke confidently as they each retired to their chosen sleeping place. 'Probably less. We can afford the rest of this evening to recover our strength.'

'Sleep well, dragons,' added Thaw. 'Tomorrow the journey really begins.'

The night was long, and Thaw could not sleep. So as not to disturb the others, he glided away from their temporary camp until he found a bald and broken hillside and, choosing the southern slope in preference to any other, settled himself down.

Above the ruptured mountain the sky was dark and crowded with stars. The falling crescent of the moon sent a shimmer of silver across the landscape, carving the jagged plain of the Injured Mountains into a bleak mosaic of shadows. Warm wind blew past from the south, dragging ash clear of the ridge tops and spilling it into the heavy air. Thaw took in its breath with a deep draught of his own, marvelling at how dead this place had become.

He was not a native of this part of the world. He'd joined Wraith's army during the Black Dragon's campaign in the north-east lands of Termanderel and come to the Heartland only when his new leader had decided finally to invade Covamere. A river dragon was Thaw, having grown up on the grass-rich flood plains of the great and meandering Term, a river so wide on its lower reaches that many dragons, on seeing it for the first time, mistook it for the ocean.

Thaw was a student of the ways of water, and of the richness it brought to the land. Covamere's landscape of lava heights and roughly sculptured plains of black rock had disappointed him. Ambition had kept him here – and loyalty to Wraith, and the responsibility he felt towards the many dragons subordinate to himself – but he'd never liked it.

Authority had always flown close beside Thaw; he was ever the leader. In his younger years he'd led endless groups of his friends across the waters of the Term to perform complex feats of flight and exploration. Hundreds of islands they explored and mapped, and the territories were recorded in meticulous detail in the regimented depths of Thaw's own mind. For as well as being a dragon of ambition and authority, Thaw was nothing if not a dragon of *order*. His phenomenal memory made him both a tactician to marvel at and a dragon to be respected – he never forgot a misdemeanour committed by a dragon under his command, nor indeed a triumph achieved. The Black Dragon had recognized these qualities instantly and soon assigned Thaw to the command of a team of dragons responsible for secret operations and subterfuge, answerable directly to Wraith. For Thaw it was the perfect role.

Ambition. Authority. Order. Wraith himself displayed those very same qualities, and yet at the end Thaw turned away from him. It was ambition, Thaw decided later, which brought Wraith down, and from this he took warning. Thus was he able to accept graciously his effective demotion when on Haven he found himself reduced to the level of a mere councillor, one of many who governed, no longer the one in charge. But soon he became restless and eager for fresh challenges. No majestic river swept through Haven – a mere backwater was this tropical idyll. Thaw was becoming bored.

Then came the rescue mission and the prospect of adventure. The world beyond Haven was changed – changed beyond measure in fact – and it needed to be charted. What better dragon than Thaw to lead the first group of pioneers into a whole new world? If he found Brace and the ruin of Aether's Cross along the way then so much the better, but surely there were many other things to be found in the turned world. The opportunity was one he grasped without hesitation, for here at last was a chance to stretch his wings wider than any dragon had before. No longer answerable to any dragon but himself, what places could he not explore, what secrets could he not uncover?

Thaw opened his wings, watching the silver light play across their black and yellow stripes. Soon the moon began to sink, and as their celestial partner disappeared from view the stars grew brighter, their hard eyes looking down impassively on the tiny dragons sprawled across the fractured land.

He thought with a thrill of anticipation, *There are such patterns to be found in the world!*

Hearing a flurry in the air behind him, he glanced back to see big Ratchet lumbering down on broad wings to join him.

'I heard you go, chief,' the giant warrior rumbled in his slow, gritty voice. 'I thought I'd give you time to think – the way you like it. But you shouldn't wander off, not without me. There's something not right out here.'

Thaw smiled and clapped his comrade on the flank.

'Good Ratchet,' he laughed, 'I can always rely on you to look out for me. But I'm not an officer any more, you know – those ranks died when Wraith died.'

'Begging your pardon, chief, but the oath I took in the Master's army was to serve *you*.'

'But the army is no more.'

'No, chief, but you are.'

'Very well,' Thaw smiled, 'have it your way, Ratchet. I must admit I feel safe when you're around, so I'm not complaining.'

They sat comfortably together for a while, until Thaw felt sleep begin at last to steal over him. He lifted himself slowly from the barren soil, his intention being to return to the camp site, but as he did so light played across his drooping eyelids, making him lift his head. A streak of white flashed in the heavens, a brilliant lance soaring from behind the mountain, sprinting up to its zenith and then falling away again towards the north with blinding speed. Flickering and silent, it shrank into the distance until it was gone.

'A night dragon!' cried Ratchet in gleeful surprise, jostling Thaw excitedly as he too clambered to his claws.

Thaw shrugged and spread his wings, expecting to see no more. Before the Turning he had been as adept at wielding magic as any charmed dragon, but he had never considered it as anything other than a useful part of his armoury, of which the greatest part was his own wit. He missed the power of the charm, but not its romance.

Another bolt of light soared upwards from the south. Soon the sky was filled with light as individual streaks became a shower and finally a storm. Ratchet danced back and forth in joy and even Thaw raised a horny brow in surprise. He heard distant cries: it seemed that Velvet had woken to the sight of the display and had roused Cumber, and now they were huddled together, their heads raised to the sky, gasping and pointing as the fleeting lines criss-crossed to form a living matrix of light. He could not see Smoke. Casting his thoughts aside, he glided back with his comrade to join them.

'Night dragons!' exclaimed Ratchet as they alighted next to the others. 'Fortune said they were real. Do you think they're real, chief?'

'Oh, they're beautiful!' cried Velvet before Thaw could answer. 'I don't care what they are – night dragons or otherwise – I could just sit here and watch them all night, couldn't you? Oh, Smoke, aren't you even excited?'

Thaw followed her gaze to where the female Natural stood casually to one side. Like her companions, she was staring skywards, but like Thaw she showed no emotion.

'Well, Smoke,' smiled Thaw, ambling over, 'what do you think?'

'I think it's odd,' she replied tersely. She squinted, scanning the heavens as though searching for something she could not quite see. 'Very odd.'

'Of course, I've seen night dragons before,' Velvet was announcing to no one in particular, 'but never a shower like this, although I've heard about them. It's wonderful, and it's magical. Oh, there *must* be some charm left in the world for something like this to happen, don't you all think?'

'I think we should get some sleep,' was Smoke's unenthusiastic response. 'We've a long way to go yet and time has a way of catching dragons out.'

'Smoke's right,' agreed Thaw.

'I'm staying here for a while – just try and pull me away!' said Velvet excitedly.

Smoke turned her back on the others and strolled back to her scrape. Thaw watched her go, curious about why she too should have remained so unmoved. She was a practical dragon, like him, a meticulous planner and pathfinder . . .

But is she even more sensitive than we give her credit for? wondered Thaw with a sudden, sickening lurch in his stomach. Warrior suspicions took control and he looked north, looked *hard*.

Beyond the curve of Smoke's back stretched the grey desert across which they would fly the next day. Beyond that, and for now beyond even the distant and gloomy horizon, were the Low Mountains and Aether's Cross, but was there not something nearer? Something . . .

Thaw peered into the night. There was a glow in the middle-distance, a flickering light trapped in the wilderness. As he watched it sputtered and died. In the sky above, the greater lights played and swooped and . . . and then did something Thaw would never have expected them to do. They fell!

Like lightning they fell, searing the far-away air with blinding, stabbing flames. Fire crashed into the desert, shattering the ground and boiling the earth. Clouds of dust and debris rose around the distant maelstrom. But the clouds did not obscure the terrible destruction, for as they grew and billowed so the lightning illuminated them from within, burdening them with pulsing, malformed hearts of light which tore them apart even as they were made. As the fire from the sky took hold so the sound it made started to filter across the desert and soon the dragons' ears were filled with the rumbling as their eyes were filled with the light and now, at last, even Smoke stood up and took in the spectacle.

They looked on in wonder and in horror, not believing what they were seeing.

The whole width of the desert was alive with flame. A wall of light had completely obscured the horizon, a wall made up of thousands of interlaced threads, the lines of fire which were made as the falling stars came to earth. The air sizzled as they plummeted from the heavens and the ground cracked as they struck it their countless blows. On they came, until it seemed that the night had retreated and a new and violent day had taken its place.

'You see!' yelled Smoke, turning to face the others. From where they stood she was a dragon silhouette against a dazzling wall of flashing white. 'They're falling, these night dragons of yours! There's no going back, not for any of us. We have to trust to nature now – we have to!'

Then Velvet, who had watched the explosive display resolutely for some number of breaths, could stand it no longer and buried her face in Cumber's flank.

'Oh, Cumber,' she wept, 'what a stupid dragon I'm being. You're the one who should be weeping. It's just another piece of the magic that's gone, isn't it, that's all, but why does it seem so sad?'

'Because it is sad,' replied Cumber, patting her sympathetically on the back of the neck.

The two white dragons wandered back in silence to their scrape, their heads bowed. Smoke too curled herself up again, leaving Ratchet fidgeting next to the dragon he still saw as his commander.

'They *are* real, aren't they, chief?' the big dragon blurted suddenly.

But Thaw found himself unable to reply. He had never before seen any beauty in the high-flying dragons which occasionally lit up the night sky, but now it seemed to him that the night dragons represented the essence of everything to which he had once aspired: order in flight and the eventual rising into an eternal hierarchy beyond the mere confines of this world. And now they were falling.

This is terrible! he thought suddenly, and as he thought it Thaw did something he seldom did – he wept, and in his tears there flickered the light of the stars that fell to the ground far away in the desert, bringing their fire briefly to the world before finally darkening and dying. Then the night was dark again and the lace of flame was no more.

The following morning was damp and cold, and despite there being a strong following wind it was in a melancholy mood that the five explorers set out from the foothills to fly north across the waiting desert. Early on, Velvet tried to revive their spirits by singing a lively mountain song, but it seemed that the clammy air struck every note dead and before long she gave up the attempt. Rivers of vapour overtook them as they flew, rushing northwards on the same wind which filled their wings.

Beneath them the grey sand flowed past, scalloped into dunes and waves which made the desert a slow-moving ocean. Squat trees crouched in the shallow valleys, their trunks fat and craggy, their leaves like spines on a dragon's back. And ahead . . . ahead was the devastation left by the falling stars.

The dragons flew over the craters in silence. They could feel the heat still radiating from the damaged ground, see the great, glassy depressions. Tortured spirals of fused sand reached towards them, clawing at the air. The graves of the night dragons.

They did not linger.

Further into the desert the vapour thickened to become a flowing mist which obscured their view of the ground and turned the sky above into a huge, anonymous mantle of white. Sounds which were already dulled grew thick and unreadable: conversation was difficult, only half heard; wingbeats were loose and hard to measure. Even Smoke, who was nearly as proficient a navigator as the great Tallow, encountered problems keeping track of her own rhythm and thus of the distance they had travelled. Soon – and with some reluctance, for it felt to her like an admission of failure – she requested that they drop below the shifting cloud to take a visual bearing again.

The cloud base was low – very low. They emerged into clear, hot air barely two trees above ground level and immediately breathed a collective sigh of relief that they had slowed their speed to a virtual hover, for directly in front of them was a sheer rock face into which they could easily have flown had they not chosen to descend.

'What made you want to stop and look?' demanded Thaw grimly.

'Just a feeling,' replied Smoke, her casual tone disguising the shock she really felt. 'A good pathfinder has to rely on instinct sometimes.'

'You're telling me!' exclaimed Velvet. 'We could have ended up flattened against that cliff if we hadn't slowed down – how did you know, Smoke, because I certainly didn't realize there was anything ahead?'

But their guide merely shrugged.

'What is this place?' Thaw pursued his enquiry. He was uneasy, pinned between the lowering cloud and the raw desert floor, no obvious way ahead without ascending again into obscurity. Ever the strategist, he was only too aware that they were vulnerable here. Trapped, even.

Did Brace and the others get past here? he found himself wondering. *Did they even make it this far?*

'I don't know,' came Smoke's cautious answer. 'I've never seen this place before.'

Thaw's response was immediate and unexpected, and all except Ratchet, who was well used to following his commander's orders without question, hesitated before responding.

'Into the cloud again. Now!' he barked, and when they simply gaped at him, not beating their wings any more than was necessary to sustain their hovering, he motioned to Ratchet and the two of them swooped beneath the other three and herded them unceremoniously back up into the billowing cloud.

'Steady on!' protested Cumber as the two big ex-Charmed warriors bullied them back upwards. 'Thaw – I mean to say, why such an over-reaction, because I for one would rather believe that . . .'

'Shut it,' interjected Thaw smoothly. 'Councillor,' he added with a half-smile. 'Look, I don't mean to scare you but we need some sort of cover while we try and work out what's going on here, all right?'

'I should think that's perfectly obvious,' responded Cumber huffily, '*councillor*. We have found a cliff – nothing more and nothing less – and we are required to fly to the top of it before we try to continue in the right direction.'

'A reasonable assumption,' agreed Thaw amiably, 'but I have a feeling our pathfinder might tell us something different. Am I not right, Smoke?' Smoke sighed heavily and nodded. Vapour rolled past, tracing filigrees of white across her nut-brown face. 'Do you want to tell us what's been troubling you this past day?' concluded Thaw, his tone kindly but firm.

'It was nothing I could put a claw on,' answered Smoke at once, clearly glad to be forced at last to speak. 'When we first struck land I didn't know where we were. Then, once we'd flown on to the mountain, I knew things weren't right – not right at all. Taking into account the distance we had to fly, on the bearing we took, I *should* have known that place where we landed. It *should* have been a place called Third Bay, but it wasn't – it was just cliffs.'

'I didn't realize anything was wrong,' said Cumber, somewhat impatiently. 'What are you saying?' Velvet silenced him with a caustic glare.

'What I mean is that the land is different now. This is not the Heartland I once knew.'

'So what you are saying is . . .' began Thaw.

'. . . that we're lost?' Smoke completed his sentence for him. 'Maybe. Yes, we may actually be lost.'

'Now just hold on there,' said Cumber hastily, 'we needn't be anything of the sort. We know when the mountain erupted it could easily have shaken up the place a bit, and last night the desert looked about the same as I remembered it from before – apart from all the stars falling – so I don't see that there's necessarily much to be concerned about, is there?'

'But we should have seen this cliff from the camp, if only on the horizon,' explained Smoke wearily. 'Believe me, Cumber – it might be here now but it wasn't here last night.'

There was silence for a few breaths, broken only by the rupturing of the wind on the cliff face, invisible beyond the swirling cloud. The world had suddenly turned treacherous around them. Then Thaw spoke again very solemnly.

'I suspect this is simply a manifestation of the strange times we are living through, we dragons. Charm is still at work, of that there can be no doubt. Can you say any more than this, Smoke?'

She shook her head. A shudder seemed to pass through the whole group then as they cast their eyes nervously over the cloud. Velvet bobbed as near to Cumber as she dared on the unpredictable wind.

'Well,' announced Thaw, 'as Cumber said, our next course of action is clear enough – we ascend until we reach the top of the cliff. Come, I will lead. Ratchet, you take the rear. We fly, dragons!'

'Anyone would think he's in charge,' muttered Cumber to Velvet as they began slowly to climb into the spiralling vapour.

'Just fly, my dear.' Had Cumber been more alert to his mate's expression he would have seen her regarding Thaw with a suspicious glare. 'Save your breath for flying.'

Up they flew, with Smoke periodically easing her way forward to verify that they were maintaining their distance from the cliff face. Upwards, with no view to relieve the monotony of the flying nor any clue as to what they would find when finally they emerged from the wind-blown cloud.

CHAPTER 7

Into the Desert

The cloud layer broke open around the ascending dragons, bringing them out into brilliant sunshine. Dazzled by the glare from the undulating sea of white vapour, they flattened their wings and stroked their way to a halt, looking around with watering eyes.

Whether by chance or otherwise, in emerging from the clouds they had also reached the top of the cliff. A broken, grey ridge stood before them, rising from the cloud as though from an ocean and extending to the limits of their vision on either side. Hovering as they were several wingspans below its peak, they were unable to see what lay beyond.

'How high we are!' gasped Velvet incredulously, only too aware of the slipperiness of the thin air against her wing membranes.

'Too high,' came Smoke's reply. 'If I counted correctly during our ascent, this cliff is even taller than the Plated Mountain was in its days of glory.'

'But that's impossible!' protested Cumber. 'The air's thin, but not that thin – and why isn't it covered in snow? You must have calculated wrong.'

Smoke shrugged, her body dipping slightly as she did so. 'I don't think I did,' she responded amiably.

'If what Smoke says is correct,' broke in Thaw, 'then something very strange is going on here.' He frowned, and Velvet found herself watching him intently.

What's driving you, Thaw? she thought suddenly.

Thaw continued, 'It is said that the tunnels near the centre of the Plated Mountain were so rich in charm that they became ... twisted somehow. Some dragons used to say that the tunnels "lost their way". I think it entirely possible that there is still charm working here in the Heartland, enough to have seriously distorted the land through which we're flying – or trying to fly. We have already encountered a changed coastline and now we find our way blocked by a cliff which didn't even exist last night.'

'Hardly blocked,' put in Cumber. 'I mean to say, we're at the top now, so we can just fly straight over it.'

'Nevertheless we must be cautious,' pressed Thaw. 'I suggest that we adopt a few basic military procedures before travelling any further. That is, if none of you has any objection.'

As Thaw spoke these words, a subtle change came over the group. Ratchet angled close against his commander while Cumber and Velvet moved nearer to each other, unconsciously closing their own ranks against the others. Smoke was left hovering alone between the two pairs. None of the moves was in the least bit aggressive, but even so a message sped among them.

Things have changed, thought Velvet with a barely disguised shudder. For that brief moment, each of the five dragon's faces was without emotion. But then an eddy whipped a froth of vapour into their midst and the moment passed.

'Come,' instructed Thaw in clipped tones. 'Smoke will continue to pathfind, but Ratchet will fly close cover on her rear flank. Cumber, Velvet, you fly next, close enough to maintain voice contact but far enough away to break for cover if need be. I will be rear patrol. Any questions?' There were none. 'Good. We move on.'

And so, with faces hard and wingbeats measured, they ascended the last short distance to the top of the cliff in the prescribed pattern. Velvet exchanged a pensive glance with Cumber, for their position at the centre of the formation defined them as defenceless. She looked back at yellow and black wings: Thaw had stamped his authority on the expedition with such ease.

'Thaw!' cried Smoke as she cleared the cliff top, cycling her wings abruptly in the thin air. 'I think you ought to see this!'

The ex-Charmed commander flew nimbly past the others to where Smoke was hovering. Without being instructed to do so, Ratchet slipped back to take up his commander's post at the rear. Velvet leaned close and whispered to Cumber, 'Did you ever feel like you were being left out?'

'Well, I suppose they know what they're doing,' offered Cumber lamely.

'Hmph!'

At the head of the group Thaw was gasping in surprise and motioning the others to stay back.

'Oh, I've had enough of this!' exclaimed Velvet presently, and she thrust her way up to where the two dragons were floating over the ridge. Both were looking down with expressions of bewilderment.

'Really, Velvet,' began Thaw as she approached, 'I must insist . . .'

'Never mind that,' she snapped, 'what are you two . . .'

But there she stopped, for she too had seen what lay beyond: nothing! On the other side of the ridge there lay nothing more than the same billowing cloud layer from which they had just emerged. In fact, the cliff was revealed to be not a cliff at all, but a sheer, slender plate of rock stretching up from the ground like a dragon's scale stood on its edge. The top of this impossibly narrow wall was as sharp as frost and jagged like a broken tooth, and the opposite side dropped away with dizzying ease into the foaming cloud. Unheard-of vertigo gripped Velvet for a fraction of a breath until she came to her senses and registered what she was seeing.

'It's impossible!' she blurted.

'I know,' agreed Smoke acidly. 'But it's there all the same.'

Cumber joined them then, so that only Ratchet, hovering diligently some distance behind them, was maintaining the military protocol so recently established. Cumber too expressed wonder and incredulity at what they had come up against, but as he watched something even stranger began to happen: the clouds began to fall away. If they had seemed like an ocean before, now they were subject to the most extraordinary ebb tide. One by one the dragons alighted on the painfully sharp rock, unable to hold themselves

72

in the air in the face of such an awesome spectacle.

Slowly at first, then at an ever-increasing speed, the layer of cloud dropped away from the ridge. Its upper surface fragmented as wind whipped it into a fury, but this turbulence could not restrain the greater bulk from its headlong descent. For a while it continued to fill their vision as far as the horizon, but presently, far away to the north, mountain peaks broke through the plunging vapour.

As they sped earthward so great tears began to appear in the clouds, gaping cavities revealing their depths. Light flared as claws of lightning snapped across the divides. The sky rumbled.

Then the first of the holes expanded, and through a patch of clear air the ground was visible again, immensely distant. As if this were a signal, more openings formed in the speeding vapour through which more and more of the pale and featureless land was revealed. Before long the clouds evaporated into the air. The last of the strands of mist boiled away, leaving spread out before them a panoramic view so immense that all the dragons were transfixed at the sight of it.

It was the Heartland, but it had *changed*. Once in the Heartland there had been a narrow belt of desert blending swiftly into the rich river land of the north; now the desert was master. It stretched, it expanded as far as they could see, reaching its claws in every direction, even as far as the far-away mountains. The expected green was nowhere; grey and bland, the desert dominated, a dead plain which beckoned to them, *I am big enough to swallow all of you.*

'Come here, Ratchet,' ordered Thaw grimly after many breaths spent simply absorbing the immensity of this daunting new vista. 'You might as well see this too.'

As the burly warrior joined them, grunting his own shock at the unexpected view, Smoke lifted herself into the air. 'I think this wall has done its work,' she announced, turning to look down upon the others. 'So we might as well carry on. I'll pathfind still, if you want me to, although this isn't the Heartland I used to know.'

'Your role is unchanged,' Thaw confirmed, joining her in

the flimsy air. 'Ratchet, to your station!' Then he added, 'Cumber, Velvet. Are you both all right?'

Velvet flew up to their self-appointed commander, beckoning urgently for Cumber to follow her, which he did with a clumsy flurry of his broad, white wings. 'We're quite able to carry ourselves, you know,' she said bluntly. 'I'm sure you're a very able dragon but I'd be grateful if you'd stop ordering us all about!'

Ignoring her, Thaw turned smoothly to Velvet's mate. 'Cumber – do you have any protest to make?'

Cumber thought for a moment before responding, then said, glancing nervously at Velvet, 'No, Thaw. You're right – we should be cautious and ... and we trust your judgement, at least as long as there may be danger.'

'Good.' The ex-Charmed warrior gave them both a thin smile. 'Now, let us proceed. Smoke?'

At his signal Smoke spun her lithe body downwards and soared away from the ridge, leading their small band back towards the earth. Velvet waited until Thaw and Ratchet had exchanged positions again, slipping past them on easy wings, before turning to her mate.

'Why didn't you back me up?' she whispered. 'We should watch out for Thaw. He's getting a bit too full of himself.'

'Well, I don't agree,' Cumber replied haughtily. 'He might be a bit overbearing but he's right all the same, and he has got the kind of experience we need. I think we should trust him.'

And so they left behind the heights of the extraordinary wall of rock, dropping down past its northern face towards the arid land which awaited them. In many ways the descent was like waking from a dream into reality, but it was a grim reality, an unanticipated peril, and promised only danger and hardship. Above them the sun was hot and cruel, and below them the looming grey soil was cracked and dry. At their backs the wall was like a barrier, cutting them off from all they had left behind. With considerable trepidation they approached a waterless place none of them knew.

Eager to avoid the cruel heat of the sun, they were grateful at first for the massive shadow cast by the receding cliff wall.

But the air was hot and dry and as the red light of evening crept across them, so too did exhaustion. Thaw suggested that they stop and rest, and then fly further after nightfall so that the next day they would not feel they had to spend too long in the air beneath the dehydrating midday sun.

'We have found no water yet this side of the cliff wall,' he reminded them all. 'This way we stand a chance of reaching whatever watering places there may be with minimum effort.'

None of his companions could argue with his logic and that night they managed to cover some considerable distance in the cool dark. As dawn lightened the sky, Ratchet and Smoke flew wide and high in an attempt to spy out any cover beneath which they might spend the hottest middle hours of the day, and perhaps even sleep. Unfortunately the desert was an unbroken sea of dunes stretching in every direction – but for the direction they flew. Far, far ahead a great rock mesa breached the waves of grey sand, but it was too remote for anyone to judge how long they would take to reach it. At Thaw's command they landed together in a steep-sided valley between two dunes to decide what they should do.

'We can't go any further today, that's for certain,' announced Velvet before any of the others could speak.

'No one is saying we should,' answered Thaw rather sharply. 'But we must make up our minds as to what the best course of action is. Any suggestions?'

No dragon spoke. They were all exhausted and in desperate need of food and – more importantly – water. They had had nothing to drink since the previous morning and in the valley of sand which enclosed them they could feel the air temperature soaring as the sun climbed higher.

'If this is what Brace and the others found,' said Smoke dismally, 'then what we're most likely to find is their bones piled in some corner of this forsaken place!'

'Don't talk like that!' snapped Velvet. 'Don't even think like that. We'll find a way out of this, or I'm no dragon!'

'I have a suggestion,' said Thaw suddenly. 'It may be possible to tunnel into the side of one of these dunes and make a crude cave. We'll still be hot, I suspect, but not nearly as hot as we will be if we stay out here for the rest of the day.'

'Yes,' retorted Velvet, 'and we won't have to worry about the heat at all when the whole thing collapses in on us and we can't breathe.'

'Give him a chance, Velvet,' said Cumber. 'It might work.'

'Well, I'm not digging,' Velvet asserted, turning her back on Thaw in dramatic fashion.

'Neither am I, I'm afraid,' echoed Smoke more agreeably, but just as firmly. 'It's a good idea but I don't want to be the one to try it.'

'I'll do it,' rumbled Ratchet, loping towards the steeper of the walls of sand. 'If you want me to, chief.'

'Well,' sighed Thaw, 'if there are no better ideas?'

There were not, and so he nodded to the great, lumbering warrior, who had already taken up a post where the sand levelled out on to the valley floor. Prodding the densely packed sand with one wing, Ratchet hauled a narrow wedge of the fine, grey material out and scattered it behind him. There was the briefest of pauses before the remaining overhang collapsed into the space the big dragon had just made.

Grunting and setting his four legs wide, Ratchet took a bigger chunk out with his right wing, then quickly followed up the movement with an even broader sweep of his left. Sand showered into the air, some of it hurled by Ratchet, some billowing from the dune as it toppled. Soon he was all but invisible in a boisterous fog of grey particles, and an ominous rumbling was building above. Just before the entire upper part of the dune wall caved in on top of him, Thaw leaped forward and hauled him bodily backwards and out of the way of the landslip. Swaying and coughing, Ratchet looked disconsolately at his work.

'I'm sorry, chief,' he apologized, his face working with concern. 'I'll give it another go, if you want me to.'

'That won't be necessary,' replied Thaw, his face like stone. 'We have no choice, dragons – we must fly on.'

Smoke and Ratchet shrugged philosophically but could not disguise the hopelessness they felt. Would this desert claim them so easily, when they had barely started on their journey? Cumber shifted his weight uncertainly, and seemed about to make some sort of response when Velvet exploded.

'You can't be serious, Thaw! We won't last another day flying in this sun! We'd be better off staying here until night, saving our energy at least. And who are you to drive us on like this anyway? There's nothing to stop us just turning back, you know! Why don't you ask what we think for a change?'

'The longer we go without water the less energy we'll have, rested or not,' explained Thaw patiently. 'Believe me, Velvet, if there were any other way . . .'

'There must be another way, Thaw! You've put yourself in charge – *you* find it!'

It took much gentle persuasion by Cumber to stem the flow of tears which burst forth then. Velvet sobbed long and hard, and the others retreated to a discreet distance in order to allow the young dragon to regain her composure. At length, she walked back over to where they stood pressed into what was left of the shadow of the opposite dune wall. She marched straight up to Thaw and said in a loud, clear voice,

'I'm sorry, Thaw. I don't agree with everything you do, but it's not your fault we're stuck out here. In this particular case I accept you're right – we have to go on – so the sooner we start the better.'

Thaw cast a quizzical glance at Cumber, who nodded in silent reply, then he offered Velvet a weary smile and said, 'Well, young dragon, I suppose that's the closest I'll get to an apology from you. Come on, then – let's go. Same formation. Smoke, lead the way.'

Desert flying was hard, demanding a delicate balance between travelling high, where the air was cooler, but not too high. The thinness of the air at high altitude demanded faster – and more tiring – wingbeats.

For two days they travelled with no food and no water. Below them the blurred grey monotony of the desert rolled by so slowly that they seemed to make hardly any progress. The sun arched its way through the sharp, transparent sky at the same agonizing pace. Its heat thumped against their backs and wings and dragged the water from their bodies like a hungry beast sucking the life from their veins. They alternated what Thaw called shadow-shifts – a technique he had learned from Wraith himself – whereby one dragon flew directly above another so as to shade his companion from the worst of the heat. At the end of the second day, as the sun dropped again at its tauntingly slow rate, so they spiralled towards the sand once more, afraid now for their lives.

Before they landed, Thaw called a brief council in the air, for it seemed that at last they had a choice of where to land. The rocky plateau which had promised the possibility of water, or at least some proper shelter from the sun, was still impossibly far away, but below them and to their left was a narrow canyon snaking through the rolling dunes. It was here they agreed that they should rest until the next night, when they would make a final effort to reach the plateau. Not one of them dared to consider the possibility that they would not reach it even then.

So down they flew into the welcome shadow of a cracked and crumbling gorge cut at random through the dry dust. Ledges and precipices tumbled away into darkness, but even in the poor light they could all see that this sanctuary would indeed provide them with sufficient shelter for as long as they cared to stay. Exchanging barely a word, they each chose a ledge or hollow and did their best to settle down for the night.

Despite her intoxicating fatigue, Velvet could not sleep. Her wings ached. Even though she held them still, they felt as though they were in the air, beating, beating. In the end she could bear the throbbing no longer and took to pacing up and down, taking care not to disturb Cumber, who was curled up and sleeping deeply at the far end of the ledge they had chosen.

Small rodents scrabbled in the dust on the opposite side of the canyon, their movements strangely comforting to Velvet as she prowled in the darkness. The tiny creatures, just visible in the dim starlight as scurrying shapes of silver, were the first signs of life she had seen since they had crossed into the desert. Their presence here meant that there had to be water somewhere nearby, but Velvet suspected that it was far down in the narrow bowels of the gorge, quite inaccessible to big, clumsy dragons. Even with her desperate thirst she could not bring herself to venture down there.

Obsessively she brooded on the way Thaw had taken command until another movement broke her thoughts, a larger, dragon kind of movement. On the adjacent ledge Smoke was pacing too, swishing her muscular tail across the ragged stone and humming softly to herself. With a supreme effort, Velvet half-leaped, half-glided the short distance to the other ledge, landing heavily at Smoke's side. Acknowledging her visitor's presence with a brief smile and a nod, Smoke went on pacing up and down, but silent now, as though Velvet's arrival had stolen her eerie song.

On the return leg of her repetitive march Smoke paused for a breath, her head cocked slightly to one side, before carrying on again. She did this several times before Velvet plucked up the courage to break into her hypnotic routine. 'What do you hear, Smoke?' she asked.

Her fellow traveller stopped and then replied, 'Things moving. Out there.'

She seemed almost in a trance, and Velvet found herself speaking to her as though to an infant. 'What things, Smoke? Animals, do you mean, out there in the desert?'

'Lots of things. All moving. Everything's moving now – everything.' Smoke shook herself free of her daze and focused in on Velvet. 'I'm sorry,' she said, her voice suddenly loud in the blackness, 'what did you say?'

Velvet moved in close to her. What little starlight there was picked out the cracked and swollen skin around Smoke's lips. She seemed in pain. Velvet guessed that she herself looked about the same, and was perversely glad that there were no pools of water around in which she might catch her undoubtedly dreadful reflection. The ubiquitous grey sand was lodged into every crack in her scaly hide, grinding painfully with each movement she made and marring its whiteness.

Smoke's light brown scales were equally contaminated, but in the strange half-light it seemed to Velvet that colours

79

other than grey and beige were shining forth from where she stood.

'Smoke,' she began hesitantly, 'I've often wondered . . . I mean, your name – Smoke. It never struck me as a particularly *natural* name. I don't mean to be rude . . .'

'That's all right,' Smoke reassured her. 'As a matter of fact there is a little story behind it, if you want to hear it.'

'I've nothing better to do,' Velvet shrugged.

'My parents were very superstitious dragons. We used to live on the south bank of Heldwater – that's the inland sea I told you about that we should have reached today. But even Heldwater isn't where it ought to be now . . . Anyway, the whole shore was lined with trees – we were forest dragons.'

'Like me.'

'Really? Oh yes, you used to live on the Plated Mountain, didn't you? It must have been terrible when Wraith burned the forest – I can't imagine how you must have felt.'

'Terrified,' replied Velvet with conviction. 'And angry too. But go on, Smoke, please. Finish your story.'

'It's not much of a story really. For five years before I was born there was an awful drought and the forest became so dry all the dragons kept close to the water's edge for fear there would be a fire . . .'

'Don't tell me, let me guess,' blurted Velvet excitedly. 'The instant you were hatched the forest caught fire and they all had to flee and so they named you Smoke in memory of their escape.'

'Well no, not quite,' laughed Smoke, gradually relaxing now in Velvet's easy company, 'although that would have made a fine tale. No, what happened was this: my parents chose the name Smoke as a kind of lucky talisman against the fire ever coming. They thought that if they made their own smoke, then the forest would never need to catch fire.'

Velvet pondered this for a while, then shook her head. 'I preferred my version,' she decided, which caused Smoke to laugh once more, only this time twice as loud.

'Oh, it's good to laugh, even here,' she chuckled. 'Thank you, Velvet – you've cheered me up more than you could know.'

'Good. So tell me, *was* there a forest fire in the end?'

'No,' answered Smoke, and again a dreaminess returned, if only briefly, to her voice. 'It rained. The night I was hatched there came the first proper rainstorm for five consecutive years, and the rain didn't stop for another thirty days.'

'Gosh,' said Velvet after a suitable pause. She looked at Smoke with wide eyes. 'So there is a bit of mystery about you after all.'

'Mystery? No, not really. But I do wonder sometimes . . .'

As Smoke's eyes grew distant Velvet was reminded of another of her natural friends, and of the mood which sometimes came over her when she was thinking of times past.

'You're very like Gossamer, you know,' she announced suddenly. 'So tell me, did you ever dabble with charm, even just a little bit? Because I think there's more about you than meets the eye, Smoke – a great deal more.'

At this Smoke shrank back, her wings tensing. No longer did she look relaxed; instead she grew wary and her eyes hardened. Here again was the distant Smoke, Smoke the loner. As though Velvet's probing had been for nothing, all of her good humour evaporated at a single stroke of the wing and Velvet found that the dragon who remained was daunting, even frightening.

'I'm a pathfinder,' Smoke intoned coldly, 'and that's an end to it. Any qualities which you detect in me are dedicated to that task and that alone. Now, please – I am tired.'

With a weary flourish of her light brown wings, Smoke flicked a layer of sand into the darkness and turned her back on Velvet, leaving her visitor no choice but to glide back to her own ledge.

What nerve did I touch? Velvet pondered as she curled up next to Cumber. Sleep was prowling her mind now as well as her body, and she hoped at last to find rest. *She knows charm, or I'm no dragon. Still, I suppose she has every right to keep it private. Such a pity – we were just beginning to get along so well.*

Night spiralled above the canyon and at last all the dragons who sheltered there were asleep. The dreams sharing the darkness with them were themselves dark and full of omens, sand shifting to spawn monsters and bury friends, and a great river racing towards a precipice of unimaginable height.

Through the dreams of them all it flowed, this river. It roared as it reached the precipice's edge, vanishing downwards in a vast explosion of spray. To most of the dreamers it was simply the essence of water, the primal source of life for which they all yearned so desperately now. But to one of them it was something else. For one dragon the water carried in its prodigious current old hopes and desires, and that dragon alone dreamed his way through the mist of the falls to see what lay within.

What lay there was old and dreadful, but it made promises no dragon could resist. Ahead it was, somewhere, if directions still meant anything in this shifting land. North, where the river flowed and the sound of charm was loud indeed.

CHAPTER 8

The Storm

It started just four days after the departure of Thaw and the others, with the death of Rangle. Fortune found the old dragon sprawled across the clumsy nest in which he had lived alone on an isolated stretch of beach overlooked by imposing cliffs. As grey in death as it had been in life, his body lay half in and half out of the waves, thrown upon the sand as though left there by the departing tide. The old dragon's body showed no marks to suggest foul play, but still Fortune could not help remembering Ledra's curious comment on the day of the departure. Her wild green eyes came into his mind and he knew she was capable of anything.

Before pursuing his suspicions, Fortune roused a small group of dragons to help him bring Rangle's body back up the beach, where the whole community, led by Quill, gathered to pay its last respects before a pair of Thaw's ex-Charmed soldiers carried him out to sea and committed him to the waves. The gravity of the moment was lost on no dragon there, for not only had the elderly councillor been generally well-liked – even if he had frequently been the butt of some dragon's joke – but his death marked an important turning point for Haven. Aria was the first to have been born here . . . and Rangle was the first to have died. The dragons of Haven were badly shaken with the reminder that not only might they be barren, but they were mortal too.

They left the ceremony in sombre mood, which was of course fitting, but Fortune felt that the emotion ran deeper than it should have done. *Out of the eye*, he thought as he was left alone on Rangle's beach. *But into what?*

83

Ledra did not attend the funeral, nor did any of her followers. A few enquiries confirmed that no one had seen them nor knew where they were, and as he returned to his nest that evening Fortune was increasingly troubled.

'Surely Ledra doesn't have it in her to kill any dragon?' said Gossamer when Fortune poured out his worries. 'And what could she possibly gain from killing poor Rangle?'

'He was a councillor. With him gone her power is increased.'

'Hardly. Another dragon will be elected soon enough. And Ledra will scarcely be the most popular dragon around when – or if – she comes back.'

'Well, yes, I suppose you're right. We'll wait and see . . . for now. But how's my favourite daughter?'

As if in response to his voice, Aria chose that moment to wake up, greeting her father with a vigorous yell. Shaking off his melancholy he gathered her up into his wings and stared deep into wide, black eyes.

'I never knew my father,' he whispered. 'But you'll know me, little one, I promise you that. I'll look after you.'

'Will you now?' Gossamer butted in with a mischievous grin. 'Well, father, you can start now: she needs bathing, and then you can try her with some of the milk I've kept from those nuts. Fatherhood isn't all sweet nothings, you know.'

'Why don't we all go down to the beach?' suggested Fortune, but Gossamer cut him short.

'I've got a better idea. You two go to the beach and I'll take a nice evening flight. It's time I started getting fit again. Take your time,' she added, smiling.

Fortune watched as she walked out to the cliff edge, breathing deep and spreading her wings as if she were a youngster venturing out for the very first time. Then up she leaped, catching the rising eddies and spiralling towards the deep blue sky. When she had gone, Fortune carefully placed Aria on his back, making sure she was gripping his dorsal plates with her tiny claws, and flew down to the small cove which lay directly below the cliff face. There he gently bathed her in the fresh water which spurted from a narrow crevice in the rock at the top of the beach, then carried her down to the sea.

Waves kissed his claws. He looked north towards Sharp, and saw once more a smudge of grey smoke in the sky above the distant island. It looked curiously *real*, too real, as though he were observing it from within some other dragon's dream.

The next morning Quill was there to greet them as they woke.

'Good morning, dragons,' she said in her warm, matronly way. 'I think we may have some problems.'

'Hello, Quill,' yawned Gossamer, rubbing her eyes with her wing as she pulled herself upright. 'Would you like something to eat?'

'Thank you, dear, but no. I'll get straight down to business if I may. Time's a tide, and there's no sense swimming against it.'

'Could we move away from the nest?' asked Fortune, quietly clambering out and on to the sloping, rocky ground. 'Aria might sleep a little longer yet if we don't disturb her.'

They settled themselves a couple of wingspans from the nest and Quill began. 'Ledra has gone,' she announced, then added, 'I see from your expressions that you already knew this, or suspected it at least.'

'Yes,' replied Fortune. 'Do you know it for certain?'

Quill nodded. 'A dragon of Thaw's saw her fly north with ten others two nights ago. It takes no great imagination to guess where she was heading.'

'Sharp Island,' said Gossamer.

'Almost certainly. Of course, she is as free as any of us to go where she pleases, even if she is foolish enough to join Hesper and his gang of thugs, but what concerns me most of all is the council. No doubt you realize, Fortune, that with Cumber and Thaw absent, and with Rangle dead and now Ledra gone too, the situation here is rather extraordinary.'

Despite his uneasiness Fortune managed to laugh.

'Well, yes,' he agreed. ' "Extraordinary" isn't a bad word,

I suppose. Things have certainly changed and changed fast – all of a sudden the council has gone from six to two.'

'What do you suggest?' Gossamer asked Quill.

'There is probably no immediate cause for concern,' the ex-Charmed dragon answered. 'After all, we can console ourselves with the fact that most of our known or suspected troublemakers have now left Haven. But despite the small size of our community the council is important. We should meet today, all of us, and discuss what is to be done. With both of those troublemakers gone, not to mention their hangers-on, the population of Haven Island has dropped faster than a wingless dragon. We must do what we can to consolidate, to bring what is left of the population together before every dragon takes it into their head to wander off somewhere.'

'There's rounding up to be done, then,' said Fortune.

'No question about it,' came Quill's instant reply, 'and straight away won't be soon enough. If I take the south side of the island, Fortune, will you take the north? Noon, on the council hill, the whole community?'

'I'll gather all the dragons from the western beaches if you like,' put in Gossamer. 'That will save you both a lot of unnecessary flying.'

'Agreed,' said Quill. 'Until later.' And off she flew.

'She certainly means business. Are you sure you're up to all this?' Fortune asked Gossamer when their visitor had gone. Gossamer stared at him for a couple of breaths and then slapped him indignantly on the flank.

'What do you think I am, dragon?' she cried. 'Some kind of invalid? You just watch me – I bet I'm on that hill before you are!'

Far from the hospitable shores of Haven, dawn was a sullen affair that filled none of the weary desert travellers with hope of any kind. It was in dry and dismal humour that they awoke one by one, and it was some time before even Thaw summoned forth the energy to speak. They grudgingly collected themselves on his ledge and listened to his attempts to raise their spirits. Before long however, Cumber summed up the mood of the group by saying, 'I'm sorry, Thaw, but much as we appreciate what you're trying to do, I think it would be better for all of us if we just set off right now.'

In the end it was Ratchet who led them up out of the canyon and into the low, dull sunlight. They started out hesitantly, partly because of their flagging spirits but also because there was a thick haze which obscured the middle distance. This was a good time to fly, while the day was still relatively cool, but the sun would soon burn its way through the haze. To their surprise, though, as they laboured on, the vapour in the air actually began to condense. The land beneath them was rising and the haze was swiftly thickening into patchy cloud as they flew north. By mid-morning the sky around them was a brilliant patchwork of blue and white.

The sun, their constant torturer, slipped in and out of view as the wind whipped the clouds into life. In the open sky it was still uncomfortably hot, but at least now there was always a cloud shadow not far ahead, a blessed haven of darker air to beckon them on. The land rose further and at last there was rock and soil visible, breaking through the omnipresent grey sand. As they lifted themselves higher into the air so their hearts began to lift too, and then came Smoke's cry from the front.

'Rain!' she screamed, her voice cracking both with dryness and emotion.

And sure enough, there ahead of them was a great bank of metallic grey cloud trailing beneath it a sheet of shimmering water. Into the water's embrace they flew, crying and laughing as they swooped through the rain storm, their parched bodies cooled and nourished and their spirits renewed. Down they plunged, rejoicing in the feel of the cool, damp air, then reared up again with mouths agape, drinking the water in a frenzy of flight and refreshment. Thaw called out, warning them not to drink too much too quickly, but they all ignored him – even Ratchet. They had crossed the desert, and survived!

The rain clouds were moving north with the prevailing wind, and so for a long time the dragons moved north with them, drenched but reluctant to leave this refuge. As far as they could see the sky was filled with the same broken cloud, and ahead the land was rising steadily and already beginning to show patches of green amid the grey rock, but still they wanted to keep their rain, this first water for too many days. It was Thaw, still in command, who finally called them down to the ground, announcing that they were all in need of proper rest.

'There's a green patch down there,' he called, spiralling around his companions as though he meant to herd them like a group of infants. 'And if I'm not mistaken this rain is starting a flood in that gully to the side. It's a perfect place to see out the rest of the day.'

This time they all agreed with him. Their mood now buoyant and their exhaustion oddly comforting, they descended towards the curved valley Thaw had indicated, the side gullies of which were indeed beginning to flood. Not long after they landed the heavier clouds, moving ever faster to the north, passed them by, but the ground was saturated and there was enough fresh drinking water pouring down the slopes to sustain them for many days.

None of them wanted to sleep, tired though they all still were, preferring to wait until nightfall in the hope of regaining something like a normal sleeping pattern. They fidgeted, conversation unforthcoming, until in the end they all congregated around Smoke, who was looking keenly north-east, her upraised wing shading her eyes from the now-gentle sun.

'Do you know where we are?' blurted Velvet, impatiently voicing the question which they all wanted desperately to ask.

'Not exactly,' replied Smoke cautiously, 'but I do recognize those mountains.'

'The Low Mountains?' questioned Thaw, and they all held their breath. Aether's Cross lay at the heart of the main pass through the Low Mountains; if that was what Smoke could see then they were within sight of their destination!

'No,' she answered, and they all sighed. 'It's very odd,' she went on, 'but it looks to me as though we've passed by the Low Mountains altogether and travelled much further north than we should have done. If I'm not mistaken – and I'm not – those are the mountains of the Spine.'

'Of course!' exclaimed Cumber suddenly, jumping up and down with excitement. 'Yes, Smoke, you're absolutely right – that *is* the Spine! How am I so sure, you're asking? Well, because I've been here before, when Fortune and I were travelling south from Torr. We're travelling north and so they're on our other side, but all the same I should have realized straight away!'

'Slow down, please, Cumber,' put in Thaw with the briefest of smiles. None but Velvet noticed that he seemed irritated both by Smoke's certainty and Cumber's enthusiasm. 'If what you say is right then what has happened to the Low Mountains? If that's the Spine then they should be . . .'

'Then they should be right here!' confirmed Cumber, his interruption, it seemed to Velvet, serving only to aggravate Thaw further. 'So you were right all along, Thaw – strange things are going on here in the Heartland. We've had an impossible wall of rock appear overnight and then vanish the next day, we've had a small desert grow so large that we could barely get across it . . . and what about that plateau we were heading for all those days? Where did that disappear to?'

'But a whole mountain range, Cumber?' said Velvet uncertainly. 'Could charm really make the Low Mountains just disappear?'

'Of course,' Thaw butted in.

'Yes,' Cumber echoed at once, nodding wisely. Thaw frowned, and was about to speak again himself when Cumber gaily went on, 'But this is different. My old teacher – Ordinal she was called, and a great dragon she was too – used to tell me time and time again that the world was turning, which of course it was, but I never used to understand her. We all know now, of course, what the Turning meant . . .'

'If I may interject, Cumber,' Thaw grated, 'while this is all very interesting, do you not think . . .'

'Yes, yes, yes, Thaw, give me a chance. I know we all know all this, but the point is that I've been wondering why it should have stopped six moons ago. You've been saying it's charm that's working all this mischief, but I think you're wrong.'

Thaw blinked and cocked his head, his expression curiously alert. 'You do?' he asked in a polite tone.

'Oh yes, completely, if you don't mind my saying.'

'Not at all, Cumber. Do go on – I am most anxious to hear what you have to say that is so enlightening.'

As Thaw spoke, Velvet caught Smoke's eye and saw that she shared her unease about the big commander. *Thaw must be watched*, their shared glance said, and the exchange went a long way towards reviving the comradeship they had started to build on the ledge in the canyon. Velvet felt her heart softening again towards this strange, intense dragon.

'Thank you, Thaw, I will,' continued Cumber, quite oblivious to the big dragon's sarcasm. 'You see, I think it's like this: nature has inherited the world, just like a dragon inherits its parents' nest when they die. But most dragons aren't really very happy with what they get, are they? I mean to say, they either move out altogether or change the place around – knock down some screens here, dig out a deeper scrape there and so on. And that's *exactly* what's happening around here: the world is remaking itself to suit the new laws which rule it – the natural laws. It's not charm working all this strange magic, Thaw. It's *nature*!'

Evidently unimpressed with Cumber's theory, Thaw grunted, 'What nonsense.' Ratchet nodded, presumably agreeing with his commander, but Velvet exchanged another glance with Smoke, and they too nodded – in agreement with Cumber.

'That makes sense, Cumber,' said Smoke encouragingly, much to Thaw's displeasure. 'And I must admit I find it strangely comforting that nature can work magic too.'

'Word-play,' growled Thaw. 'Nature's nature and charm's charm, and that's an end to it.'

'That may be,' acknowledged Smoke smoothly, 'but *this* –' and here she indicated the entire surrounding landscape ' – is now a natural world, Thaw, and the sooner we all accept that the better, don't you think?'

Thaw's mood might have darkened further at this point but, just when it seemed that his frown would crack the scales along his crest his expression relaxed and his wings drooped.

'Ah well,' he sighed expansively, 'I suppose you're right at that. But I'm not like you, Smoke. I knew charm once, and I miss its strength . . . and its order. Cumber knows what I mean. And you too, Ratchet.'

Again Ratchet nodded, but Cumber shook his head vehemently.

'No, Thaw,' he said, 'I'm afraid that's the difference between us, because I don't miss it. I don't miss it at all.'

Fortune thought later that he'd had a premonition of what was to come, but one so late and so ill-formed that he did not at the time recognize it for what it was. It came shortly after he left Gossamer to head north. As he flew towards his first goal – the well-populated bay known rather unimaginatively as Palm Cove – he fancied that he heard a sound over the distant rush of the sea.

It was another water sound, but one much more violent than the gentle sighing of the waves. It thundered in his ears, a rasping, hissing roar which swelled to a crescendo and then died away as quickly as it had come. It left him puzzling over whether it had been a noise inside his own head – or had he really heard it? The din of a colossal downpour, or perhaps a mighty river breaking itself against impenetrable cliffs.

The air was odd. The sky was a white haze, cooling the sun and softening Fortune's shadow as it rippled across the waving palm-tops. Yet the wind was hot and strong, as though it blew independent of the weather which filled the sky above.

The heavens want a storm, thought Fortune, unsettled by the contradictory elements. The heat of the wind, which was rapidly building towards a gale, was uncomfortable. He felt nervous.

Dragons flew out of the haze, very many of them, flying south from the sea. They were spread across the blurred sky in a long, straggling line, their wings beating various times and their individual courses wavering within the flock. Despite these minor perturbations their progress was relentless and before Fortune could draw breath they were over the coast and separating into four smaller formations, each pulling away in a different direction. The nearest of the groups carried on flying due south, heading straight for Fortune.

As they came for him, he thought only of Gossamer and Aria, grateful that they had flown west and he north, hoping that they would spot the approaching trouble and be able to escape it. On his own behalf, he permitted himself a grim smile, for the oncoming dragons were close enough now for him to be able to recognize their leader.

It was Hesper.

Rainwater was flooding off the thin soil of the valley uplands. They had landed halfway down the valley side where the ground flattened a little, briefly trapping the hectic flow of a thousand tiny rivulets. Leaving the others to their discussions, Velvet wandered down to the pool which was gathering in a depression nearby. Overflowing, the pool released water as a single, winding stream to continue its journey down towards the slowly flooding plain far below.

Velvet drank from the clear, fresh water, scarcely able to believe that she had woken that morning parched and sure that she was soon to die. The surface of the pool rippled and danced in the warm sunlight and its edges lapped over her claws.

Then she looked closer. Bubbles were rising near the far shore and she found her curiosity opening her wings for her. With a few easy strokes she was across to the other side and stretching her neck out over the water to see what was happening. Sure enough, at one point amid the ripples there was a steady stream of bubbles breaking the surface and popping cheerfully. She laughed, entranced.

Then something darted across her vision and the line of bubbles moved, tracking across the pool. Beneath the water flashed a silvery shape, then it was lost again into the darkness. More bubbles broke out to the right, and then to the left, and before long there were hundreds of the shapes speeding to and fro, gradually collecting into a single shoal filling a corner, then a quarter and then fully one half of the pool. They swam and turned and then arrowed towards the exiting stream, whereupon they fled precipitously through the rapids, downhill, and were gone from sight. But still the bubbles came, and still the silver shapes appeared, a never-ending source of them, filling the pool and the stream beyond with their living, darting energy.

'Fish!' exclaimed Velvet as a small group of the creatures paused long enough for her to be able to make out fins and shining tails and gaping eyes. Bubbles streamed from their gills and they glowed from within, but before she could examine them more closely they sped away to the side and were lost into the anonymity of the shoal.

Alerted by her cry, Cumber flew over to see what was wrong.

'Nothing's wrong,' she replied enthusiastically. 'Look – fish. Thousands of them, and more with every breath.'

'Don't be silly,' he scoffed. 'This whole valley was as dry as the desert before the rainstorm, so I don't see how there can possibly be . . .'

But Velvet gently guided his head with her wing until he too was looking down, mouth wide open, into the frothing water. Uncharacteristically lost for words, he stared soundlessly at the frantic activity which was going on beneath the surface, at the thousands of fish which seemed to be coming from nowhere.

'From nowhere,' he muttered, agitated now and fidgeting on the shore, which was shrinking still as the pool deepened and widened.

'What's happening?' said Velvet, thrilled by the discovery.

Cumber did not at first reply. Instead he stretched his white wings out over the water and closed his eyes. Though a Natural, he retained enough memory of the workings of charm to be able to sense the presence of some of the larger deposits of magic which had been abandoned here and there as the world turned. It was for such abandoned charm that he now probed. And he found it!

'Much charm,' he blurted, opening his eyes with a start. 'It was locked in the valley side. I was right – the land is moving by natural forces, reconfiguring itself to suit the new laws, but in doing so it's releasing some of the abandoned charm. Mantle warned us to be wary of its powers, but look what it's doing here – obviously the valley has shifted recently, and now the rain is carving into the hillside, and it's broken into the magic's lair. See what it's doing!'

'What? What is it doing?'

'It's *creating*, Velvet. It's making life! Isn't it incredible?'

Awe-struck, Velvet narrowed her eyes and peered as hard as she could into the water. The intensity of her gaze and a sudden burst of sunlight through a break in the cloud gave her an unprecedented view deep into the pool, and she gasped in wonder at what she saw there.

The silt on the bed of the pool was boiling. Unseen forces were pulsing through it, lifting its particles from the loose rock of the hillside and pumping them into the swirling water. There the grains were coalescing, gathering together into solid, streamlined forms which jerked and flexed and finally filled with a light which seemed to come from nowhere. Then, with a sudden, vigorous snap, the brilliant forms became living fish, fleeing into the stream, glowing still for a brief time before they finally locked themselves into the real world and became flesh. All this both Cumber and Velvet saw in a flash of sight and insight, and they knew that what they were witnessing was one of the final pieces of the puzzle of the Turning, a final truce between charm and nature in which wholly new creatures were being born.

As the sun retreated behind the clouds again they looked up, focusing on the wider world and then looking into each other's eyes, where they saw tears shining like beacons. Shining out like the glow of creation.

'Oh, Cumber,' whispered Velvet, 'isn't it beautiful?'

'Yes,' he answered with conviction, 'the most beautiful thing I've seen. It's charm at work, and it's beautiful.'

Quill saw that Ledra was among the newcomers appearing in the sky above her. She called to her fellow dragons, the first group she had contacted to summon them to the meeting, not to panic and to stay near her. They were a motley group of five Naturals who lived in shy seclusion in a shallow bowl of land filled with fruit groves. Caught unawares, she perused the approaching flock, trying to determine their intentions.

A dragon whose life had been dedicated to the protection of others, Quill invariably found it easy to make decisions. If she was in company then her every action was designed to help one or more of the dragons she was with; even if an especially large number of dragons fell under what she saw as her care still the decisions came easily, for she would simply substitute the good of an individual for the good of the whole group and act accordingly. Quill's was a world filled with decisions, all of them predetermined by her own carefully controlled rules, all of them implemented with efficiency and compassion.

As an ex-Charmed however, she found life without magic rather less easy to manage, just as she found it difficult to accept that she would never see Covamere, her beloved home, again. Most of her healing powers had been derived from some kind of charm – from the simple curative earth charms she had used to ease aches and pains to the dramatic fire charms with which she had restored severed limbs and even pieced together dragons' shattered minds – and now that the magic had gone she felt greatly weakened. She had thrown herself wholeheartedly into her new role as councillor because she was less able to help dragons physically.

This transformation had been a success in all respects but one – she was now never satisfied with what she achieved. So much of what she had done at the healing centre in Covamere had been of a practical nature that she found it almost impossible to be content with helping dragons in other, less tangible ways. Many times Thaw – who had become a close friend since their arrival – had reassured her, reminding her that even in those days she had done as much spiritual healing as she had physical. But even he could never fully convince her, though his words were always comforting. Compared to what she had once been, now she was useless.

And useless was precisely what she felt as Ledra and a group of five ex-Charmed dragons circled overhead, spinning faster and faster until their wings were a blur and it seemed that their tails met their mouths. Vapour puffed where their wingtips cut the air and the wind whistled through the centre of the hoop made by their spiralling bodies.

Energies left dormant for many moons began to rise from the ground, spitting like angry sprites, darting up towards the dizzying formation of dragons. The sky began to glow.

All across the turned world the land was moving. With slow grace the shifting scales of the Heartland were grinding across each other, their motion driven by the imperative to settle into an easier, more natural configuration. Narrow streams of abandoned charm, their flow interrupted by the pressing activity of the soil and in the deep rock, were leaking out into the twisting ground, bringing to the process an unnatural velocity. Thus the movement of mountains and the filling of oceans took not aeons but days, their blinding speed wholly of charm; a curious marriage, but one of undeniable power.

In this way there rose great cliff walls, their upward momentum created by pressure ridges formed when two mighty plates of land crashed together, and then sustained to an impossible altitude by the abandoned charm which was still bound up in the rock. The magic was strong enough to hold such ridges intact for only a day or two, so weak and perforated was it: the residual charm would soon succumb to gravity, allowing the risen land to slip with unnatural quiet back to earth. The ridge which the travelling dragons had encountered had been one such formation; its silent and magical collapse had occurred in the secrecy of night and so had passed unobserved.

Ridges, plateaux, inland seas and precipitous mountains; all these things were born and died over and over during those restless days. Old names faded away: Heldwater became a lake of salt and then was consumed by the vast, grey desert which hurried across the continent. Rain pursued the sand, crackling from the sky as moisture-laden charm broke free of the dryness which had trapped it, leaping skywards to form cloud upon cloud upon cloud. The Heartland – or whatever that place had now become, for the old names no longer held any power – nearly drowned in the floods which followed, until new mountains emerged from the water, sending up new and craggy backs like monsters breaching from the sea.

Nature and charm at work, their ultimate end unknown, creating the new world between them. The world beyond the Turning.

But the strangest aspect of the creation was the silence. The magic dulled the great, tearing sounds of stone as it was ripped apart deep underground, it absorbed the growl of the speeding seas as they surged up hills and across barren wastes. As though the world were somehow ashamed of the unholy partnership of forces which it had employed to carve its face anew, it imposed this silence upon all that occurred. Silence – and darkness too, for only when the sun had passed into the next corner of the world did the land shift again, bringing about the next great round of changes in the brief space of time before the dawn returned.

Through one such dark and secret silence the five explorers slept, unaware but for their dreams of the changes going on around them, unaware that the desert which had so nearly claimed them was no more, that in its place a huge salt sea had risen. Creatures other than fish poured now from the flooding valley where they slept, their creation simply a tiny piece of the greater puzzle which was the reshaping of the skin of the planet. Amphibious serpents thrashed in the shallows, sucking air past their gills and gaping into the mud which called them clear of the water. Insects melted from the coarse grass which had sprung up around the growing reservoir, scraping their legs and leaping high in clumsy imitation of flight.

Far down in the valley, where the swelling lake was gradually beginning to scale the lower slopes, other beasts were made, budded from the clay of the reservoir bed, brought life by a frantic release of charm as the water combined with the ceaseless turmoil of the land beneath. Larger they were, and altogether more mobile than the flopping, jerking creatures that swarmed amid the fast-flowing streams. New to this world, intoxicated by the explosive life-force which coursed through their veins at their birth. They began to search for prey.

*   *   *

Fortune was surprised when, instead of challenging him, Hesper and his companions paused a few wingspans short of where he was hovering. Then they began to circle, slowly at first, gathering speed. Soon he could barely make out individual dragons amid the blurred and merging shapes.

Get away! a voice shouted in his head. But it was too late.

A light grew at the middle of the circle, a pulsating glow which seemed to be approaching from a huge distance but then was suddenly all around him, enveloping his wings and crushing his ribs so that it was impossible to breathe. He cried out, stricken with panic.

They've come back to kill us all!

But he did not die. The light expanded further, pulling him into its throbbing centre until he was a part of it, and then his lungs filled with air again in a single, violent thrust as he was hurled through the sky at incredible velocity. He felt the wind tearing past him like a many-clawed beast, yet at the same time he felt separated from the real world, as though something had enclosed him within a bubble outside of time and reality, a bubble in which only he existed.

A bubble of charm! he thought with a curious mixture of horror and ecstasy.

The flight was as short as it was surreal. Before he could think any further the wind crashed to a halt and the light, against which he had closed his eyes, winked out. Something hard and rough thumped against his breast and he snapped out his claws automatically, trying to gain purchase on whatever surface this was. Distant thunder shook the air and he opened his eyes.

CHAPTER 9

Prey

Cumber woke suddenly, groping for a dream. He had been flying, and the sky had been filled with spray . . . but that was all he could recall. The dream slipped away like a speeding night dragon and his awareness was left black and empty.

Black – it was still night. Clouds obscured both moon and stars and it was only with the greatest difficulty that he made out Velvet, sleeping barely a wing's width from his side. Black and silent, except . . . except for two voices, whispering behind him. Dragons, but what were they saying?

'Are you sure you heard it?' That was Thaw, his deep voice confident and commanding.

'I heard it, chief, and I didn't like it. I'm telling you there's something down there.' Ratchet's gruff baritone, of course.

'Well, let's not wake the others just yet,' cautioned Thaw, his voice growing muffled for an instant as though he had turned his head away, perhaps to peer down the slope. 'Silent flight, please, Ratchet: just scout to the south for now, where you thought you heard the noise. Be back in one hundred breaths, no more.'

'Right away, chief.'

Cumber heard nothing as Ratchet lifted soundlessly into the dark sky. He waited patiently, his heart thumping as he tried to guess what the two warriors thought they had detected. Like most dragons, he had little fear of other animals, but he was nervous about what they might find here in this strange and altered land. He was about to wake Velvet when Ratchet returned.

'Nothing, chief. But I still don't like it. There's a smell.'

'You were trained for your strength, Ratchet, not your snout.'

'All the same, chief.'

His curiosity finally getting the better of him, Cumber spread his wings and performed a passable impression of a dragon just waking up. Yawning and smacking his lips, he ambled over to where the two soldiers had stationed themselves.

'Did I hear you two talking?' he inquired brightly. 'Something wrong? I thought I saw Ratchet scouting around, so I wondered if you'd spotted something out there.'

Thaw paused for a breath, then shrugged and answered, 'Ratchet just thought he heard something, that's all. I'm sure it's nothing, Cumber.'

'Hmm,' grunted Ratchet, obviously less certain of that than his commander.

'Well,' said Cumber, 'I suppose it's always worth checking these things, isn't it? I'm glad we've got a couple of military dragons out here with us, dragons who know a few procedures and that sort of thing.' Cumber was a little surprised to find that he was in fact glad of this. Realmshock and the memory of the battle of the Plated Mountain had blunted some of the adventurer in him; suddenly he *was* glad to have protection, he *was* reassured by the kind of strong, fighting dragon of which he had once been so wary.

Even I am changing, he thought philosophically. *Well, there's a thing!*

'You might as well get back to sleep, Cumber,' suggested Thaw. 'I don't think there's anything to concern yourself with, and if anything should happen then rest assured that . . .'

But there he stopped dead. From somewhere beyond their camp there suddenly came a loud shriek, made even louder by the depth of the silence that had preceded it. There was a pause, then a second shriek, this one much closer and truly ear-splitting. The first howl answered the second, and then a third joined, and a fourth, until a cacophony of crude voices filled the night with a dreadful, ululating song. It was like no sound the dragons had heard before, not any of them, and with brutal abandon it snatched Velvet and

100

Smoke clear of the profound sleep which had claimed them. They sped to the sides of their fellows, staring wildly into the gloom, trying desperately to see what terrible creatures were out there.

'What is it?' sobbed Velvet at last, for the longer and harder they listened the louder and wilder the howling became. The voices rose higher, then broke and barked and shrieked anew before ascending once more into the same, unbearable screaming. None answered but Ratchet.

'Bad creatures,' he said simply. 'Out there, coming nearer.'

'We must fly,' urged Smoke, stepping back from the rest of them and opening her wings. 'Now.'

'Wait,' replied Thaw quickly, his voice strangely hesitant. 'We don't know what's safest – after all, they might fly too . . .'

'Only dragons fly!' countered Smoke impatiently.

The approaching howls separated, and before any of the dragons could blink they were surrounded by the noise. Even Smoke, her wings poised to take her into the sky, was paralysed. The fear of the unknown had become a beast itself, harrying them and snapping at their flanks, hypnotizing them with its horrifying, rhythmic approach.

When Fortune opened his eyes he found a shelf of porous, black rock beneath his claws, so like the rock the Plated Mountain was made from that for a breath or two he thought he had been transported back there, perhaps even back through time itself to the moment of the Turning. But the soft rumble of the sea made him lift his head and he saw that he had not travelled nearly so far.

Far enough, though, it would seem.

It took him only a short time to work out where he was. The sky was the same, the sea was the same, but the land was very different. Black and lifeless where it should have been bounteously green, this could be only one place: Sharp Island.

A quick look around confirmed his suspicion. He had been deposited on the southern shore with a clear view of Haven, floating far away through the haze but unmistakable

101

nonetheless. Behind him the rock rose steeply towards the sharp ridge which had given the island its unwelcoming name. All was barren, a complete contrast to idyllic Haven. Hesper had sent him here somehow, and now . . . now what was he to do?

He had no time even to ponder the question for suddenly the air crashed open all around him and dragons dropped from holes in the sky. Balls of light gyrated in the empty spaces from which they materialized – which then snapped shut with explosive pops. Some, like Fortune, came alone; others came in larger groups, among them Quill, who appeared with both wings draped protectively around two cowering Naturals. Panicking momentarily, Fortune cried out with relief when he saw Gossamer fall to the hard rock a wingspan's distance from him; Aria rocked to and fro as her mother landed heavily but clung on tenaciously, mewing in fear. He rushed over to help Gossamer to her feet, brushing the black lava dust from her hide.

'I'm fine,' she reassured him.

'It was Hesper,' said Fortune angrily.

'And Ledra,' called another dragon before he could continue.

'That's an old charm, that one,' said some knowledgeable ex-Charmed. 'Quite a crude piece of magic really. In the old days a charmed dragon could have wielded it by himself with both wings strapped to his flanks. Took a lot of work for Hesper, though.'

'That's right,' confirmed Quill, her two Natural charges still sheltering at her sides. 'I'll wager it's taken him all this time just to store up enough charm for that one simple trick.'

'Well,' came a sturdy cry from somewhere behind her, 'it'll do him no good. I'm not stopping here, that's for sure! I say we head straight back for Haven and send him packing again!'

There was a general clamour of agreement which Quill silenced with an upraised wing. 'Wait a minute, dragons, he'll have thought of that. All the ex-Charmed here – help me for a moment.'

Bending forward, the ageing healer urged her fellow

dragons to stretch out what she called 'the ghost of your charm-sense' in an effort to detect any charm in the vicinity. After much frowning and heavy breathing, they reluctantly concluded that there was none.

'He used it all up,' came one cry.

'Or taken it with him,' came another.

'The latter's more likely,' said Quill. 'He'll be preparing his defences now or he's a bigger fool than he looks.'

'I still say we should just go straight back!'

'I think we ought to attack him!'

'Let's have done with him!'

'No.' Gossamer's voice floated through the outbursts but at length she was listened to. 'Why do we have to go back at all? There are a hundred islands here. Why fight over territory when there's plenty to choose from? If Hesper and Ledra want it so badly then I think we should just let them have it.'

Her words shocked the assembled dragons into silence – and angered many. This approach had not occurred to any of them but Gossamer, and for a breath or two none felt able to argue with her logic.

'It's the principle of the thing,' offered one young Natural. 'He just shouldn't get away with it, that's all.'

'Haven't we all done enough fighting?' urged Fortune, taking Gossamer's lead. She pressed herself against him, grateful for his support. 'Quill?'

'Hmm.' The prickly dragon was evidently torn and, for once, in need of more time to decide which course of action would be for the best. But then the decision – and indeed all immediate decisions other than to flee for safety – became irrelevant. Finally, in cataclysmic fashion, Fortune's storm struck the Western Sea and the archipelago of Haven.

The same, constant wind that had been blowing for so many days past suddenly and brutally accelerated to become first a gale, then a typhoon. Wave crests shattered, drenching the dragons and forcing them back up the steeply shelved beach of rock. Clouds hurled themselves up from the horizon and pounced upon the island chain. Sea and sky became one, a continuous exchange of water obliterating any boundary between the two. Day turned to a heavy, brown twilight scored by the occasional flicker of lightning high up in the boiling heavens.

The marooned dragons were taken completely by surprise, for no natural weather phenomenon could ever have produced such a tidal wave of changes so quickly. Prey to the storm, they struggled inland over the streaming rock in search of any shelter to be found on this barren isle. In their midst scrambled Fortune and Gossamer, clinging to each other and to their daughter lest one of them be swept away. Yet, despite the undeniable wrath the elements unleashed, Fortune found himself wondering what else was to come.

This is just the beginning, isn't it? he asked the raging sky.

They were utterly new to the dragons, these monsters, for never before had the world seen wolves. They were huge, each beast fully half as big again as Ratchet, himself the biggest of the dragons; even above their howling the dragons could hear the snapping of branches as their shoulders scraped against the overhanging trees. In the blackness it was hard to make out their shapes, but their size and ferocity were overwhelming and would never be forgotten: they were fat and greasy, their coarse pelts sagging over rolls of flesh and great bulges of bone. They stank. From their snapping jaws there poured a breath to rival that of the basilisks, a steaming, sickening vapour which was like a vomit in the air. One of them crashed straight into Smoke with its first leap, but it was not the force of the blow which knocked her unconscious – it was the poisonous stench of its breath.

But this first wolf, by far the largest of the four, did not pause to savage Smoke. It turned at once upon Ratchet, the strongest dragon, who was already beset by two other wolves. Cumber and Velvet could only look on in horror as dragon blood sprayed black across the dark sky, its arc horribly clear despite the meagre light.

'Get away!' Thaw screamed at them, ducking a blow from the fourth wolf and launching himself into the fray. 'Go now, save yourselves!'

There was no time to think, only to respond, and both Cumber and Velvet responded in like manner: they turned upon their ravening attackers.

The fight was a tangled, ferocious affair. Dragons unused to being prey; giant virgin wolves with no memory of this world, nor of any purgatory which might have preceded it. The dragons sought only survival, the wolves knew only hunger, and between them they turned the freshness of the valley slope into a bloodied battleground. Teeth sheared flesh and claws raked through fur and scale. Through it all the harsh wolf voices continued to sound, though their howls swiftly degenerated into broken snarls and grunts; for these newborns, voice represented life, and they were prepared to relinquish neither.

Cumber and Velvet struggled valiantly against foes superior in every way. The wolves seemed to sense that only flight could save the dragons, and so they took every opportunity to clamp their wings down, or else to leap upon them and restrain them bodily from fleeing to the air. Once Velvet broke free, only to be hauled down by her tail and returned to the mêlée. Ratchet and Thaw claimed most of the wolves' attention, and it was undoubtedly this fact which saved the lives of Cumber and Velvet. This fact, and one other.

The wolves were fighting a battle of attrition, wearing their opponents down rather than going for a swift kill. Had they tried they could probably have slaughtered all five of the dragons with little extra effort, but they were fresh to the world, as yet unpracticed as hunters, and so the dragons survived for far longer than they might otherwise have done.

Then, as Velvet fell back briefly from the jaws of one of the reeking beasts, she saw a shudder pass down its spine. All the bones in its back seemed to dance for the briefest of times, and then they were still again. As the creature's eyes glazed over, she took the opportunity to reach in and deliver a devastating blow across its snout with her clawed wing. The wolf's blood spattered across her wing membrane and she stilled the urge to vomit. Again the beast's spine trembled, and a cracking sound issued from somewhere deep within its belly.

No sooner had she gained this minor victory than a second wolf knocked her to the ground and bit deep into her flank.

She cried out in pain and in an instant Thaw was there, butting the slavering creature with cruel sweeps of his head, slicing through the creature's substantial neck with lowered horns. The wolf howled even louder and then it too shook and its eyes filmed over. Thaw paused, and watched with mouth agape as the wolf's shoulders bulged like tumours from its back and then dropped down beneath its pelt once more. A massive tremor shook its whole body and then, to the utter amazement of both Thaw and Velvet, it *contracted*.

Fur exploded from the body of the wolf as its body twisted and swayed ... and shrank! Its howls were now howls of agony, for the dragons could only guess what pain it was experiencing as its every bone cracked and bent. Looking up, Velvet saw that the same distortions afflicted the other three, and that Cumber and Thaw were gradually falling back, leaving the wolves to perform their eerie dance. She limped over to where her companions stood aghast, holding their wounds and breathing hard. Beyond the circle of ground where the wolves were writhing, Smoke was slowly coming round to witness this incredible turn of events with an expression of both disbelief and fascination on her face.

The wolves, blood-stained and hideously naked of fur, were growing smaller with every breath they took. Their bodies had been made too large for the mean spirits which inhabited them. Some malicious quirk of the abandoned charm which had brought about their creation had conferred upon them a grossly wrong physical stature. Now, the initial charm quite used up, dominant nature was taking its revenge and cutting them down to size – literally. They stood no taller than the dragons as their legs buckled: they were only half as big when they struggled again to their feet. Their skin glowed a sickly pink in the inadequate light, and their scattered fur lay all around them in black clots.

For one of the wretched creatures the transformation was too much, its body for a long while remaining grossly over-sized while its head narrowed and its legs contracted. Its eyes bulged from its shrunken skull as though they were about to burst then all of its legs broke like twigs under the weight of its huge body. The luckless creature crashed to the ground and died, but not before a set of massive internal organs had spilled, bursting from a suddenly contracting underbelly.

As if this were some kind of gruesome signal, the three remaining wolves grew suddenly silent. Their bodies had apparently stabilized – at a size approximating to one quarter of the bulk of an average dragon. Lurching across the gore-strewn ground, they fled the watching dragons, throwing not a single glance behind them as they scrambled away beneath the cover of the trees and away into the night. Into the darkness they sped, and ultimately out into the world, where they would gradually learn their true place and breed and grow sociable, yet remain forever bitter, forever angry with a world that had promised them such power . . . and then taken it from them when they had scarcely been born.

As for the dragons, they were too shaken to do anything more that night than nurse their wounds, some of which were grave. Between them, Cumber and Velvet had suffered only superficial cuts – although both were heavily bruised. Smoke was badly concussed and kept drifting in and out of consciousness, but had no obvious injuries other than a graze along the side of her head. Thaw was covered with blood, and bore several deep gashes down his left flank, as well as innumerable smaller cuts across most of his body. Though he was badly wounded, his battle training carried him through shock and out into a private limbo which prevented him from admitting to his companions the true extent of his suffering.

'It's mostly the blood from those monstrous creatures,' he said with forced casualness when Velvet urged him to let her help. 'It's Ratchet who needs help most.'

Poor Ratchet. Both of his wings were shredded, tatters of skin hanging from exposed bone like broken leaves. Like Smoke, he was only partly conscious, but unlike her he had suffered terrible injuries. One of his forelegs was crushed, his neck was torn and bloody, and hundreds of scales had been ripped from his back and flanks, leaving red and weeping skin exposed to the air. In great pain, he groaned his way into restless oblivion. Though Cumber washed his wounds as best he could, and Velvet whispered to him that everything would be all right, as the night wore on he grew quieter and stiller, and it seemed probable that he would not see another dawn.

In this way the dragons wandered through the wasteland of the night, hardly daring to believe that there *would* be another dawn, and even if there were that any of them would see it. But dawn did come, and see it they did, even poor Ratchet. Over the valley lifted the sun, revealing to the dragons the latest and most fundamental changes they had yet seen to the landscape they had once trusted to remain still. Their sense of wonder dulled by nightmare, the dragons could only look on with blank and weary expressions as new sounds filled the valley and new sights reared above the horizon, clean sunlight glinting with a thousand reflections off the towering spectacle now confronting them.

A wall of water.

A huge stone structure clinging to the face of the waterfall.

The sound of the river.

'What's happening?' whispered Velvet, staring up at the strange and shining vision. Yet even her curiosity was blunted and automatic: she could hardly have cared less what it was.

'I don't know,' replied Cumber, his voice pitched low, just for her, 'but whatever it is we have no power over it. We have no power at all now, we dragons; the world turns on without us playing even the tiniest part.'

The roar of the waterfall was loud but distant. Mists rolled but did not approach the exhausted dragons. The panorama which had risen during the night waited but did not draw any nearer. A plaintive, wailing cry drifted through the damp air.

'Let's just stay here, then,' said Velvet, closing her eyes and huddling against her mate. 'Let the world do what it must. Let's just rest.'

Above them, unseen, two stars streaked together across the sky and then separated; one headed north, the other turned towards the Western Sea as though it had found some inviting target among the many chains of islands which were slowly disappearing beneath the rising waters. The seas rose into the sky, and dragons sheltered where best they could, dwarfed by the giant peril which had beset them, able only to wait and watch.

CHAPTER 10

Veil

Another world . . .

It rotated lazily beneath Ocher's silver gaze. The hard, red light it reflected blanched the basilisk's pale body like the glow of some mighty fire, yet a fire which blazed with no heat. All was cold here, cold and dead.

There had been life of a kind, once, back in one of this world's many pasts. The basilisk recalled those times now, times when ponderous battles had broken across barren deserts, each one a clumsy skirmish in the greater war which had finally tipped the planet out of true, shattering its many moons and wiping the slow-thinking, slow-moving creatures from its surface once and for all. Another Turning that had been, on another world. The Red Planet.

Ocher spiralled down towards the dust, its myriad senses probing sterile wastes for signs which it knew had to be there. It was to this place that Veil had retreated long ago, the only one of the six basilisks to leave their native world to search for an inner peace – probably unattainable for one of its kind. Across the cold seas of space it had journeyed, finally settling here beneath the dust of the Red Planet, choosing like its siblings the counterfeit death of eternal sleep. Like Ocher and the others it had slept here for aeons, and as far as Ocher knew it slept still.

Ocher dispatched sensory scouts ahead of its plummeting body to seek out any trace of life in this deserted world. As they departed the basilisk felt its skin contract to accommodate the missing senses. Thin vapour streamed from the end of its prehensile tail; the scant atmosphere stung with a frigid embrace.

Although the body which Ocher inhabited was truly immortal, and although Ocher had been able to wield charm throughout its reign in the world – indeed all the basilisks had been grand masters of the arts of magic – the basilisk form was not in itself charmed. What it did possess however was a skin of living senses, an outer membrane formed from a host of parasitic intelligences, each unique, each continually evolving into new and more elaborate forms. Where most natural creatures had five senses, and those which had been charmed perhaps six or seven, the senses of the basilisks numbered in the millions.

Each of these senses was in fact an entity in its own right, but one permanently attached to the basilisk's body, trapped in a symbiotic relationship which brought each of them eternal life. The sense-beings fed from the basilisk's blood, drawing basic nutrition from whatever their host ate; in return they sustained the basilisk's body, adapting its entire metabolism according to its current needs. Thus whatever environment or physical state the basilisk might find itself in, the sense-beings effectively recreated its body to suit. For this reason and this reason alone, a basilisk could never die.

Even so, all the basilisks had attempted suicide time and again, only to be thwarted by this skin of senses. If a basilisk stopped eating then its metabolism was adjusted to draw energy from some other source; if it tried actually to injure itself then it would find its mutilated body regenerating at blinding speed. Always the sense-beings – individually as ruthless as gaolers, collectively as powerful as gods – found a way to promote survival. Currently, as it sped towards the dry and sterile surface of the Red Planet, Ocher was drinking sunlight. The solar energy was just enough to maintain its life force, but if it proved insufficient once it reached the ground no doubt some other means of survival would be employed. The basilisk would live on. Always the basilisk lived on.

It struck the ground with a great concussion that lifted rubble from the crater floor for some distance around. Senses worked ferociously to hold its disintegrating body together, successfully of course, and within a few dragon's breaths of its violent arrival, Ocher moved clear of the wreckage of the landing site and swept away across the desert in pursuit of its sibling, which, its returning senses reported, was hidden only a short distance away.

Veil had always been the least adventurous of the six, so it was odd that it should have selected the most remote hiding place of all of them. Veil pondered this now as it sensed Ocher's approach and concluded that perhaps it was not so odd after all. The others, in choosing to remain on their native world, had thereby chosen to remain near all the echoes of their pasts. But Veil had cut itself off from such concerns, preferring to make a single, epic journey to reach the ultimate seclusion which the Red Planet promised.

For millennia Veil had slept, cocooned beneath a cradle of iron, itself a visitor here, having fallen from the sky before even Veil had come. The sleep had been a welcome blank in a mind too full of past failures. For Veil, all of the basilisks' existence had been a failure, from the earlier times when ambitions had brought them to the high places of the world to more recent ages when they had quarrelled constantly, and then fought titanic battles that levelled mountains and drained oceans, making even the labour of the trolls seem like mere insect-bites on the skin of the world. After that they had sought only escape, both from each other and from the eternity in which they were imprisoned.

Yes, Veil had slept, but recently it had woken, for strange tremors had overtaken the heavens, touching even the orbit of this distant world. Sentinels which it had posted among its millions of senses had awakened it abruptly to the awesome sight of stars whipping sideways in the black sky. The Red Planet's two tiny moons had circled each other like dancing nymphs and whirled away on new and erratic paths. Far away, the minute, blue star which was the world of its origin had shuddered and Veil had known that it was turning. It had not slept since.

And now Ocher was here.

They did not speak. Communication between them was practically instantaneous, so sophisticated were the senses by which they interpreted the universe. So fearsome were their intelligences that responses could be accurately judged long before questions could ever be asked. Nevertheless, communicate they did on their own, aethereal level and the discussion in which they engaged, had it been conducted in a more conventional way, might have been described as heated.

... *Veil. You have slept long, basilisk. Yet you live still. Would you not have it otherwise?*

... *Ever the dreamer, Ocher. I sleep to forget, for my memory is clearer than ever yours was. Always you were confused by the past, so that the future to you was always a confusion too. For me it is clearer: the future is doom, nothing more, for ever. So I sleep.*

... *The future doom? Perhaps, Veil. Or perhaps not. Dreams may yet become reality. It is that for which we must strive – escape may yet be in the future for us all.*

... *I turn my back on your futures, Ocher, as I have already turned my back on the world.*

... *But the world has turned.*

... *You tell me nothing I do not know.*

... *Many things have turned, Veil. The past is clearer to me now, and so is the future. I see many things I did not see before.*

... *Ocher the Charmed! Dreamer you are, nothing more!*

... *Charm is no more, Veil.*

... *Indeed? That is – interesting.*

... *There is more, if you would but open your mind to it.*

... *Proceed.*

... *Veil, I know you best of the six. We are opposites. Where I look out, you look in; always we have disagreed. We argued over what the future might bring and never could we agree. Yet always we agreed on what we wanted: oblivion! Escape! Charm is no more, Veil, but it has left a legacy: the abandoned charm, the magic left behind in the final exodus. It is wild, Veil, this abandoned charm, like nothing I have seen before. It lives, it creates – and it destroys!*

... *You believe it has the power to destroy us?*

... *Veil, yes.*

... *I must dwell on this. Leave me now. I will inform you of my decision when the sky is bright again.*

*   *   *

The encounter was over in less time than it would have taken a dragon to snap its claw. Ocher retired from Veil's presence strangely uncertain of how its sibling would react. They had argued so often with each other that their responses should have been predictable down to the finest detail, yet it had been so long since they last met. Veil was familiar, yes, but also different in many ways. Unpredictable.

Time changes, thought Ocher, and the thought was a revelation. They had shared the world for an eternity, and all the worlds before, and yet this was the first time they had been separated from each other for such a great length of time. *Even for the Deathless, there is still the capacity for change.*

Veil emerged from the shadow of the iron boulder just as the small, hard sun crept above the jagged horizon. Its body was almost identical to Ocher's, lean and pale. Featureless silver eyes glared out at its sibling from a broad reptilian skull. Two muscular arms clawed their way through the red gravel, dragging bloated belly and lashing tail behind. Sliding up to the other, it halted in the low dawn light and exhaled. Its breath – certain doom to any creature except another basilisk – clouded about its angry face and obscured its fearsome expression.

. . . I am displeased that my rest has been disturbed, but you, Ocher, are not responsible for that. Greater events than your coming have returned me to sensibility, not least of them the Turning. I do not believe I will sleep again until those events have run their course.

. . . Then you will come?

. . . I believe that we will never find the peace you yearn for, Ocher, but I do believe that this abandoned charm is a force which the Deathless might use to their advantage. True death will never be ours, and sleep can never last, but perhaps this rogue magic might bring about an intermediate condition. I have thought hard on this matter, and I have come to believe that we might induce a state which I will call coma. *True eternal sleep, nothing less. For that I am prepared to labour.*

. . . And for you this will suffice, Veil? Do you not yearn for the ultimate escape?

. . . I yearn for little, Ocher, as you well know. But I am prepared

114

to strive to achieve a lasting peace for my soul. If eternity teaches us anything it is that time cannot be wasted. If this venture fails I will return here, if not to some more distant world; if it succeeds I will never have to strive for anything again.

. . . Your motives, as ever, are weak and dishonourable, Veil. But I welcome your support.

. . . Come then, dreamer. I will humour you once more, if only to cure the insomnia which has descended upon me now, for I do not believe you will leave me in peace now that you have found me again. You have a destination?

. . . Of course. Already I have begun to marshal the abandoned charm. Even now it is gathering at the place where we shall soon make our glorious exit from eternity.

. . . Dreams, Ocher. Pathetic though your obsession is, I am strangely comforted to find you unchanged. Come.

Unchanged, reflected Ocher as they soared up together from the surface of the Red Planet. *Am I still what I have always been? Has time worked none of its charm on me as it has so obviously worked it on Veil? Never was Veil so amenable to my demands. Can it be that the time has truly come?*

Unable to answer its own questions, Ocher focused its myriad senses outwards from its own soul, ahead in the direction they were speeding, towards the familiar blue and green world of their origin. As the world grew large again in its vision, Ocher spread the net of its perception across the region it had chosen for the Gathering, and was pleased at the depth of power which had already begun to build there. The abandoned charm was flowing in at ever-increasing speed, only to find itself trapped by the hasty barricades which the ancient basilisk had erected to contain it. Soon those barricades would need to be strengthened, but Veil was here to see to that.

Much had changed on the world's skin. Storms spiralled across the oceans; lands drowned beneath the rising water; mountains marched. Tiny details grew large beneath the basilisks' probing senses, and both found their gaze drawn, if but briefly, to the northern Heartland. There they saw a place still reflected bright in both their memories, a place once high and remote in the upper passes of the Spine, but which the shifting of the land had brought earthward. The colossal mountains had twisted south and bent their backs towards the new sea covering the Heartland. Accessible again was a place long since abandoned, long since despised by the basilisks.

On a river it stood, at the head of the waterfall known only as the Falls of the Deathless, the stronghold which had been their retreat before they had all fled to the sanctuary of sleep. The citadel.

As the fringes of the atmosphere licked against their pale bodies they separated. Veil arrowed north towards the Gathering place to watch over the massing charm, while Ocher turned around the curve of the world, heading down towards the vivid blue of the great Western Sea. Soon its silver eyes were full of the white of foam and the thrust of wave and the circular chain of tropical islands. Blind to all but its quest, it sought.

PART TWO

CITADEL

CHAPTER 11

Archan

The air was white. Surrounded by rushing water, the citadel of the basilisks clung to the sheer face of the Falls of the Deathless, its complex form a dazzling mixture of grace and barely restrained power. Its towers and ramparts hung cantilevered in awesome defiance of gravity, its lower parts solid and bold behind the constant spray, its highest spires invisible in the mist and the dazzling light of the sun. All around its foundation was motion – the constant, breathless motion of the pounding waterfall – yet to the centre of the flood it clung, a permanent stone in a liquid setting, wondrous to behold.

The streamlined blocks from which it was made were pearly and rich with deep and hidden colours. No brash rock fortress this but a towering monument to beauty and precision. To each side of its agate buttresses the falls curved away into the mists of their own creation, while the body of the citadel surged up into the spray-filled sky. A constant dew made it shine above the precipitous waters; the magic in its form made it flex into the wind as though stretching from sleep. Seemingly alive, it burst from the torrent like perfection newborn.

Many were its towers, each resplendent with a different and subtle hue. They twined around each other, like vines as they lunged upwards into clouds of vapour, thick at the base but narrowing to sheer pinnacles as they rose, losing themselves in the haze above the maelstrom below. Patterns of smooth-sided cavities chased their way up these organic turrets; some of them were windows, others were reservoirs of charm, bright and hard and jealous of the prize they held,

119

for now magic was hard to find and even harder to keep.

One of these depressions glowed more fiercely than its neighbours, its sharp blue light burning into the quartz of its guardian tower and bringing a cold and wintry aura to its surroundings. Immediately above, its translucent frame cut with angry shadows from the light of the trapped magic, was a delicate opening in the wall, a window. And out from the window there looked a dragon.

Archan was her name and she was near to death. Her mortality bore down upon her with the weight of the whole sky, yet its proximity had not weakened her; on the contrary, the more years she gathered beneath her wings the more she was buoyed up. During her darker moments – of which she had many these days – it seemed that she was crushed between this buoyancy and the descending sky, and that nothing in her many powers could break her free. But then she would remember who she was and where she was, and she would be reassured that a route to freedom did exist, and that the means to take it would, eventually, come her way.

As she gazed out of the spiral eye of the basilisk window, she believed that such means had just arrived.

Many years before the Turning Archan had retreated to this forgotten stronghold locked high into the mountains of the Spine and made the citadel of the basilisks her home. Once a vital member of Halcyon's worldwide dragon parliament, she had long since turned her back on all that had filled her life with power and conflict.

Of course, now she lived for more than such trifles. Much more . . .

Dragon Leader Halcyon's government in Covamere had consisted primarily of the Great Council, and beneath that a vast network of dragon underlings – envoys and marshals, judges and captains. The business of the parliament was public and accountable to all, and for many years Halcyon held sway with honest speech and open wings. But behind the honour was that part of government with which Halcyon had never been comfortable. The need for it he readily admitted, but always he expressed his dislike of the subterfuge necessary for its success. It was the Secret Council.

Ten they were, their complement changing as dragons came and went but their number remaining constant. Ten dragons spread over the world, their minds linked by charm, their business to share rumour before it could become fact. By calling in instantaneous reports from his fellow Secret Councillors, Halcyon was able many times to prevent revolutions by despatching his forces to the appropriate part of the world before trouble could really start. His lesser subjects were in awe of his apparent omnipotence – he was known as Halcyon the Eye – and those close to him, who knew of the existence of the Ten, were respectful of this power and rarely dared challenge it.

It took a very special dragon to become a Secret Councillor, and for many years dragons suited to the task gradually found their way into the ranks of the Ten. But time moved on, the world began to turn, and one by one they fell away. Towards the end only Halcyon and Mantle were left, suffering the pain of their comrades' successive deaths – for, as each of their fellow Councillors died, the survivors were granted the briefest glimpse of the burning light awaiting all dragons when the last wingbeat has been struck. In a way, they died a little, too. Then Halcyon himself was slaughtered by Wraith, and Mantle flew away on his own great quest to plant the Seed of Charm in the secret spaces behind the stars. None of the Ten remained.

Except Archan. Archan had faked her own death some years before the Turning – an elaborate, triumphant forgery of charm and wit that convinced her colleagues she was dead beneath an avalanche. She lingered still, old but quick, and with plans that were very much alive.

Always in the Secret Council she had been the one to question. Many times there had been consensus but for her: nine said yes but Archan it was who said no; she was the difficult one. Halcyon, she fancied, had respected her for it – although he was ever a difficult dragon to gauge – but she'd soon found that her attitude irritated her fellows. Before long she'd found herself voting contrary to the majority out of pure stubbornness, with no regard for the issues at hand, and before long she had isolated herself from all friendship.

But that mattered not, for she was by nature a solitary dragon. Halcyon showed no desire to dismiss her and none of the others had the courage to suggest such a move to him, and so she began to enjoy her role as stirrer of trouble and obstacle-maker. Each time the Council convened she spent more time planning her next gambit than attending to the agenda. She relished the challenge; it became her life.

Her infancy on the western continent of Ocea had been a traumatic time. She was barely four years old when a dreadful plague ravaged her home settlement of Sylon – a dry, sprawling collection of nests and shelters built on the periphery of a great desert. Most of the young dragons of her generation perished, their flesh wasted to nothing in a matter of days. The single image remaining from her early years was that of the skulls of infant dragons littering the dusty ground, grinning at her with bleached and sand-swept teeth. Death stalked the community like an invisible predator and Archan was one of the few youngsters to evade it.

Unsurprisingly, she grew up solemn. Soon she left Sylon to live quietly in a mountain settlement so remote that it had no name of its own. In those days she had still not heard of Halcyon – indeed her new home was on the opposite side of the world from Covamere; further from the centre of the dragon empire it was not possible to get. Regarded as something of an eccentric by her neighbours, she lived a solitary existence in a large network of caves unconnected to the main cavern complex. Physical congress was something from which she consistently shied away and no male dragon came near her, deterred by the powerful waves of hostility she emitted if ever a dragon came too close. Not that she was not beautiful, nor desirous of a mate, for she was both. But her standards were high and no dragon, not even those whose minds she would eventually share across the curve of the world, possessed the peculiar qualities she sought.

In the privacy of her isolated cave, Archan built herself a world of charm into which she could retreat. She spent years modelling and remodelling her body in a constant striving for physical perfection, and she honed the kinds of magic in which most charmed dragons only dabbled, especially the difficult techniques of thought transfer. Across the world she sent her mind, wandering through jungle and desert, across sea and prairie until at last she struck a comparable intellect: Halcyon! At once he recruited her to his Secret Council, and suddenly she found herself able to communicate with like-minded dragons without the distraction of their physical presence. On Council duty she roamed the skies of an entire hemisphere, breaking free from the isolation of her cave but not from the solitude of her world, and she loved her new role. Life became perfect for Archan; she never wanted it to end.

But end it did, all too soon. Foreth died first, prey to the madness which was beginning to sweep through charmed dragon settlements the world over. Suddenly the Secret Council was nine and no dragon came forward to take Foreth's place. Then fell Hock and Reciter and the Council was decimated. Archan suffered secret tantrums, lancing fire charm into the walls of her cave, furious that her perfect world should be so disrupted. It was only then that she learned that change was a necessary part of the world's workings, but it was not a lesson she was prepared to accept. With anger born of fanaticism she conjured a spell which mimicked the death-throes of her own mind and cast it into the circle of the remaining seven dragons; as far as the Secret Council was concerned, Archan too was dead.

Uncertain of where she was heading, she flew west, fleeing the sun if not the very wingbeat of time, crossing oceans and rising high over mountains until she found her unlooked-for goal: the citadel of the basilisks.

As she approached it seemed to her that the river from which it rose was a river of time and that its creators had set this place in defiance of its flow. The notion suited her mood and so she entered, and explored . . . and stayed.

Over the years she had learned independence and gained the strength and wit to manipulate her world. That such achievements should lead only to death was not proper, not in Archan's mind. Time might flow like a river, but Archan would build a dam. If she had to halt the very spinning of the world, she would cheat her own mortality; no skeleton would she become, staring vacantly up from the dust of the world. She would seek the immortality the basilisks had so far hoarded as their own ... and she would find a mate with whom to share eternity. Her meticulous study of the citadel's treasures quickly demonstrated the feasibility of her grand scheme: there *was* a way, if she could only live long enough to see it to fruition.

For engravings found in the many vaults of the citadel described the ritual of the Gathering, a complex recording of sigils and spells – most of them authored by Ocher – which she painstakingly translated. And if she read the signs right in the changing world outside the citadel, conditions were almost perfect for the Gathering to proceed. All that remained was for her to find her elusive partner. Then, by infiltrating the final ceremony the two of them would become heirs to eternity. Deathless they would be, like the basilisks before them. Immortal.

She looked out from the turret and saw a ragged band of dragons. Archan wondered if among these was the mate she had sought for so long. She sensed further change in the heated air and opened her mind wide to these newcomers.

Already the Deathless are gathering, she thought, glancing briefly skywards, *and now strangers come*.

'Chitraka!' she called suddenly, and the creature was there at her side, its golden head bowed in submission. 'Go to them!'

No sooner had she spoken than the beast was gone, a yellow blur vanishing through the distant vaults of the tower's spiral ramp, wailing as it ran. Archan rocked back on her slender wings, waiting.

Beneath the new sunlight the citadel glistened. None of the dragons knew what it was, but all recognized the power which emanated from it. Abandoned charm sparkled up and down its countless spires, sending beams of energy through the mists to fall across their wings with welcome heat. Such a mighty edifice none of them had ever before seen, and to a dragon they were struck with awe, even Thaw, who had seen many marvels in his travels across the world.

As the sun rose so the mantle of spray dropped further, unveiling more and more of the fortress, although its upper battlements remained hidden by brooding cloud. It lay across a wide expanse of water, a broad river whipped to foam by the ferocity of the falls. Thaw found himself strangely comforted by its presence, for in its immensity it reminded him of his native Termanderel and the mighty river which gave that land its name.

If only a dragon could be like these great rivers, he mused, his thoughts floating as the effects of his wounds sapped his strength. Then he shook his head vigorously and glared at the emerging apparition of the citadel. He thought he could see movement near its base, a flash of yellow as though a seam of gold had opened up beneath the sunlight. But then the mists closed in again and the motion was lost.

'Thaw?' demanded Smoke sharply. 'Did you see that?'

'I don't know what I saw,' replied the ex-Charmed commander. 'But I think something may be coming our way.'

A line of waves was breaking on the surface of the swirling river. As they watched, a slim, bone-like structure rose from beneath the water, supported on trembling filaments of charm. It curled out from behind one of the lower turrets and curved over the water, twisting and stretching until it slithered up the shore near where they stood. It was a bridge. Its surface was sheer as opal and rang like faeries' laughter as the wind struck its taut body.

Speeding down the sloping part of the bridge, something yellow was racing towards them, accelerating as its pathway flattened out. The dragons drew together, cautious and fearful. Thaw and Smoke stood instinctively before the unconscious Ratchet, hoping to offer him some protection before he died, while Cumber and Velvet held each other close and trembled despite the heat of the morning wind.

Archan's warden leaped from the bridge and stopped short of the group of dragons, prowling to and fro on four slender legs. Only Thaw recognized the creature, for he had once seen their like hunting zirafae on the southern savannahs of Termanderel.

'It's a chitraka!' he exclaimed, his words loud even against the bellow of the waterfall. At the sound of his voice the

125

creature ceased pacing, jerking its small head high and pricking pointed ears in the direction of the watching dragons.

It was long and sleek. Its body was half the size of Thaw's, and indeed bore an uncanny resemblance to that of the ex-Charmed for it too boasted yellow and black stripes; in place of dragon's scales however was a pelt of luxurious fur. Its belly was light in colour and spotted rather than striped. A long, serpentine tail lashed the air and it, like the creature's rounded head, was held high. Slitted eyes stared ferociously back at the uncertain dragons.

'What's a chitraka?' whispered Velvet. 'Is it dangerous?' After the terrible episode with the wolves she was suspicious of new creatures.

'I don't think so,' came Thaw's cautious reply. His composure returning, he looked along the bridge. 'I think it's been sent to take us across. Ugly brute,' he added.

'Over there?' snorted Cumber. 'I'd rather fly.'

'You might,' snapped Thaw. 'Ratchet cannot.'

Cumber flinched, and Velvet was disappointed to note how subservient he was becoming to Thaw. Had the fight with the wolves knocked all fire from his spirit? 'Ratchet is dying, Thaw,' she responded curtly, then she felt a great draught of air across her tail and turned to see the chitraka speeding past her and over to where Ratchet lay. She lurched forward, but Thaw restrained her with an outstretched wing.

'Wait,' he hissed.

The yellow and black creature sniffed for a while around Ratchet's prone body – so still that it might have been a corpse – then it stopped suddenly, its legs set wide and its tail held high and brittle. The wind ruffled the longer fur which sprang from its heavily-muscled shoulders as it stared with startling intensity back across the bridge, towards the citadel. Then it sprang.

Both Velvet and Smoke raced forward as the creature pounced upon Ratchet, silvery claws extended as though to rip out his heart . . . but Ratchet was no longer there! A shock-wave of scalding air knocked them back on to their haunches as with a terrifying screech the chitraka sprinted back over the narrow bridge and vanished into the haze.

Wind whistled like a retreating voice and the bridge sank away beneath the waves.

'Come,' said Thaw, breaking the paralysis which had gripped them all. 'Let us join our comrade.'

'It was a charm of transition,' he explained as they coasted through the moist air towards the citadel. 'Evidently the bridge was purely for the benefit of the chitraka. Something has taken Ratchet – we have no choice but to follow.'

'But . . . such magic!' protested Velvet, flying as close to Cumber as the buffeting wind would allow. 'Surely the charm has all gone by now?'

'Don't be so sure, dragon,' responded Thaw imperiously. 'Were you Charmed like me, you would feel the power in this place. This is a nexus, a focus for abandoned charm. The reservoir of magic here is vast beyond even my reckoning. You should feel nothing but awe to be in its presence.'

'Hmph,' muttered Velvet, quite unimpressed. 'And that told me, I suppose. Cumber, don't you think Thaw is getting a little too overbearing. Cumber?'

Velvet's voice startled the young ex-Charmed out of some waking dream. 'What? Yes, Velvet, whatever you say, dear.'

'No sense from any of them,' grumbled Velvet as they drew near to the citadel.

The closer they got to the structure the more they felt dwarfed by it. Here the spray hung in vast, undulating sheets of moisture, wrapping tendrils around organic towers and seeming to draw them out across the water. The sound of the crescent falls was an overwhelming thunder and the air tasted fresher than any they had ever known.

Thaw led the way, for he alone seemed to know where to go. He flew between two contorted spires, each the colour of obsidian, then emerged with his companions into calmer, drier air. To each side, enormous bastions of black stone plunged into an abyss, their bases lost in the spray. Ahead, the focal point of this strange holding area, loomed a crystalline steeple laced with veins of gold and silver. Beads of water rained down its slick outer surface, chasing transparent patterns around the single, circular entrance which beckoned to the hovering dragons.

Cautiously, their wings wide and ready for flight into the open sky, they entered the citadel of the basilisks.

Archan let out a long, controlled sigh. She had decided to bring them all here, even the one with the terrible wounds, since she was uncertain of what part they might play in the significant time soon to come. The wounded dragon she had healed during his brief and magical journey across the river, although she was sure now that he was not the one. The two females she could discount at once, but females could be useful nonetheless. They would live for now. Of the two other males only one was of any real interest, but to kill the other would so disrupt the group as to make her previous decisions worthless.

One male, this *Thaw*, was intriguing. Archan observed him as he led his companions through the mist and into the citadel, aware of the fact that she herself was guiding his wings but impressed by his fortitude, his strength of will. His thoughts were complex, too complex for her to glean on this first, tentative meeting of their minds, but she suspected that she would enjoy congress with Thaw.

Time is already running short, she mused as the chitraka loped up the ramp and curled up in the warm coils of her tail. *I do not have long to decide. If I must ultimately be alone then so be it, but still I would explore other possibilities. While there is time.*

She raised her smooth and gleaming snout to the sky and scented the wind outside her observation tower. Much was moving on that wind, much that was not natural. The Deathless were gathering; time was indeed running short.

CHAPTER 12

Inside the Citadel

'Ratchet!'

It was Velvet who spotted him first. The big warrior was sitting in a slab of shadow, blinking slowly and looking around with a bemused expression. The entrance chamber flowed around the visitors like a gigantic rack of pale bones which had melted and then set again; Ratchet sat at the far end, where the undulating floor rose sharply to become a curved and shining wall.

Velvet launched herself boldly across the dust-crowded space between the entrance and the deep recess where Ratchet was waiting. Bars of light flickered across her pale wings as she flew through the powdery air. The ceiling was lost in a shimmering haze; none of the dragons could determine whether it was natural light or charm by which they were seeing the interior of the citadel.

'Ratchet,' she repeated as she skidded to a halt before her companion, her claws scrabbling to grip the glossy, white curves of the ribbed floor. 'We thought you were . . .'

'Dead?' grunted the big dragon. 'Yes, me too. But apparently not.'

He opened his massive wings and flexed them experimentally. No scars showed on his body, and not a single bloodstain marked his scales. His eyes shone. He was fine.

'Good to see you recovered,' bellowed Thaw, alighting next to Velvet. He frowned as he cast his gaze across his colleague's unblemished hide then squinted up into the watery light. 'Full of charm, this place. Curative charm, it would seem – we should be grateful.'

'Yes indeed,' agreed Cumber enthusiastically as he

struggled to gain purchase on the slippery floor. For Cumber this problem was compounded by his own uncontrollable excitement. 'Can't you feel it, all of you? What a find! In fact, I'd even go so far as to say that I can feel more charm in this one chamber than I've ever felt in any . . .'

His exuberant speech was cut short as he slipped from the rib to which he was clinging and tumbled several wingspans away down a gentle slope. The others laughed companionably, all except Thaw, who continued to stare up into the light.

'What is it, Thaw?' asked Smoke presently, noticing their self-appointed leader's distracted air.

'Hmm? Oh, nothing. I was just . . . looking.' Thaw shook himself as though to clear his head of some unwelcome thought, then turned back to Ratchet. 'Are you ready for duty, dragon?' he demanded briskly.

'Steady on, Thaw,' began Velvet, shocked by his brusqueness, but it was Ratchet himself who waved her to silence.

He announced, 'Thaw's right to ask. I'm healed now. I'm all right.'

The big warrior lifted himself to his feet, swaying a little as he did so. But he soon regained his balance and immediately took up a post at Thaw's flank. As they stood there together, these two ex-Charmed warriors, it occurred to Velvet that they looked invincible. The broken light of the citadel painted their scales with resilient bands of light and shade and it seemed to her that she was looking upon dragons who might last forever.

The same light played over her own, white body, as well as over Cumber's and Smoke's, but it made them appear less substantial, more fragile. Vulnerable. She moved close to Cumber, who had by now clambered up from the gully into which he had slipped, and caught Smoke's eye. Her fellow Natural was frowning, and Velvet knew that she shared her unease. Then together they followed Thaw's gaze up into the light and saw Archan.

She descended through a striped mist, beams of light slipping across her creamy scales and describing her form with a purity no natural illumination could have matched. For as she dropped the haze cleared a little and the source of the aethereal light was revealed: thousands of tiny, individual light charms were embedded into the upper walls and ceiling of the entrance chamber, each charm a nugget of pure magic glowing with fierce and unique colour. None was the same, and there were more colours in the fractured air than in a hundred rainbows.

Archan's pale, slender form flew down through the colours, reflecting the exquisite patterns of light and shadow as she drew near to the watching dragons. Long, slim wings held a serpentine body, a constantly moving coil of muscle over which a milky skin of minute scales flexed like liquid. She had no legs, only wings and a whip-like, seemingly boneless torso which all but Thaw found a little disturbing. Thaw was enraptured, for to him Archan was astonishingly beautiful. She was just perfect, fluid motion.

The dragons stepped back gingerly as she neared the level of the floor. Supple beyond measure, her neck twisted round upon itself, revealing her head to be little more than a pointing of its furthest extremity. Her mouth was held barely open, a fanged slit in a face otherwise without feature. The air rippled about her non-existent lips: there was fire inside her.

She had no eyes.

All but Thaw had retreated now as she landed on the uneven floor. She touched down directly in front of him, her unreadable face cocked to the side as though she were appraising his worth. Then, with a gesture that thrilled Thaw and repelled his companions, she tipped her sightless gaze towards the other dragons and contemplated them with a blank yet intense scrutiny. All but Ratchet – who had fallen irresistibly asleep – withered beneath that eyeless glare; all felt belittled. All but Thaw.

Velvet found herself clinging to Cumber, her wings wrapped around him in a tight embrace. A bitter wind seemed to howl through the chamber and its origin was the place on this incredible dragon's face where her eyes should have been. At their side, Smoke stood resolute, but inside she trembled.

'Welcome to my citadel,' purred Archan, her slitted mouth

pouring out the words as though they were flames. 'I am Archan.'

And then the mood changed.

Suddenly the chamber was filled with a golden light, a warm glow which bathed the weary dragon explorers with restorative power. The light redefined Archan's essential form and what had been a leer became a smile, what had appeared threatening now appeared welcoming. Caring. Creamy wings opened wide to take in these wanderers and it was with gratitude that the dragons acknowledged their own fatigue and sank into the shadow they cast, joining Ratchet in his easy slumber. The last thing Velvet saw before she drifted away was an eyeless face peering down at her, but she was too exhausted to pay it any further heed, and finally she allowed herself to be delivered into the light.

Last to sleep was Thaw, and if his companions had seen a change in Archan for the better then he saw something glorious become still more glorious. As the light expanded to claim him he imagined that it was not into sleep that he was falling but into a single scale on Archan's flawless hide, falling, falling, to become a tiny dragon mote fixed like a stone in the liquid of her body. With tremendous reluctance his eyes closed against the sight. The dreams through which he flew were wild and full of passion.

And not entirely his own.

The sound of the waterfall crashed into Cumber's ears and jerked him awake. He lurched to his feet and rubbed at his eyes with one of his broad, white wings. Water splashed against his face, shocking him to alertness. Behind him, Thaw was wielding charm.

'I thought that might do the trick,' came Thaw's deep chuckle, and Cumber turned to see the ex-Charmed commander leaning nonchalantly against a wall of crystal. To the side of the laughing dragon the wall was peeled apart to form a gaping, vertical slot through which the crescent falls were clearly visible. Blue charm flickered around its newly-made edge like a host of sprites.

'Did you just do that?' exclaimed Cumber.

'Is it so hard to believe?' replied Thaw, snapping the

window shut again without even blinking. Errant magic wriggled into the seamless crystal wall, firing minute stabs of light out into the chamber as it fled. Thaw smiled, his ease and humour throwing Cumber quite off balance – his former severity had gone. All was silent.

Cumber shrugged. 'The charm won't last,' he said, 'and I for one see little need for dragons to use it any more.'

'But that is where you are wrong, Cumber,' came a rich, sensual voice from the far side of the small chamber. There was poised Archan, resting on a complex knot of coils, her wings tucked efficiently away within its folds. 'The time of charm is far from over. Look, your wounds are healed.'

Swiftly examining his flanks and wings, Cumber grunted acknowledgement. Presently he inquired, 'Where are the others – where's Velvet?'

'They are resting,' responded Archan smoothly. 'Do not fear for their safety. But, Cumber, I am concerned for you, that you do not understand the truth about this place.'

'How do you know my name?' asked Cumber with cautious curiosity. Although he was still wary of this strange dragon, he felt more and more intrigued by her. She had remarkable presence, of that there was no doubt, and she had here such a store of charm! *What happened to her eyes?* he wondered, gripped.

'Thaw has been most enlightening,' explained Archan with a gracious nod.

'The power here is beyond belief, Cumber!' blurted Thaw suddenly, and with uncharacteristic passion. 'Archan has revealed only a fraction of it to me, and already I am struck with awe. Come with us, and see what sights there are!'

'We have a mission,' warned Cumber, uncertainly.

'With that I may be able to help you,' came Archan's silky reply.

'And the magic?' prompted Cumber.

'You decide. If you wish, it can be yours.'

'I shall decide,' agreed Cumber.

Golden claws tapped restlessly on a floor beaded like frozen dew. The chitraka prowled the width of the ramp, her purr an undertone beneath the distant hiss and rumble of the waterfall. Head bowed, stride easy, she loped to and fro in blind obedience to the most recent command of her mistress. For the chitraka, to obey was everything, even when the commands brought her pain, as often they did.

But not this time, thankfully. This time her task was simply to guard. Loyal, she would obey. The dragons would not escape.

Up to now, the only dragon she had ever known was Archan. A mere cub when Archan had swooped into her life, she remembered only as the vaguest of blurs the tiny family which had once embraced her. Golden faces still occasionally flickered across her consciousness, pressing into her limited intelligence with warm insistence and stimulating yearnings impossible to fulfil. Those faces she had long ago abandoned – or been abandoned by, she did not know which – and she had been a creature alone until the surrogate had appeared. The dragon, Archan.

An irresistible urge to imprint her loyalty on to this curious, flying beast compelled the chitraka to remain in Archan's presence thereafter. Her new mistress was cruel and strict, but she was *there*, and sometimes she was kind. Sometimes she tantalized the chitraka with spells that crawled through her flesh like the ghosts of the family she had never properly known. If she knew that these spells could as easily be made to burn and hurt her, then that knowledge only made the occasional ecstasy more thrilling. Bound ever closer to her mistress, the chitraka who had never been named lingered, her loyalty growing with every day that passed.

But beneath the loyalty, something else . . . in some deep place she knew she was being abused. Too weak to fight back against the might of a charmed – or even ex-charmed – dragon, too slow of thought to devise any strategy other than compliance, the chitraka fed in agony off the crumbs of wrath she felt in her bones. The wrath spread ever deeper into her crude soul. Addicted to the treats of charm which Archan occasionally bestowed upon her, she allowed the anger to fester until it grew to catastrophic proportions, until it sucked at her every waking breath.

As much a prisoner as the dragons she had been commanded to guard, the chitraka watched them wake.

The chamber was wide but very low. No sooner had Velvet woken and struggled to get up than she cracked her head against a drooping outcrop of some silvery material. Ducking irritably, she glanced around.

The room was made entirely of metal. The ceiling – which Velvet now regarded with a mixture of respect and annoyance – was a jagged patchwork of silvers and bronzes, rough and ugly in its undisciplined tumble through the space immediately above her head. The floor was smooth gold, and showed their reflections: dragons trapped beneath their claws. The distant walls were lost in a grey haze, but nearby a ramp crept up from the floor, eventually to pierce the dark, craggy ceiling. Beyond this sullen exit a pale shape loitered, its eyes glistening green.

The same thing that came to greet us outside? wondered Velvet as she turned to nudge her two companions awake. Smoke was already stirring, but Ratchet took a little longer to rouse. He looked on, his face unreadable, as the two females marvelled at their newly healed wounds.

'Still tingles a bit?' he commented at length. 'That's charm for you.'

'Where are the others?' demanded Velvet sharply. 'Well,' she went on when neither of her fellows responded, 'let's take a look around, anyway.'

They moved up the shallow ramp, wings and claws moving cautiously over the smooth floor. While they ascended they heard the purring of their guard over the constant, distant sound of the waterfall, but as soon as they reached the top the purring stopped.

Framed in an oval chasm, suspended between two floor levels, the three dragons found themselves confronted by the chitraka.

She appraised them with her intense, green gaze. Far from threatening, Velvet found her presence here strangely reassuring, for behind those eyes she believed she sensed a desire not to hurt but to help. Motioning her companions to remain where they were, Velvet took an extra pace forward so that she directly confronted the creature.

'We can be your friends,' she began hesitantly, seeking her words with care. 'Are you here . . . to stop us leaving?'

The chitraka did not reply, nor could she, devoid as she was of the power of speech. The dragon's voice was soft; Archan's voice was sometimes soft, but even then the chitraka could detect a hard undertone, an echo of the crueller blows Archan inflicted. But this dragon was . . . different.

'Go on,' whispered Smoke. 'I think it likes you.'

At the sound of this second voice the chitraka's ears pricked forward and the rich, golden fur on the nape of her neck sprang erect. Muscles bunched beneath her supple hide and the trust in her eye was replaced by wariness.

'It's all right,' soothed Velvet. 'We won't hurt you, I promise.'

'No – most likely it'll hurt us,' growled Ratchet under his breath.

Slowly, carefully, Velvet extended her wingtip until it reached nearly to the chitraka's shoulder. 'Please,' she said, 'let us pass by. We just want to find our friends. Perhaps you could help us.'

For the chitraka this was a wholly new experience. Understanding Velvet's every word yet bound by the words of Archan, the chitraka was trapped in a dilemma. There seemed no reason for her not to trust these new dragons – indeed, she sensed they represented a chance for a freedom she could scarcely define, let alone imagine – yet the command of her mistress was undeniable. What possible course of action was left open to her?

'Look out!' bellowed Ratchet. He hurled himself forward just as the chitraka extended long, golden claws from both of her front paws and slashed at the space where, had he not managed to pull her clear, Velvet's throat would have been. He was about to turn on the creature, which was after all less than half his size, when suddenly he stopped short, drawing back hurriedly and dragging the protesting Velvet with him back down the ramp.

The chitraka had transformed into a demon. Her claws whirred repeatedly through the air with a sound like lightning and her body had become a black and gold blur of frenzied motion. Driven by some cataclysmic fighting instinct, she thrashed down the ramp after the retreating dragons, spinning and whipping down the slope until she had forced them again on to the level ground. Only then did she stop, her limbs contracting with equal suddenness to resume their former composure, after which she loped back up the ramp as though nothing had happened. By the time the dragons had caught their breath she was pacing again, head lowered, eyes fixed now on the floor.

'Well,' announced Smoke, peering out from behind Ratchet's reassuringly ample bulk, 'it looks like we're stuck down here.'

'It's fantastic!'

Cumber's exclamation was understandable, yet even his enthusiasm utterly understated the wonder which was the central core of the citadel of the basilisks.

The three dragons hovered in cool, damp air a short distance from the chamber in which Thaw and Cumber had awakened. Archan had led them out through a spike-lined exit portal – the spikes had bent around as the dragons passed, following their progress down the long, winding tunnel as if watching them, though they bore no eyes. Before long they found themselves entering a space where the air was colder and filled with flickering light. Then it was that they emerged into the core.

'This is the heart of the citadel,' explained Archan, but her guests had already determined that for themselves.

Simply, it was a hollow tube extending the entire height of the massive construction and located directly in the path of the waterfall. One half of its immense, curved width – and it was easily ten trees in circumference – was formed from a strange substance Cumber could not identify but which looked for all the world like flesh. Its surface was rich and translucent, filled with criss-crossing veins of colour and mottled patches of light and shade and perforated with countless dark tunnel entrances. Subtle movements pumped beneath its skin, as though the very structure of the citadel were alive.

The other half was made from the waterfall itself. Here the

cascading waters were wrapped upon themselves to create a vertical channel which curled round to merge with its fleshy counterpart in the space beyond. Some massive charm was pressing the waters into this unnatural configuration, magic still powerful despite the traumas which the Turning had inflicted upon the world. Cumber looked out into this divided and dizzying cylinder and it seemed to him more vital, more real than anything he had ever seen before. More wondrous. And yet . . .

'The heart,' Archan had said, and Cumber thought she was probably right. But as he gazed out upon the staggering vista he realized that if this really were the heart of the place then it was a heart cold and devoid of life, despite the phenomenal forces that powered it. There was no place here for a dragon to alight, no hint of warmth or comfort to bring a dragon solace should he need it, in short, it was a heart without a soul.

Perhaps this place has many souls, Cumber thought uncertainly, but here and now, after the initial rush of exhilaration, he saw nothing but emptiness in this echoing void. Then, as he began to absorb the sheer scale of the edifice, he found that he did not even know where he was.

'What is this place?' he demanded suddenly. 'Who built it, and why? And who are you, Archan? What do you want from us?'

Archan's eyeless face smiled. Cumber's scales tightened against his skin as her unearthly gaze moved across his body; he felt as though she were testing him somehow. At last, and to Cumber's great relief, she turned her pointed head away and spoke, projecting her voice into the cylindrical chamber so that it boomed out over the roar of the water.

'Aeons ago the basilisks thrived. They were six – the Deathless they called themselves. It was they who built this citadel, built it as a monument to eternity, for the basilisks were blessed with the greatest of gifts: immortality. They lived here for many ages, until at last they grew bored and moved on. No dragon knows where they are now. But the citadel survives, despite everything it survives.

'When I came here the basilisks had long gone, but much of the charm which they had bound up here survived – and survives still, despite the Turning – for the citadel has soaked up abandoned charm like a sponge in the sea. But this place holds more than mere power – it holds memories.'

'Memories?' interrupted Thaw. Cumber noticed that the warrior listened avidly to Archan, opening and closing his claws as she spoke as though trying to catch the very words spilling from her slitted mouth. For his part, Cumber was still wary, but her story compelled him to listen and he could not drag his attention away.

'Indeed,' continued Archan smoothly. 'Over millennia the basilisks gathered all manner of things from all over the world – and occasionally from other worlds too. The collection they amassed here has no rival anywhere. I myself have taken barely the first wingbeat on a flight through its splendours; there is enough here to keep a dragon enthralled for eternity.'

'For eternity?' echoed Thaw.

'Indeed.'

'So what is this collection then?' demanded Cumber. He was simultaneously intrigued and repelled. What little he knew of the basilisks was confined to a few vague tales told by Ordinal his teacher, and more recently his distant perception of Fortune's encounter with one of the ancient immortals at the very instant of the Turning. Then, when the world had seemed a mere speck of dust blown on winds of chance, the basilisk had been the enemy not just of dragons but of all creation, for at that moment it threatened to crush the Seed of Charm and end the history of this fragile world in a single, lethal breath.

But it did not do so, he reminded himself. And entwined with the threat and the incomparable power, had he not sensed . . . sadness? An immense, all-conquering despair which had finally driven the wretched creature from the world altogether, driven it away to . . . *Where is it now?* he thought with an involuntary shiver. *And what would it do if it knew of the intruders in its palace?*

Cumber shrank back slightly as he felt Archan's blind gaze pressing against him once more. The noise of the cataract crashed in his ears and he felt his head grow momentarily light. At his side, Thaw's heavy wingbeats thundered to the same rhythm as the captive waterfall, striped vanes sliding through shafts of eerie light. A sharp, acidic scent drifted past his snout.

'There is too much here for any one to see it all, mortal dragon,' purred Archan, 'but I will show you something of the glory of the Deathless. Come.'

Her supple neck curled round to the left until it pointed directly at one of the myriad cavern entrances which pierced the curved and precipitous walls of the core chamber. Then, with a single flick of her narrow, creamy wings she led the two curious ex-Charmed dragons into a dark, sombre tunnel. It led down towards the level of the river, and grew only darker and more sombre the further they passed into its embrace.

A lengthy exploration of the metal cave confirmed the dragons' suspicion that they were trapped down here; at the furthest perimeters of the gloomy enclosure the ceiling lowered dramatically until it met the floor in a ragged and ill-formed junction. There was no escape.

As she glided back towards the base of the ramp, Velvet saw that Smoke and Ratchet had already returned there and were deep in conversation, apparently unaware of her approach. She fluttered the trailing edges of her wings, silencing the rush of air across their delicate membranes, and turned into the ramp's shadow, alighting there and straining to make out their words.

'. . . simply have to leave tonight,' Smoke was saying. 'There's too much here for me to bear.'

'It still amazes me,' came Ratchet's growl. 'But I'll help if you need it.'

Before they could go on there came a clattering on the slippery deck of the ramp. The chitraka was descending. Velvet slipped from the shadows and rejoined her friends as the golden-furred creature moved gracefully into their presence.

They remained utterly still as it approached each of them in turn. Even Ratchet held his breath as it sniffed at his wings, evidently respectful of the sharpness of its long, hooked claws and mindful of the unexpected speed of its former attack. Smoke flinched visibly when transparent whiskers brushed against her flank and Velvet saw that every muscle in her dull, natural body had tensed against the threat of attack.

But she's scared of more than just attack, Velvet thought with a flash of insight. *What is your secret, Smoke?* Are *you Charmed? Is that it?*

But before she could pursue her thoughts the beast was upon her.

CHAPTER 13

The Deep

Dazzling plumes of spray engulfed Ocher as it struck the surface of the storm-tossed ocean like a falling star. The heat it had generated during its ever-accelerating dive from distant space flooded the roiling waters like a firestorm and superheated steam exploded from the point of impact with ferocious energy. Shock waves pressed the sea into an immense, shallow bowl and a great mushroom of vapour lifted up to meet the belly of the storm clouds, spitting and hissing as the sound of the detonation shook its way into the distance.

Underwater, below the storm now, a maelstrom of bubbles pursued the basilisk as it continued its plunge towards the seabed. Though it knew the hopelessness of these attempts, still it tried such futile means of self-destruction at every opportunity; this time, as always through eternity, it survived.

There is hope in this mission, however, it thought with determination as it descended.

The light swiftly deteriorated, bringing a blue drabness to the surrounding water. More powerful senses activated themselves at the periphery of the basilisk's consciousness, some of them utilizing sound waves, others tasting chemicals, a few employing the shreds of charm which still drifted here in the icy depths. A shoal of bony, transparent fish moved past like ghosts, their eyes shocked wide, phantom tendrils wavering beneath their perforated forms. The weight of the ocean tried to crush the basilisk's body but its sensory skin compensated, developing exotic elements with which to rebuild its outer shell against the mounting pressure.

The dull echoes of Ocher's steady probing located a mountainside far ahead, one of many tall pinnacles which stood proud of the seabed in this part of the world. The roots of islands. With a flick of its prehensile tail it swung towards the edifice, still moving deeper, traversing until it swept past one of the lower cliffs of the mountain and beyond to its opposite side. Here it paused, sounding charm.

Ocher counted over one hundred mountains rising hard and spindly in a tortured crown from the seabed. Despite their immensity, they were set in a perfect circle. Not all of their tops, Ocher realized, pierced the waves far above, but many did.

The basilisk swam towards the centre of the circle. Here was the central peak, a staggered and fragile claw poking through the cloudy sand. Invisible at its summit was a reef; below was a bleak landscape of sand and porous stone. Here the basilisk stopped.

. . . Mediel.

The name slid gracefully from its mind and filtered out into the deep. It knew the other basilisk was here, somewhere, but the overwhelming pressure of the water blurred perception and made weak abandoned charm even more difficult to wield. No reply was forthcoming so Ocher called again.

This time it sensed movement down where the spire of the subterranean mountain met the black sand of the sea bottom. Descending cautiously, it focused all its useful senses in an attempt to probe the terrain ahead. Something was in motion beneath the sand, something huge . . .

. . . Mediel. We must confer.

Still there was no response, but now the sand itself was moving. A giant dune which some wayward current had built against the base of the spire vibrated once and then shook itself, sending an enormous cloud of silt out into the waters in a ponderous, billowing explosion. Senses already dulled grew duller still and the basilisk struggled to perceive what it was that moved within the cloud.

Suddenly a long, mournful cry echoed through the deep, and Ocher knew that this was not a basilisk.

Slowly the cloud of silt opened up, parts of it turning over and beginning to fall back towards the bottom of the ocean as though drifting back into some eternal sleep. Revealed within was a massive body of flesh, dark and sombre, with flattened fins and a rounded back made craggy with growths and barnacles. As it emerged from the confusion it opened a maw the size of several dragons and gulped at the water as though it had not tasted food for an aeon.

It has not tasted food at all, realized Ocher with wonder. *It is new to this world altogether.*

The monstrous beast thrust against the press of the ocean with its huge fins and began to pull itself free of the dispersing cloud of debris. With a single, mighty lunge of its flukes it surged towards the basilisk, its wrinkled eyes closed against the immense pressure. Ocher slipped to the side, perceiving the creature's entire metabolism as it thundered past wailing its melancholy song.

It yearns for the surface already, it thought, amazed. *It is an air-breather, this giant of the deep. Such a contradiction even charm could never have conceived!*

The filaments of abandoned charm which had called this behemoth into existence had already dispersed their power into the act of creation, making this newcomer to the world a truly natural creature; though unnaturally made, it held no magic of its own. As the basilisk observed its ascent towards the far-off surface waters, it found room in its overburdened spirit to marvel at the ingenuity of the cosmos, for never in its infinite life had it encountered such a splendid beast.

Turning its senses away from the rolling, receding shadow of the newborn ocean dweller, Ocher found itself face to face with Mediel.

. . . I have observed you, Ocher. You have changed.

. . . The Deathless do not change, Mediel. They grow older, they weary, but change? I think not.

. . . I would disagree with you, but I myself am proof of your argument. I have not changed, Ocher, whatever may have become of you.

Ocher closed its mind to its fellow for a brief period of contemplation. Mediel was going to be more difficult than Veil.

Of the six, Mediel had always been the outsider. Through the aeons the Deathless had wavered alternately between ferocious loyalty to each other and equally violent animosity ... all except Mediel. Mediel had always displayed at best antagonism and at worst warlike hostility towards its fellow basilisks. Even during those times when they had built and lived together in their various citadels across the world and the cosmos, Mediel had participated as a functioning member of the group for only the shortest of times, usually shutting itself away in some remote tower or dungeon the instant the opportunity had presented itself. A loner, and possessed of a ferocious temper, Ocher had endured but never relished its presence.

... *The world has turned, Mediel, or had you not noticed? The Deathless do not change but times do, and now the time is right* ...

... *I have already perceived your plan, Ocher, and although it holds a certain ... intrigue ... I find I am unable to rouse the smallest jot of enthusiasm for such a travesty. You should go, before I grow angry.*

... *Such an easy solution.*

... *But satisfying.*

... *Will you not be swayed?*

Mediel did not reply to this final plea, instead whirling round in a mass of spinning bubbles and thrashing silt into its sibling's face. Ocher held back from losing its own temper, knowing that to do so would in turn provoke the other into a typically blind rage from which it would not be diverted. Instead Ocher held its position in the icy crush of the ocean deeps, searching for a crack in the scales of hostility which this particular basilisk wore so proudly.

... *You have read my intentions fully, Mediel?*

... *Of course. As ever, you seek oblivion. To be eternal is dreadful enough but there is no pride in the end for which you yearn. At least bitterness has a flavour – death has none.*

... *We could argue for a comfortable span of millennia about that. But consider this, Mediel. Does not vengeance have the sweetest flavour of all?*

... *You play with words, Ocher. State your mind, if it is not as muddy as these waters.*

... I seek oblivion for us all, Mediel. For the six Deathless Ones.

... You waste my time with what I already know.

... We have already wasted eternity – a little more will not harm.

... State it.

... My proposal is just this: if you participate, you will not only end the nightmare of your own existence but you will also bring about the destruction of the five beings you despise most in the whole of the cosmos. What sweet revenge would that be for you, Mediel, who alone of us all wish your fellow basilisks dead with every waking breath, every wrathful blink? That wish can be yours, now that the world has turned. Now that the Deathless are gathering again.

... And if I do not participate?

... I have reason to believe that the cataclysm requires only five souls to be present at the end. In short, Mediel, we do not need you. I offer you the chance, nothing more.

... Why?

... I have not yet visited all of the others. One may yet refuse.

Ocher contracted itself as though against attack, guessing that Mediel would rant and protest while underneath it pondered the proposal. But Mediel responded almost at once.

... Ocher. I have decided.

... Mediel?

... You manipulate me. Yet I will join the Gathering, for I sense that the promise of revenge is a true one and its prospect I cannot resist. But I warn you, Ocher, if I am to have any control over your death then you may be assured that I shall make it as painful and prolonged as I am able, as just punishment for the insult you have paid me in daring to exploit my desires.

... I expect nothing less of you, Mediel.

... You wish me to go north?

... Veil is there already. It will explain the function of the new citadel at the crest of the world. I will join you both soon. The others shall be with me.

Without further comment, Mediel launched itself violently up through the sea, bubbles of steam spurting in its wake as the friction of its passage stressed the water beyond endurance. As it departed Ocher enjoyed the thrill of con-

146

frontation, discovering that the sharp edge of possible failure which was pressed against its throat cut with a pain both frightening and exhilarating. Never had it played against such odds.

Is this a taste of what it is to be mortal? it wondered.

The cavity left in the seabed where the sea monster had been born was already filling up again with sand, but now new concussions began to rock the drowned terrain. The mountain spires shook, sloughing off great scales of rock and punching dense, reverberating groans out into the ocean. The land was still moving, and moving faster. Time was racing like a hungry predator and the Gathering was only half complete.

CHAPTER 14

On Sharp

In his dream, the world was reduced to a spire of rock trapped fast in the grip of a faceless monster whose form was so unstable it could not be perceived. Then he saw that the rock was not rock at all but coral, an immense claw of coral reaching up through the monster's very veins to breach its skin and emerge struggling into heavy air. Within the coral was a network of secret channels leading to places long hidden; the sponge of its structure was a maze with a million entranceways, from which there fled a million exits, a porous labyrinth which did not trap but liberate.

A maze, he thought in wonder, *but not the Maze.*

Blood slowly filled the hollow channels, surging up from the obscure shadows around the base of the spire, filling the body of the monster containing it and bringing it life. The monster turned silver eyes on the minuscule dragon who observed it from afar and breathed death. The dragon realized that the monster had lived forever.

Then the dream began to fragment as rods of light seared from the dark sky, illuminating the horror of the beast and piercing its skin with their radiance. Where the light impacted, the monster shrank back, gradually relinquishing its grasp on the spire of coral which was also the world, until it had grown small and pale in the dragon's vision. Ice crusted over its diminished form and it became trapped beneath a wall of crystal, prowling angrily but unable to escape its prison.

Light continued to streak downwards, slashing brilliant stripes across the dragon's eyes. One slash was brighter still and hurt to look at. With it came a sound.

* * *

Fortune lurched free of brief, shallow sleep and snapped his head around to see where the sound was coming from. All about him the storm crashed, but above the noise came a sudden explosion. A line of fire streaked from the clouds and hammered against the surface of the ocean with a sound like the end of the world. Water plumed and spread out into the rain and wind and a series of massive waves lifted broken crests and careered towards the shore.

'Up the slope!' shouted Fortune desperately as it became clear that the beach on which they were sheltering was about to be swamped. Slowly the other dragons responded – some too slowly. The deluge dragged four unfortunates down into the maelstrom and sucked them back out to sea, their wings flailing helplessly as vicious currents pulled them under and beat them against concealed rocks. Their bodies did not reappear.

In a rush of terror and grief their companions hurled themselves upslope, howling with anguish at the loss of their friends. In despair they found themselves once more fully exposed to the raging elements. They dropped their heads and turned into the wind, waiting for the flood waters to subside. Overhead the tempest rampaged, whipping rain ahead of galloping wind and launching bolts of lightning as thick as tree trunks through the tortured air. The sound of the thunder was constant and unbearable; the sea was all but indistinguishable from the sky, so wild and fractured were they both, and the blue darkness gave no clue as to whether it was night or a bleak and gloomy day.

Slowly the waves retreated and the dragons descended again to the relative safety of the lee beneath the outcrops of black rock lining the beach. They were grim-faced and silent in grief, trapped on this barren isle. And still the storm raged unabated.

In desperation Fortune persuaded the sorry group to move across Sharp to the less exposed northern shore. At the time it seemed a good plan, but the trek exhausted them all and it transpired that the wind did not care where it directed its wrath; here they were just as exposed as they had been in the south. Now they were all too tired to move any further, and with no food to speak of and no prospect of there being an end to the dreadful weather, their very survival was in the balance.

Gossamer crouched behind the protection of Fortune's wings, her own wings bundled tight around Aria, who was wailing inconsolably with hunger and fear.

'Fortune! Gossamer!' It was Quill, battling her way valiantly through the gale to join them. 'We have to try flight – it's the only way we'll ever get clear of this weather. If we can just get above the clouds . . .'

'Out of the question!' shouted Gossamer, poking her snout from beneath Fortune's wings. 'Well, for us at least. I'm not risking Aria's life.'

'There are already several dragons discussing the possibility,' Quill persisted, her lined face heavy with the scowl she wore. 'Your thoughts would be welcome, Fortune, adept as you are in the air.'

'Oh, Quill,' groaned Fortune. 'I have flown in blizzard and through fire, but I cannot fly now. If there are some who want to try . . . then I wish them luck. But that is all, Quill – I can do no more.' Rain sliced across his frown and he bent his head again.

Quill appraised this young dragon family as she turned disconsolately away. Ever the carer, she felt nothing less than devastated if a dragon refused her aid, or even her advice. Long years of toil in the healing caves of Covamere had given her strength in addition to her native compassion, but strength did not lessen the hurt she felt when other dragons suffered. Now, as she leaned into the storm, squinting her eyes half-shut against the pain of the lashing salt spray, she felt weak and very, very old.

Covamere had been perfect for her, an enclosing community in which she had been born and which she had never thought to leave – before the Turning. Exploration was not a word with which she was familiar, unless perhaps in reference to the inner territories into which a suffering dragon sometimes retreated; then she would journey to bring that dragon back. But now Covamere was destroyed and she was homeless, although as much as that she felt simply *unprotected* these days. She had spent her former life underground, massively shielded by rock and charm.

She missed Covamere, and she missed the magic.

She always found flight an unwieldy and exhausting procedure, even more so now that she was forced to achieve it by wholly natural means. Even after so many moons on Haven the sky still seemed to her a frightening and empty void. In a strange way the storm was almost comforting, for it reduced the vacuum of the sky to a cavern of cloud, a ceiling . . . threatening in the extreme, but oddly welcome nonetheless. Deep in her heart, Quill longed to be underground once more. She longed to be home.

But those days are over, she mourned as a sudden discharge of sheet lightning flashed whiteness over the sky. *So much is over*.

The wind blasted her against the rock outcrop then doubled back to force her out again on to the steep slope of the shore. She hunched over, her ragged wings furled tight against her flanks as static energies flickered over her scales, reminding her briefly of lost fire charm. Glancing into the gale she saw another dragon clambering up the stony shore towards her, his own scales crackling with tiny lights. Blue and green sparks skated down the spines on his back and his bared teeth glowed as though they were aflame. Incredibly, his wings were spread.

'Quill!' the dragon was shouting. 'Quill, don't go yet!'

'Who says I'm going at all?' she retorted. She was confused, for the roiling air of the tempest obscured both this dragon's face and his voice; though she knew every dragon of Haven by name, this one she did not recognize. 'Speak your name, dragon! Who are you?'

The other approached further, slipping several times as his claws failed to grip the treacherous rock, until presently he was virtually snout to snout with the old healer.

'It's me,' he drawled. 'V-Vox!'

Quill groaned inwardly, for this was a dragon for whom she had little time. Though she confessed that there was little actually to dislike about him, she found it impossible to ignore the scandal of his past and for this reason alone had always avoided him.

Vox was a murderer. The year he came of age, he was flying west of Covamere with a young female dragon, the daughter of a prominent member of one of Halcyon's many councils. Their friendship was not popular with her parents, Vox having been born into a lowly mountain family with few connections and – so it was judged by many – limited intelligence. 'Vox the Uncouth' he was called but evidently Choliel, the young female, saw something attractive in his rough, slow-talking ways and for most of that summer they flew frequently over the broken mountains to the west of the settlement, enjoying each other's company and exploring the boundaries of adulthood together.

Then, one day, Vox returned without her.

He offered no story other than they had argued and she had flown off. But Choliel did not return home. Dragons searched . . . and after three days Choliel's body was found on a remote mountain top, her slender neck snapped in two.

Vox never denied the charges against him nor put forward any explanation for Choliel's mysterious death. Though nothing could be proved, Halcyon himself decreed that the young dragon should suffer the penalty of ten years without charm. The binding spell was a complex one, and in the end it was a member of the Secret Council who administered it, though she lived on the other side of the world. She was Archan.

Vox sat unmoving as magic flowed from far around the globe to neutralize the charm he had previously been able to wield. Archan's spell was both powerful and delicate, taking two full days to wrap itself completely into Vox's system. During that whole time he did not move one muscle. The final humiliation was the colouring of his every scale to the detested purple of the outcast dragon. A charmed dragon who wore purple scales was universally shunned, or worse, in some settlements, attacked. This wretched colour was originally the mark of the evil clan of the Nistri, one of the earliest known races of charmed dragons who had lived far in the south and who, among even more grisly rituals, had practised cannibalism and blood sacrifice; its imposition was in many ways worse than the crippling effect of the excising of charm.

The ten years of Vox's sentence were almost over when the world turned, and suddenly all charmed dragons suffered his fate: they too were made Natural. But none of them bore scales the colour of twilight, and still by most he was shunned.

Even by Quill, even by kind, caring Quill.

'P-Please listen to me, Quill. I don't b-believe any other dragon will.' Vox's face was earnest and, it seemed to Quill, still very young, though she would have expected the years of hardship to be etched into it. In his gaunt features she saw a certain strength and, it startled her to note, a directness and even . . . honesty?

'Be quick about it, Vox, whatever it is,' she snapped, impatient as much as anything with her own wayward thoughts. 'We cannot linger here.'

Pathetically grateful that Quill had even bothered to reply, Vox blurted out what he had struggled up the shore to say.

'I've lived without charm for longer than any of you,' he explained abruptly. Then, his voice halting and uncertain, its tone a constant question, 'b-but that means I can feel it better. I've always been able to feel it, even when I couldn't work it. Like a b-blind dragon who finds that his hearing has got better, you know?'

'We have little time, Vox,' interrupted Quill irritably. 'Say what it is you want to say and then let's be moving.'

'B-but that's it,' pleaded Vox. 'We mustn't move on. We c-can't fly in the s-storm, Quill – it would kill us!'

Glancing back at Fortune, whose head was still bowed low against the driving rain, Quill shrugged and said, 'Many things are possible. Fortune has flown through worse than this, as have others.'

'B-but they haven't! This is no ordinary s-storm!' Vox was getting quite agitated now, jumping up and down and scrabbling to keep a grip on the rain-slicked rock. A wave crashed against the shore below them, its sound burrowing into the rock at their claws and making the ground shake. 'Look at the sky – there's . . .'

As he spoke, Vox gestured upwards with one, purple wing. Then he froze, his mouth dropping open as he saw something wholly contrary to what he had been trying to demonstrate. His proof would have to wait, for there in the sky, floating with impossible ease amid the veritable hurricane which the elements had become, was a dragon. Quill followed his gaze skywards, and as Fortune looked up so did the rest of the refugees, each one marvelling at what they saw.

It was Ledra, of all dragons – a Natural. Cocooned in a wavering shell of charm, she was hovering in the treacherous air with her wings furled around her pale belly. The egg-shaped charm which contained her was sheer, almost transparent, although every so often darts of lightning chased across its surface and betrayed its form. With a beatific smile shining from her face she spoke, her words amplified by some secondary magic so that they thundered out of the sky, overriding the cacophony of the storm with formidable power.

'Dragons!' she announced. 'Join us, and the power of charm shall be yours again. Ledra and Hesper make you this promise: that all shall possess the magic, Natural and Charmed alike. The Turning was but a break in the pulse of the world. All things return, not least of them the charm. Far from a world of natural dragons, it shall be a world of the Charmed. See, I am the living proof that this is so!'

So saying she unfolded her wings to reveal not two but four legs curled against her belly – the four of the Charmed! She had changed. She was no longer a natural dragon; now, it seemed, even she had the magic.

The effect on the cowering dragons, both ex-Charmed and Natural, was astonishing. One by one they emerged from their various refuges and opened their wings to the storm.

'Help us!' several cried, and, 'Save us, Ledra!' To them all Ledra nodded comfort and blessing, and as they gathered beneath the glowing shell of the spell which kept her aloft, the magic sent beams of energy lancing into them and recreated the flight charm about their own bodies, drawing them slowly up into the air until a great wing of dragons, some bewildered, many triumphant, had formed itself in the very clutches of the storm.

'And you?' jeered Ledra triumphantly, staring straight down at Fortune. 'Would you refuse me now?'

Ignoring her, Fortune cried out to his former companions in a desperate attempt to bring them back to his side. 'Don't believe what she tells you, dragons! You are being deceived – there is no future for charm, not until the world turns again many lifetimes from now.'

Rain slashed him, beating his words back into his up-turned face. Glancing down he saw that two other dragons had remained earthbound along with him and Gossamer – and of course little Aria. Unable to recall the name of the purple dragon, he pleaded with Quill to help him convince the others to reject Ledra and her certain folly.

'They will not believe you,' mourned Quill. It seemed to Fortune that her attention was as much with her nervous companion as with those dragons in the air. She radiated towards this other dragon an odd mixture of curiosity and hostility and Fortune could not readily judge their relation-ship with each other, if relationship there was. The purple dragon remained silent, his head lowered, and he was mut-tering unintelligibly to himself. Quill, he saw, was weeping.

'Oh, but there is nothing we can do,' she wailed. 'The urge to fly is too great for any of us to resist, but . . .' and here she looked again at the dragon who loitered at her side, '. . . but resist it we must. There is more to this storm than mere squall and scourge.'

Before any of them could muster further argument Ledra had turned in the air and swept through the midst of the hovering crowd of dragons to take up position at their head.

'Come!' she cried. 'We go to Hesper, and you shall all see the secret of the charm which had gone and which has returned to us! Come! Follow!'

Like beads of fire they dwindled into the violent distance, leaving the five remaining dragons to huddle yet closer together beneath the crumbling rock in the hope of repelling a storm which grew steadily worse. As hail began to drum against the precarious shore so the light failed further, its retreat sending despondency into their hearts. Only light-ning illuminated now, and its light was cruel and brief. No magic remained to comfort them in the claws of the hurri-cane, only the warmth of each other's bodies and the hope – surely vain – that some far-off dawn would see a change in the weather at last.

Dawn came, and it seemed to Fortune that the storm had abated somewhat. Still it lashed the rock, driving flakes of pumice into the air and sending rain slicing against their bodies like claws, but the sky was less heavy, the cloud base higher. The sun skulked on the eastern horizon as though fearful of the day it had invoked, but gradually it rose and though it failed to warm it did force its yellow light into the coldness of the tempest and, for a time at least, Fortune dared to hope that the wind might eventually die away. Stretching his wings, grunting with the sharpness of cramp, he poked his head out into the rain and surveyed the scene.

The shore dropped away from their refuge at a steep angle, but . . . was it not even steeper than it had been the previous day? Fortune thought it was. And the shoreline was nearer. In the night, somehow, Sharp Island had moved . . .

'Um, s-sir?' The voice came from behind him and he turned to see the purple dragon loitering at his flank. They had sheltered close, all of them, grabbing sleep in fitful bursts, but little had been said during the darkness. They had all turned in on themselves during that terrible night, shutting eyes and ears and hearts against the fury of the storm. For a time, Fortune had even forgotten that Gossamer and Aria were still with him – much to his shame this morning.

The dragon repeated his greeting and Fortune wiped rain from his eyes to find the newcomer smiling nervously and ducking his head. 'Um, sir, you p-probably don't remember who I am.'

'Vox,' replied Fortune at once, the name flashing into his mind like a night dragon rising in the heavens. 'That's right isn't it? And you're, er . . .'

'Outcast, sir.' Vox looked down at his claws and shivered slightly, the motion disturbing the long, bristling spines which stood proud of his dorsal plates. 'But I've served my p-penance, honestly I have, sir. I only want to help now, if I can.'

'I'm sure you can, Vox,' replied Fortune. Like Quill, he had ignored this young dragon over the past moons, having heeded only the stories which were told about him and never bothering to investigate the dragon himself. Now, in his company, he found Vox disarmingly pleasant.

Then Quill and Gossamer woke from their shallow slumbers and shuffled over to where Fortune and Vox stood huddled beneath the lip of the outcrop. Aria clutched instinctively to her mother's back, even though she was still fast asleep. The sun had risen further and the torrential rain had become a heavy shower; water still cascaded from the overhanging rock and poured down the shore into the sea but at least it was no longer driving into their faces.

Overcome by a sudden impulse, Fortune opened his wings wide and drew all his companions – including Vox – close to him in a huge embrace.

'The storm came back,' he announced to no one dragon in particular. 'Just like I said. I knew it would.'

'Oh, Fortune,' laughed Gossamer, the lightness in her voice transparently false but welcome nonetheless. 'Do you think we hadn't noticed?'

'Ah, but Hesper was right, wasn't he?' put in Quill. 'It wasn't just the storm that came back.'

Gossamer yawned loudly. 'Quill's right, my dear. All that Mantle told you cannot have been true. We know the magic went when the world turned, but for how long? Maybe the world is already turning back again. What are we to do against the likes of Hesper and Ledra, against such powerful charm?'

Fortune shook his head, tutting loudly.

'My darling Gossamer,' he began, 'you of all dragons should know . . .'

'I'm about to get a lecture about how charm isn't necessarily as powerful as a dragon might think,' Gossamer confided in Quill. 'But Fortune, the fact remains that the magic is with us again, and there's very little we can do about it.'

'P-pardon me . . .' came a small voice at their sides.

'And another thing . . .' began Fortune simultaneously.

'Pardon me,' the outcast repeated, 'but I would like to speak.'

It was Quill who encouraged him. 'Go on,' she urged, for in his expression she saw that he was a dragon with truths to tell and secrets to unburden.

'If I m-may,' Vox continued hesitantly, 'I'd like to tell you what I think is happening. I'm g-good where charm's concerned, you see . . .' He began by relating his wretched history, sparing none of his own shame in the process but simply presenting events as they had happened – except he still refused to speak directly of Choliel's mysterious death. The others listened sympathetically, for whether or not he was guilty of his alleged crime was not an issue here – he was simply presenting his credentials to his new companions, and his honesty went a long way to reaching their hearts.

'You can sense charm at a distance?' prompted Gossamer as he halted briefly.

'All charmed dragons can – or could, before the T-Turning. Some better than others,' confirmed Vox. 'My handicap made me b-better than most. I had to work harder at it, I suppose.'

'So did you sniff out this charm of Hesper's too?' asked Fortune. The more he listened to this dragon the more he liked him, although an inner voice warned him to be cautious. *Halcyon himself convicted this dragon of murder*, he reminded himself. *He could be more dangerous than he seems*.

'Sort of,' responded Vox eagerly. As he spoke he relaxed, the twitch in his muscles and the stammer in his voice slowly calming as he felt at ease in this new company. 'But it's not Hesper's charm. It never will be. M-Mantle was right: this magic, it's just the abandoned charm he spoke of. You must know that, Fortune – there's nothing strange about it at all.'

'But the abandoned charm is scattered all over the world,' put in Quill, clearly unconvinced. 'It exists only in tiny pockets – there isn't enough to be of any real use.'

'Yes, but something has changed.' Here Vox paused, glancing round at each of the others in turn. 'I think something is g-gathering the abandoned charm together, pulling it towards a single place. The charm is being focused, being concentrated. All Hesper's done is used the power of the flow. But it won't last, the magic – it'll all be gone once the flow dies away again. Then it really will be over.'

'Quill?' Fortune prodded his fellow councillor, seeking verification of Vox's theory.

'Well,' the old healer said slowly and thoughtfully, 'I think young Vox might actually have something there. But of course, a dragon is bound to ask the one question he has raised and not answered.'

It was Gossamer who completed the thought. 'Who – or what – is gathering the charm?' she asked softly. As she spoke the wind fell away almost completely, leaving their ears singing in practically clear air. 'And why?'

'I don't know,' admitted Vox, 'but it explains the storm. The wind is full of charm, blowing n-north as far as I can tell. The wind *is* the charm, soaked in magic. It's not n-natural, this storm of yours, Fortune. But I suppose you knew that.'

'Yes,' murmured Fortune. 'I think perhaps I did.'

'So what does this mean for us?' demanded Gossamer suddenly. The low morning sun glanced across her white face and made a warm glow in the half-cave which had been their protection throughout the night. Today – just possibly – they would not need its shelter. Perhaps today they could take to the air themselves.

'Well,' answered Fortune, 'for me that's obvious. Hesper and Ledra have lured our friends away with false promises and evil intentions. It's up to us to lure them back again.'

'And just how do you plan to do that?' Gossamer felt a surge of energy fill her body as she saw returned to Fortune's eyes the very light of purpose which had been lacking in all their time on Haven. The sun cupped his face like the wings of an old friend, filling its young, noble features with warmth and wisdom. Only now did she realize how deep his frustrations had run there, how much he had yearned for the freedoms he had once enjoyed. *No*, she corrected herself, *not freedoms. Adventures!*

'I don't know,' he replied happily, gazing deep into her eyes. For a few breaths it seemed that only the two of them were present in the shadow of the outcrop, that only they mattered. Then, with a lusty wail, Aria broke the silence and suddenly they were all laughing, even Quill and Vox, although no dragon knew quite what they were laughing about. 'I don't know,' repeated Fortune, 'but I suppose we'll think of something.'

The sun dimmed as it rose into cloud but nothing could properly extinguish it that day, and although later the rain returned and the wind whipped hard again, it was as nothing compared to the storm's former rage. On its back the charm sped through the sky, heading north.

CHAPTER 15

The Halls of the Deathless

Archan led them on through a huge, light-filled gallery. Thousands of exhibits filled its every contour, ranging from monstrosities such as a troll's skull to minuscule works of art fashioned by the basilisks themselves. All were held in place by artfully sculpted ribs, which were themselves items of display in this museum of the Deathless. Dark and sombre, these reaching fingers led both the eye and the wing out along richly textured buttresses and spindly members to focus the eye on the exhibits themselves. The light of charm poured out over the collected memorabilia of a thousand lifetimes.

Cumber stared long at the troll's skull. The troll stared back at Cumber with a gaze as deep as an aeon. Though its flesh had long since wasted, the smooth, grey bones of its skull gleamed in the dusty light of the hall, a dewy coating of charm imbuing them with eerie phosphorescence. It loomed before the dragons like a mountain face, the gaping cavern of its mouth large enough to swallow them all with ease, had the creature been alive. Tusks like stripped redwoods jutted across their flightpath, towers of ivory tattooed with a patchwork of scars.

'It's incredible!' marvelled Cumber, beating the dry air with steady strokes. 'But why hasn't it vanished like the rest? The bones of the trolls have long since sunk into the ground – I saw it happen myself.'

'Charm, of course,' answered Thaw dismissively, more interested in the ferocious complexity of the basilisks' sculpting of every surface in this enormous chamber. 'It's been held captive here against the flow of time. Archan, how long did it take the basilisks to create this place? Years, centuries?'

'Aeons,' came Archan's reply. 'They lived here for tens of thousands of years, and this chamber is but one tiny scale on the hide of their citadel. They never completed it, of course. There is so much still to be done here.'

'Aeons!' echoed Thaw. 'To have such time . . .'

'This is the pelt of a kerak,' proclaimed Archan, indicating a long, gnarled thread of dried skin. 'Such creatures lived when dragons were young. Their bodies were so thin that they could cut through their prey simply by constricting them. They usually killed by decapitation.'

Further on she demonstrated with some pride a hollow tube through which cascaded a river full of rich, orange light. Sparks flared inside the stream, each trapped within a perfect liquid sphere.

'Fire in water,' she explained. 'Its charm had deteriorated by the time I came here, but I have restored it to something approximating its former glory. It has no function, but it is an interesting exercise as I think you will agree. I like to think the Deathless would be pleased were they to see it now.'

'It is beautiful,' confessed Cumber.

'It's a marvel,' agreed Thaw. 'As are you, Archan, to have repaired it so flawlessly.'

Some way down the endless hall the intricate arrangement of the supporting ribs narrowed the flight space into a constricting channel. The three dragons coasted through the tunnel of air thus formed, two of them pale and luminous in the chalky atmosphere, one striped yellow and black, his body cutting through the dust like teeth.

Thaw was inspired. He had been removed too long from the high rank he enjoyed beneath Wraith, and his thoughts since the Turning had grown uncharacteristically reflective – a dragon of action, his new role as councillor and advocator of peace had blown against his instincts like an unwelcome crosswind. He yearned for new challenges.

And what greater challenge for a dragon of action than that offered by this citadel of the Deathless? What treasures still existed in the world which were not kept here? Once, the young Thaw had mapped an entire archipelago: now, here, were whole worlds to map, worlds and histories, all contained within a single edifice, all laid out beneath his gaze and awaiting rediscovery. Such wonders!

Red flakes of rock from the surface of another world; the petrified remains of a tree which had once stood as tall as the Plated Mountain; the captured dreams of a slaughtered faery council, thirteen hundred minds embossed into a shred of flawless crystal. The gatherings of the world, of many worlds, brought here by the Deathless, by the ones who owned the power to pursue any dream they cared. The ones with the power – and the time – to *know*.

To map all that there is to know, thought Thaw with mounting excitement. *I care not that this path has been flown before, for the Deathless abandoned it only half-explored. So much still to be done – so much a dragon could do!*

Suddenly Thaw turned on Archan, his eyes burning like beacons from his hard, yellow face. Her own face was blind and unreadable as he spoke but it was clear that she was listening to all he said with the utmost intensity.

'Archan!' he exploded. 'You have hardly even begun to restore this place to what it might be! Think of what you could achieve if you possessed the power of the Deathless.'

'Power, Thaw?'

'Yes!' By now Thaw was almost beside himself. Cumber looked on with unfeigned surprise – he had never seen the warrior so impassioned about anything, least of all a dusty chamber filled with ancient relics. 'Don't you see, Archan? Somewhere in here is their secret. Somewhere in here is nothing less than the power of immortality, the route to eternity. What could dragons not do who owned that power? What could they not achieve? Having learned everything that there is to be learned, what glories could they not aspire to, what victories could they not win? What could they not conquer?'

'And the basilisks?' Archan's question was dry and quite free of the emotion vivid in Thaw's ranting.

'Forget the basilisks! From what you have told us their minds were petty and unimaginative. They preferred to squabble among themselves rather than seek the true glory

162

of their eternal state. But they have shown us the way, Archan. And we must follow!'

'We?'

Cumber inhaled sharply as Archan approached Thaw, her creamy wings cycling through the air with hypnotic grace. For an instant he was convinced that Thaw had so offended her she would strike him dead as he hovered there, but before he could cry a warning the exotic dragon had wrapped her long, sinuous tail around the warrior's striped hindquarters and pulled his body against hers. Sucking charm from the very fabric of the hall in great gulps of light, she folded her wings around them both.

Suspended on a web of magic, the two dragons embraced in the museum of the basilisks, while behind them Cumber became filled with a sudden and abject terror which caused him to flick his white wings sideways and retreat through the slender passage of air until he was careering back the way they had come. His wings thrashed with hard, urgent strokes as he swooped this way and that, his mind growing confused as the labyrinthine passageways opened up to admit him.

Ancient and impassive, the troll watched him exit the hall.

As the chitraka moved, so did Smoke. She lunged towards Velvet, her teeth bared ready to tear at the glowering chitraka, but before she could reach her companion Ratchet blocked her path with his heavy, square body.

'Wait!' he hissed. 'Look!'

Smoke looked ... and listened. Velvet was humming softly to the creature, whose eyes were closed, their lids flickering with hidden motion. The song she sang was a plaintive mountain song – had she been better acquainted with the missing Volley she would have known the song was a favourite of his – and the effect it was having on the fearsome chitraka was remarkable. Muscles unclenched beneath its striped, golden hide, hackles lowered on to its shoulders; peace fell across its whole form like a fall of softest snow.

Tentatively, Velvet reached out a wing and stroked the

163

creature's head, swallowing hard as it twitched slightly. It began to purr. The young dragon continued for many breaths, humming and calming the chitraka until she finally gathered her resolve . . . and stopped.

Slowly it came out of its trance. Smoke and Ratchet stepped forward as Velvet edged back towards them, tensed for a second attack. But it never came. Gradually the chitraka's eyes opened and the dragons saw that in place of the former blaze of fear and anger was a new fire: one of trust.

It has intelligence! marvelled Velvet, the knowledge striking her with a sudden jolt. *Its mind is simple but . . . it knows!*

She moved forward again, her head cocked slightly, trying to formulate some kind of greeting with which she might further strengthen the bond which had started to form between them. But she had no need of words. The chitraka loped to her side and pressed its flank against hers, lashing its serpentine tail and issuing a deep, contented growl. Then it lay down in the shadow of her wings and gazed placidly up the ramp down which, scant breaths before, it had been racing with murder in its heart.

'Well,' exhaled Smoke, 'we seem to have made a new friend.'

'We should still be cautious,' warned Ratchet. 'I don't trust that Archan, and this is one of her beasts.'

'Don't worry, Ratchet,' Velvet smiled. 'I have a feeling we can trust this one.'

The chitraka listened ecstatically as these three dragons discussed her loyalties. Powerless to speak, she was content to let them debate; her actions would prove her decision.

For this one dragon, this . . . *Velvet* . . . had in the space of a few short breaths shown her more kindness than Archan ever had. This dragon exuded a deep and passionate concern for her fellows, and now it appeared the chitraka was counted as such. Perhaps even one of her family. And for an orphaned creature fostered by a dragon who cared more about the dry and soulless basilisks than ever she did about a living creature, this was a revelation. The sun rose inside the chitraka's head and it had the face of a dragon, the face of Velvet.

'So what shall we call you?' demanded Velvet suddenly, her voice full of warmth and humour. 'I suppose you have a name, but since you can't tell us we'll have to think of one ourselves.'

'What about "Gold"?' suggested Smoke.

'Too boring.'

'"Dancetail"?' offered Ratchet with unexpected poetry.

'No,' replied Velvet quietly, her insight deepening as she regarded the chitraka closely. 'I've got it. There's an old mountain word that will do just nicely – "Mokishi".'

'That's a name?' puzzled Ratchet, his massive face screwing up in confusion. 'What does it mean?'

'Liberty.'

The chitraka purred and nuzzled the kind dragon's flank. A name! At last it had a name!

Cumber checked his headlong flight, his heart thumping against his ribs. Having regained the open airspace of the core, he was now unsure of where he should go next. The only two tunnels he knew in this giant crossing place were the one which led back to the museum and the one from which they had earlier emerged.

Why did she separate us from the others? he wondered. *Some kind of test? If so, Thaw seems to have passed.*

Behind him the trapped cataract thundered through the artificial confines of the charm moulding it into a half-round channel of water. Hundreds of boulders jutted forth through the torrent, breaking it into a wild pattern of spray and foam, single rocks locked in defiance of the waterfall's inexorable flow. Cumber glanced over their contours and, for the briefest moment, ghostly faces were reflected across them. Old faces, with silver eyes and moist, deadly breath. The faces of the Deathless.

They were six, these ancient watchers, and whether the illusion was a fabrication of his own anxious mind, or whether they had appeared by some trick of charm, Cumber could not tell. Their pale features floated in the rocks as though trapped behind some translucent skin and he was reminded briefly of a dragon he had once imprisoned in similar fashion, so long ago now, it seemed. They blinked slowly, with stars reflected in their hard, metallic gaze.

The illusion lasted a mere breath, but before it faded Cumber saw their features melt and fuse into new shapes, new faces. The faces of dragons, one creamy white, the second yellow ... and a third, a young, bright dragon face with black eyes and dark skin like a brittle autumn leaf. He looked out from the water's flow with open curiosity and overwhelming confidence. His body melted into the rock – it seemed that he had no wings. In his eyes Cumber saw reflected a vista of stars, one of which was moving like a streak of fire.

Who are you? wondered Cumber, but even as his mind worked the vision departed and he was left staring again at lifeless boulders. Still gripped by fear, yet filled too with a strange joy at the vision, he tipped his wings into the spray and arrowed down towards the base of the falls where, perhaps, he would find some direction.

At all costs I must find the others. Maybe there's a map somewhere. What is this Archan up to?

Down he flew, unaware that watching his departure from a distant tunnel entrance was the very dragon he feared, her new disciple at her side. They followed his descent with stretching necks until he was almost vanished in the haze, then they too spread their wings and pushed languorously out in pursuit, their wings beating in perfect time.

The ramp led up to a small antechamber adjoining the main entrance hall to the citadel. The floor was slightly concave and folded into a series of shallow scallops; it was like walking across a gigantic seashell. The ceiling was low – barely one tree high – and studded with tiny, gem-like lights. They watched the dragons like eyes. Smoke regarded these overhead stars with trepidation.

'Remember, Ratchet,' she whispered, her voice pitched so that only the big warrior could hear. 'I cannot stay here. It's too much.'

There was another way out of the antechamber, one which did not lead to the entrance hall. This second exit tunnel was positioned halfway up the far wall and Velvet was hopping up and down, flapping her long wings clumsily in the confined space in an effort to see what lay beyond.

'It's very dark,' she announced. 'It certainly doesn't look very welcoming. It looks like it just goes down and down – and there's a funny smell.'

Reluctant to probe the unwelcoming tunnel's depths, they made their way back towards the main entrance. The chitraka followed them with long, graceful strides, her claws retracted now so that her padded feet made no sound on the shining floor. Smoke lagged behind the others as they made their way out into the huge and airy space, and presently Velvet dropped back to join her. They walked in silence together as the chamber opened out around them until finally Velvet spoke.

'Tell me to mind my own business,' she blurted all of a sudden, 'but are you Charmed?' Smoke stopped dead, her breath choking in her throat. She coughed several times, spluttering as Velvet clapped her on the back with one of her wings. 'Well?' persisted Velvet, determined not to be evaded, 'are you? It could matter a lot now, you know, looking at where we've ended up.'

By now Ratchet had rejoined them. Mokishi, the chitraka, prowled at the periphery of the group, casting her acute gaze all about the chamber, guarding. Ratchet cleared his throat.

'Maybe you should tell her, Smoke,' he rumbled.

Smoke regarded Velvet for a long moment, then shivered slightly and nodded her head. She smiled, but it was a smile quite without feeling. In her eyes Velvet recognized the same haunted, distant air she had perceived several days before when they had sheltered together in the desert canyon.

'It's nothing, in a way,' said Smoke hesitantly. 'But then for me . . . it's everything.'

'Tell me,' whispered Velvet, her voice gentle.

'The story I told you – about how I was named – that was true enough. I was born into a storm, Velvet, and the storm has never left me. I'm different, you see.'

'Charm?' prompted Velvet, her curiosity well and truly aroused. 'There is some charm in this story of yours, isn't there, Smoke?'

'Since you've guessed it I may as well tell you. To be honest, it's a relief – I told Ratchet here a little of it but even he doesn't know the whole story. Perhaps now the time has come to relate it all.

'I am half-Charmed, although that is only the start of it. My mother was attacked by a charmed dragon before she met my father, and the egg she bore became fertile as a result. My father took pity on her and became her mate and helped to raise me as his own. He loved me so much.' Here her eyes began to fill with tears and she sniffed loudly. 'But that's far in the past. The main part of my story begins much later . . .

'Being half-Charmed I have a well-developed charm sense. I cannot wield charm but I can detect its presence with great accuracy – greater, I fancy, than many a charmed dragon. But I feel it as a kind of pain, like hot claws digging into my mind, and the more charm there is the more it hurts. There is a great deal of charm here, and I am in pain now, even as I speak. This talent – though few others of my clan knew of it – made me feel like some kind of freak, and so I left my home when I was young. I never saw my parents again.

'I flew far, never settling down, building my body and my flying skills until there were few dragons who could match me. Charm sense gave me skill in navigation – made me the pathfinder I am, in fact – but it could not bring me peace. Eventually of course I found my way into Shatter's army and, well, the rest you know, more or less. But that was after, after . . .'

'After what, Smoke?' pressed Velvet.

'After I met the Black Dragon.'

'*What!*'

'It's true. I can hardly bear to speak of it but I must. I know that now. I lived for a time in a small Natural settlement east of Heldwater, not too far from where I was born. It was a close community and I never really fitted in; in fact, I was about to leave when he came.'

'Wraith?' blurted Velvet.

'Him. He rounded up the Naturals, every one, and bound them into cages of charm, just as he imprisoned the dragons of Aether's Cross, I suppose. But something went wrong – the magic he was using was not right, I could tell that it was ... distorted somehow. Anyway, the cages collapsed into a dreadful firestorm and all the dragons died. Wraith was not pleased.'

'But what about you, Smoke?' Ratchet asked the question. She had already told the big warrior of her charm sense, and of the immense pain it was causing her here in the citadel, but this tale of her past – and Wraith – was new to him. He was captivated.

'He had spared me alone out of all the Naturals,' she replied, sobbing as sudden tears burned her eyes. 'Oh, I suppose he sensed my special ability and spared me out of curiosity. At the time I thought he loved me.'

'*Loved* you?' Velvet was aghast.

'It is not so strange an idea. He was beautiful, Velvet. There were such colours in his wings, colours I had never before seen, and he seemed so gentle, so kind . . .'

'The Black Dragon? Smoke! How could you have . . .'

'Don't judge me!' exclaimed Smoke, hot tears coursing down her distraught face. 'You were not there – you can't know what he was like then. Don't you think I hate myself now? Can you imagine the horror I felt when I saw his error bring about the deaths of all those poor dragons, or even later when he brought war to the whole world? And I fought *against* him in that war – can you imagine what that was like, to have such hatred for the only dragon I had ever . . .'

'Ever what, Smoke?' asked Velvet, fighting to keep her voice under control. Deep in her heart she knew that Smoke was a good dragon, and she loved her all the more for having the courage to tell such a terrible story, but this confession was hard to comprehend, and even harder to forgive.

Yet who am I to forgive? she berated herself. *Who am I to judge? Fortune and Gossamer both spoke of the Black Dragon's awful beauty – could he not have seduced me too, had the circumstances been right?*

'Did you bear eggs?' asked Ratchet, the soft tone in his normally rough voice completing Velvet's shame at her own reaction. But Smoke shook her head. 'My parentage made

169

me barren long before the Turning sterilized dragons. Freaks do not have young.'

Velvet exchanged a glance with Ratchet, but the complexity of their thoughts made it impossible for either to read the other. *We must support her now*, seemed to be the common message, backed up by Ratchet's gruff statement, 'With the pain you're in, we must have you out of here right away.'

Smoke did not reply, only lowered her head to the ground and hitched in a great, sobbing draught of air. As she continued to cry, Mokishi wandered up to her and nuzzled against her coiled neck. Smoke accepted the comfort without words, spreading her wings and embracing the golden creature as though she were an infant dragon, perhaps the infant she had never had, could never bear.

All her companions could do was to leave her there for as long as it would take to purge her sorrow, but as they settled down to wait a breeze began to move in the chamber. Velvet looked up to see a pale dragon shape speeding down towards them from the dizzying glow of the distant ceiling.

'Cumber!' she cried joyfully, opening her wings and launching herself up to meet her mate in the dusty air. They tumbled briefly through beams of light and then alighted together next to Ratchet. Already Smoke was drying her eyes with her wings and sniffing away the remains of her tears, Cumber's arrival having prompted her to cut short her grief. As she approached the group, the chitraka loping close behind her, she smiled nervously at Velvet. Velvet returned her smile with a broad grin of her own, at which Smoke's tears started to flow yet again until leaping forward, Velvet threw her wings around Smoke and hugged her close, scarcely able to stop herself from weeping in sympathy. 'It's all right, Smoke,' she whispered. 'We'll look after you now. You have to move on now, you have to fly away from it all.'

Cumber looked on in puzzlement, but Ratchet refused to enlighten him. 'I daresay your Velvet will fill you in,' he proclaimed. 'It's not my place to say any more.'

At length the two females disentangled themselves and joined their companions. Recent news was swiftly exchanged, as well as the shared conviction that Archan was not a dragon to be trusted.

'She separated us, tried to trap us down here, and the sky knows what evil she's doing to Thaw!' said Velvet angrily. 'We have to leave this dreadful place, if only for Smoke's sake.'

Cumber cast her a quizzical glance but she waved him silent. *I'll explain later*, her look said. 'Yes,' he agreed, 'I suppose we ought to get out of here, but as for Thaw ... I'm not altogether certain whether or not he's ...'

But before he could finish the sound of paired wingbeats filled the space around them, and suddenly Archan and Thaw were *there*, having appeared from the empty air as though by magic.

Of course, by magic, thought Cumber irritably. *They are obsessed with it, both of them.*

'Whether or not he's what?' demanded Archan, her voice rich and sensuous.

'Whether or not he's on our side any more,' retorted Cumber, his voice sounding braver than he felt. Something about this great, eyeless dragon struck fear into his very soul. *She is a monster!* he thought with something close to panic.

'And what if I am not?' replied Thaw smoothly. He hovered at Archan's side, the rhythm of his flight matching hers perfectly. 'Although I was not aware that there were any sides, Cumber.'

'We have a mission,' persisted Cumber doggedly, 'in case you'd forgotten.'

'We're leaving now,' added Velvet. 'We've wasted far too much time here already – through no fault of our own I might add.' Here she glared venomously at Archan, but if the ancient dragon felt any emotion she displayed none. 'Are you coming, Thaw?'

'Where are you going, dragons?' laughed Thaw with a confident chuckle. 'To find your friends at Aether's Cross? Well, I wish you luck in finding the place. The land has moved, in case you'd forgotten. Great Smoke couldn't even find the Low Mountains –'

'I can find Aether's Cross,' responded Smoke with bluster.

171

'Given a lifetime or two, you might. Stay here, dragons. Here is the whole world laid out for you to see. There is no need for sides. Stay.'

'We're going,' repeated Velvet, turning her back on the two flying dragons and hustling her friends away towards the glow of the entrance.

'I can show you the place you seek.'

Archan's voice cut through the dust and the haze like a claw, stopping the departing dragons in their tracks. They turned slowly to regard their enigmatic hostess with deep suspicion.

'Why would you help us?' demanded Cumber.

'You did not question me when I cured your wounds,' came the silky reply. 'There is no need to question me now. You are free to go, of course, but first – do you not wish to see the way ahead? I can show you, if you have but the patience to tarry a little longer.'

'It's a trick,' whispered Velvet to Cumber, but in the end it was Smoke who decided.

'You can show us the way to Aether's Cross?' she barked. Archan did not reply, simply inclined her head: yes. 'Very well. Despite everything we will stay long enough for you to show us. Despite the fact that you kept us prisoner, despite the fact that . . .'

'Prisoner?' repeated Archan with astonishment in her voice. 'Oh, I see what you mean. I cannot be held responsible for the actions of my dear chitraka. She roams at will and, I'm afraid, if she chooses to take up station in a certain place there is little a dragon – even myself – can do to get past her. But that will be of little concern to you now as I see she has . . . shall we say, *adopted* your little band?' Velvet was certain she detected a flash of anger in her voice, but Archan was already going on, 'Come, dragons. You are my guests for as long as you wish to stay. Come with me now and you will see the greatest achievement of the Deathless. And you will find the way to reach the treasures you seek. Come!'

Thaw's expression was unreadable as he flew off with his new companion. As he circled down and up his path crossed that of Mokishi, and with a casual blow from one of his trailing legs he cuffed the creature to one side. Archan nodded her approval – he was learning well how to treat his servants.

The others consulted about what they should do, quickly agreeing that, despite everything, Archan seemed to offer their only real chance of ever finding the Cross.

'I can bear the pain a little longer,' said Smoke. 'And this way we can perhaps leave on good terms. I would hate to anger her – her power is great indeed.'

'That's true enough,' replied Cumber with conviction. 'So is it settled then?'

It was. Together they lifted into the haze and followed Archan and Thaw towards a far-off slit in the wall of the chamber. On the ribbed floor below, the chitraka bounded along in their wake, easily matching their pace through the air with her own huge strides. Somewhere above them the waterfall thundered with its constant voice, louder now than it had been for many, many years.

CHAPTER 16

Descent

For the rest of that day the storm was like a restless dragon, now settling and permitting the watery sun to prise its way through thinning cloud, now rearing back and pouncing once more with renewed energy on the sea. The periods of relative calm were welcome to the dragons urgently seeking food and proper shelter on the barren island of Sharp, but the relapses were as violent as ever the storm had been, and seemed even more so after the quiet that came before. But as the sun reappeared for the last time on its slow descent behind the dim western horizon, the clouds finally became a fragmented mist which soared high above the wind and dissipated into the heavens. Stars blinked with surprise as their eyes were exposed once more and suddenly the night was clear.

Cautiously, Fortune led his companions out from beneath the shelf of rock which had been their shelter throughout the worst times of the day. They looked around and up, scarcely able to believe that the hurricane had indeed passed them by. The sky seemed far away and huge, a dark cowl sprinkled with bright, white dust. Before them, dim in the faint starlight, stretched the jagged plateau which was the centre of Sharp.

'Food first,' announced Quill briskly. 'And then you can start weaving your plans, Fortune. But I'm short of ideas, I'm afraid – does anyone have any thoughts?'

'I do,' suggested Vox at once, eager to be of use. Then he hesitated as all eyes turned to him.

'Go on, Vox,' said Gossamer with an encouraging smile.

'Well, it's just that I flew over Sharp a few m-moons ago – back when a lot of dragons were scouting around. I remember seeing a place near the middle of the island. It looked like a b-big, black hole in the rock.'

'Doesn't sound very promising,' muttered Quill, unimpressed. 'A hole, you say?'

'Yes. I think it might have been a w-well.'

'Hmph!' Quill snorted. 'Water's not the problem, young dragon, not after all that rain.' To prove her point, she gestured with her wing at the numerous craters filled with fresh rainwater.

'I know,' Vox persisted, 'but if it is a w-well then there might be something g-growing there, something we could eat . . .'

'Well, leaves can have curative powers I suppose,' acknowledged Quill.

'I'm not sure what it was you saw, Vox,' said Fortune carefully, 'but it sounds like as good a place to start as any. Are we agreed?' All nodded consent and so they set off, Vox leading. Fortune felt a thrill run through his body as the warm night wind played across the taut surfaces of his flight membranes – what a release it was! He swooped across to where Gossamer was flying with deliberate care.

'How's my daughter?' he asked, anxiously craning his neck to inspect the tiny bundle of wings which clung to her back.

'Sleeping, my love. I think your storm has worn her out.'

'She's not the only one.'

The flight was a short one. Presently Vox called out and circled back down towards the ground. All was dark, but darkest of all was the roughly circular patch of utter blackness which gaped below them, an immense hole set into the broken surface of the plateau. The dragons alighted at its lip, exchanging wary glances and tipping their heads forward in a vain effort to see what lay in its depths.

'It doesn't exactly look welcoming,' said Quill, still unconvinced. 'The air's clear now – why don't we just fly out to sea a little way and try fishing?'

'Maybe we shall,' replied Fortune. 'But first let's just see what this has to offer.' He squinted into the blackness, his curiosity well and truly afire. The deep place reminded him of the Maze, although he sensed that there was little or no charm here; it was simply a hole leading down, down . . .

But down to where?

'Who's c-coming with me?' demanded Vox suddenly, gripping the edge of the hole with his claws. His wings were spread and trembling, ready to take him down.

'I'll come,' replied Fortune. Then, in response to Gossamer's quizzical expression, he added, 'It's all right, my dear. I don't think there's any danger here.'

'No,' she answered at once, 'it's not that, it's just . . .' She paused, scenting the air. 'Nothing – you go, Fortune. But don't be long, please.'

'I won't!'

Joining Vox he opened his wings and together they jumped easily down into the pit. They found themselves descending through a straight, vertical shaft, confined enough to force them to fly one above the other. Vox went first, with Fortune looking over his wide, purple wings as they floated down.

The weak starlight swiftly decayed and soon they were in darkness . . . except suddenly Fortune noticed a pale glow emanating from the sides of the pit. Straining his eyes in the eerie light, he could just make out some kind of growth – a fungus perhaps – coating the curved walls. It brought green, shadowless life to this peculiar underworld and Fortune remembered his dream, remembered the silver-eyed beast which dwelt beneath the sea . . .

'Something tells me,' he whispered, his voice echoing strangely around the pit, 'that we're not going to find a great deal to eat down here.'

A glance upwards revealed the distant entrance as a dark blot held by softly-glowing walls. It looked very far away. Looking down, he was relieved to see that a floor was approaching, and before he could draw breath again his claws touched rock and he was standing next to Vox. Air pressed against his ears and the sound of the ocean rumbled all about them.

'We're below sea level,' observed Vox. 'Where do you think this goes?'

Fortune followed the line of his gaze to see that the vertical tunnel down which they had ventured intersected with a crossing place, the junction of three horizontal passageways. Each of the three stared blank and black; none offered any clue as to where it might lead.

'I don't know,' replied Fortune slowly. 'I've never seen anything quite like it.'

These new tunnels were also roughly circular in section, but unlike the accessway, which was made of the same volcanic rock as the rest of Sharp Island, they looked oddly fibrous, as though they had been grown rather than carved. Fortune shuddered – he did not like the look of them at all.

'Just a moment,' blurted Vox as Fortune tugged at his wing, urging him to leave. 'Let me concentrate.'

Fortune held back as Vox thrust his snout towards each of the three tunnels in turn. As he did so he rocked slowly from side to side, humming tunelessly and gulping air in deep, considered draughts. At length he relaxed and turned back to his companion.

'Well,' he announced, 'I don't know what this place is but there is charm here after all. A long way off though. That must be why I didn't spot it from the air.'

'Charm?' queried Fortune dubiously. 'Are we in danger?'

'No. It's weak, and far away – or spread thinly perhaps. Too thin to tell what's making it. But the tunnels are interesting . . .'

'Hardly. Come on, we'll find nothing to eat down here. Our only hope is to use the better weather to reach one of the other islands.'

No sooner had Fortune spread his wings than Vox urged him to close them again. 'Wait, Fortune. These tunnels – they could help us.'

'What do you mean?'

'Wait here!'

And without further ceremony Vox launched himself into the nearest of the three passages. Fortune cried out after him but was too late – all he saw was his odd companion's dim form fading into blackness at the limits of his vision. He called out several times, his voice hoarse and nervous in the heavy air, but there came no reply. Since he was disinclined to follow there was no choice but to wait, but before long, with no obvious prospect of Vox's return, the damp and gloom began to press in on him and his unease grew. Looking up towards the tiny fragment of night sky, he shivered and wondered if the others were safe.

The ascent back through the shaft was arduous but uneventful. The closeness of the walls meant that Fortune had to scoop air past him in steady, muscular strokes, and by the time he reached the surface again he was out of breath. Gossamer and Quill rushed to meet him, anxious to know what had happened to Vox.

'I don't know where he thought he was going,' lamented Fortune when he had filled them in. 'He's a strange dragon, that one. And his stammer's gone,' he added as an after-thought.

'There's more to him than meets the eye,' suggested Quill. 'We should go down there.'

'All of us? Is that wise?'

In silence Gossamer stepped forward and turned Fortune's head to the south. He squinted into the night . . . and then his wings and shoulders slumped. There on the dark horizon fresh storm clouds were building.

'We need shelter,' whispered Gossamer. 'Real shelter, Fortune. I'm scared, scared for us but most of all I'm scared for Aria. She's so tiny – she needs warmth and food. We have to hide from this storm of yours, because otherwise I'm afraid . . . I'm afraid she might die.' Her mouth quivered as she said this. Fortune gazed at the small, starlit bundle wrapped tight on Gossamer's back and felt a bubble of fear swell and burst inside his heart.

How can my thoughts leave her even for an instant? he wondered, guilty at having left his mate and daughter so exposed on this barren isle. *What can be more important than these dragons whom I love?*

'Take us down there, Fortune,' murmured Gossamer. 'At least we'll be out of the storm.'

He nodded and led them carefully to the edge of the shaft. Quill flew down first, followed by Gossamer and Aria and finally Fortune. As he descended into the weird green light of the pit he felt as though not just the storm but the whole world were receding in his wake. The strangest thought came to him, that the air leaving his wings was speeding back in time towards some distant history where dragons had never existed, and could never exist. The shaft led down, but it led also into the future, and at that moment it seemed to Fortune that the future was a place where nothing was certain, not even its own, fluid past.

The tunnel fitted Vox perfectly, and he glided with growing confidence through the spaces beneath the seabed.

Confidence was not something he was used to dealing with. During his years as outcast he had learned to keep his head lowered, his eyes averted, his hide toughened against the glares and insults which were continually hurled at him, not to mention the occasional physical assault. Many times dragons had tried to drive him away from the Plated Mountain, but he had no other home to go to and so he stayed, eventually taking to wandering in the forbidden zones which were scattered throughout the enormous, girdling forest. To stay in these places was dangerous, being as they were thin patches in the skin of the world where the Maze occasionally broke through to perform weird and violent acts of magic, but Vox's charm sense was so acutely honed that he managed to avoid these sporadic outbursts.

There were other fascinating things there, too, for beyond the net of the Maze he found he could sense another net, a lacework of tunnels which he could not access. Deeper places which spanned the world and were not made by dragons. They called to him, these unknown tunnels.

And of course, the mountain reminded him of Choliel.

The day she died was one he remembered with black despair. He could remember everything so vividly that it was as though those terrible events were still going on, trapped inside his mind in some endless looping chain of time. The truth about that day he had never told any dragon, not even Halcyon, not even when those wise and penetrating eyes bored into his own, demanding that he lay aside the falsehoods he had constructed.

Tell me, dragon, Halcyon's eyes seemed to say. *Spare me no detail. Protect no dragon. Hide no truth. Be honest.*

But Vox resisted, for although the truth was plain enough in his own mind he could see no way of bringing it forth into the real world. Instead he said nothing, lowering his head in the manner which would soon become second nature. Halcyon passed the sentence he was bound by his own laws to pass, but even as Vox was led away those eyes burned into him, and Vox knew that Halcyon knew.

Knew that he had not murdered Choliel, that he was no more capable of murder than he was of revealing what he had witnessed on that fateful day. Knew that there *had* been a murder however, and that the killer still flew free. And perhaps Halcyon even knew, as Vox did, the name of the murderer.

The day had been bright. Choliel was gorgeous in the brilliant sunlight, her young body rich with veins of charm and glowing hard against the whiteness of the clouds through which they soared. She was one of the few dragons who did not judge Vox by the reputation of his family, who did not laugh when his voice stammered, nor tease him about the way his wings folded so clumsily against his flanks. He loved her, and hoped she loved him.

One of their favourite spots to meet was a tall pinnacle of rock west of the Plated Mountain. Broad and smooth-sided, a wide plateau flattened its summit. A dragon could bask there all day long without fear of interruption. The sociable Covamere dragons preferred places less isolated for their courtships, but for Vox and Choliel, dragons kept separate in public life yet desperate for each other's company in private, it was perfect. Their secret rendezvous.

The murderer must have been watching them all that day, awaiting his chance. The young lovers flew all morning, and by the time the sun was high they were exhausted. They lay at the top of the pinnacle with their wings spread wide, soaking up the noon sunshine and talking in low, intimate tones. Thinking back over that afternoon, Vox realized that he had known they were being watched, but that he had for some reason ignored the sensation.

Perhaps it thrilled me, he thought much later, during one of the long, lonely nights he spent in a forbidden zone. *Perhaps it was exciting to think of another dragon being jealous of me.*

Towards the end of the day Vox grew thirsty and flew down from the spire of rock to the small lake which lay at its base. He was gone for the shortest of times, barely long enough for the clouds which had been sweeping overhead to reach the foothills in the middle distance, but when he returned to present his love with a carefully bundled leaf bulging with drinking water he found a scene which stopped his heart dead in his chest.

A dragon was crouched over Choliel, dark wings spread wide against the setting sun. Vox did not recognize him. His body was the colour of dried blood, a red so deep that it was almost black; as the sun's rays soaked them, it seemed to Vox that the scales were growing darker and darker before his eyes.

Soon this dragon will be black all over, he thought hysterically. He dropped the waxy leaf, spilling the water about his claws.

Choliel was pinned to the rock beneath this dragon's massive claws. Choliel! Vox's mind, often a little slow, flooded with the realization that he had just flown straight into his worst nightmare. His heart in his mouth, he started moving towards the dragon he loved when he saw that the stranger had too many legs: vestigial limbs were twitching at the root of his neck, flashing with charm and wavering into near-transparency at their tips. Fear flashed through him and at the same time he was repelled. Choliel was squirming, whimpering with fear as the dark dragon pressed his talons into the soft skin about her throat.

'Let her go!' Vox intended to shout but his voice quavered. The dark dragon laughed, his voice rumbling like an earthquake.

'Those who are touched by Wraith may not be left to go free,' he bellowed.

Touched? What has he done to her?

'Vox,' cried Choliel pathetically. 'Help me, please.'

But already it was too late. With a great roar, Wraith raised his foreclaws and slashed them down across Choliel's slender neck. Her head fell away from her body, which jerked once and then lay still.

In that terrible moment, unable to comprehend what had just happened, Vox stared at Wraith's dripping claws, following the arc of their motion as the dark dragon swung them up again into the red light of the dying sun. Then the claws began to wave to and fro, hypnotizing him. Blood trickled on to the plateau, tapping out a deadly rhythm on the flattened rock.

'Wraith prevails,' whispered the dark dragon. 'You have

181

not seen me. I was not here.' Charm lanced from his mouth in the form of tiny shards of fire, discharging themselves into Vox's hide and vanishing between his scales like running water. With a gasp of air Wraith launched himself into the dusk, striking the air with his mighty wings. Soon he vanished into the lowering cloud.

Vox remained where he stood, tasting the charm with which Wraith had tried to alter his memory. He had countered the magic at once, for although it was powerful in the extreme it was badly directed and easy to deflect. The dark dragon had been distracted, aroused . . .

He took her, and then he killed her . . .

Snatching at the flavour of Wraith as the magic evaporated from his scales, Vox understood that the black dragon had done this before, often. Hidden in the charm was the horrible scent of *routine*, the knowledge that this was a crime perpetrated time and again, that the dark dragon loved . . . and then killed. Over and over.

A thought came into his mind: *May the sky help any dragon he loves and does not kill*, and Vox shuddered, but then his thoughts could proceed no further. The shocking wound which Choliel's neck had become stared back at him like a blind, red eye and all the tenderness he felt for his love was stained with horror. He lurched into the air, fleeing east towards the mountain and the hard questions which would eventually lead to his conviction for murder.

Always one of two things stopped him whenever he was tempted to reveal the truth of Choliel's death. The first was simple doubt that he would be believed: the dark dragon was a stranger, and would likely as not never be seen in Covamere again. Most of Vox's accusers were friends of Choliel's parents and as such were more than keen to see the rude, forest dragon brought to some kind of justice. There seemed little chance of his evading conviction under such prejudice and overwhelming evidence, however circumstantial.

But there was a second reason. At the really crucial times, when he could easily have broken down – such as when he was brought before Halcyon – he found rising into his mind an image which clamped his mouth tight shut: *yellow eyes, burning from a hard, dark face.*

If he betrayed Wraith, and if the dark dragon were found, then he would be dealt with by Halcyon. Not by Vox. This was not the way of the forest dragons, the way of vengeance. The only way Vox could retain his right to avenge Choliel's death was by enduring whatever punishment Halcyon might see fit to impose upon him, and then tracking Wraith down himself. *Yellow eyes, burning, and my love beheaded . . .*

He would endure. No punishment could be so terrible that it would take away from Vox this right. The notion fitted the simplicity of his mind and so it was that he withheld the truth even from great Halcyon, thus becoming one of the few dragons ever to have denied the probing of that mighty dragon. His charm was locked beyond his reach and in his outcast state he roamed the forest, mourning his Choliel and planning his revenge.

But the world turned, and though Wraith came back to Covamere, grown mightier than Vox could possibly have guessed, it was the Maze in its death throes that finally consumed the Black Dragon. Vox had been forced out of hiding when the forest was razed by Wraith's warrior dragons, and during the eruption of the Plated Mountain he found himself swept up with the small group of dragons who managed to escape to the sanctuary of Haven. Learning then of Wraith's death, he retreated back into his life of solitude, confused and uncertain of his place in the world.

Wraith was gone, but Choliel was still murdered, unavenged. Even as Vox coasted through the tunnel beneath the sea, feeling its route hugging him, this thought accompanied him. Sister tunnels reached into the rock all around, invisible, tantalizing. This one passage seemed clean and good but beyond . . . was there something unpleasant lurking behind its accommodating face? He could not tell.

Where am I going?

But the uneasiness passed. Suddenly he felt as though a great cloud were beginning to lift itself from before his eyes, and he flew with renewed determination. In his heart he felt that somewhere in the distant future he would find the solution, the missing scale in the puzzle of his tragic life.

* * *

High above, ferocious lightning emblazoned the angry sky. Beyond the distant shaft entrance, the torrent of light was just visible as a blurred, circular flare. The event was high and remote, and had little to do with the cavernous crossing place in which they sat, waiting for Vox to return.

After much debate, Quill had scraped a little of the fungus from the lower wall of the shaft and tasted it. The stuff was bitter but she kept it down and they all ate of it, although Gossamer refused to give any to Aria, fearful of possible side-effects in one so young. The infant dragon whimpered in her sleep, and Fortune took consolation from the fact that she was still able to slumber.

He said lamely, 'We'll know when she's really hungry. We won't be able to hear ourselves think.' The attempt at humour bounced, strangely without echo, into the tunnels, and neither of his companions laughed. Presently they dozed, while overhead the storm thumped, sending fresh water cascading down around them.

Fortune woke suddenly into the phosphorescence, his eyes wide and bleary in the odd, flattening light. Something was scuffling in one of the tunnels. 'Vox?' he whispered, keeping his voice low in an effort not to disturb the others. 'Is that you?'

'Yes,' came the reply at once, putting an abrupt end to the suspense. 'These tunnels are amazing!'

'Never mind the tunnels,' hissed Fortune. 'Did you find any food?'

'You could say that,' came the triumphant reply, and before Fortune could say any more there came from the tunnel entrance a burst of light that momentarily blinded him. Gossamer and Quill – and a startled and screaming Aria – awoke with a jump, and as they all blinked into the painful glare, Vox stepped forward. 'Look what I've found,' he announced with bashful pride.

Beneath the veined cowl of the pale, woven tunnel there flared a crescent slice of charm. It pulsed, a flickering, blue chunk of moonlight long ago captured by some cunning magic and trapped in a loop of time. This fact Vox explained to them all later, but for now it was simply a marvel, and a marvel most welcome in these gloomy, timeless depths.

It floated at Vox's side like a loyal servant, flooding the chamber with its cool and glorious light.

More welcome even than the light charm was the pile of food which Vox had somehow managed to drag back through the tunnel to the cross-roads. Berries and tubers and fish, and even a broad basin cut from a tree trunk and filled with the milk from giant tropical nuts.

'Where did you find it all?' cried Fortune, leaping forward with unrestrained glee. 'It looks as though it's all come . . .'

'From Haven,' replied Vox matter-of-factly. 'Yes – that's where I've been.'

'You mean this tunnel . . .'

'Goes to Haven. I guessed when I saw it – I could feel it – but I wanted to be sure. Eat, please – I've had enough already.'

They needed no further encouragement. Aria fed blissfully on the milk while her elders devoured almost everything else. Fish bones scattered across the weave of the floor and fruit husks were left empty at their claws. Their hunger reared, its full strength unrealized until now, and they ate until their bellies were full and their senses dulled. All else was subordinate to the feast, and if any intruders had stolen their way into the gathering they would have been quite ignored, so single-minded were these weary, hungry dragons.

Gossamer was first to sit back on her haunches, slowing her giddy senses as she pulled Aria close against her breast and warmed her with folded wings. The infant gurgled happily and stared back up at her with dark eyes, the smooth corners of her mouth turning in a way which filled Gossamer's heart with joy. How precious she was, this little one.

And unique, she reminded herself, the thought unwelcome in such an intimate moment. *No other infant dragon but Aria. Is she the future now?*

Fortune flopped at her side, grinning broadly while a thin trickle of milk rolled out from between his crinkled lips. In the background Quill belched contentedly.

'Well, Vox,' announced Fortune, 'you're a marvel! I don't know what we would have done without you.'

Vox looked nonplussed at this unconditional praise, and squirmed a little in the glow of the floating light charm.

Nevertheless, he managed to look pleased with himself. 'My pleasure,' he replied nervously.

'Yes,' agreed Quill, slightly begrudgingly but with some warmth all the same. 'Well done, Vox. Now, Fortune, do you have any ideas about how we should proceed from here?'

'One or two,' smiled Fortune. 'Vox – why don't you tell us about this tunnel you've found?'

And so Vox told them, about how the faintest of charms was woven into the skin of the strange, pale tunnel whose walls were like a mesh a dragon might weave from twigs to keep the wind from his nest, about how the tunnel dipped far below the seabed before rising again to break the surface in a hidden corner of Haven Island which no dragon had yet discovered – until now.

'But we scoured Haven,' protested Quill. 'Surely we would have found such a place.'

'It was held closed with a charm,' shrugged Vox. 'No dragon ever thought of looking there, and the magic was too weak to be noticed. There are trees all around the spot, so you wouldn't even see it from the air.'

'Are Hesper and Ledra there?' put in Gossamer. 'And all the others – what about them?'

'I think they're all there,' affirmed Vox. 'But the island has suffered. The storm. Many nests have been destroyed.'

'Did they see you?'

'I was very careful.'

'Can you take us there?'

'Of course.'

There was a collective sigh. Quill, Gossamer and Vox all looked towards Fortune, all eager to know his mind. Dragons they knew and loved were on Haven and they might save them from the folly into which Hesper had tempted them. Did they have any choice but to try? Fortune thought not.

'We should have a plan,' he said doubtfully. A fresh cascade of water showered behind them as he spoke and distant thunder resounded through the cross-roads chamber.

'Why?' smiled Gossamer. 'You've never bothered with plans in the past.'

CHAPTER 17

River in the Sky

The sky glowed as though some abysmal predator had lifted its claws and scratched a thousand parallel grooves across its skin, opening the way to dreadful fire beyond. Ocher regarded the sight with something approaching astonishment, for each scratched line was a stream of charm speeding north from wherever it had lain dormant: astonishment, for the sheer scale of the event. Ocher had released it, the abandoned charm, channelling it north, ever north . . . but there was so much!

Magic liberated from deep below the cold southern seas; magic from the dawn of some long-forgotten time when the world had been but a single thought in the mind of some mighty beast; magic which remembered the cataclysmic wars of the extinct trolls; tiny charms which had once been the living breath of dryads and faeries. Reservoirs great and small emptied themselves at the basilisk's command, spewing forth their contents into the sky.

Ocher entered the river, thinking itself immune to the wonders which surrounded it. And yet . . .

Symbiosis was an integral part of the basilisk's very existence. What were its million senses if not parasites . . . and what was the threat of the hybrid *bringer-of-shadow*, such as Wraith had almost brought to pass with Ocher's unwitting aid before the Turning, if not the ultimate joining of species? Now another sharing had occurred within Ocher – the presence of the vestiges of the Maze of Covamere. Now that its jumbled store of memories had found some coherence beneath the soothing, rational light of the Maze, Ocher found itself actually enjoying the process of recollection more and more with each breath it took. This time, after another aeon-long period of slumber, after yet another Turning, it had woken feeling truly refreshed.

Can it possibly be that Ocher is not ready to die?

The thought pierced the basilisk with unwelcome sharpness. Had it survived an eternity of desperation eventually to find peace with its deathless state? Could it be that now, having set the process of final dissolution irrevocably towards its end, it was having second thoughts?

It turned its mind swiftly from such distractions. Like a boulder, it would remain unmoved while the river of charm cascaded past it. Beyond the troubles and emotions of this tiny world it *was*. Beyond the effects of its actions on the short-lived and flimsy creatures which roamed the world, it *was*. Only north mattered now, north and the remaining three basilisks.

Tellere. Bacht. Geiss.

Tellere was nearby and not likely to refuse Ocher's offer of release, and nor, Ocher considered, was Geiss. Both, in the end, would join the Gathering. And Bacht? If any of them had been a leader, Bacht had been. And Bacht, like Ocher itself, had always argued fiercely that the ultimate goal of the basilisks should be suicide. Although in recent times Bacht had grown unpredictable . . .

And there was another problem: Ocher did not know where Bacht was. The Maze, with its memory of all the places in the world, and all the strands linking them together, had helped Ocher to locate all its fellows except Bacht. Tellere was close by, sleeping in the lowest dungeons of the citadel they had once built in the great mountains of the Spine, and that was where Ocher was now headed. Geiss, by a coincidence Ocher found reassuring, had concealed itself very near to the point where all the abandoned charm was now gathering, the very place where Ocher had already dispatched Veil and Mediel, the very place where, at last, the Deathless would die.

North. The crest of the world.

Already charm was being focused and primed to do its work, and soon the power of even the basilisks would be unable to restrain it any longer. Then the basilisks would gather in the north to work the last great magic this world would see. *But unless I can find Bacht then it might all be for nothing! What if the charm destroys itself and we are immortal still? Five will suffice, but would a circle of six not guarantee success?*

Panic was not an emotion the basilisk was familiar with, but the stakes were high. Blood thundered like hot metal through its indestructible veins. Ocher forged a way through the airborne torrent of charm, casting out over the sea towards the citadel.

A changed continent rolled by beneath it as it flew. The open mouth of Heldwater was closed now, its waters lost either to the rain or to some subterranean cataract. Ahead, the land rose but not so high as once it had; the Low Mountains had collapsed altogether as the peaks of the Spine had crashed down from the north, themselves dropping earthwards so that their once-proud alps were now meagre in comparison.

Behind, the Western Sea was pinching shut, bringing remote lands and islands close to what had once been the Heartland, lifting the seabed towards the sky and liberating realms which had long rested hidden below the waves. The sky rebelled as the land seethed beneath it, sucking the confused water from the seas and hurling it back down upon the earth as storms erupted far across the globe. Winds surged up from the south with renewed fury, their energies marshalled by the unnatural elements which had in part provoked them. In part, for at the heart of this worldwide storm was the beating presence of nature, eager to mould soil, sea and sky into the forms it desired. There was much that the wild, erratic power of the abandoned charm did of which the forces of nature approved, not least the explosive acts of creation which were bringing forth new creatures and new kingdoms, but in essence the process was one of conflict. Against the death throes of charm the natural world set all the strength at its disposal to ensure that it prevailed: wind and rain, hurricane and tempest, earthquake and tidal wave.

Storm.

*   *   *

Palm trees bowed before the hurricane, segmented trunks aching and finally splintering as the leaves were torn from their crowns. The air was filled with sand and spray, a lethal blend of elements that ravaged skin and scale as dragons battled their way towards some shred of safety. In the sky a broad band of charm began to infiltrate the roiling cloud, but for the moment no dragon was aware of it.

On the north shore of the island of Haven was a narrow box canyon, a virtual cocoon within which a large group of dragons huddled, shaking with fear and desperate for a leader who might take them to safety. They had been brought back from Sharp Island safe in the spheres of magic which Ledra, suddenly and miraculously charmed, had woven about them. And all had rejoiced, ex-Charmed and Natural alike, that the magic had returned and there were still dragons who could wield it for good.

But the joy had been short-lived. No sooner had the spheres deposited them on the shore of Haven than they had disintegrated, their magic melting into the sand like snow in spring. And the storm had struck again, its power worsened, its wrath unimaginable.

Into the canyon they retreated, Ledra no longer at their sides, Hesper nowhere to be seen. Rescued and abandoned, they cowered as entire trees were uprooted from the crumbling ground at the crest of the canyon walls. They cried out in fear as the sea swelled ever higher, crashing further and further up the nearby beach until it frothed at their claws and cut off the only way out of the trap. Their retreat became a prison, their only hope of escape now to fly. The sky was even more dangerous than the sea, filled with flying debris and the crackle of lightning. It would be suicide to enter such a maelstrom.

Tired, losing the hope they had gained when Ledra had first come to them, the dragons of Haven turned in upon themselves and waited for a saviour.

Ledra's first reaction when the flight charms she had constructed failed was to remake the magic, but to her horror the power was no longer there. Having sculpted her body anew, Hesper had schooled her swiftly and efficiently on some basic techniques and then sent her to fetch the dragons from Sharp while he remained on Haven with the core of his gang, his loyal thugs.

'But if we sent them away,' drawled one of the slow-witted dragons, 'why are we bringing them back again?'

'I am now their saviour,' explained Hesper in exasperation. 'This way I can be sure of their loyalty.'

Protected by Hesper's charm, Ledra flew through the storm to Sharp and effected her rescue. But no sooner had she reached Haven than her new-found abilities evaporated into the seething air, leaving her fearful and confused. Hurriedly instructing her new charges to remain in the box canyon until she rejoined them, she made her way quickly back to the lush grove where Hesper and his gang awaited her.

'They are safe,' she shouted over the howl of the wind. 'But the charm has gone!'

Hesper's cronies sat up sharply at this, and Hesper himself scowled at Ledra. 'Nonsense,' he crooned. 'You are a Natural, my dear, so naturally – if you'll forgive the expression – your powers are limited. Stick with me and I will keep you strong.'

Pacified for the moment at least, Ledra drew closer to the circle of dragons. But the storm was accelerating and as foliage and banks of soil were torn from the hillside the grove grew less able to shelter them.

'We should join the others,' barked Hesper at length and none argued, for here they were becoming more and more exposed. They struggled through the cutting wind and flailing undergrowth, making for the box canyon.

It was a short trek, but on the way two dragons died, stout warriors from Covamere caught and crushed inside a fist of palms which had been wrenched from the soil. The rest increased their speed, concerned now for their own lives. Soon they reached the crest of rock which dropped sharply into the three-sided canyon, but before they could descend Hesper called a sudden halt. 'Look!' he exclaimed.

The sea had reached halfway into the canyon. All the dragons whom Ledra had rescued were clinging to the back wall, clearly trapped. Most seemed frozen to the spot as though hypnotized by the oncoming peril.

'Why don't they fly out?' cried Ledra, darting forward, but Hesper stopped her.

'No, they . . .' he began to say. Then he looked up, and he too froze.

'What is it?' questioned Ledra. She looked up and saw it too.

A ribbon in the sky, a wavering presence which could not be described as light but was simply *there*, floating above the jeering clouds with a grace quite in opposition to the fury of the storm. Like a river it flowed, currents vying for supremacy along its prodigious length, its beginning and its end lost in the distance beyond sight. A river of charm in the sky, beautiful.

Both Ledra and Hesper were captivated by it. They stared long at it, awed and excited by its promise of magic. Urged on by an equal lust for the power of charm, they both felt as though the river were drawing them upwards, inviting them to enter its stream, to taste its pleasures. Temporarily oblivious to the hurricane which was destroying the island about their very claws, they pressed against each other, necks stretched, heads raised, drinking in the thrill of it.

'Boss!' came a cry from the cliff edge. One member of the dragon gang was leaning out over the precipice and calling back to Hesper. 'We've got to get them out of there. The wind's impossible and it's too steep to climb.'

Hesper and Ledra turned slowly together, gradually, reluctantly, returning their attention to the natural world. Then, like a scene played out slowly for the benefit of some infant dragon, events unfurled themselves with eerie sluggishness. Neither moved to intervene. They simply watched. Screams were carried on eddies and updraughts to their ears, but they did not respond.

A great wedge of sodden soil collapsed from the far side of the canyon top, depositing its mass of roots and mud on to the dragons trapped below. Several of Hesper's followers leaped over the side, finally electing to assist their fellow dragons. No sooner had they jumped than a vicious thrust of air sucked them back against the face of the canyon wall, slamming their bodies with astonishing force against the crumbling rock. Their bodies dropped with the last of the avalanche into the canyon.

A massive shockwave pounded up through the ground and a huge split opened directly before Hesper's claws. The remaining dragons of his gang were caught on a tilting finger of rock, and though they reached out to both him and Ledra, neither dragon raised a wing to help. Slowly, with a dreadful tearing sound, the rest of the clifftop sheared away from the hillside and collapsed into the box canyon, taking the flailing dragons with it.

There was a massive impact, and an angry fountain made as the falling cliff met an enormous incoming wave, then the storm rolled in again and brought trees and all manner of debris into the ruined canyon. The sea rose still further and drowned the site before Hesper or Ledra could even reach the new cliff edge.

They peered down. No sign of dragon remained. Up in the sky the river of charm beckoned. Together they answered its call.

CHAPTER 18

Ascent

Even Smoke, whose sense of direction was almost impossible to deceive, found herself growing uneasy as they took turn after turn, moving ever higher, flying up through the wide and shining vessels of the citadel towards the topmost corridors where once the basilisks had prowled. Archan led them. As they ascended the glossy interior became more and more filled with light until they were almost blinded and none of the basilisks' painstaking etchings and details could be discerned. Charm permeated the entire structure and grew more concentrated. Smoke felt the pain in her head grow more intense; she thought that soon she would be able to bear it no longer.

Just when she was beginning to despair, the ascending ramp over which they flew levelled out and they entered an expansive chamber filled with a blue, hazy glow: daylight, at last.

'We are near the very top of the citadel now,' proclaimed Archan. 'There to the side is the chamber I really want to show you – the chamber where some of your questions may be answered – but before you see it, I fancy you might enjoy the spectacle which the east window has to offer. Come.'

Obedient, for it seemed that they had no choice but to comply, the dragons followed Archan across the enormous, glowing space towards the source of the watery light. Here the air was filled with the scent and touch of spray and with the roar of the waterfall. To breathe was to drink a fine mist, a vapour soft and enriching and overflowing with magic. All was magic here at the citadel's crest.

The window widened itself in the blank wall before them

like a dragon unfolding its wings. The magical, oval opening thus formed created a stunning effect, for it was as though the citadel peeled itself open to admit them to its very substance. The light swelled then retreated, leaving their eyes moist and tired, but they did not remain tired for long, so astonishing was the sight which met them as the clouds of vapour dropped away into the torrent, far, far below.

They stood along the lip of a great, arching window cut into the side of a mighty tower of stone. But, impressive though it was, it was the view which captured their attention. Across a sea of mist, the whole upper battlements of the basilisk citadel were visible in astonishing detail. This was a sight they had missed when first they had approached the fortress, for these high towers had been shrouded in the same clouds which had now fallen away. Revealed, they were a wondrous sight.

The towers – there were thirteen – leaped from the transparent fog as though striving to touch the sky itself, reaching up into the heavens like young dragons eager for their first flight. Each was exquisite as an icicle, sharp as a claw, sculpted and moulded into a filigree of light and beauty and sparkling with sunlight and magic. But that was not all, for beyond even the perfect, physical splendour of their marvellous forms, the towers danced.

Their motion was a constant rhythm, like the rush of the waves upon the shore or the stroke of a dragon's wing in flight. They grew and stretched, and sank and melted, constantly reforming, ever-changing, their shapes fickle and indeterminate as the power of some mighty charm moved them in the air above the churning waterfall. Now tall and slight, now bunched and ready to surge skywards again, they clutched at the sky with graceful strength, every breath a new creation, every pulse witness to a new, fragile structure, soon to be no more.

Long they had performed, the dancing towers, and the span of those aeons the dragons sensed now as they watched with open-mouthed wonder the marvel of their ceaseless motion. It was Smoke who first realized the true direction of their movements.

'They are here and not here,' she gasped. Her scales

shivered in recognition of what she saw since she could scarcely believe the idea that came into her mind. She turned to Archan. 'They are dancing through time, aren't they? I'm right, aren't I?'

'Yes, dragon,' came the silky reply.

And indeed Smoke was right, for the basilisks' skill was such that they had built these upper towers with a solidity which existed only in the physical world. Rigid in three dimensions, their structures were fluid in the realm of time so that to watch their dance was to follow their endless movement back and forth to different moments in the different histories of this restless world. It was not that they grew – they simply journeyed back to a time when they had been larger; they did not really become small and slender but merely travelled to an age when such would be their nature. *Simply, merely*: such concepts the creator basilisks might have used when conceiving and constructing this, their most artful of whims, but to the watching dragons there was nothing *simple* or *mere* about the dancing towers. They were nothing short of miraculous.

Velvet could not draw her eyes away from the sight. Each time one of the towers shrank down towards the mist she felt compelled to watch for just a little longer, spellbound by the perfect metre of the dance, to see what form it would take next. To witness the elaborate choreography of thirteen towers had an effect akin to hypnotism. Velvet fancied she saw bodies twisting in the writhing shapes of the towers, scales cut in the engraved patterns, dragon faces peering out from their crystalline flesh. She was overwhelmed by the anticipation that something might appear that she would actually recognize. She was entranced, as were they all.

But slowly the mists returned to cloak the towers once more in their sleepy embrace, concealing their endless dance through time. A soft groan of infinite sadness floated out from where the dragons stood rapt, a groan which came as much from their souls as from their mouths, for this was a moment they might never recapture. The loss was a heart-felt ache, and it was with strong and private grief that they all turned away from the east window to see where Archan would lead them next.

The next chamber beckoned them with a rich, warm glow of its own, but they all believed – even Thaw, who saw little now beyond the thrall of Archan herself – that compared to the dance it would seem squalid and uninteresting. It was in this frame of mind that they entered the Chamber of the World.

The space was round and domed and unsupported by any kind of column across its entire, prodigious span. The lower part, where the curved walls rose vertically from an intricately tiled floor, was encrusted with an elaborate mosaic of shimmering crystal; as the walls rose they merged into a ceiling which was quite black and decked with stars. For all the dragons knew, they may have been real stars. It seemed that here was another hall of the basilisks' museum, and at its centre was a single exhibit: a massive, circular platform, half the height of an average dragon yet as wide as a small lake. And on it was the world.

Had he been there, Fortune – who had once perceived the world in a similar way – might have made sense of it more quickly than his friends, for here was the world peeled open and laid out like the skin of a fruit. Of them all it was Thaw, a dragon with a mind for mapping, who first realized what it was, and the realization sent him leaping into the air, darting back and forth over the enormous, flower-like chart as he began to make sense of its contours. Slowly the function of the thing dawned upon his companions and they too took tentatively to the air, hovering over the map and staring in wonder at the seas and clouds and continents laid out in miniature beneath them.

'It's like being a night dragon,' exclaimed Velvet, her voice swallowed by the massive vault as she looked down upon mountains and forests and rivers like scratches in the soil. 'Like flying higher than a dragon could ever fly.'

'Indeed,' agreed Archan. 'It is splendid, is it not?'

'It's fantastic!' enthused Thaw. 'And . . . by my wings, it's moving!'

This secondary revelation was less surprising than it might have been, given the recent and still-vivid sight of the dancing towers, but it was an astonishing discovery nonetheless. The map was *alive*: as they watched the dragons saw weather patterns crawl over its flattened surface, saw storms collide far away in the Western Ocean, saw lightning crackle seemingly a thousand trees beneath them. And more, they saw the land itself moving.

The continents were bucking like restless beasts, trying to throw off skin which had held them trapped for aeons. What the dragons had suspected they now saw revealed as truth: the world was turning still, and in the process all the geography they had known was changing to something utterly new. Lands reformed themselves before their incredulous eyes, seas emptied, others filled, mountains burst through from deep underground. The world, reborn.

'Hard to find the place for which one searches, when all is changing,' mused Archan, and suddenly all their attention was on her.

We were brought here so that we might complete our quest! thought Velvet ecstatically. *She is going to show us the way!*

'Aether's Cross,' Archan continued. 'One of many places vanished into the rhythm of the world's dance. Gone, but not destroyed. Not yet.'

'How do you know?' asked Thaw, his voice as enraptured as if he were addressing a goddess.

'I know because the Deathless tell me. There is more beneath the world than a mortal dragon can know, but the Deathless left us the Chamber of the World that we might begin to seek one of the many ways forward. Your Cross is buried here, dragons, have no fear, and it may be unearthed. But the question occurs, which of you is worthy to bear the knowledge?'

As she spoke, a burst of light intruded from some high and hidden opening, casting a network of flickering beams across the upturned wings of the hovering dragons. They glanced at each other, suddenly horrified, for in the evil light Archan had grown all at once mighty and dreadful, and the eyeless glare of her perfect face bored into each of them with power beyond reason. Below them the world boiled, and the storm which had beset the seas marched with astonishing speed towards what had once been the Heartland. Here the air itself was alive, split by multiple lines of light: the river of charm, speeding north. What they saw on the map they heard beyond the chamber walls. The magic was coming.

'Which of you is worthy?' repeated Archan, her wings now wide and livid in the uncertain light. 'Time is speeding, dragons – think fast, for you can be sure that I shall!'

All were confused except Thaw. Where the others saw only the cruel set of Archan's coiled body he saw the dragon he adored. Deep inside he knew that she was working magical seduction upon him, but he did not care, for what else was love? He alone responded to her challenge – Thaw, the great military strategist who had ever ignored the wiles of love and beauty. His whole being was bound up with this one, awesome dragon so that he had no control over his actions. His heart thumping in time with the thunder, he stretched his wings wide over the world and joined Archan in the static-ridden air. Charm and light crackled over them as they embraced, and if any part of his mind still counselled resistance it was in that instant consumed.

The others looked on. As one, they knew instinctively that they had been tricked, that Archan's invitation had been nothing but a game. She had no intention of revealing the new location of Aether's Cross to them – if indeed she possessed such knowledge. In the midst of wonder they had suddenly but one objective: to escape. As though she had read their minds, Archan began to mould charm into the body of her new consort, lifting ice-sharp blades of bone from his flanks and deepening his jaw until it held fangs white as chalk and serrated down their entire length. Both dragons growled, their lips curling back, murder in the set of their every muscle.

A glance chased around the group. Smoke was in agony: of them all she was most aware of the river of charm which was descending upon the lowered mountains of the Spine – and not least on to the basilisk citadel. The pain was so great now that she was almost ready to swoon and saw little of what was happening. Ratchet: torn between loyalty to his master and a nameless, irrational loathing of Archan, which welled not from his thinking mind but from the very depths of his strong and simple soul. And thinking now that he must fight them both to the death if his friends were to stand any chance of fleeing with their lives.

Cumber was certain that Thaw's ambition had tipped him over the edge. Intoxicated by what he saw as Archan's beauty, lulled by the fabulous trappings of the basilisk citadel, he had at last succumbed utterly to the alien power of Archan's ambition. What frightened him most was the sudden blindness of Thaw's gaze, as though he, like his chosen partner, had lost his eyes. *They care for nothing but themselves*, he realized with a deep and icy dread. *We've got to get out of here!*

And Velvet. Of them all she saw closest to the truth. She saw the way Archan had pounced upon Thaw's hungry heart, how vulnerable the apparently capable commander had been. She saw their lack of concern for any other dragon just as Cumber did, but she saw more. She saw that they had reached a decision: they seemed swollen, *elevated*, pumped up with their own power and their own ambition. They were gods now, these dragons, and as such they would rule all who fell beneath their shadow. They would dictate the terms by which all would live . . . or die.

Thaw is the one, Archan had decided. But now . . . it seemed that he was not!

She had grown more and more convinced that she was destined to spend eternity with Thaw. He was almost as ambitious as she, and he was not unattractive, with his well-muscled body and striking markings of yellow and black. Like her, he had seen a new horizon here, and it was one over which he was prepared to fly. Desperate to fly. She had promised him immortality and he would not rest until she had fulfilled that promise. Together they would absorb the talents of the basilisks and live forever, the only two dragons ever to have flown free of the ultimate gravity: death. Except . . .

Except he is not *the one!*

Everything about him had seemed right, but now there was something dreadfully wrong. Archan could see that now and she was glad, for the simple knowledge had prevented her from making a terrible blunder. *He is too old!* She needed a partner with ambition to be sure, but one whom she could mould exactly as she desired; Thaw was malleable – but not malleable enough. This she realized the instant the storm struck, and she nearly abandoned both him and the citadel there and then, cutting her losses and flying north with the flow of charm.

But then, almost casually, she tracked a few of Thaw's thoughts and discovered that his yearning for immortality, now planted, was stronger than she had realized. She probed deeper, exploring the set of his mind and the shape of his heart, and it was then she decided that he might have a role to play after all. Not the role she had at first anticipated, and certainly not one which would bring Thaw what he dreamed of, but a glorious role all the same.

What Archan conceived then was more a gamble than a plan, one which even she had to admit promised little hope of success. *But it must be the right dragon or no dragon at all,* she decided bitterly as the lightning slashed across the faces of the dragons lined before her. Tasting the air, the magic which filled the air, she sent her consciousness out into the swirling cloud and crashing thunder and measured the rate of flow of the abandoned charm. In its motion she detected the overwhelming scent of the Deathless, that spice which had filled her lungs here over the years and without which she now felt she could not live. The miasma drugged her and thrilled her and she inhaled it like the sweetest poison.

The Gathering is imminent, she determined, *yet I still have time. Thaw will give me what I need and eternity will still be mine!*

But what of Thaw's companions? With so much charm flowing around and through the citadel, she knew that unless she took extreme care some dreadful chain of coincidence might easily draw out the already long odds against her plan working. Magic, as she knew only too well, joins events which might otherwise remain entirely unconnected, and the histories of these four intruders were too close to that of Thaw for her to be able to risk their mingling further. They would have to be dealt with. Now.

Vox led his companions quickly through the tunnel. The walls heaved and creaked as they beat their wings, pale surfaces dimly visible in the wavering light of the crescent charm which flew with them through the corridor; the storm had to be great indeed to reach these depths. The dragons were all painfully aware of the immense weight of water poised above their heads, ready to crush them like insects. The only direction was on, but soon on became up and their ears sang as the air pressure relaxed from around their skulls.

'The sea is deep here,' said Quill. 'It will be an age before we reach the surface again.' But barely had she spoken than light blossomed ahead – daylight, though it was flashing from white to blue even as it grew in their vision. Rain began to lash against their faces and behind them the tunnel grumbled like the intestine of a restless giant. They emerged into the storm, and its wrath had doubled since last they had fallen beneath it.

Haven lay around them, but it was flattened. Where the storm met the sea none could determine, for the horizon was no more. Waves as high as the highest trees reared over what was left of the island, yet even they appeared misty and insubstantial for the very air itself seemed made of water. Rain and hail exploded from the lightning-torn heavens, cutting soil apart and shredding it into sodden particles which turned swiftly to mud. What few palms remained standing were leafless and bowed, groaning and cracking as one by one they gave in and fell lifeless to the soaked ground. Gone were the golden beaches, gone into the rising ocean, and as far as the dragons could determine Haven itself would be gone soon as well.

They clung together, unable even to crawl, let alone fly. All speech was in vain for the storm had such a voice as none of them had heard before. It was as though the sky had fallen to earth and was thrashing there in blind rage; it was like the end of the world.

Gossamer was terrified. Reaching up with her wing she dragged Aria off her back and held her tight beneath her belly, managing to protect her from the worst of the tempest. What could they do now? A glance back at the tunnel from which they had emerged revealed the dreadful sight of a river of mud rolling into its cavernous maw, dragging behind it an entire hillside of debris until the opening was quite gone. Of Hesper and his disciples there was no sign, and whether they had flown to safety or been consumed by the heaving earth the cowering dragons did not know.

Gossamer thought with a strange calm, *This is really the end*.

Then an almighty rumbling began deep in the ground and a long, straight channel opened in the clouds. The dragons could see it quite clearly, as though some invisible claw had reached into the sky and carved a passage of clear air straight through the storm, starting in the south and slicing directly over Haven towards some distant, northern goal. Lightning prowled the edges of the divide, occasionally darting out across the void but seeming wary. Miraculously, the sinking, muddy slope where they crouched lay directly beneath this channel, and so they were left shivering in a narrow canyon of motionless air, protected from the hurricane beyond by imperceptible walls.

Over the sea the channel's presence pushed the waves down to a perfect mirror and pressed back the clouds. And into its emptiness rushed the river of charm. Tired of the war being waged against it by the forces of the natural world, the abandoned charm, beyond even the command of the basilisk Ocher, had at last wielded its own magic, cutting into the storm in order to create a clear passage north for itself. Into this lightning-edged canyon the charm descended, concentrating its many strands into a single rope of barely-visible light. Uninhibited now by the weak yet irritating onslaught of wind and rain, it increased its velocity tenfold and created a thunder of its own as waves of air fled its edges in a stampede of charm.

Relieved to be under the protection of this phenomenon yet uncertain of its durability – not to mention terrified that it might hold an anger beyond that of even the storm – the dragons pulled apart slowly, faces raised in wonder. Vox and Quill scented desperately, stretching out what was left of their charm senses in a combined effort to calculate both the strength and the origin of this welcome, frightening intrusion. Whether their fear honed their senses or whether the river of charm itself somehow amplified them was not important, for both exchanged a glance and said as one,

'The land is moving!'

Sure enough, far in the distance at the end of the channel of calm, a shadow loomed. Slowly it approached, parting the sea before it as the invisible force had parted the clouds, then accelerating until it bore down upon the remains of Haven with dazzling speed. A wall of stone, the edge of a continent, was racing towards the dragons through the water as the space between it and Haven contracted like a clenching muscle. A titanic wave stood in its path, pressed on by its relentless approach. Its sound was beyond all comprehension.

The dragons slumped, for they had reached the limit of their endurance. The storm had come and that had been bad enough, but it had waxed and waned so often that they were incapable of any further response. Nothing could be predicted now – all was a random chain of disaster upon disaster with neither pattern nor sympathy. The world had turned away from charm and into . . . insanity.

The continent which had once been the Heartland bore down on the island of Haven, poised to crush it beneath its moving mountains, and all the dragons could do was stare it in the face, wings wide to embrace the mortality which had finally descended upon them.

The citadel trembled and even Archan registered surprise; nothing had shaken this bastion before, so deep-sunk were its foundations. The storm roared, pounding the tower's exterior like an angry god. Blue flame reached into the chamber, supple lightning searching for a target. It struck the centre of the map and sparks rained upwards towards the dome of the ceiling.

With a grating sound like a monstrous tooth being drawn, a crack split the curved chamber wall, speeding around its circumference in pursuit of its own tail. Charm scintillated along its length. The crack met its origin, completing the circle with a spitting sound which grew into a mighty rumble. Wind barked, slapping the amputated roof away from its supporting walls and dragging it out into the sky. Light poured into the Chamber of the World, steely storm light punctuated by massive discharges of rich blue lightning.

Rain soaked the dragons and splashed across the basilisk map; it was repelled before it struck the surface by a protective charm.

Smoke was first to bolt. Straight upwards she flew, breasting the broken wall with three powerful strokes of her wings. There she stopped, lifting her head into the gale and squinting against the rain. Her mouth dropped open in wonder and for an instant she forgot completely about her intention to escape.

The sky split slowly in two. The same gorge of clear air which had opened over Haven opened over the citadel. The dragons still hovering in the remains of the chamber saw clearly the ribbon of stillness separate the clouds, but Smoke's view was more stunning yet. Looking out over the citadel heights she saw the dancing towers continue in their strange ballet, vivid in the clean, sharp air and oblivious to the drama that was going on around them. She saw the thunderheads peel open as the swathe of still air forced its way through them. She felt pain and realized that within the stillness flowed a massive stream of charm. Glancing left and right, she saw the land *fold*.

The citadel was moving. The *land* was moving, and the sense of motion was astonishing. The entire mountain range was speeding through the gorge of clear air as a whole new continent expanded in its wake; it was like riding on the back of a titan, a troll-giant the like of which the world had never seen. Ahead, the sea suddenly rose into view, then contracted, accepting the momentum of the Spine as it advanced southwards. And there on the horizon appeared a chain of dots, now small but growing bigger with every breath. Islands.

'Haven,' murmured Smoke. 'We're going home!'

The air on which she hovered had grown calm as the gorge had opened in the clouds; now the blue flicker of lightning began to recede too. Red light erupted from below her. She flicked her gaze down to see Archan and Thaw floating on a bed of angry, red charm, fire licking from their throats, claws long and silver. They advanced steadfastly upon her companions, flames prowling around them in a living pyre.

CHAPTER 19

Dungeon

The mountains of the Spine descended upon the Western Ocean, but already they were losing their momentum. Charm succumbed to simple friction until finally their weight held them still. Around the world the continents slowed and stopped. All charts bar the one, ever-changing map in the basilisk citadel, were now obsolete, for the skin of the world was made anew.

The silence after the uproar was unbearable. Over both Haven and the citadel the walls of the storm closed in again only to find they no longer had anything to fight. The abandoned charm had at last been sucked into the river and isolated from the natural world. Those few places where the magic remained – the basilisk map, or the deep parts of buried Covamere where once the world had opened on to the Maze – were places belonging entirely to charm, where the magic was for ever. Rare magic that crossed between all the worlds and was always in the same place, ineradicable.

The storm continued to thrash for a brief time, as though battle-crazed, unaware that its foe had fled, then it too fell silent. Natural forces, weak by comparison to the charm which had once ruled the world yet with prodigious strength when combined, pulled back into equilibrium, content that their work had been done. Still the river of charm filled the sky, but now that its first task was done it was aloof, no longer a gatherer but a transporter. Nature surrounded it, content now to escort it north where its arrival would herald the final death throes of the charm it bore.

Ocher surveyed the changed land as it dived down towards the citadel. It noted with passing interest that the abandoned stronghold was inhabited by a dragon now, a dragon almost as solid as Wraith had been. Other dragons busied themselves in its towers too, but they were ghostly compared to this . . . *Archan*. And also to another . . .

There was a second dragon, a dragon resting motionless on the island to the south. The lower reaches of the mountains of the Spine had become sea cliffs, licked by the rising waters of the new ocean. Just off this virgin coast a small island floated. Ocher recognized it as the very island beneath which Mediel had lain concealed. A pleasing coincidence, and one which reinforced the basilisk's conviction that the Gathering would succeed. But this dragon . . .

So that is the future for these frail creatures of the air, mused the basilisk with wonder. *Such a beautiful fate for such . . . mortal creatures*.

Touched by curious new emotions – was there jealousy of these dragons in its hard and ancient heart? – Ocher plunged down into its citadel. Unlike before, when its every such descent had been a futile attempt at self-destruction, it steered an accurate path between the dancing towers, aiming its streamlined form down towards the deepest part of the stronghold. Tellere, like the others, would shortly be journeying north towards certain doom.

The basilisk wondered, as it fell, if there might not be other choices than doom for Ocher.

Archan's heartbeat quickened as the streak of silver flashed across her charmed vision. A basilisk! One of the Deathless had returned, and its coming convinced her that this critical moment must not be stained with blood. The death of any dragon now would tip the delicate balance of her plan into an abyss of confusion. This complicated matters, but her narrow, determined heart told her that it was true.

Detecting Archan's hesitation, Smoke flicked her wings and dived towards her adversary. Thaw sprang from his place amid the writhing red flames and butted her hard in the stomach, knocking her sideways on to the tiled floor beside the raised map platform. Ratchet raced to her side, helping her up and glaring at his former commander.

'Have a care, *chief*,' he intoned. 'You would not want to make an enemy of your old comrade.'

But Thaw only laughed and rejoined Archan in the midst of the flames. The eyeless dragon was motionless, apparently unconcerned by events around her.

'Let's go, Cumber,' pleaded Velvet, tugging at her partner's wing. 'It's Thaw she wants, not us. We've got to get out of here!'

But Cumber hesitated. He could still sense the stream of magic swarming through the sky above, and its presence made him feel suddenly, devastatingly sad. Despite the awesome presence before him of Archan and Thaw in their lake of fire, despite the obvious peril they were in, still he was forced to wonder if he had not been wrong after all about charm.

How can we go on, any of us, without charm? he thought mournfully. He turned to Velvet as though to demand an answer from her, but before he could speak Archan acted.

The decision came easily to her, and as she activated the opening in the floor she thought of Wraith. *The Black Dragon took many prisoners*, she mused. *I merely follow his example, though I will prevail where he did not.*

Archan inclined her head, tugging at the interlacing charm which filled the air of this Chamber of the World. Conscious of the value of the chamber and its contents, the basilisks had set many magical triggers in its fabric. Never had an intruder dared to violate this place, but had they done so they would have been swiftly dealt with. Now Archan turned the defensive charm to her own ends.

A great semi-circle of floor dropped away. With a yelp Cumber tried to open his wings, only to find them clamped to his side by restraining magic. Velvet clutched at him with her hind legs as she too plummeted through the opening, but all resistance was useless. Ratchet fell with them, as did Smoke, still winded from her encounter with Thaw. Into darkness they fell, necks curled over instinctively as bleak rock raced up to batter their helpless bodies.

More magic bounced them without injury away from the walls of the chasm, guiding them with a curiously gentle touch down into the blackness. Light quickly failed above, although a dim glow was growing beneath. It rushed up towards them until at the last moment the supervising charm buoyed them up and deposited them softly on a damp and stony floor.

They had no doubt about where they had been sent. A watery light struggled towards them from a distant slit in what they presumed was the far wall of the dungeon. The floor was strangely hot, the air humid. The sounds of their claws on the damp stone echoed like the ring of metal off the unseen ceiling. Rousing themselves they moved cautiously towards the light until they reached a narrow, vertical slot in the dripping wall. After an apprehensive glance at his companions, Cumber thrust his snout through it, craning his neck so as to look around.

The window led outside, but it was so narrow that no dragon could ever squeeze through it. A soft rain fell against Cumber's face as he looked out on to a circular yard filled with half-light and gloom. Shelves of stone and finely carved buttresses soared up from this tiny plot, merging into the larger shapes which loomed against far-off sky; clearly they were trapped in some deep and forgotten corner of the citadel, where even the day was reluctant to venture.

In the centre of the yard, caught by a thin beam of light, was a pedestal. On the pedestal rested a lumpy form which was at once strange and familiar. Cumber squinted through the drizzle, trying to make it out.

Tapering, craggy, it was made of stone and crouched on the smooth-sided pedestal like a beast about to pounce. Moss and lichen had long since swarmed across its back, turning its grey lines to a green patchwork. Its flanks bore vertical grooves, and as Cumber looked closer he saw that into the grooves there fell a constant drip of water – clearly the statue must have been here for a very long time for such erosion to have occurred. Odd that it was . . . familiar.

'What do you see, my dear?' urged Velvet from close behind. Cumber jumped, banging his head against the side of the window. He withdrew back into the cell, rubbing his head irritably with his wing.

'Do you have to shout?' he muttered.

'Is there a way out?' demanded Smoke, ignoring Cumber's petulant air.

'No,' sighed Cumber. 'At least, I don't think so . . .'

Then he stopped. A scuffling sound echoed far away to their left. They froze. There was a pause, then the scrabbling sounded again, this time much nearer.

Archan learned of the imminent Gathering from the basilisk map, for beneath its surface she had seen both the glowing points of light which were the awakening basilisks and the wavering thread of the river of charm. Soon she would have to travel north with the magic, very soon. But first . . .

I shall have a mate!

At last Archan knew why she had never found the perfect dragon – he had not yet been born! But he would be soon, very soon, and Thaw would be his sire. *You are too old, Thaw, and set in your ways. But you are still of use.*

Absently Archan dissolved the platform of fire on which she and Thaw were floating. Now that Thaw's troublesome companions had been despatched to the dungeon she felt that her thoughts were clearer than they had been for some time. The controlling charm she had woven into Thaw's mind was already growing weaker – magic was so frail now! This made her uneasy, for his loyalty was less predictable without the indomitable influence of charm. No matter – his gaze remained that of a dragon obsessed and though he said little Archan was confident that her hold over him would last as long as was necessary.

She watched him now as he flew to and fro over the basilisk map, striped wings luminous in the dusty air, and it occurred to her again that he was attractive, something more than a mere instrument. The unnatural sight afforded by her basilisk-enriched senses enabled her to see beyond his striking yellow and black markings and some small way into his soul. There she saw the inner Thaw, the ambitious, intelligent commander with sharp mind and powerful wing. She saw the outline of his past, saw how his youth had been bound up with the landscape in which he had grown up: the flood plains of the great river Term. The river flowed through him like a guiding spirit, directing his mind and shaping his future.

This is his river, she marvelled, considering the mighty

waterfall within the embrace of which the citadel lay. *He has come home.* Sensing his destiny in this way, she saw him as vulnerable and so, to her surprise, beautiful. She saw that, given time, she could actually grow to love him.

No! she berated herself. *He is not the one. I cannot allow myself to be diverted from the one, true course. The fate of one, small dragon cannot compete with the call of eternity!*

Thaw had his part to play, to be sure, but to complete the task Archan had need of another . . .

Opening her creamy wings she lifted herself above the giant, moving chart, joining Thaw in his flight. The land rested, its contours settling into new configurations; the storm had died away. She plucked at the charm which, despite everything, still filled her head and gave her the ability to see though she had no eyes. Those organs she had plucked out shortly after arriving at the basilisk citadel. Their sight distracted her from using instead the more subtle senses the Deathless themselves used when they built the citadel. Dragon charm was all but gone, but basilisk charm at least remained in her mind, and she retained the gift of sight where she should have been blind.

She set that gift to work now, casting it over the flattened and minuscule world in a search for what she hoped was there. Over mountains and seas her blind gaze roamed, crossing and recrossing the great river of charm which wound its way ever north towards the crest of the world. Having begun on the continent which surrounded the citadel itself, she was about to expand her field of vision when suddenly her attention was dragged back to the immediate surroundings. There, just off the new coastline which flanked the remains of the Spine. An island. And on the island . . .

There! The final piece of the puzzle! Thaw I have chosen as sire and now this dragon . . . she will carry the egg.

Basilisk senses had revealed to Archan the last fertile female dragon in the world. A dragon whose eggs would be owned by one alone. Archan.

Against all hope the dragon for whom she had really been waiting had come to her very claws.

*　　*　　*

211

The misty rain crept down from the remains of the mountains of the Spine, shrouding the cliffs with haze and closing upon the dragons who lay in a stupor on the shores of Haven. Hot and moist, the air invigorated them and brought their gaze back up from the dead, black sand towards the sky. Before them loomed the citadel of the basilisks, a mighty, sculpted boulder set uncompromisingly in path of the prodigious waterfall which now poured itself out over the edge of the cliffs and into the waiting ocean. The citadel was a short flight away and already it beckoned . . .

Aria lay between Fortune and Gossamer. Quill and Vox sat a little to one side, both of them enjoying the warmth of the air. Quill was singing an old, healing chant in a low voice. It was that song Fortune would remember later when he tried to recall the strange and dreadful events that were about to unfold.

They had lain there for some time, uncertain of what they should do now. It seemed that Hesper and his gang had gone, either lost to the storm or fled; Haven, once a tropical idyll, was now a ravaged wasteland of sand and broken palms. But none of it mattered, for it seemed to Fortune that he had finally rejoined the real world.

'Don't you feel it, Gossamer?' he whispered, nuzzling his love as she brought her body closer against his. Aria wriggled pleasurably between them, looking around with wide and fascinated eyes. 'It's as though everything that happened on Haven was a dream.'

'Yes, my love,' responded Gossamer at once. 'I thought I'd woken up once before, just before the storm first struck, but now I can see even that was an illusion. If I didn't know better, I'd say charm was still at work.'

'You remember what Mantle told us?'

'To be wary of the abandoned charm? Of course.' Gossamer looked down at Aria, caught the direction of her tiny daughter's gaze and then looked sharply upwards. 'Look, Fortune,' she murmured, 'do you see that?'

The sky directly overhead was rippling, as though they were seeing it through a skin of moving water. If they looked directly at the phenomenon its motion seemed to cease, but as soon as they looked away, catching it in the corners of their eyes, it was impossible to miss. A river of charm, flowing relentlessly north through the air above the citadel.

'And look at those towers!' exclaimed Fortune. 'They're moving too.'

Excited now, he lifted Gossamer to her claws and together they strained to make out the upper spires of the citadel through the haze. Though all detail was lost to the mist, nevertheless they could see clearly the constant movement of the dancing towers.

'It's beautiful,' cried Gossamer, irrationally happy.

Then the rogue charm was upon them.

Aria bleated once as the sand in which she lay was sucked away in a single breath, leaving her suspended on the rogue flight charm; once this magic had held a beast the size of a mountain aloft in the old skies – now it snatched up the helpless infant dragon. Fortune and Gossamer whirled round instinctively at the sound of her plaintive cry, but already it was too late. Before they could take a single pace towards her she had been lifted ten trees high in an invisible cradle of magic. Her small wings, quite incapable of flight, flapped hopelessly at the air; her cries could no longer be heard.

'Aria!' howled Gossamer, blind even to Fortune as she opened her wings and pumped her way into the sky more ferociously than she ever had in her life.

She powered her way up towards Aria's bobbing form but with each stroke she took the charm carried the infant dragon further away. She could not catch up. Tipping her head down she cried to Fortune, who was close on her tail, 'Get her back, Fortune – for the sky's sake, get my daughter back!'

But even Fortune, who had learned the art of flight from mighty Tallow, could not match the pace of that old and wily charm. It sprinted ahead of them, a casual outrage, bearing Aria away towards the cliffs, towards the citadel which lay waiting in the grasp of the waterfall, up towards its ramparts, towards its highest peaks. Towards the dancing towers.

The noon sun gazed down dispassionately as Quill and Vox, alerted by their friends' distress, clambered their way into the air to follow Fortune and Gossamer on their desperate pursuit of Aria through the mist.

'Who's there?' called Velvet bravely.

'Velvet?'

Moving shadows resolved into the shapes of dragons – hunched and weary dragons. They emerged from the gloom and into the weak light of the window. The sound of their claws on the stone was hard and brittle, and the expressions borne on their faces were ones of utter exhaustion. Four thin, pale dragons stepped into the light, and at their head was Brace. When they saw who had come into their prison relief spread its wings to cover their fatigue.

Cumber crashed into Brace with the force of a whirlwind, knocking him clean across the floor and into the wings of Scoff, who croaked a hoarse welcome and embraced them both with all his strength. Then big Tallow lumbered over, closely followed by Volley, and together the two forest dragons joined the celebration. Tears flowed freely and wings reached out to touch, reassuring dragons that their fellows were really here. Accounts of their respective adventures were begun and straight away interrupted by more emotions than words could express.

'Where is Werth?' demanded Velvet suddenly. Werth, the matronly female who had played such an important role in the development of the Flight, and who had attached herself so strongly to Tallow after the Turning, was nowhere to be seen.

'She died,' said Volley, glancing at Tallow. 'We will speak of it later, but for now we must attend to ourselves, or she will have died in vain.'

'There is no food and only a little water,' explained Tallow in a low and desperate voice. 'It is good to see you, my friends, but I fear you have not come to rescue us.'

'*We* were supposed to be the rescuers,' added Brace bitterly.

'No food?' exclaimed Velvet suddenly. 'But how long have you been here?'

'Six days,' replied Brace heavily.

'But where have you been?'

Brace blinked at her, uncomprehending.

'We've been here, Velvet,' he said. Then he coughed and smiled. 'I see you couldn't wait to follow us.'

'Couldn't wait?' responded Velvet. 'But it's been six moons, Brace. What were we supposed to do – give you up for dead?'

'Six moons?' whispered Brace.

'Now wait,' announced Scoff, breaking into the conversation. 'We left Haven ten days ago, by my reckoning. Been prisoners six. Like Brace said.'

'That's right,' confirmed Tallow. 'I do not make mistakes in such matters. We see the dawn, even down here, and ten days it is.'

'But that can't be!' exploded Velvet. 'I mean, it's six moons since you left and that's that. It just can't be!'

'Yes it can,' said Smoke quietly.

All eyes turned to her, the members of Brace's group frowning a little, for this was a dragon none of them knew.

'Tell us, dragon,' Scoff said encouragingly.

'Well, I can't explain it exactly,' sighed Smoke, 'but I can guess. This place of the basilisks – it distorts time somehow. We know that, because we saw those towers: the dancing towers. Something has happened to slow down the passage of time here, to keep it apart from the rest of the world.'

The others nodded, shocked but relieved that there was at least an explanation which seemed to make some kind of sense.

'The world has certainly been turned on its head,' said Tallow in his slow, methodical way. 'Perhaps time has moved as well as the land.'

'You saw the land moving too?' questioned Cumber, his brow lowered, his expression one of ferocious concentration.

'What's the matter, Cumber?' asked Velvet.

'I think perhaps Smoke has only got it half right, my dear. Tell us about your journey, Brace, if you would.'

And so Brace told them. His voice cracked often, for his throat was dry, and occasionally Tallow or Scoff added some detail that he had forgotten. As they listened, the others realized that Brace and his party had experienced a journey almost identical to their own, the land twisting beneath them as they flew north so that had seemed to bypass the Low Mountains altogether, to find themselves instead at the Spine and the citadel of the basilisks.

'We even saw night dragons falling from the sky,' said Brace mournfully, 'behind us, not long before we arrived here.'

'But we saw that too!' blurted Cumber excitedly. 'Only we saw it *ahead*! Don't you see – we can only have been travelling a day or two behind you at most!'

'But I don't understand,' quavered Velvet. In the aftermath of all they had endured this was all rather too much for her. Her body was shaking almost uncontrollably.

But Cumber did not notice. A conviction had been growing in him, and though he was not sure *how* he knew what he knew, he felt sure it was true. 'Smoke was almost right,' he went on hurriedly, 'but you see it's not the citadel that's frozen in time, it's Haven! All that time, all those moons we were living on and around the island, almost no time was passing in the world outside, so when we left in pursuit of Brace we were actually flying right on their tails! It's so obvious!'

'It is?' ventured Volley who, like Velvet, was somewhat confused.

'Cumber may be right,' agreed Scoff. 'Doesn't help though. We're still stuck.'

'And Fortune and the others are locked away in Haven,' added Smoke. 'There's no chance of us finding Aether's Cross now.'

'Did Archan promise to help you search for the Cross?' asked Brace suddenly. 'Us too,' he went on grimly as both Cumber and Smoke nodded. 'I suppose she was just lying to us all along, tempting us here just to imprison us.'

'But why bother?' protested Velvet. 'What good are we to her down here? Why hasn't she just killed us?'

'Wraith didn't kill,' put in Smoke quietly.

A thoughtful silence fell upon the group then, into which Ratchet slipped a comment. 'What about Thaw?'

'Yes,' said Smoke acidly. 'Thaw.'

She and Cumber quickly filled the others in on Thaw's

behaviour during and after their flight, and in particular about his reaction to Archan.

'Sounds like seduction,' suggested Scoff. 'She's the type.'

'I suppose so.' Brace frowned, and then sighed, a long, hopeless sound. 'But none of this is of any great help to us. Wonderful though it is to see all you dear dragons again, and fascinating though these theories are, the fact remains that we are trapped here with little hope of escape.'

'Nonsense,' blustered Cumber, marching across the dungeon towards the window, where Velvet was sitting, staring sadly out into the drizzle. 'We'll be out before you know it, Brace, don't you worry. I've escaped from worse places than this in my time . . .'

'Had charm then,' said Scoff.

'There's always another way,' came Cumber's echoing reply. He started to scrabble around by the window, distracting the melancholy Velvet. Her hope had all but gone. She smiled wanly at him and for the first time he noticed how exhausted she was. 'Oh, my dear,' he cried, 'you're shivering.'

The words brought Volley hastening towards Velvet as she made to answer Cumber with a reassuring shake of her head.

'You come with me,' announced Volley, gathering up the young dragon in his wing. 'And you – Ratchet, is it? Let me take you over to the water hole while these good dragons set their minds to our predicament.' And off he led them, exhausted Natural and warrior ex-Charmed following meekly in his step as he took them away into the blackness.

'Tell us about Werth,' demanded Smoke suddenly. Cumber nodded sympathetically. Though he had known Werth but a short time, he had developed a certain respect for her straightforwardness and concern for her fellow dragons. And she and Tallow had seemed so well matched.

'There is little to tell,' sighed Tallow, the subject clearly upsetting for him. 'We diverted from our course briefly to look at the ruins of the Fortress. It has fallen, like everything else.'

'Closed forever,' put in Scoff.

'A grave, that place, now,' continued Tallow. 'I saw the

troll which lay beneath it awaken, and I saw Shatter's army leave its mouth. And I saw Werth die beneath its shadow.'

'But what happened?' asked Cumber as he returned from the window to listen, captivated by the uncharacteristic melancholy in Tallow's voice.

'She was born there, so she of us all wanted to return. She was foolish – simply foolish. She tried to dig down to a place she thought she could see through a gap in the rubble. The ruins collapsed. She was crushed.'

His gloom filtered through the dank air, its shadow colouring their hearts and clouding their hope. They sat in silence for a long while.

Of them all it was Cumber who brightened first. 'Well,' he announced briskly. 'We had better find a way out of this dismal cell, and the sooner the better as far as I'm concerned.'

'It's no good,' sighed Brace, heaving himself up and stretching his wings. 'We know everything there is to know about this cell. Believe me – there's no way out.'

'Rot!' beamed Cumber. 'Now, let's have another look through this window at least. You never know what we might find.'

CHAPTER 20

Miracle of Flight

Rogue charm.

When charm held dominion, when the matrix across which the entire cosmos was stretched was the Maze of Covamere, magic infiltrated every pore of every structure of the world. Of every world. Continents and creatures, skies and seas, all danced to the beat of charm. Like thoughts in the mind of some unimaginably vast, living entity, charm flashed constantly through the web of the world, stimulating, building, creating, *living*.

Now nature thrived and, obsessed with its own stewardship, it allowed the last shreds of charm to slip forever beyond its grasp, to retreat to places where it could remain undisturbed. Most of the magic which survived the Turning joined the great river of charm in the sky; that which remained was either bound up in ancient spells, or else lingered in places of special power. A little still floated free however, uncertain of its place in the natural world. Rogue charm.

One such shred of magic moved among dragons. Slender, ghostly, it carried with it the strength of its long history. Aeons before it had borne aloft an ancient creature – now extinct – which had ruled the sky long before the dragons had come. Solitary that creature had been, with neither parents nor offspring to lend its lonely existence origin or destiny. It had lived, and it had died, its name and form forgotten many ages since. But its magic had lived on.

Alone now as its master had been then, the charm floated high above the waterfall, bearing its prey towards the dancing towers of the basilisks.

*　　*　　*

'Haven,' said Cumber suddenly. 'We have to trust that Fortune will find a way.' The others – Brace, Scoff, Tallow and Smoke – all looked at him quizzically. Cumber was peering out through the narrow window slit and up towards the distant sky.

'What do you mean, Cumber?' asked Tallow slowly.

'Haven was the eye of the storm – Fortune was more right than he knew – and Fortune's still there, I'm sure of it.'

The surety was a welcome stranger to Cumber, for he had felt none since entering this basilisk place. After Archan's overwhelming presence, and her terrible power – especially the power she exerted over Thaw – he found the cloying darkness of the cell strangely comforting. Here he could think clearly; here the world seemed straightforward again.

Back underground, he pondered. *Magic was ever the stuff of the underworld.*

And Fortune was near, Cumber was certain, and – perhaps – in a position to help. Charm bubbled in the sky, refusing to lower itself back into the futile lives of these tiny dragons, but Cumber could feel its presence, however remote.

'You think Fortune can help us?' prompted Tallow doubtfully.

'If he can't, no dragon can.'

Volley returned then, bringing with him Velvet and Ratchet, both of them refreshed.

'There's a drinking pool a little way over there,' Velvet informed Cumber as he gave her a swift embrace. 'You should have a drink at least.'

'No time for all that,' replied Cumber urgently. 'We have to send a message to Fortune, and quickly.' As he said this he smiled wryly – it was not so long ago that it was he himself who had responded to a message from the trapped Fortune.

'And how exactly are we supposed to do that, Cumber?'

Something blotted out the sun.

Ocher sped down the narrowing well of the citadel ramparts towards the tiny yard where Tellere lay sleeping. Having scoured the entire complex it had finally located its companion of old at the bottom of this dismal pit. Fine drizzle misted the air around it as Ocher swooped down to the pedestal, extending its prehensile tail to form a cushion of flesh which absorbed its impact with the hard ground. *A safe landing*, it marvelled. *Once I would have scoffed at such a thing.*

Narrow windows stared back at Ocher as it circled the statue, dark in the dripping walls of the citadel. Dungeon windows. It spared a cursory glance for the dragons who gazed at it wide-eyed from the lowest of the slits, then turned its attention fully to the stone basilisk.

Tellere was crouched on the mossy pedestal, its body almost wholly petrified. Erosion had ruined its flanks and fungus bloomed in its every wrinkle; dull and apparently lifeless it squatted beneath the grey rain. Ocher came nearer, lifting itself up until its silver eyes were level with the closed lids of its sibling. Opening its mouth, it exhaled. The breath which issued forth rolled across Tellere's motionless form in a visible wave through the damp air, scouring the various growths to burn away the coating of lichen and fungus. Pitted stone was revealed, colourless and drab.

Beginning at Tellere's coiled tail, Ocher swept its gaze across the basilisk statue's entire body until its mirror eyes came to rest upon the head. Nothing moved but Ocher's own flanks, drawing in and out as lethal breath passed between its lips. Then it rested its head against Tellere's, so that their brows touched.

Extending one of its long, metallic claws, Ocher raised a hooked forelimb towards its own right eyelid, pulling down on the resilient flesh with the sharp tip. A second claw pursued the first, stabbing tenderly at the silver orb like a striking serpent. Healing charm busied itself about the wound, but not before a single drop of clear fluid had gathered itself at the brim of the basilisk's lower lid. It hung there, suspended, then dropped into the finely etched line which marked the meeting place of the closed eyelids of Tellere. There it stayed, briefly, before slowly disappearing, absorbed into the statue's ancient and petrified flesh . . .

Ocher retreated, awaiting the result.

Cracks raced down Tellere's back and into each crack the gentle rain fell. Steam rose from the crevices, pressing them further apart until one by one chunks of stone began to fall away. Fire glowed within, joining the rain to form a cloud about the pedestal, a cloud within which there was sudden movement. Fire, a lancing explosion of light and a shower of broken rock across the yard. A sound like a falling cliff.

Tellere, the fourth of the Deathless, had woken.

There was no glory in this flight, no freedom, no ecstasy. Beating his wings as he never had before, Fortune raced through the mist in pursuit of his abducted daughter, blind to all but the narrow vision which had closed about him. The sky was a tunnel of thick, resistant air, a syrup through which his wings refused to move, a hostile fog which might as well have been a blanket of rock for all the progress he was making. Red clouds pressed against the corners of his eyes from the pressure of blood in his head.

But he would bear anything, if only he could catch up with Aria.

There was no below, no above, nor even behind – although somewhere in his speeding thoughts he knew Gossamer and the others were close on his tail – there was only ahead. *I am the fastest,* he thought desperately. *It's up to me now.* At the end of the tunnel, beyond the wave of charm on which Aria rode, dark and frightened, the towers of the citadel loomed. This close, their endless dance was the writhing of insect claws, the closing of fangs upon innocent air. Their sound was that of lashing tail and hissing breath; their movement was unpredictable – dangerous.

A crystal turret speared the sky directly in front of Fortune, catapulted upwards by some unimaginable imperative and forcing him to swoop drunkenly to the right to avoid being caught in its slipstream. He banked hard, dorsal scales scraping against the charm-hot surface of the erupting tower, eyes squinting hard past the sparks tumbling from its hide. He saw its prismatic form swelling as he rushed past, then saw it decay as fast, falling away again as some future catastrophe eroded it back into the depths of another time. Though he could not comprehend the true nature of what he saw, Fortune instinctively understood the fluidity of time in this outlandish region of the sky. Haven he had guessed was isolated from the natural river of time; what anomalies he might experience here he could not speculate.

Through the dancing towers he weaved his way, rearing back as one reached out for him with scintillating fingers, darting forward across the path of another as it tried to impale him against the sun. His wings throbbed but the pain existed in another world; here such things did not matter, only Aria mattered.

'Aria!' he cried out as he rounded the curve of yet another plunging spire to find her, incredibly, balanced barely a single wing's width away. His shout turned to a howl of anguish as he overshot, and he pounded his wings outwards in a vain attempt to slow his velocity. Into the down-draught of the tumbling spire, on and down he fell, reaching up towards his daughter with a single, flailing wing. He had been so close!

Treacherous currents clamped his outstretched wings against his body as though angered by his audacity. *To fly here?* they seemed to say. *Such boldness should not go unpunished!* Managing to free his wings a little, Fortune flicked their tips out into the turbulence just in time to prevent himself from crashing into the upraised teeth of the falling tower, which was melting into the waterfall like ice in spring. The water, released now from behind those particular foundations, exploded over him and knocked him back out into clearer air. Dazed, completely disorientated, Fortune extended his wings fully to find them limp and unresponsive. Shining walls of stone swept past as he fell. Aria was gone.

Before the husk of stone which had formed its sleeping self could even strike the ground Tellere had recreated its body in the air before Ocher. They exchanged no thoughts, nor even wasted their murderous breath on words. Not for Tellere the banter of its siblings, not for Tellere the easy combat of the mind. Tellere fought.

Catching the other basilisk completely off guard – a phenomenal achievement considering the intimate parallels of their minds – it grew a tough hide of grossly extended scales and spun its way across Ocher's path, scything through bone and muscle like an avalanche. Ocher fell into a hundred separate pieces, silver blood jetting across the shattered pedestal and sizzling where it struck the deep puddles which were gradually filling the yard.

Into the water dropped gore and myriad exotic fluids; steam rose in gouts, its smell foul. From their restricted vantage point the imprisoned dragons looked on in amazement. As they watched, Ocher rebuilt itself.

Guardian senses thrown clear by the ferocity of Tellere's attack quickly reintegrated themselves and knitted a sketch of a basilisk into the mist. The water which had accepted Ocher's scattered parts surged upwards, an inverted rain which fell into the organic space, dragging with it both flesh and form. Anatomy pulsed through the air, exploding from some internal point of creation as, in less time than it took Cumber to blink, the apparently vanquished basilisk was constructed anew. The agony in its face was unforgettable to the watching dragons and, as Ocher turned to face its opponent, they understood in a single blast of insight something of the torture of immortality.

Tellere, its body new and shining from its own recent rebirth, floated before its sibling, taunting it with a flashing smile.

'Will they kill each other?' whispered Velvet, fascinated. She had squeezed into the narrow space next to Cumber. It seemed that some exchange was occurring, some conversation which she could not hear, and it occurred to her that the outcome of that conversation might very well have a great deal of bearing on their current circumstances – if not their entire futures.

'They cannot die,' responded Cumber. 'They are basilisks. They are immortal.'

Is this *what Archan wants?* thought Velvet with a shudder. *And Thaw?*

Outside the rain fell more heavily, cloaking the ancient duellists and making their movements heavy and mysterious. Then, through the shower, there came flight. There came a dragon.

* * *

Rain cascaded past Fortune as he recovered, pumping his wings against its warmth. Barely one tree below him creatures were hovering in the gloom.

Basilisks! he thought, the sight jolting him into sensibility. *Two of them!* He knew at once that the nearer of them was the one he had encountered over the Plated Mountain. Then it had come so close to crushing the Seed of Charm – the key to the turning of the world and the future of magic in it. Now . . . did it still want to destroy? *The other basilisk must be one of its siblings. Were there five, or six?* The old stories were hazy, unrelated to these solid monstrosities which prowled beneath him. He stroked the air, fearful to proceed, curious to know what these beasts were doing here. He did not need to wait.

As though they had reached some decision, the two basilisks turned their blunt snouts up towards the sky and thundered past Fortune with blinding speed. He flicked his head with their motion as they sprinted past, catching the eye of the one he knew as it moved through his field of vision.

Dragon, came Ocher's voice in his head. *She is the one. At the crest of the world . . .*

Then it was gone.

'Fortune!' came the call which finally folded his wings altogether. 'Down here!'

Ocher had not expected to fight. Tellere had always been the most taciturn of the Deathless and had never before displayed such a temper. Its vicious attack had been predictably futile but the pain it had inflicted had been real nonetheless. To be torn to pieces, even for an eternal, is to know agony.

. . . Enough, Tellere! Do you not know why I am here?

. . . Your purpose I have divined of course, Ocher. But you have disturbed me where none should have trespassed. This was my final choice, as well you know: to sleep for the remainder of eternity.

. . . No answer that, Tellere.

. . . Not for you to judge, I deem. To be stone is to experience if not death then stillness, and that is all we can hope for, despite your vain dreams.

. . . Not vain, Tellere. Look into the sky if you doubt the power is there.

. . . Abandoned charm has no power, however well it may be focused.

. . . Veil and Geiss already trust its strength. As should you, Tellere.

. . . No, Ocher. I will sleep.

. . . Here? Now?

. . . You have broken my repose, Ocher. This place is soiled now beyond cleansing. You know I must now find another sanctuary – you have angered me more than you can know.

. . . Not like you, Tellere.

. . . Let me speak of the basilisk you do not know, Ocher. Let me speak of Tellere. Minds can be hidden, even the mind of one Deathless from another. Much about Tellere I have kept secret from you and our brethren, including this: once I too tried to initiate the ritual of the Gathering. Before the Turning it was, before we parted even, when we considered ourselves enlightened. When we built this citadel. Neither you nor the others of our kin knew of my experiment, but try I did all the same. Charm I gathered from the borders of the Realm, from the edge of the Maze, from all the junctions between the worlds, for there the charm was at its most powerful.

. . . Why did you not complete the ritual? Why did you never tell of this before?

. . . The ritual was flawed and I abandoned it. As for my secrecy – think of it as a game, Ocher, a means of releasing an anger which has built for too long. The charm I gathered was wild and passionate, as once I was when worlds were younger and we were still old. Do you remember those times, Ocher? Or is your mind as polluted as always it was?

. . . I remember clearly now, Tellere. Can you say the same?

. . . I can, Ocher. I always have. Did you not know the source of my anger, nor its depth?

. . . I did not.

. . . But I shall relent, for I believe you mean to go through with this. My secret knowledge I will share: there is one thing, Ocher, without which no Gathering can succeed.

. . . Tell. What do we need?

. . . Dragon.

A decision made, their minds locked in deep exchange, Ocher and Tellere fled for the sky. Faster than lightning can split the clouds their thoughts moved between them, puzzling and solving, drawing back from the horrors which prowled the borders of Ocher's complex plans, lunging for the half-truths which Tellere had uncovered when it had first attempted the ritual. Ocher could not resist glancing at the hapless dragon in its path as it leaped skywards, meeting its frail gaze as both basilisks left the citadel behind. It threw what it hoped was a clue at the strange, flapping creature and wondered at the threat it – or at least its kind – posed to the Deathless. And the one, last hope it offered.

. . . Ocher, the Gathering will succeed or fail on the presence of these dragons. They did not exist when first I tried. But now they do and they are vital. But if it fails . . .

. . . If it fails?

. . . Bringer-of-shadow will come.

'Cumber!' Fortune scrambled through the dim and water-logged yard to where Cumber was frantically waving with one white wing through a window.

'I knew you'd find us!' beamed the young ex-Charmed from within the prison. 'Did you see that fight – did you ever see such a . . .'

'Fortune!'

Pressing his face through the narrow slit Fortune peered into the darkness within to see Brace bounding towards him. They bumped horns and Fortune wept with delight to see first Gossamer's brother, then his old friends Tallow and Scoff and all the other prisoners crowding the single opening.

'You're all alive!' he repeated over and over, scarcely able to contain himself, but then his heart turned over with a dreadful thud and he dragged himself from his friends' clumsy embraces into the rain outside. 'Aria!' he wailed into the heavens, flailing his wings hopelessly in the puddles.

'What about her?' called Velvet sharply, instantly con-cerned.

'Who's Aria?' came Scoff's quizzical tones.

As Cumber explained in a furious undertone, Fortune told

through his tears what he had seen. Brace and the others quickly shushed Cumber as it became clear to them the gravity of what had happened, and the devastating effect it had had on Fortune.

'Where's Gossamer?' barked Velvet.

'I don't know,' sobbed Fortune. Velvet reached out to him through the slotted window; never had she seen a dragon look more wretched and bedraggled. It was as much as she could do to restrain her own tears.

'It's all right, Fortune. We'll get her back,' she choked.

'Of course we will, old fellow,' agreed Cumber in a more businesslike way, 'and to do that we'll need to get out of here. Fortune, it's about time you got a grip on yourself and rescued us, don't you think?'

The sound of his old friend's tumbling words brought Fortune round a little, and he managed to hitch in a great, juddering breath. 'But what can I do?' he managed to say, trembling now as he struggled to compose himself. 'I can't think about anything except . . .'

'Then here's something to think about,' interrupted Cumber briskly. 'We're trapped in here, and Brace and his lot are near exhaustion. There's no food, only water, and if you don't get us out pretty soon then we're all going to die in here, so if that's not an imperative situation then I don't know what is. So what are you going to do about it, eh?'

'All right, Cumber. Just give me a moment.' Fortune lowered his head to the ground, resting his snout briefly in the shallow water before raising it again. Cumber was deeply upset to see that his friend's eyes were hollow and haunted, but behind the sorrow was the fire of purpose and it shone from the shadows like a pale, flickering beacon. No warmth was there, not yet, but there was determination and that was enough for Cumber.

Something moved in the shadows behind Fortune. Catching sight of its reflection in the streaming wall, he whirled round to confront it. Head lowered, shoulders high and prickling with golden fur, the chitraka watched him warily from beneath her lowered brows.

CHAPTER 21

Tower

Before she implemented the desperate shred of a plan which had illuminated her mind, Gossamer hurled an order at Quill and Vox. In the corner of her eye she had seen Fortune knocked out of the sky by the collapsing tower and knew that he was in need of help.

'Both of you,' she screamed, 'follow him – help him!'

If there was any thought in their heads of refusing her command, it was swept entirely away by the blaze of light which seemed to swell in Gossamer's eyes as she flicked her gaze across them. Exchanging the briefest of glances, her two companions wheeled around and ducked into the treacherous airspace around the dancing towers, arrowing down into the spray of the waterfall in pursuit of the tumbling Fortune. No sooner had Gossamer thrust her tail to the side to regain her former course than they had vanished from sight. She lifted her head and struck out for the sun.

Her heart was raw. It seemed to her that it had shrunk to a taut and trembling nugget, one quite incapable of responding to anything other than the abduction of Aria. The search for Brace, the fury of the storm, even her love for Fortune – all the essential concerns which had driven her up to now were unwelcome intruders. Her daughter had been snatched away by cruel magic and nothing could challenge the presence of that fact at the core of her soul. At this instant she cared for nothing else in the world but Aria's safe return. Nothing at all.

Instinct took her high. A memory surfaced as though from another age, memories of an erupting mountain where altitude had proved her ally once before and she acted without thinking upon its whispered advice, soaring above the citadel until the towers directly below her were points of angry motion on a field of mist – which she scanned for her daughter. And found her!

Aria was a dark mote carried on a bed of undulating air. The mischievous flight charm held her motionless between the rise and fall of the spires, protecting her from the currents which would otherwise have dragged her across their teeth. Gossamer bobbed lower, the tiny infant dominating her vision. The world about her had ceased to exist. She descended, her mouth dry, stalking the charm with strong, silent beats of her white wings.

A tower surged towards her, an expanding circle of glistening amber, but it fell away again before reaching her, leaving a trail of spent and hissing charm in its wake. More towers ascended and receded but they seemed easy to avoid, as though something were guiding her. Now Aria was only three trees away. Gossamer paused, hovering in the damp air, her breath still in her throat as it had been for what seemed like a lifetime: there was no need for breathing when such prizes were at stake. Her heart galloped, a thumping engine of fear in a body otherwise empty of emotion.

The rogue charm wavered . . . and failed. Powers which had lingered since distant dawns of distant times finally gave themselves up into the beckoning river and collapsed into useless shards of energy. Light bristled momentarily about Aria's prone form and then she fell, her tiny wings flailing like uncertain leaves. A tower of crystal leaped up to meet her.

No voice visited Gossamer's throat, so filled was it with the breath which would not move. She transformed her own wings into narrow, ineffectual blades and fell along with her daughter, giving herself up to gravity in a final, desperate attempt at rescue. Together they plummeted towards the rising spire and together they entered the maw which yawned suddenly in its side, passing from the bright, moist air to the darkness within. The spire continued to grow until it reached an ecstasy of form, a trembling pinnacle which stood poised at the limits of structural possibility

. . . and froze there. The charm which had erected it still flowed through its skin but it had been redirected. Time raced in the tower, but no longer for the tower's sake.

Mokishi, the chitraka, was only briefly distracted by the arrival in the pit of Quill and Vox. She marched boldly past them and straight up to Fortune, whom she regarded with her sleek head cocked querulously to one side. In this dragon she sensed the same compassion which she had discovered in Velvet – and something more. Knowledge of charm, or the memory of its influence at least. Once charmed herself, and still possessed of the merest fraction of her former skills, she bent her head and purred loudly: a greeting. Fortune glanced at Cumber, his face asking the question he hesitated to speak.

'Yes,' replied Cumber excitedly, 'she's safe enough, we think. Velvet befriended her and she seems to like our company now, although I didn't expect to see her down here, I must confess. Hello, Quill – who's your friend?'

Fortune looked back to see Quill and Vox dawdling in the rain behind him. They joined him beneath the dubious shelter of the crumbling stone parapet which crowded the narrow window, clearly nervous in the presence of the strange chitraka but willing to trust Cumber's assessment.

'Perhaps she can help,' came Velvet's voice from the depths of the cell. 'She must know this place pretty well, I imagine.'

'Well?' shrugged Fortune, looking down at the great, golden beast. 'Can you?'

Mokishi backed away, lashing her long tail slowly from side to side. All the time she retreated she kept her green eyes locked on Fortune's, until she reached the broken pedestal where once a basilisk had slept. Then she turned and sprang with easy, muscled grace on to the ruined stone. Dropping her snout she sniffed at the pedestal, tossing her head occasionally to throw off the rain – which was intensifying into a downpour. She scoured every pore of the fractured surface as though searching for some specific scent. The dragons watched, puzzled.

Dissatisfied, Mokishi bounded down and began to prowl

231

the yard itself, padding carefully through the deepening puddles and scenting, all the time scenting. Some areas she surveyed with a mere cursory sniff, others she examined over and over again, returning to some spots frequently, narrowing her search until finally she stopped. Water had filled a shallow well here, turning it into a miniature lake. Mokishi crouched, her powerful limbs gathered against each other, her ferocious green gaze locked into the depths of the pool. There she remained motionless, her curious search completed.

Wordlessly Fortune moved across the rain-soaked yard to where the chitraka squatted. He circled the remains of the pedestal with caution – the basilisks had scared him and he feared any lingering charm – until he too could peer down into the water. He saw nothing.

'Quill. Vox,' he called softly, anxious for no reason he could determine to keep his voice low. The sound of the rain nearly drowned his words. His companions joined him obediently, Quill obviously confused and wary. But Vox . . .

Vox was trembling. Fortune watched him closely as he joined them at the edge of the pool, watched the way he clenched his purple wings to his flanks, the way he held his jaw tight closed, the fierce concentration in his eye.

'What is it, Vox?' he whispered.

Vox did not answer at once. He simply stared into the pool, his eyes growing wide and scared, the trembling overpowering his body until the rain scattered from his scales, as though with a life of its own.

'What is it?' repeated Fortune.

Vox turned to him, misery distorting his features.

'It's Wraith,' he answered.

The dream flowed through her like blood, or like a river, and quite when it transformed into reality she could not tell. She knew only that she held her daughter again, and that they were both safe.

Aria was the warm island of life to which Gossamer clung while the dream moved past her with a different heat. A *magical* heat. The dream was a river, and the river was charm, and the charm was time, and within the flow they lay, two dragons comfortable in their defiance of the powers which washed past them. In the dream Gossamer saw many pasts and many presents, and she saw many futures.

She saw ancient times when tiny beings had swarmed over the world, conquering the land with the vast network their minuscule forms combined to create. She saw their uncompromising predation, the way in which they swallowed every living thing which dallied in their path. She saw the perfect, uniform hive they created in their wake, a flawless, repetitive gestalt which turned the skin of the world into a single intellect with insight far beyond the individual organisms which were its cells. And she saw how these entities finally met the sea, and how the water consumed them, etching like acid back into the world-hive and turning the dreadful, mighty conquest into so much dust. So they perished, nameless ones, many Turnings past when neither charm nor nature ruled.

Whether they were memories from some other realm she could not tell. She saw their flow and how they mixed into the events of the present – and extended beyond into myriad futures which had not come to be and yet which swarmed through the river of time like migrating salmon, driven by single-minded instinct and oblivious to all but the one, final destination.

Flashes of recollection brought her images of the flying monster whose charm had abducted her daughter, showed her the last breath of a dying troll as it tipped a boulder into the snow, betrayed some far-off time – past or future she could not say – where the clouds grew bright with fire and something greater than a night dragon fell from the sky. A dragon moved in the glare of the disaster, dark and wingless.

All these moments, all these memories both gone and to come, flowed in and around Gossamer and Aria while the tower of time into which they had been sucked remained motionless, locked into a single, solid form which defied gravity with impossible ease and resisted the river which battered against it, trying to pull it forward again, battering its ramparts in a series of vain attempts to push it back.

While its twelve companions continued to dance some

greater power kept the one tower utterly still ... and Gossamer slept.

Wraith's elegant, black snout lifted clear of the confines of the water, breaking delicately through the membrane of tension to emerge into the rain. It was transparent, clearly unreal, yet both Fortune and Vox backed away from it with slow, deliberate steps. More of Wraith's head rose through the violated pool, growing paler and less substantial the further it entered into the real world. Fragments of charm clung in vain to its dripping contours as it began slowly to melt away into the rain; soon only the eyes were left, glowing yellow in the dank oppression of the pit. Eventually they too faded.

Drawing his breath with difficulty, Fortune crept towards the water's edge and peered down. Clear as air now, the water revealed a single, minute scale resting at the bottom of the shallow pond, pale and lifeless.

'A basilisk scale,' he whispered to himself, although Vox heard his words and joined him, puzzled and curious.

'*Was* it the Black Dragon?' Vox asked, the memory of his encounter with Wraith like a set of jaws clamped about his throat. The tremble in his voice caused Fortune to regard him with renewed interest.

'No,' Fortune answered, 'just his memory. He knew this basilisk, I think. He's gone, Vox.'

'Yes, he's gone.'

What do you know of Wraith? wondered Fortune, but before he could pursue his suspicion the chitraka was there again at his side, sniffing eloquently at the water. She raised her head and stared straight into Fortune's eyes; the intensity of her gaze – the glimmer of intelligence behind it – was disturbing and also ... *thrilling*. Fortune's eyes flickered from the chitraka's to the pool and back again. Then he understood.

'The way out?' he demanded.

Excited now, Mokishi bounded up to the window and, to the surprise of the watching dragons, squeezed her slender frame through the narrow slot, a feat which even Velvet, the slimmest of them, could not have achieved without the aid of magic. Fortune and Vox joined Quill at the window, struggling to follow the chitraka's progress into the gloom of the dungeon.

'Well, come on,' announced Cumber suddenly, his voice echoing around the cell, 'let's follow her, for the sky's sake – we might only get one chance at this!'

Leaving Fortune and the others to peer in as best they could, the prisoners followed Mokishi through the shadows until they reached the drinking pool, a half-circle of smooth stone jutting from the end wall of the cell. Here the dressed stone of the walls met a natural formation of limestone to create an arched ceiling which flared out from the far side of the pool. Stalactites fronded the arch, many spindly and fragile, a few longer and more robust. They seemed to be pointing down into the water, reflected in the smooth mirror of which were their twins, reaching up towards the air; the reflection looked like a fabulous city, a miniature construction of spires and battlements which looked . . .

'It looks just like the citadel!' exclaimed Velvet. 'I didn't notice before.'

'Didn't look like this before,' explained Scoff dryly.

But before they could consider the significance of this transformation, the air was suddenly filled with a blur of gold as Mokishi sprang out over the pool and crashed through the water's surface, shattering the illusory citadel into a million shards of crystal and showering the dragons with icy water. Gasping, they staggered back, then rushed forward again to see what had happened to their strange new companion.

Deep blue light fell heavily across the ribcage of the tower when Gossamer woke into a kind of dusk. Before she registered anything more than this single colour – *Twilight! Magic time!* – instinct snapped her head down to confirm what she felt within her wings: Aria, rescued!

She could remember little of her headlong flight between the dancing towers, and even less of her entry into this one tower, although it seemed to her now that they had not so much entered as been dragged through the opening and into the deep blue space inside. Holding Aria tight against her breast, she inspected their surroundings.

Unlike the complex labyrinth of the basilisk citadel itself, this peripheral tower possessed no separate chambers, no corridors, nor any changes in level or form whatsoever – it was hollow, a simple void – and Gossamer floated in it. Another flight charm, trapped here perhaps from some older aeon. The blue light came from below, its source invisible in the distance, its effect on the supporting ribs breathtaking. The light rolled across the tower's skeleton, throwing into gentle relief a series of organic spirals which swooped through Gossamer's vision as if they themselves were in flight. Arrested in the throes of some unimaginable motion, the tower held itself poised in the beauty of the dusky illumination, clearly anxious to uncoil itself and resume the dance, but not yet, not yet . . .

Despite her ordeal, Aria lay quiet and comfortable in her mother's embrace, and now that she had made at least an initial assessment of her surroundings, Gossamer turned her attention more fully to her daughter. Her heart swelled as she stroked her wingtip across Aria's small, perfect face, and the tears ran freely as the infant dragon's eyes crinkled in response to the sight of her mother, the warmth of her body, the sound of her heartbeat. Her gaze was wide and strangely knowing, and Gossamer thought she would burst with the love which filled her like a charm.

Love is *magic*, she thought deliriously. *That is the future for charm in this world.* Chuckling a little at such nonsense, she hugged and fussed Aria until the little dragon squirmed in protest, wriggling inside her wings.

All else was still. Gossamer felt her blissful calmness gradually melt away, leaving her alert and nervous. Swiftly she reviewed the incredible events of the past few days, finding in them neither sequence nor pattern. The Turning she had been able to accept, for it had centred upon a massive and universal logic which could not be denied. But the storm . . . the storm was chaos. Neither sense nor structure emerged from her brief analysis of the effects of Fortune's storm (strangely she still thought of it as being somehow *owned* by him) upon the world.

Chaos, she thought. *The world beyond the Turning has lost all reason. What can we now predict; for what can we now dream?*

The voice which interrupted her thoughts was soft but insistent. It rolled across her senses like the sweetest honey, like the clearest scent; it was like the voice of her mother and father melded into the purest of songs. Tears came to her eyes as she heard it, though later she could not recall what emotion it was which had accompanied them.

'Nothing can take away your dreams, dragon,' it whispered. 'And there is order, if you know where to look.'

'W-who's there?' stammered Gossamer. Her heart thumped fast and slowed only slightly as she took a series of deep breaths, trying to still its pounding. A warm breeze wafted past her face, like the draught of a dragon's flight, though she saw nothing which could have disturbed the air thus. Nothing but rich blue light and the complex skeleton of the tower. 'Who are you?' she repeated.

'Call me Cloud . . .'

Air moved past again, this time from behind. It gathered in front of her, collecting into a lens which grew before her eyes until it had formed a broad oval of shadow hovering between the far wall and the central space where she and Aria floated. Movement twisted the oval out of true, pinching it and sending pulses of vapour swirling across its perimeter. Its edges were blurred, fading into the lighter, clear air beyond. Though it was dark, at its core there was a hint of light, burning dim and orange.

Speechless, unable to react, Gossamer simply stared. The voice was surely just another manifestation of the chaos which surrounded her, an irrelevant wonder in a world turned on its head; still, it soothed and revitalized her with a power so vibrant that she felt nourished in its presence. Whatever it was, this spirit, this entity, Gossamer knew without question that it was unassailably good.

'*Cloud*: as a name it is inadequate, and I shall bear many names when my time in this world eventually comes, but it will suffice for now. It is the name dragons will use for me regardless of any influence of mine, so as such it is fitting.'

Gossamer heard the words but they meant nothing to her. She could not help but love the voice but she did not understand its message, if message it bore. She had Aria; now she just wanted Fortune and freedom and an end to the chaos.

'Chaos is a question of perspective. Shortly you may reappraise your views. For now you need only listen.'

'Who are you?' whispered Gossamer, not expecting an answer.

'A name you have heard, but names say little. I do not yet exist, dragon, but soon I shall. I am . . . an alternative.'

'An alternative to what?'

'I am afraid you will find me very . . . elusive. This I cannot help, for it is a function both of my nature and of the unusual circumstances in which I am forced to present myself to you. I have no place in your past, dragon, but I will have a place in your future. As for the present . . . as I said, I simply do not yet exist. This tower has proved useful however, for here the flow of time has been made malleable enough for me to manifest myself. To show myself to you, dragon.'

'Why to me? What do you want?'

The orange light dulled a little, and the edges of the oval cloud grew even less distinct. Distortions rippled across its nebulous form like waves through water. Gradually it reintegrated itself, reforming its vague boundaries and forcing fresh light out from within.

'I am reminded that my presence here is unwelcome. The new world is not yet ready for me, and what is left of the old rejects me utterly, for I am its heir.'

'Heir to what? To charm?' The longer the faint voice spoke the more Gossamer was enthralled. She felt tired, but a tremendous sense of purpose, of destiny, was growing in her. She felt as though she were in the presence not of an intelligence but of all that was to come; she felt as though she were talking to the cosmos itself.

'Forgive me,' continued the voice as though she had not spoken. 'My intention is not to confuse you. Not at all. I bring you a message, dragon, and you must bear it on to others of your race who may interpret it correctly.'

There was a pause then, long and pregnant, before the voice went on.

'You perceive disorder, dragon. Be reassured that beneath

the chaos there *is* order, a greater order than any you might now imagine. The world that has emerged from the Turning is an infant newly birthed. It is blind and clumsy, it has yet to shake off the yolk of the egg which has nourished it; it is confused and uneducated.

'The message I bring you concerns the world, and the Turning and the place of dragons within and between the two. New life is bursting through the soil, a great diversity of species, each one desperate to make its mark upon the skin of the virgin lands. All these things and more you and your kin have experienced, and in your hearts you know that you do not belong among all these creatures of the new world. Dragons belong to the old world, to the world before the Turning.'

'Charmed dragons, yes,' protested Gossamer, 'but Naturals . . . ?'

'*All* dragons. In the river of time you are but a single droplet, and history will make no distinction between Charmed and Natural. But do not despair, for it is hope that I bring you. Though you do not belong, you must survive. The reasons for this I cannot speak of, not yet, but the natural world must not forget you. You must forgive the Turned world its tantrums – its *storms* – for they will pass. Seas are rising, continents are moving – though it has a past, it is not one that offers meaning or relevance. It is *new*, dragon, and has everything to learn. It is vital that dragon ancestors survive.'

'But how?'

'The answer lies within your wings, dragon.' As these enigmatic words drifted through the tower, a tremendous flare of light erupted from the lens . . . *Cloud?* The light broke into two distinct beams, each of which quickly solidified into recognizable forms: twin rivers flowing through glowing air.

The vision was more real than anything Gossamer had ever experienced; its clarity was such that in seeing she also *comprehended*. It – and the concept it presented – was *bright* beyond belief.

A river of charm, and a river of time. They co-existed – for now – but soon they would converge. This event the vision showed, and the brilliance of the conjunction nearly burned Gossamer's eyes from their sockets. She looked away, grimacing, and when she looked back the vision was gone ... or nearly gone. A tiny dragon shape, a dragon ghost it seemed, dwindled at the exact point in space where the rivers had collided. Then it was that she knew.

'It's Aria isn't it?' she blurted with sudden terror. 'Something dreadful is going to happen to Aria!'

The voice softened to the merest breath of air. 'I shall not return until the time of the Gathering is over,' it whispered. 'Until then you, and all living souls, will be alone. Until the sky falls ...'

The lens was fading, its edges evaporating into nothingness as the light at its core died. 'Tell me!' blurted Gossamer. 'Please tell me what I must do! Please!'

But the voice spoke no more. Blue light washed upwards and into the void left by the retreating cloud and as it did so the tower began to groan, preparing again to yield to the forces pressing against it.

The answer lies within your wings.

The bizarre exchange with the unearthly voice had served only to increase Gossamer's confusion. The awe which she had felt in its presence was swept away by the terror it had engendered in her with those ambiguous words: ... *within your wings.* She looked down with tears in her eyes at what indeed lay there, afraid of the nameless horror about which the voice ... *Cloud* ... had warned her.

The tower creaked and a filament of light stabbed through the tower wall, slicing a new opening to the sky beyond. Pale wings cycled against mist, accepting the twilight colour of the interior as they passed into its embrace. Tail coiled, neck taut, Archan flew into the tower.

CHAPTER 22

Transformation

No sooner did Archan sense the tower's arrested motion than she was in the air. The answer was there, in the tower – all of Archan's instincts told her it was so and she would not be denied this fragile opportunity. What power it was that had stopped the dance she did not know, nor was she interested. She wished only to seize the moment. Thaw, enraptured by the incredible detail of the living map, ignored her as she accelerated away through the broken roof and into the mist.

A dramatic yield-charm allowed her to gain access to the tower with little effort and a great deal of spectacle. All Archan's power was coming from the basilisk chamber now, borrowed magic still reluctant to join the river in the sky. She hung in the still air, watching Gossamer and her daughter as they turned to face her. The tower strained around them, preparing to launch itself once more through time. It trembled in anticipation, as did Archan, for here at last was the spark to the fire of her destiny. Here at last was the mother of her chosen one.

Not the older dragon, of course, though she was herself still young. No, she did not bear the startling aura which surrounded the infant. Archan concentrated upon the younger dragon, honing the vestiges of basilisk charm which still enabled her blind eyes to perceive the world. Small and brown the infant was, unremarkable in many ways . . . yet possessed of such *presence*. Aria's eyes shone like beacons in the clear air, throbbing with a potential Archan had never before known. In that first instant when Aria was revealed to her, when not even the merest scale of doubt obscured her unearthly vision, she knew that here was the one. Here was the gateway to eternity.

Those eyes! Archan yearned to do nothing less than raise her claws to those young, fragile eyes and wrest them from their sockets. To render the infant sightless would divert all her power into Archan's own blind sockets. Such a fitting mutilation would it be that Archan could scarcely restrain herself from performing it.

But she checked herself. The infant was even younger than she had anticipated, and much charm would be needed if she were to produce the offspring Archan so desperately needed.

A companion! At last, a companion with whom to spend eternity!

Archan dragged charm from the Chamber of the World and wrapped it around the frozen tower, knitting its raw energy into the sweet fabric of the time-defying structure. At the limits of perception the other great river, the river of time, boiled.

Gossamer looked on warily as Archan prowled the perimeter of the tower. The blue light turned the cream of her fine-scaled hide to deep moonlight, cold and magical. Featureless but for the glint of her fangs, Archan seemed a dragon carved from flexible ice, supple as winter and deadly as snow. What she wanted here Gossamer could not guess, but she was filled with fear.

Perhaps I could bolt for the exit, she wondered. But the opening through which Archan had entered had somehow healed over again. They were trapped.

Folded within Gossamer's wings, Aria stirred, and as she moved so did the tower. Aria's wide, dark eyes gazed out upon the spectacle. Tiny still, yet on the brink of self-awareness, she drank in the events which presented themselves to her with the hungry desire of the infant. Absorbing, learning, she began to *know*.

She saw the fire race up one of the many spiralling ribs which braced the tower's interior, a frantic blue flame which began in the unmarked depths and reached its zenith at the tower's dark peak. There it exploded, showering sparks over the watching dragons and heating the air until it sizzled.

The rib along which it had chased glowed bright white like a tear in the flesh of the cosmos, a split through which something else was visible. Aria's eyes turned into the slit and saw what lay beyond.

River!

The name leaped into her innocent mind, and as it did so she felt the awesome power of the river of time reach into the world through the tear it had created. The tower juddered, desperate to be swept away again into the dance with its twelve siblings, but Archan had given the river another task to perform first. It splashed across the empty space towards Aria and Gossamer, droplets of hissing energy cascading from its tendrils as it rolled through this alien environment. A current of pure time, made manifest in the natural world.

As soon as it reached Aria it tugged at the hold Gossamer's wings had on her small body. Gossamer struggled for many breaths to maintain her grip but the river was too much for her and Aria was dragged under its waves. A whirlpool it became then, a colossal, vibrating cone of energy still linked to the rib which had spawned it by an undulating thread of light. Gossamer was thrown back, crying out in anguish against the roaring which had overwhelmed her senses. Aria had been taken from her again, and this time she was power-less to intervene.

But for Aria, all was light. The whirlpool span around her, dizzying her and filling her with time's indomitable strength. She felt the relentlessness of its flow, the constancy of its direction, the infinite possibilities of all the pasts and futures it held between its banks. She felt it slip between her scales and through her pores, she felt it entwine itself around her heart and mind, she felt it pumping strange new juices into her body, filling her with its power, changing her . . .

New ideas swarmed through her mind; with each breath she took in this circular torrent she felt a new part of herself locking into place. Time itself was a new concept to an infant dragon, not to mention notions of birth and death. These basics she learned first before being bullied on into language and motion. Then love, hate, the quest for truth. Betrayal. On she tumbled through the river of time; each wave which thrust her forward was a year, each tide in which she floundered a lifetime. The entire process an education, a revelation.

The waves whipped faster. Disorientated now yet curiously *stable* despite her surroundings, Aria gave herself over to the experience. Not that she had any choice. Her body was tampered with. Time eddies prickled through her limbs, stretching and filling them as they did her wings. Her own future entered her bloodstream, injecting new power into her heart and expanding its chambers with the span of history. Her lungs grew strong, her muscles taut as the magic of the river forced them towards the future, taking her infant body and escorting it into adulthood. For a blinding, terrifying instant it seemed to her that it would not stop, and that her own death were visible in distant mists, but suddenly the pulsing in her bones faltered and ceased and the crashing sound of the whirlpool descended into a whine which began slowly to fade.

The rings of light which had encircled her folded into themselves and collapsed back into the single strand which had summoned them. This in turn was sucked back into the slender rib from which the entire conflagration had sprung. With a crack the rib closed its glowing wound and silence fell.

Archan and Gossamer floated on the invisible platform of charm which spanned the tower. Between them, her head bowed, floated Aria. A chain of fire still lingered about her, the fitful sparks of the vestiges of charm which had kept the whirlpool intact. Slowly it died away, leaving only a dragon. A *grown* dragon.

Archan was awestruck, overwhelmed. Though she had released the power she had not anticipated its beauty. In its presence even she felt belittled. And overjoyed.

Gossamer felt . . . numb. She had glimpsed fragments of her daughter's transformation through the veil of the spinning bands of energy but had not comprehended what it was she witnessed. Now, with the magic faded, all was made clear. The face which Aria now lifted to confront her mother was the face not of an infant dragon but of a dragon fully-grown – a dragon older than Gossamer was herself. Yet it was still Aria, her daughter. Astonished, repulsed, strangely thrilled, Gossamer stretched out a tentative wing to touch her. Aria reached out bashfully in return.

They never completed the gesture because suddenly Archan was there. She rose up through the magical platform itself to stand between mother and daughter, facing the grown Aria. Gossamer did not yet know Archan, but she sensed the immeasurable evil which was gradually overwhelming her soul. Pale wings obscured her view of her violated daughter and she reacted as any mother would – she attacked.

'Get away from her!' she screamed, almost incoherent. 'What have you done to her, you monster!'

Archan flicked her head upwards, calling charm from the citadel. A gap immeasurably wide opened up between the two dragons and Gossamer found herself flung outwards through a void until she was twenty, thirty trees away. Gathering her wits and strength she thumped her wings against the charm-hot air, speeding back across the gap which had so suddenly appeared, desperate to return to where Aria floated. But as she flew the gap remained as wide as ever, though her wings hammered. On she flew, in vain, pouring her whole heart into the effort, tiring swiftly yet drawing no closer.

Her back still turned to the flailing Gossamer, Archan appraised Aria. Those same dark eyes (yet they glowed, too – such a contradiction) stared back at her, betraying an intriguing mixture of confusion and composure. She was elegant – not beautiful but with a face compelling in its intensity. Her body was small and lean, its wings broad; the body of a natural dragon highly skilled in flight. *She has travelled in time*, thought Archan ecstatically. *She has journeyed forward to meet me, that my quest shall not be in vain!*

Aria looked on quizzically as Archan's wings opened to embrace her, and remained mute as she was folded into their creamy luxury. Their hearts thundered together as Archan's flight charm carried them to the tower's perimeter and out through a sudden wound into the misty air beyond. As they exited Aria cast her gaze back into the blue darkness, struggling to make out the distant shape of her mother beating hopelessly against the shackles which held her in limbo. Then the tower flashed out of her vision as it was dragged back into the looping dance through time from which it had been temporarily suspended.

Her mother was gone then. Was this creamy goddess her mother now? Though she was now grown and fully aware her education was totally lacking in real encounters and so she had no precedents for anything she was experiencing, no measures against which to make her judgements. Truly naïve, she had no choice but to trust her new companion.

I shall observe, she thought. *And by the actions of this dragon shall I learn proper ways to behave. She shall be my tutor and I her pupil. My true education begins now.*

Hot wind smothered Gossamer. Caught up as if in a deluge, she was flung against a soft, yielding surface which she guessed to be the wall of the tower. Time screamed inside her head, tugging at her as it tried to haul the tower backwards towards some distant history. Splinters of crystal grew across her vision, regenerating as erosion and decay began to reverse themselves. All around her time was poised to run backwards.

The scream became an inaudible whistle which hurt her very mind, and she realized that it was an alarm. There was an intruder here: herself. She was not welcome and would be dealt with summarily.

Light unfurled in a sudden starburst and she was spat through the mouth of the tower like an undigested morsel of food. Speeding air was replaced by crashing water as she glanced against the waterfall; thrown clear again she tumbled in the spray, a tiny dragon shape flurrying on a wind a thousand times its superior in strength and wit. As Fortune had before her, she folded her wings and submitted herself to the angry elements.

All was white before her eyes, a cloud which whirled and dizzied her, a cloud . . .

Help me!

No response came, despite her desperate hope that the mysterious voice of the Cloud would return to her.

Somewhere out of sight the tower hissed its satisfaction and the dance resumed.

Down she fell until the mist-ridden updraught from the base of the falls opened her wings and buoyed her up again. Reluctantly, for she had little enough energy left, she flapped against the breeze and lifted herself clear of the spray, her wings working an automatic rhythm while her mind raced: where to go? The part of the citadel towards which Fortune had plummeted was lost to her now, and even the tower from which she had just been hurled had already turned to a different form, and was turning still. Down was defeat.

Up, she decided before argument could ensue, and as if to applaud her resolve a shaft of sunlight broke through the spray and illuminated the side of one of the citadel's highest turrets. A tiny shadow vanished into its tip as Gossamer looked up, the movement enough to satisfy her. *Aria! I won't let you be taken twice!*

Wingbeats strong and confident, Gossamer began her ascent.

Mokishi burst from the pool of water in the yard, an explosion of drenched yellow and black fur. Panting hard, clearly distressed, she limped up to Fortune and butted him towards the window. Once there, she opened her great jaws and emitted a mournful howl, then glanced at Fortune.

'I think she wants me to tell you she's out!' called Fortune into the darkness. He could see nothing in the depths of the cell and guessed that Brace and the others were still crowded around the drinking pool. 'There must be a tunnel after all. I just hope you can all swim.'

After a breath or two Cumber's face bobbed up at the window, eyes wide with excitement. 'Of course!' he exclaimed, catching a horn on an overhanging parapet as he bounced up and down in glee. 'An underground escape route. Of course, if we still had a bit of charm around I'd have spotted it at once, but as it is I suppose we'll have to make do with . . .'

'Cumber,' smiled Fortune, 'just get on with it.'

'Hmm? Oh, yes, of course.'

As soon as his friend had disappeared again Fortune

turned back to Mokishi. The golden creature was shaking badly; her tail drooped and her flanks were heaving. But as he smiled at her she raised her head and uttered a single, soft purr. 'Are you all right?' he asked, and by way of reply the chitraka nuzzled him and prodded him back in the direction of the pool to await the arrival of his companions.

Ratchet was first to appear, floundering up out of the waterhole with a great show of effort, then one by one the others emerged in varying states of exhaustion.

'Phew!' announced Cumber with feeling as he, the last of the group, broke clear of the water and scrambled out on to the rough stone floor of the small yard. 'If I didn't know better I'd say that beast left a trail for us down there.'

The chitraka bowed her head and the dragons were left to guess at what she had really done for them. Only she knew the sacrifice she had made in the lightless depths of the flooded tunnel. The last shreds of charm she had been conserving in her heart, the shreds which tied her to what scant past she had with a forgotten family of magical creatures, those she had scattered in her wake as she swam, leaving a trail of sparks which the dragons, even more clumsy underwater than she, could follow to safety. The charm had been forgotten up to now, almost insignificant so weak was it, but at the last she had rediscovered it and found for it a use. Now that it was gone she felt drained and ready to sleep. Perhaps, soon, ready to die.

No regrets, ran the simple track of her thoughts. *I die free, and as a bringer of freedom to others. That is enough.*

'Thank you, er . . .' said Cumber, bending his head towards the chitraka.

'Mokishi,' prompted Velvet in a whisper so loud that it echoed around the yard and raised a chuckle or two from the group.

'Er, Mokishi, yes. Well, everyone, here we all are again. So what should we do next?'

There was a brief silence during which no dragon seemed keen to speak. Then all eyes turned to Fortune and he felt again something of the pressure he thought he had left behind on Haven. *They rely on me*, he mused, *but what have I left to give them?*

'For my part the answer is simple,' he sighed, 'and for the moment I can look no further ahead than this: I must find Aria. She and Gossamer are all that matter to me now; everything else must wait.'

'Agreed!' cheered Cumber, his enthusiastic good humour doing little to raise spirits in the thickening rain. The clear space which the river of charm had opened in the sky appeared to have closed up again, bringing with it not the fury of the storm but the dull oppression of constant drizzle. 'Now, Quill, where did you say you left Gossamer? And you, what did you say your name was?'

'V-Vox.'

'Yes, Vox – so, was it you or Quill who saw her last?'

Surprised at this sudden interrogation, Vox lurched forward clumsily. As he did so he trod inelegantly on Smoke's trailing wingtip, causing her to yelp with pain. 'Oh, I'm t-terribly s-sorry,' he stammered, self-consciously raising a wing as though to hide his shame.

'It's all right,' replied Smoke, hastily rubbing at the bruised membrane. 'Tell us, please – did you see where they went?'

'Into the tower,' he blurted, clearly uneasy. Dragons stared quizzically at him from all sides and it seemed to him momentarily that among the faces was Halcyon's, bearing down in judgement. But then the illusion faded and they were just dragons – no inquisition this, just ... *friends*? 'I thought I saw one of the t-towers stop in m-mid-air,' he went on. 'I think they w-went inside.'

'That's settled then,' put in Cumber swiftly. 'We take each tower in turn and search it from top to bottom. We're good flyers so we should be able to force our way in, even if they are speeding up and down like mad things, don't you think? Of course, if anybody disagrees then I'd welcome ...'

'But Archan said they were travelling through time, Cumber,' protested Velvet. 'Wouldn't it be dangerous?'

'Archan told us all many things.' Brace's voice cut through the air like a claw, silencing the others and bringing his stony expression to their immediate attention. 'First of all, Fortune, you are right, of course – we must find Gossamer and Aria. My niece,' he chuckled softly. 'But we cannot

249

trust *anything* this Archan has told us. She has misled us, imprisoned us – what else might she do to us in this evil place?

'I don't plan to make a speech – for which I'm sure you'll all be grateful – but please, I beg you, let's not forget our greater mission. Every breath we linger here the dragons of Aether's Cross are one step nearer to oblivion. Fortune – your task is clear, and we will help you all we can, but if time moves on and Aria is not found then I must move on too . . .'

Here Brace stopped. Lifting one, shaking claw to his eye he brushed a single tear on to its sharpened tip. He stared at it in surprise, then murmured, 'Well, well,' before concluding his speech. 'I don't say this lightly, Fortune, for Gossamer is dearer to me than any dragon, but if they are not found by tomorrow then I must go on. I made a vow and I cannot stop now. Please, do you understand?'

Brace's voice was taut now, choked with tears, and Fortune was painfully aware of the conflict he was bringing upon himself. Though his words were brave, his face seemed suddenly very young and Fortune was reminded of how young they all were, this little band of dragons which had already experienced so much. *And which is soon to be split again*, he thought with sudden premonition.

'Of course I understand, Brace,' he answered, touching the younger dragon's flank with his outstretched wing. 'But where will you go? If Archan does not know how to find Aether's Cross then who does?'

'I will find it,' came Brace's stubborn reply. 'There must be a way.'

Fortune noticed Vox watching Brace with strange intensity, but he was distracted by a coldness against his breastbone: the yard was slowly filling with rainwater.

'We'd better go then,' he sighed. He forced a smile. 'Any suggestions as to direction, Cumber?'

'Well, all things considered, weighing up all aspects of the predicament in which we find ourselves, and taking into account the underlying peril should we decide on a course of action which might . . .'

'Up it is then,' chuckled Fortune, and up they flew.

CHAPTER 23

Thaw and Aria

Thaw felt as though his mind had been released from a great clamp. Archan was gone from the Chamber of the World. Clouds roiled beneath him; through their shroud he could just make out the mighty river Term. He was hovering over the north-eastern segment of the basilisk map where the remnants of a storm passed over Termanderel, his home-land. Following the thread of the river, he saw that it reached down along the flank of the Spine to the new southern coast of what had once been the central Heartland. To the citadel.

This waterfall is the outpouring of my past, he marvelled, *and these are the very waters in which I sported in my youth. Were I to journey upstream from the falls I would find my home. But can I bear to leave this place now? Can I bear to leave . . . her?*

The dilemma was agonizing, for he knew only misery and horror would result were he to stay. Yet Archan ruled him so – he *loved* her so, though he knew she was a monster. But could monsters not be changed? Perhaps he could help her to become a dragon of true worth and nobility . . . if he had the whole of eternity.

Ah, eternity. Now there *is a reason to stay!*

Though the debate went on in his mind and in his heart, Thaw knew that he could never leave. The endless span of immortality stretched out before him like a visible stream of light and he knew that its siren call was too tantalizing to be ignored.

Eternity, then. With her.

Thaw had never before known the security of love. Ever a

dragon of action he had always led others, never worshipped them. Inevitably couples had met and paired in the many and varied groups of dragons he had commanded over the years, from the informal youth tribes with whom he had charted the river to the now-decimated colony of Haven, but he had always remained aloof. Not for Thaw the distractions of desire; in such things he saw only disorder.

But Archan had changed him. Here was a dragon with true power, and an ambition to match his own beat for beat. Here was a dragon who flouted traditional notions of beauty and created an elegance of a kind never before seen. Her slender, white form filled his heart as her aroma filled his senses. As for his own feelings ... where once he had thought of love as merely a contrivance of lust and confusion, now he perceived it as a mighty force, a pattern of feeling so complex yet so *ordered*. For Thaw now, love was destiny – the two concepts were inseparable. Archan was his future, and the future would never end.

Soon she will return! The thought was intoxicating. *I must be ready for her!*

Thaw glanced around, seeking a place where he might await his new partner for, though they had not yet consummated their relationship, the pairing was unshakeable. Rain blew in through the ragged space left when the storm had torn away the roof; now the chamber's dome ended halfway up its curve in a line of broken mosaics and shattered stone. Thaw regarded the inner skin of the dome, marked with thousands of tiny, white motes which glinted even through the drizzle. He remembered the dying night dragons, the stars which had fallen to earth, and found himself mourning charm. *But there will be charm again*, he determined. *How many Turnings might an immortal see?*

Eventually he selected a platform of dressed stone protruding from the far side of the map pedestal. He landed lightly, preening his wing membranes in the glossy reflection thrown up by the polished surface and admiring the lighter stripes which spanned his underbelly. He had to look his best for when his queen returned. Presently he heard wingbeats high in the sky outside the chamber – evidently she planned to enter through the open roof. Opening his wings wide he lifted his eyes to the heavens, his heart bursting with new love.

For Aria the short flight across to the chamber from the tower was a revelation, for of all the new sensations which crashed against her the one which struck with most power was simple perception. Myopic infant eyes were opened to a world thrown into dizzying focus. Light poured across her like living energy, illuminating all she saw: sky, cloud, wall, window, dragon wing, the sparkle of distant charm – all these things, for the first time, she *saw*.

She wept, marvelling and wondering, innocent to all but the sheer beauty swelling up around her. Smiling with ridiculous candour at Archan she flexed her wings wide and swooped drunkenly to the side, practising the skills of flight which she had never actually learned, yet which filled her body as though they had always been there. She breathed deep, revelling in the speed of the air in her lungs; she bit at her tongue, savouring the metallic taste of blood. All at once sensual and aware, she began to absorb the world around her in a frenzy of aerobatics. Songs began to spill from her mouth. Rejoicing in her new life, she cavorted and cried out for the simple joy of being.

Suddenly aware that Archan was watching her she halted abruptly, pounding the air with her long, sleek wings and panting hard. 'What is it?' she blurted, the words strange in her mouth. 'Do I go too far?'

Archan offered her a thin smile and advised, 'Your reaction is to be expected, however, you might . . . restrain yourself a little, given whom you are about to meet.'

To meet someone! Another dragon? Her mother again?

Pulling herself into loose formation with her new mentor, Aria dipped her head by way of apology and then giggled. When Archan coughed her disapproval she straightened her face and followed the exotic creature up and over the broken crown of the Chamber of the World.

Thaw jumped when he saw two dragons appear from behind the broken parapet. There was Archan, his sinuous love . . . and another dragon, a dark-scaled stranger with the longest

253

tail he had ever seen, and a face not pretty yet made beautiful by the exuberant expression it bore.

As Thaw watched Aria descend, Archan lowered herself through the air behind him, a look of intense concentration distorting her normally smooth features. Confused – and a little disturbed – by Aria's unexpected presence – Thaw was quite unaware of the charm Archan was beginning to dredge from the pores of the map, dark charm from the deeper spaces where even the basilisks had rarely ventured. Primal charm this was, too old to join the river in the sky and deformed now by the immense age which pressed upon it. It was never meant to be raised from its virtual grave but raise it Archan did, binding it into a spell which she caressed with her wingtips until it took on a hot and glowing life of its own. Livid orange light fired the undersides of her wings, lifting her physically into the air again and thrusting her forward towards where Thaw stood trembling on the platform he had chosen.

The perfect place, thought Archan coldly as she assessed Aria's position over the map. *Perfect!*

Thaw saw Aria's expression change from one of innocent curiosity to one of wide-eyed wonder as she looked past his shoulder at Archan, but even then he did not look round. Had he done so he might have saved himself – and Aria – but he was enraged by this unwelcome intrusion. Rational thought was wholly gone from his mind; all he knew was that a second dragon had trespassed upon his territory at the most crucial of moments. That Archan herself had brought the stranger here he did not even register.

Then the charm bit into him.

Fire burst against his flanks, racing up his tail and sinking flaming fangs into his hind legs. Up his belly it sped, devouring his wings and forelimbs and spreading across his neck and face until it covered his entire body. Orange agony thrust spikes deep into his flesh and as he opened his mouth to scream it poured down his throat. Crawling over his skin and scales like an army of blazing worms, the fire converged upon his screaming mouth and emptied itself into him. An eyeblink later the pain was gone and he snapped his mouth shut. Flames growled deep inside him.

Aria watched this not with horror but with fascination. Her experience was so limited that she had no way of assessing the merit of anything she observed. As the fire seemed momentarily to consume Thaw she smiled, for she had never seen anything so pretty. Then the fire was gone from the outside of his body, only to reappear within. Behind his eyes.

Thaw advanced on Aria, stepping out across the miniature world, his claws skating on the repelling charm which coated the basilisk map. Aria cocked her head to one side, dropping lower and lower as she hovered. The flames licked out from Thaw's eye sockets, lean and orange, delighting her with their ever-changing dance. Closer he drew and she laughed, for as he leered at her the fire spilled from his jaws again. It spread over the map's invisible protection to form a cocoon which rose up behind her, cutting off her retreat. Not that she wanted to retreat, for she was spellbound.

Thaw drew nearer. Now the heat given off from his eyes began to blister the sensitive skin on the underside of Aria's throat. The pain was another novelty, but one which sent her scurrying backwards, cycling her wings over the map in sudden retreat. Thaw's mouth belched orange fire and he lunged.

Aria's long tail dragged against the map's coating of charm and sent a shower of angry sparks exploding into the air. Her wingbeats faltered and she hovered clumsily before the advancing Thaw, dropping still lower as he narrowed the distance between them. Charm snaked from his out-reaching claws and grappled with her tail, binding it with stinging fire and holding her fast before his advance. Pain turned to another new sensation – fear. Thaw's eyes glowed white.

Aria's fear became panic. Thaw's wings unfurled right in front of her, blanketing the sky and killing the light. Bars of shadow flickered across her upraised eyes as he loomed over her, the jerk of charm from his claws locking her tail to the map so that she was pinned there, wings flailing, spinning helplessly while he enfolded her. With an agonizing thump his body struck hers. Then the real agony began.

* * *

Archan looked on as Thaw's wings collapsed around his prey. What little she could sense still of his mind was a torrent of pain. Fired by his anger but ultimately driven by the charm she had invoked he had abandoned all reason and descended into a pit of blackness even she could not conceive. As the two dragons writhed in the air, the horror of the attack largely hidden by Thaw's cloaking wings, Aria's tail remained fixed in the bed of charm so that they spun round and round like a clot of leaves caught in a whirlpool.

Aria's plaintive moans Archan found it easy to ignore; not so Thaw's grunting. Despite everything, despite the sure knowledge that this was right, that this was the one, true way for her to meet her ultimate destiny, she found that she was jealous of the new-grown infant.

Jealous! she thought angrily. *I shall not let it be so! Thaw is useful – nothing more. It is his offspring I shall truly love.* There *shall be my destiny, not here.*

But it was hard to remain aloof, for part of her *did* desire Thaw and was ill-pleased that Aria should have gained his attentions, however unnaturally. And that part was powerful enough to rob her of any pleasure she might otherwise have gained at witnessing this atrocity. As the appalling violation was played out before her, she found that she was sickened, not at the act itself but at the animal nature of her own feelings towards Thaw. *If this is love*, she thought suddenly. *Perhaps I am better off on my own. Have I not survived this far?*

Then she thought of the basilisks and of the lessons they taught about eternity, for even they had craved the companionship of fellow immortals, if only from time to time. She could not remain solitary forever; this way had to be the right way, however much pain it may cause her now.

Resolved, yet racked with unexpected fury, Archan looked down as Thaw concluded his assault and fell away from Aria. He opened his wings wide and lifted himself up to the cracked perimeter of the open roof where he alighted, perching amid the rubble. The fire dying, he rested his smoking body, apparently devoid of emotion, leaving his victim limp and suspended against gravity by the network of charm laced around her body. Bruises covered her breast and flanks and blood traced a thin line from her mouth. Her belly seemed to glow, as though the fire had entered her. Her eyes were open and glazed over.

Turning her attention only briefly to Thaw, Archan glided over the hissing lake of charm and lashed her tail against Aria's. With a curious splashing sound the charm which still bonded the tip of the young dragon's tail to the map separated and her limp body floated free. Archan sent a pulse of basilisk magic into Aria's body, probing for what she hoped was there.

Archan rarely made mistakes. Acutely attentive to the world around her, she made up for her lack of normal vision by honing her other senses – both charmed and natural – to an unparalleled degree. Few dragons ever crept up on Archan. But Gossamer did.

She appeared on the skyline behind Thaw, landing some distance from the ex-Charmed warrior with her usual lightness of touch. Belatedly, Archan swung round and analysed her with her many senses; she found her full of wrath yet weak. A poor adversary and certainly one quite incapable of hindering her escape. She contemplated the situation – should she kill her too, instead of just Thaw?

Then she heard the wingbeats. The other dragons, still far below the Chamber of the World but approaching fast. How had they freed themselves from the dungeon? But there was no time to wonder. There was no time now for anything but flight.

Before Gossamer could begin to assess the situation Archan had extended her sinuous tail and wrapped a dozen powerful coils around Aria. Filling her wings she rose steadily up through the massive hole in the roof, pausing when she was level with Thaw.

'Your visit has been worthwhile,' she said to him, her voice a dreadful taunt. 'But I do not know what your friends will make of your . . . actions.' Then looking across to Gossamer she called, 'And as for your daughter, she has proved useful, too. Perhaps you may reclaim her one day. If you can find her.'

No sooner had she said this than Archan inflated her

wings to what seemed an impossible degree and shot straight upwards into the sky. Two faint lines of charm stabbed down towards Thaw as she ascended, but Gossamer did not see them fall. Climbing vertically, Archan parted the clouds until she was a tiny speck against the wavering line of the river of charm. Then . . . then she struck the river and grew bright, a night dragon born in the brilliance of day whose light exploded and then accelerated north along the line of charm, arrowing into the distance and vanishing before even a single breath could be drawn.

Then Fortune came, rising up behind Gossamer and falling upon her with relief and also grief. They were swiftly joined by Cumber and the others. The reunion of Brace with his sister was agonizing as the incredible truth about what had happened to Aria in the tower became clear; there was only horror to share, no tears of joy. Gossamer could not know what had happened to Aria here in the Chamber, even though there was an appalling suspicion swelling in her heart. She glanced across at Thaw . . . but Thaw had gone.

Around the broken rim of the curved walls the dragons gathered, all happiness at their escape from Archan's prison quite gone when they learned of the magnitude of the challenge they now faced. For not only were they still charged with finding the mountain pass of Aether's Cross, though the mountains themselves no longer existed, but now there was an innocent dragon to be rescued from the claws of a monster. And where Archan had taken Aria none of them could guess.

CHAPTER 24

The Map

The over-reaching curves of the chamber sheltered the resting dragons and offered them protection from the night, if not from the horror of their dreams. The black of the night was a welcome void into which Fortune hurled his screaming heart. It was as though the chaos brought by the storm had infiltrated his pores and the cracks between his scales, creating turmoil within. The stars were hard and distant and offered him no help; he did not know where to turn.

Gossamer had told him all she had seen, right up to the moment when Archan and Aria had vanished into the river of charm. She had not seen what happened in the ruined chamber before Archan and Aria fled, but she harboured the gravest suspicions, especially about Thaw's part in it. More than that she would not say, not yet.

Her account of Aria's trials centred on her experience inside the frozen tower. Fortune listened agog as Gossamer described the whirlpool of energy which had surrounded their daughter, and he comforted her when she wept over what she perceived as her own inadequacies.

'I did nothing, Fortune. Our poor Aria – while I just looked on.'

'Hush, my darling,' he soothed, hugging her so tightly that he thought he would suffocate them both. 'There was nothing you or any other dragon could have done.'

Gossamer's vivid account chilled Fortune's blood. She spoke of the helplessness of the tiny dragon infant, of the glimpses she had caught of Aria's body stretching and growing under the spell of the captured time-stream.

'She is *grown*, Fortune. This monster, this Archan has stolen our daughter's infancy from her!'

It was a crime which Fortune could scarcely comprehend, so unjust was it, so *incredible*. What dreadful scheme could Archan possibly have been implementing – or did she do it to satisfy some appalling desire to subvert the natural order? This latter notion he rejected, for Cumber's analysis of Archan's character suggested to him that she was anything but an arbitrary worker of evil. That she *was* evil he had no doubt, but she surely worked to a plan, a logic of which only her own twisted mind was aware.

But where is the order to her actions? he thought hopelessly as he scanned the unsympathetic sky. *Where is an end to the chaos?*

The stars did not reply, they simply rippled and dimmed behind the endless trail of charm that raced ever northwards.

He did not sleep, not properly, experiencing instead an intermediate dream-state in which he wandered through the turbulent airspace around the dancing towers. Ahead – always ahead – bobbed Aria, constantly out of reach and taunting him with a song in a language he did not understand. Each time she appeared from behind the oscillating towers she had changed: now she was an infant, now full-grown, now ancient and wrinkled. One time she seemed nothing but bone, a dragon skeleton cackling at him through a veil of fog. Later the visions left him and he passed the rest of the night in an emotionless limbo, hearing nothing, seeing nothing, feeling . . . nothing.

Dawn brought new dampness to the miserable surroundings of the broken Chamber of the World. The drizzle had stopped during the night but as the sun rose the sky turned steely grey and mist billowed up from the falls; everywhere there was moisture.

At the first hint of grey light three dragons gathered beside the basilisk map. Each confessed to having been shocked from sleep by a voice uttering words none could recall. They were Tallow and Vox and Smoke.

'I feel uncomfortable here,' confessed Tallow, his deep voice slow and methodical. 'There is more charm than I care to consider.'

'I too,' yawned Smoke. 'Charm is pain to me, Tallow. My distress is more real than you can know.'

Vox nodded wisely, for he too knew the association of magic with pain. 'What are we to do?' he whispered, glancing out into the shadows where, as far as he knew, the rest of their company slept still.

'Fortune and Gossamer need our help most now,' suggested Tallow, 'yet Aether's Cross still lies buried. Alas, even my skills cannot find a way forward.'

At this Smoke turned, more alert now and appraising Tallow with cool eyes. 'I navigate too, Tallow,' she said. 'But I feel that the answer still lies with Archan. Tell us what you know about her. You have said little of your own capture. Perhaps there is something we may learn.'

'There is little enough,' said the big dragon slowly. 'As Brace himself has told you, we were easily tricked, much as you were. Archan spent much charm in ensuring our capture was speedy. Were it not for your arrival we would have perished here.'

'Hmm,' mused Smoke, looking around. 'It was from this chamber that she finally consigned us to the dungeon. Where were you taken, Tallow?'

'Here also.'

Smoke nodded, unsurprised. Vox listened intently as the two dragons spoke, the conversation a steady exchange of concise statements, an economy of language he welcomed. A dragon of few words himself, especially during and since his ten years as an outcast, he found himself growing comfortable in the presence of these two great navigators. And as he grew comfortable he found himself thinking. Thinking hard.

'Forgive me,' he said, interrupting their talk. 'But s-something has just occurred to me.'

'Speak, dragon,' responded Smoke with a smile which Vox, unused to kindness, found almost overwhelming.

'W-well,' he stammered, 'everything seems to come back to this chamber. And I was thinking about the tunnels we went through between Sharp and Haven. They weren't like any tunnels I've been in before.'

'Made by charm?' suggested Smoke. She, like Tallow, had heard briefly of the trials of Fortune's group on the islands during the storm, but the details were new to them both.

'If they were, it wasn't like any charm I've ever encountered. It certainly was not dragon charm.'

'Basilisk?' suggested Smoke cautiously, casting a wary glance at the map which huddled at their backs. She had a sudden sensation that it was listening to them. But Vox shook his head vigorously.

'No,' he affirmed. '*That* charm I can taste now – it's in the air all around us. No, this was d-different. And I don't think the t-tunnels were made at all, not in the way you or I would make them. They weren't dug – they g-grew.'

'Grew?' asked Tallow suspiciously. He, like most natural dragons, was uncomfortable with the idea of caves and tunnels. A dragon of the sky, he associated the underworld with magic and ritual, and fear.

'Well,' sighed Smoke, 'be that as it may, we still aren't getting any nearer to a plan.'

'B-but I think we are,' interjected Vox, his eyes growing wide as he scanned the interior of the chamber. 'I think it all f-fits together somehow – we just need to work out how.'

'But it's all such a mess,' lamented Smoke.

'No, it isn't. S-somewhere in here is the answer, all the answers, laid out as clear as anything for us to . . .' Vox broke off, opening his wings and pulling back his neck. He looked as though he had just been slapped. 'Of course,' he breathed. 'Of *course*. It's right here!'

'What's here?' rumbled Tallow, glancing hopefully at Smoke.

Vox did not reply, simply bounded forward and glided up on to the lip of the map. His claws contacted the perimeter of the protective charm and were instantly cloaked in a gentle filigree of magic, crackling blue and green in the dim, grey light. Then he turned and said,

'The whole world is here. Literally. Anything we care to find is *here*. We need only discover how to look!'

Tallow and Smoke, the greatest of dragon navigators,

exchanged a meaningful look and said as one, 'All right. Where do we start?'

Fortune was the last to rise. As he left the shadowy cleft in which he and Gossamer had passed the night he saw all his friends gathered near the great basilisk map. Dull light echoed through the chamber, although it seemed to Fortune as he approached that the surface of the map was aglow, radiating a faint, blue-green light into the cloying mist. When he joined Gossamer at the periphery of the group he saw that this was indeed so – there was charm at work here.

'What is it?' he demanded.

'Aria,' Gossamer replied defiantly, as if daring him to contradict her. 'They think we might be able to get her back.'

With a rush of air Vox flew back from the shadows of the far perimeter of the chamber. The grey light dulled the shocking purple of his scales and skin and Fortune remarked how . . . normal he looked. His eyes were bright and glistening with both excitement and exertion.

'It's beginning to make sense,' he announced enthusiastically. 'All we need to do now is find the trigger points for the different levels.'

'What's going on?' whispered Fortune to Gossamer. In her expression he saw the same, granite anxiety he carried inside his own heart, a block of despair that made every thought an effort, every word an ordeal. But she, as did he, forced herself to go on. And behind the block . . . a shred of hope?

'Last night I thought all was lost,' she explained quickly, her voice low and anxious, pitched for his ears only. 'Everything was gone – Aria, the Cross, all hope for ourselves and our kind, although I'm ashamed to say I shall care nothing for this wretched dragon race of ours if I don't find Aria again. But these dear friends – I think perhaps they've found something.

'It's the map, Fortune. Vox and Smoke – and Tallow as well – have been examining it very closely. Apparently it mimics the real world precisely, even down to the weather. To all intents and purposes it *is* the world.'

'But how can that . . . ?' interrupted Fortune.

'Ssh, listen. On the face of it, very little. But Vox thinks the map has many layers. It doesn't just show the surface. He thinks the map must know where Aether's Cross is, if only we can find the spell which will release the information.'

'Spell? How can we work charm when . . .'

'Oh, can't you feel it, Fortune?' blurted Gossamer, a fragment of her former gaiety shining through her bleakness. 'This place is *buzzing* with magic!'

'Hmm. And Aria?'

'She's here too, I'm sure of it. And it's all connected, Fortune. Aria, the Cross, there *is* a pattern.'

At that moment Vox cried out, his voice ringing off the bed of charm and resounding about the circular chamber. 'I think I've got something!'

He was hovering over the southern part of the map, a great sea laid out beneath him in azure splendour. The dragons clustered around the nearest point on the map's circumference, hopping and straining to see what it was he had located.

'I can't see anything,' grumbled Cumber, shouldering his way to the front.

'Stay where you are, Cumber,' called Vox, his gaze intently fixed on a point in the ocean directly beneath him, his occasional stammer quite forgotten. 'I shall need you in a moment, but it's not here we should look . . .' and he pointed with his outstretched tail to the curved chamber wall, '. . . it's over there.'

There on the crystalline wall was a dark shape. It looked like a shadow which might have been cast by a dragon's head, but nothing projected from the wall to cast it. Cumber turned to speak to Vox, but just before he opened his mouth he realized that he was standing next to Fortune.

'My dear friend!' he gasped, as though he had not seen Fortune for an eternity. 'I'm so pleased to see you with us. Velvet said to let you sleep, and then Gossamer woke and she said the same, but even then I wanted to come over and tell you how sorry . . . I mean to say, how much I want to tell you . . . I . . . oh dear, what in the sky are we to . . .'

'It's all right,' smiled Fortune, touched by his friend's obvious distress. 'The best way you can comfort me is by helping Vox in whatever it is he's up to. I'm fresh out of energy at the moment, I'm afraid.'

'Yes, yes, of course, old fellow.' Cumber's eyes shone as he jumped forward and called to Vox, 'I say, er . . .'

'It's Vox, you fool!' hissed Velvet, suddenly appearing at her mate's side. She flashed Fortune a dazzling smile then butted him gently on the chest. 'It's going to be all right, Fortune,' she said eagerly. 'Really it is.'

Tell Gossamer, he thought suddenly, seeing the grimness slowly leaching back into her face, recognizing the troubled set of her wings.

'Vox – of course,' continued Cumber. 'Well, dragon, how do you think we should tackle this dilemma? Are you thinking what I'm thinking?'

'About that shadow?' Vox replied. 'Yes. I saw something like it once before, years ago when I was in Covamere. It was in a deep tunnel. I was exploring. Guards found me in the end but I was young and they let me go. It was a forbidden area, you see.'

Brows were raised as Vox spoke. Clearly there was much more to this dragon than first met the eye. His reputation as a murderer had all but died within the group for, having met him and talked with him, none could believe him capable of such an act. But the mysteries of his past would have to wait, for he was speaking further.

'I know now that I must have been very near the place where the basilisk was sleeping. The basilisk you met, Fortune, in the Maze. I could feel the charm – not so much strong as . . . *particular* – but I was young and foolish and it didn't scare me. Anyway, the guards found me before I could stray any nearer. I don't think they knew what was there.

'But I saw something just as I was being led away. It was sticking out of the wall just above me. It was a carving, a creature's head. A basilisk's head. And it cast the same shadow as is on that wall over there.'

'But there's nothing there to cast a shadow,' piped Velvet, her voice thin and nervous in the ensuing silence.

'Nonsense,' blustered Cumber, taking the lead. Vox,

continuing to hover over the map, nodded to the young ex-Charmed.

'Go on, Cumber,' he urged. 'You know what to do.'

And to his surprise, Cumber found that he did. Suddenly he was aware of the thickness of the air in the chamber. For the first time since the Turning he felt something of the old feeling, the feeling he had experienced when he had used the Realm to draw fire charm into the world. Though the charm was gone from his own mind and body, the magic of the basilisks lingered here with prodigious power. And he knew that he could tap into it.

Approaching the strange shadow with deliberate caution, he opened his mind to the possibility that there *was* something there. *It exists*, he thought calmly. *If only I can find out how to see it.* Half-closing his eyes lessened the distraction of the surrounding wall; now only the shadow itself occupied his attention. Without realizing it he crouched slightly, spreading his wings as though performing a slow and intricate dance. He held his breath. *There?*

He began to see something wavering before his straining eyes, a vague form rippling as though seen through a heat haze. When he tipped his head to the side it vanished. There! Settling his gaze he found the object again and advanced slowly. It grew more clearly defined, a silvery projection reaching out towards him with gaping mouth. He had only to deviate a fraction of a claw's width from the correct path for the thing to vanish altogether, but he managed to keep his course true and came closer and closer until it was practically touching the end of his snout. Taking a deep breath he extended his neck and tapped it softly.

There was a sighing sound underneath the map. Vox rose a little into the air, uncertain what would happen, ready to bolt if necessary. The sigh became a hum, then a loud drone which suddenly cut off. Then the skin of charm protecting the map's surface began to melt away, splitting first into six part-circles before gathering at points on the perimeter. Six pale nuggets of glowing charm separated themselves from the raised platform and floated out to the boundary of the chamber. One struck the wall just above Cumber's head and as it did so the air opened with an audible pop, just as it did at five corresponding points around the chamber. At last the hidden object was fully revealed and it was, as Vox had predicted, a sculpted basilisk head, thrusting clear of the dark stone and staring across at its five siblings which were now uncloaked, spaced at equal distances around the chamber. Bleak and silvery, each was unique; clearly here were the likenesses of the Deathless.

The dragons gasped. Each of them, even the Naturals, could feel the release of massive charges of magic. Their awe was not so much at the power itself but at the obvious control under which it had been placed. *But is it really any wonder?* thought Fortune as he tasted the charm in the damp air. *Here they have modelled the world, and to do so must take strength indeed.*

'Now we can really get to work!' cried Vox triumphantly as Cumber stepped back proudly from the statue he had uncovered. 'What shall we look for first?'

There was a flurry of activity then, for while some of the dragons were still confused, most understood at least in principle what Vox wanted to do. Fortune found himself content to let others do the work for the moment, and so he retreated with Gossamer and Velvet to where Cumber was lounging beneath the basilisk's head.

'Quite impressive, if I do say so myself,' Cumber was saying nonchalantly. 'Of course, I know I've never been a great fan of charm but it can have a certain elegance, even I must admit, on occasion.'

'That's quite enough, Cumber,' snapped Velvet. 'Think about our poor friends for a moment, please. Remember what they've been through.'

'No, Velvet, it's all right,' soothed Gossamer, though her face remained sad and distant. 'Let's just see what our pathfinders can do.'

'But that's just it,' moaned Velvet. 'What *are* they doing?'

'Cumber?' prompted Fortune. He too was curious, for while he sensed that the spirit of adventure which had seized the group was good he was unsure where it would ultimately lead. If indeed it would lead anywhere.

'You're sceptical, Fortune, that much I can see,' grinned his white-scaled friend, 'but let me reassure you, old fellow.

You see, we believe that this map, just like the real world – has many layers. I mean, the basilisks are perceptive far beyond anything we can comprehend, so if they were going to make a model of the world it follows that they would build in far more detail than we could ever conceive.'

'I suppose so.'

'I know so. Now, we all know that time has been made to play some rather peculiar tricks around here – you more so than most I'm afraid to say. But now we might be able to work that to our advantage.'

'Cumber,' sighed Velvet. 'What are you talking about?'

'Just listen and I'll tell you,' groaned Cumber. 'My dear,' he added when he caught sight of Velvet's withering glare. 'Look, currently the map is set to reflect the world as it is in the present – what we see on the map is actually happening outside. But the basilisks would not be content with that. They have lived forever, if we can imagine such a thing – and I for one can't imagine a worse nightmare than the whole of eternity stretching out ahead of me, and behind me for that matter – but anyway, they would surely have constructed the map in such a way that it might also show the past. Maybe even the future too, if we could find out how.'

'You think we can turn time backwards on the map?' said Fortune slowly.

'Yes.'

'So it will show us what the world used to be like? Yesterday, for instance? Or even before the Turning?'

'Yes.'

'But I still don't see . . .' protested Velvet.

'I do,' smiled Fortune. 'If we can configure the map to the time just before Aether's Cross was destroyed, we'll be able to see where the Cross used to be – where we all remember it being. Then we can watch what happens to the land between that time and the present. We should be able to track Aether's Cross to the precise point on the world where it is now!'

'Brilliant!' exclaimed Cumber.

'And what about Aria?' said Gossamer in a small, dull voice.

Fortune turned to her with anguish on his face but before he could speak Vox called to them.

'Come here, all of you. It's even easier than I'd hoped!' The four dragons trooped over to join their companions. The group had divided into two parts – Vox, Tallow and Smoke were hovering over the central part of the map while the others were crowded on the lip of the mighty pedestal. 'Join us,' added Vox, speaking directly to Fortune. Gossamer joined her mate in the air as he flew across the miniature seas to join the pathfinders.

'I'm working charm,' warned Vox, and when Fortune looked he saw the faintest bands of light emanating from the six basilisk heads. They converged on Vox, painting his purple hide with the subtlest of rainbow colours. 'The controls are difficult, and I can deduce only the crudest of them, but I think I can do it. Watch.'

Looking down, Fortune gasped. This was the first time he had really looked at the map and he was unprepared for the sheer realism of the spectacle. Below him was the world! If he ignored the shadowy chamber which encroached at the limits of his vision he could imagine himself flying thousands of trees' height above the land and sea, his wings gripping air impossibly thin and carrying him higher than any dragon could truly fly. Directly below was a huge cloud of dark soot, a stain of ash which covered a continent and cast an immense shadow across the surrounding oceans. As he watched he saw that it was shrinking, receding towards a single point as though being sucked into nonexistence.

'Time is running backwards now,' breathed Vox, concentrating as he manipulated the tenuous charm which he had drawn from the basilisk statues. 'You are watching the eruption of the Plated Mountain. You are witness again to the turning of the world.'

Fortune's breath lodged in his throat as the pall of ash and smoke accelerated towards its source. The cloud grew tiny, travelling faster until it disappeared. A great flash of light crashed against his eyes and briefly he saw the mountain opened like an enormous wound. Then, with incredible speed, the wound healed, the light died and storm clouds bubbled, themselves shrinking and racing away eastwards.

Night and day flickered beneath them, fog gave way to cloud and sun and time moved further back towards younger times.

'Look further north.' Gossamer's voice broke the hypnotic state into which Fortune had fallen. Jolting himself he looked away from the Plated Mountain and across the plains of the central Heartland. There was Heldwater, peaceful lake where Cumber had fallen prey to Realmshock, there were the foothills of the Low Mountains. *These lands no longer exist*, he thought with amazement.

The hills rose into mountain peaks, separated by a single pass, the mighty gorge which once the troll lord Aether had carved through the mountains. Steep-sided, breathtaking so deep was it, the canyon wound its way back into the heart of the mountains, narrowing until it flared out into the one wide space in all its track. Aether's Cross.

'My home,' murmured Gossamer. Wind buffeted her wings. She looked around to see Brace hovering at her side.

'There it is,' he said. 'Now. Now we'll see. Vox?'

Vox nodded. He had taken the map back to a time shortly before the earthquake had closed the Cross. Now he flexed the strands of charm so that they pulled the miniature world forwards again, slowly, very slowly.

Tremors shook the Low Mountains. The watching dragons fancied they could hear the rumble of rock upon rock, but none could be sure. Avalanches splashed white across the upper slopes and then, suddenly, the gorge began to pinch itself shut. Cliff walls clashed together like jaws and with dreadful ease the canyon of the Cross disappeared from view.

'Watch closely now,' muttered Vox, unable to look himself so intent was he upon his delicate task. He accelerated past the instant of the Turning and then slowed again, focusing on the days just gone, when the whole world had folded.

Nothing happened for a breath or two, then the entire continent of the Heartland jerked as though struck a titanic blow from beneath. Storm clouds raced, moving with unnatural speed and emptying a deluge upon the land. Between their fleeting shapes the dragons saw mountains buckle under their own weight, saw seas drained from below, saw the Heartland consumed as if by an unseen predator.

Saw the Cross dragged deep underground.

'There!' exclaimed Brace. 'Stop it there!' Vox complied, arresting the flow of time so that the map was temporarily frozen. 'Can we see underground?'

'I think so.' Frowning, Vox investigated one of the strands of charm he had not yet wielded and found the trigger he sought. Abruptly the nature of the map changed: although the land remained in place it became translucent, enabling the dragons to see far into its depths. After a brief search they found the distinctive shapes of the Cross tunnels. They were indeed buried, the corridors of a prison itself taken captive.

'When is this?' barked Brace, making a half-turn in the air and straining his eyes in an attempt to improve his view. He was fascinated – there was the swell of the Great Chamber, there the intricate lattice of Wraith's cells, each cavity in the rock visible like a bubble in ice.

'This is now,' replied Vox. 'This is where Aether's Cross is right now.'

'But *where* is it?'

There was a series of gasps as the truth of the situation dawned upon each of them in turn. There was the Cross, and there, above it, were the complex curves of the basilisk citadel. It was *here*. Directly beneath them and locked forever in impenetrable stone, Aether's Cross was imprisoned a thousand trees deep beneath the citadel of the basilisks.

It was utterly unreachable.

'It can't be,' cried Brace. 'It can't be true!'

Gossamer wept, and pushed Fortune roughly away when he tried to comfort her. They tussled awkwardly in the air until they finally fell away together, landing on the far side of the map. Fortune held her close, but though she sobbed into his wings she did not yield to his embrace. At that moment he felt that she was further away from him than she had ever been. Looking up he opened his mouth to bellow a great lament into the sky, but stopped short when he saw yellow and black striped wings opened across the gaping roof space.

CHAPTER 25

The Way to the Cross

Like Fortune's, Thaw's world had turned dark. But whereas Fortune's darkness was one of the spirit, Thaw's very eyes had been burned from their sockets by the fire which Archan had thrown at him. He was blind. He was a shadow of her now, a lost victim of her dreadful love, eyeless like she but without the depth of charm which lent her the miracle of sight.

He felt the wrench as she left the chamber, felt the heart torn from him. In that single breath as his sight was destroyed, his last moment of vision was of her creamy wings opening wide into the heavens . . . to take away not him but Aria, wrapped in her sinuous tail. In that instant he saw his future. Not for Thaw the endless panorama of eternity, not for Thaw the great search for order he had dreamed of. Now only mortality remained. She had rejected him and left him blind in punishment for his crime.

What have I done! he thought wretchedly as he let himself fall heedlessly from the shattered roof of the chamber. But though his thoughts raced wildly across this territory of despair he faltered at the final edge of self-destruction and his wings beat to break his fall. Finding himself at the very base of the waterfall, deafened by thundering spray, still he could not bring himself to cast his body into the torrent. Here the rocks were raw and ready, he knew, and had he entered the stream he would surely have been dashed to a thousand pieces . . . but something held him back.

That night he stumbled aimlessly between the intricate ramparts of the citadel, guided only by the rush of air and scent of water. His thoughts would not settle – each time he tried to consider the future his inner eye (its power of vision still horribly vivid) reminded him of his unspeakable violation of Aria. Nothing would erase the sight of her struggle nor the sound of her pleas, and as the night crawled by he embraced ever more tightly the mortality he now knew was his. *At least I may die*, he thought. *That way I can be free*.

Then the knowledge came to him: he could not die yet, though he wanted to. *But first I must help them*.

Thaw spent the rest of the night beneath the cataract, growing cold in the mist and sleeping not at all. When instinct informed him that morning had come, he lifted his wings and headed back for the Chamber of the World, its charm guiding his sightless flight.

Gossamer was first to respond to Thaw's entrance. Accelerating up to where he hovered over the assembled dragons, and pausing for not a single breath, she battered her wings ferociously against his yellow and black scales. But he weathered unresisting the great storm of blows she unleashed.

'What have you done?' she wailed. 'What did you do in here, you monster?! Look where you've brought us all! Where is our hope now? I'll tell you – it's buried beneath the ground with what's left of my home! What have you done, Thaw?'

As her blows rained across his hide, Thaw held his position and lowered his head until Fortune and Cumber between them managed to wrestle the distraught Gossamer away. Leaving Fortune to console her as best he could, Cumber took up station next to the great, striped warrior, a frown set upon his face.

'What brings you back here, Thaw?' he demanded. He winced as he looked into the blackened sockets where once the eyes of his former companion had shone. He cast his gaze across Thaw's scorched body. Despite all that Thaw had done against them, still he pitied him. 'Tell us you were bewitched,' he whispered, desperate to believe that Archan had worked magic upon him.

'Whatever charm Archan may have held over me, I offer

no excuses for what I have done,' replied Thaw, his voice loud enough for all to hear. 'I have come now because I believe I might help you in your quest. You may listen to me or not, as you choose.'

'Why should we listen to you?' blurted Velvet, her normally forgiving nature clouded by her deep-rooted suspicion of Thaw. A glance at the weeping Gossamer served only to strengthen her dislike of the warrior.

'Because I have already studied the map, and I know some of its secrets.' This silenced Velvet's protests, for she knew as well as the others the importance of the basilisk map to their quest.

'We have already found Aether's Cross,' called Vox, the charm he had been wielding over the map temporarily suspended. 'We cannot reach it. What more is there to know?'

'You have done well, dragon,' replied Thaw. 'But you have not looked deep enough.'

'What do you mean?'

'No way to reach the Cross, you say?' Thaw smiled, a black leer which revealed the remains of shattered teeth. 'Ah, but you are wrong, dragon. There is one way you may reach it. And I alone know what it is.'

'Then tell us, you monster!' shrieked Gossamer suddenly, baring her teeth at Thaw as he cycled his wings above her upturned face. 'And then go! Just go . . .' She buried her face in Fortune's wing again.

'Just tell us, Thaw,' Fortune repeated.

Thaw hesitated for a moment. He was impatient to die and therefore he needed to do what he had to do swiftly, without error. Despite his blindness, the nearest of the basilisk sculptures drew him into its sphere of influence by the pressure of charm around it. He flew straight to it, reaching with his head to suck pale fire from its open mouth even before he could halt his headlong rush. He redirected the fire charm into a narrow slit, which none of them had yet noticed, in the side of the map pedestal. This action he repeated at each of the other five sculptures.

Hovering once more above them, he drew breath. 'What is your name, dragon?' he asked, clearly aiming his question at Vox. Vox told him. 'Hmm. You were outcast, were you

274

not?' Vox did not reply; he expected Thaw to know him at least by reputation. 'Well,' Thaw continued, 'whatever your faults I suspect that you of all these dragons will know what to do now. I must go, I fear, before I outstay my welcome.'

'But what must we do?' demanded Vox. Even as he spoke Thaw began to turn in the air above them, but falteringly, as though his body were not his own to control. Then a shadow fell across the big warrior, a dark shape silhouetted against the low, dull sun. It was Mokishi, the chitraka, crouched on the broken wall, glaring at him with rich, green eyes.

I must tell them the secret of the map! Thaw was thinking desperately, the words fighting to gain release from his throat. But Archan's lingering charm had infiltrated his system again and it did not want the secret revealed. Then there was a scent on the air ... *The chitraka!* Pure hatred surged through Thaw as he scented the gold and black beast. He remembered how her fur was striped, as though in mockery of his own splendid hide, and how that had angered him. She was a mere servant of Archan's, subservient to all dragons. *Yet she dares to stand above me! Of all Archan's slaves she should have incurred the wrath, not I!* He could barely control his rage ... but then he checked himself.

This is madness! he thought. *This creature has done me no harm. It is Archan's evil working on me still. Her magic remains and I am its prey. I must tell them – I must!*

'Do not distract me in this way!' he bellowed up into the heavens, his voice anguished. Below him the watching dragons exchanged puzzled glances. Thaw tossed his head from side to side as though engaged in some internal struggle, then he bolted to the side.

Mokishi darted back to let Thaw past, but the big dragon swung drunkenly aside. Like a dragon possessed, he arrowed towards the prowling creature, his injured mouth opened wide, his face a mask of horror. The chitraka sprang the opposite way, unnaturally fast, to avoid a clash with this mighty dragon. But Thaw responded as quickly, closing the gap between them until the chitraka was trapped between his enveloping wings and a jagged spur of stone. Cornered, she whipped around, claws flashing in the pale sunlight.

'Stop!' It was Ratchet's voice which broke the silence, and the sound of his heavy wings as he lumbered upwards. To whose aid he flew none could tell for certain – perhaps his former commander's, or perhaps that of the creature who had first escorted him into the citadel, when he had been near to death. Whichever it was, he moved faster through the air than his great bulk might have allowed, forcing his way between Thaw and Mokishi.

It was Thaw who struck first, gathering up his taloned forelegs to deliver a stunning blow against the coiled chitraka ... except he struck Ratchet instead. Charm-honed claws raked through metallic scales and exposed flesh. Scales showered down upon the basilisk map. Red blood splattered Thaw's striped hide and he cried out, half-realizing what he had done. Ratchet, his motion suddenly arrested, folded his wings and would have fallen had not Thaw's own forward momentum knocked him back on to the splintered edge of the wall. There was a sharp crack, and shards of stone joined the rain of scales and blood. Ratchet's neck twisted unnaturally to the side and his lifeless body fell limp, hanging grotesquely from the wall like some monstrous exhibit from the basilisks' darkest halls.

'No!' screamed Thaw, the shock of this latest atrocity purging Archan's evil magic from his system in a single, cleansing wave of horror. But before he could even consider the results of his actions he found that he had fallen upon the chitraka.

Mokishi was ready for him. She had never liked this dragon. He had sneered at her, and even cuffed her. He was too much like Archan, this one. Now she was as much a victim as Thaw, swept away by her own fighting instinct. Predators by nature, it was the careful introduction of charm into their systems that had brought intelligence and control to the chitraka species. But despite every effort to deny it, their aggressive origin remained close to the surface. In short, chitrakae had dreadful tempers. Blinded beyond reason by her own primal nature, Mokishi succumbed to the instinct which had ruled her ancestors and which ruled her still.

Long claws flickered out from padded feet and fangs

unfolded from jaws thrown wide in fury as Mokishi whipped her body into the frenzy of motion which Velvet, Smoke and poor Ratchet had witnessed earlier. Except this time she did not stop. Her claws opened a hundred wounds in Thaw's body before his even made contact. By his overwhelming weight and momentum Thaw forced her back, despite her speed, against the stone spur, pinning her body flat and ravening at her throat with his own, broken teeth. To the dragons watching aghast in the chamber below, it seemed that they were tearing each other to pieces.

Abruptly the fight ended. Thaw fluttered away from the wall, leaving Mokishi sprawled on the ragged stone. He landed heavily in the shadows on the far side of the map, and while Quill and Cumber raced around to tend to him, Velvet flew swiftly up to the scene of the brief and bloody confrontation. Averting her eyes from the sight of Ratchet's body, still dangling from a spike of rock, she landed next to the chitraka, expecting the worst.

Mokishi was still alive, barely. 'It's all right,' soothed Velvet between her tears. 'Oh, you did nothing to deserve this, you poor dear. All you did was help us and this is what we do to you in return.'

The wounded creature nuzzled her affectionately before dropping down on to the jagged stone again. Her breathing was raw and laboured; a pool of blood was growing beneath her. Velvet looked down to see Cumber and Brace attending to Thaw in similar fashion. *What dark place have we come to?* she wondered. *Where there is no hope for life, only death and despair?* And in appalling confirmation of her grief, as she held Mokishi close to her, the chitraka died.

Below, Thaw was struggling to speak.

'Have to tell you . . .' he murmured.

'Ssh, now, don't try to speak, old fellow,' replied Cumber, clumsily trying to staunch one of the hundreds of injuries to the warrior's hide.

'Let him speak!'

Fortune moved quickly to Thaw's side.

'Saw the night dragons fall,' whispered Thaw, his voice gurgling in his torn throat. 'Much charm dead. But some survives . . .'

Quill, once the most skilled healer in Covamere, gently halted Cumber's attempts to stop the bleeding from Thaw's wounds. To comfort the dying dragon she held his head and urged him to go on.

'. . . not abandoned charm, not dragon charm. Troll. That's what you need now . . .'

'Troll charm?' Fortune demanded, listening intently. The big dragon lurched, and a torrent of blood escaped his flank. He settled back, his ribs no longer moving, the breath slowly escaping his body in a long, wheezing exhalation.

One final word Thaw, dragon warrior, spoke before he died. 'Trollvein . . .'

'He was a great dragon before he came to Haven, and even afterwards, for a while at least,' murmured Quill. 'I knew him when he commanded the respect of thousands. Lately there have been barely a hundred. And now, for Thaw, none. We should not be too hard on him.'

'There is no time to be hard,' cut in Brace's voice. He had flown across to join them at the last, aware that Thaw's dying words might aid them in their quest. 'What does "trollvein" mean?'

Neither Cumber nor Quill knew, but both turned their heads towards Vox, who was weaving to and fro over the map a short distance away, muttering to himself. It appeared that he too had heard Thaw's words and now he was searching, searching . . .

'Trollvein,' he whispered as he flew.

Mist once more obscured the distance. Outside, all was liquid movement: the endlessly tumbling falls, the dancing towers and the rain which seemed to have become a constant in this changed and natural world. Doubt that they would ever leave here again prowled among them like a phantom.

Tallow and Volley, by far the strongest among the group, had wrestled Ratchet's body down from the ledge and folded his massive wings around to form a cocoon. Quill attended to the two corpses – Ratchet's and Thaw's – cleaning their wounds as best she could and arranging and rearranging their wings until she was satisfied with their final appearance. As a healer of many years, she was as experienced with failure as much as with success, with death as much as life, and lavished much care on the bodies. Her companions waited respectfully for her rituals to be completed.

Finally she was satisfied, and nodded to Tallow. Again he and Volley applied their strength and with the help of Brace and Vox they hauled the bodies out of the Chamber of the World and into the bigger space beyond. Here, early light from the huge east window illuminated fine tendrils of mists drifting in from the damp sky outside as though come to claim weary dragons' souls. Through the mist they took their companions until they reached the lip of the window. Again Quill took the lead.

'Our friends are dead,' she began. 'Once we would have consigned their bodies to a great circle of charm, but such circles no longer exist. We have all grieved for the loss of charm in our many ways, yet how much greater grief do we feel now at the deaths of our friends. They have been taken, and nothing can bring them back to us.'

She spoke then about each of the two in turn, remarking on Ratchet's bravery and loyalty and on Thaw's strength of command, which had failed him at the last when he himself had fallen into the thrall of another. As her eulogy progressed however she grew more and more uncertain, for so many of the old forms of funeral rite relied upon the charm which had abandoned them. Eventually she halted, halfway through an old poem which seemed suddenly inappropriate.

'Um,' she stammered, 'would anyone like to say anything more?'

Her companions shifted uneasily. Then Gossamer boldly made her way to Quill's side. Her eyes were red and puffed, and her wingtips were trembling, but she managed to compose herself before saying, 'You cannot know the fears I harbour. But Thaw is dead now and cannot be judged. We must remember how he was, not how Archan made him.'

Here she faltered, and Fortune darted forward to comfort her. But she waved him back, continuing, 'Quill fears that there is no place to send these dragons now that the magic has died. None of our Natural rituals seem right, either. We are on our own here.' She caught her breath, looking around sadly at the group. 'There is no power we can invoke to help us.'

They all pressed forward as she gestured out of the window with her wing. 'I suggest we simply send our friends into the one place where we can be sure they will find peace. Into the cloud,' she said. There below, shrouding the lower half of the citadel and the rumbling waterfall, was a bank of cloud rolling like a brilliant, white sea. Luminous with hidden sunlight, it swelled up towards them then retreated, then surged again as though eager to claim its prize. *Cloud*, thought Gossamer. A strange excitement dulled her sorrows.

The ceremony concluded, all that remained was to push Thaw and Ratchet out over the precipice and into the mist. Their wings expanded as they fell, blown open by the rush of air and giving a brief and glorious impression that they somehow awakened to begin this last, mysterious journey. Then they fell together into obscurity, and the mourners were glad that they would not see them consumed by the waterfall.

They were about to leave when Velvet appeared, panting hard, having departed the proceeding halfway through Quill's speech – overcome by emotion, most of her companions had assumed. She landed heavily at the window's edge, a bundle of fur gathered in her hind legs. It was the chitraka.

'She deserves the same,' she said defiantly, and none argued.

As Mokishi's slender, golden form tumbled down to follow the two dragons into the cloud, Velvet whispered these words: 'We'll meet again one day. Then maybe we can truly be friends.'

Slowly the dragons made their way back to the Chamber of the World. Vox was first to leave for, sad though he was, he had had little love for Thaw in the short time he had known him on Haven. Ratchet he had never met before today. Besides, something was burning in him: Thaw's dying words. *Trollvein*.

By the time the others arrived in the chamber Vox had

taken up his station again over the map. 'I think there's a way after all,' he called.

It took but a few breaths before all the dragons were positioned as Vox required. Keen to occupy their minds with something other than grief, all were enthusiastic in following the outcast dragon's instructions. *They listen to me,* marvelled Vox as they scampered at his command. *They trust me!*

He addressed himself to the group at large. Vox's growing confidence filled Gossamer with hope despite all that had happened. The mysterious voice she had heard in the tower came to her mind, though she could not quite yet bring herself to believe its words: *From the horror will come salvation.*

Well, she thought bravely. *We have experienced the horror. I must have faith that what is to follow will be good.*

'Trollvein,' said Vox, his voice booming through the Chamber of the World as if he were the most experienced of orators, his stammer quite gone. 'This is what Thaw said, and I have pondered its meaning.'

Vox made a half-turn and tipped his head up, drawing a faint line of charm from the basilisk head beneath which Cumber was stationed. A tingle ran down Cumber's spine and he shuddered, but the sensation was not unpleasant and he stood his ground. The dragons exchanged puzzled glances.

'There is no danger,' Vox reassured them, then he pulled identical magic from each of the other five heads in turn until he was bathed again in a glowing sphere. 'Trollvein: we have already found one. All we need to do now is find the *right* one.' He stared at Gossamer. 'Have you not guessed?' he smiled.

'The tunnel?' she blurted, the instinct coming from nowhere. 'The one you found so strange?' Vox nodded and Gossamer began to understand.

'Trollvein,' Vox repeated. 'Simply this: *the veins of the trolls.* We know the trolls lie buried across the world, and their bodies are being reclaimed – but more than just their bones survive, much more.

'We found a tunnel which ran between Sharp Island and Haven. I thought it odd at the time – it seemed to have grown rather than been cut, either by dragon or by water. And it *felt* odd. I am very sensitive to charm and it felt most peculiar. Most peculiar. I am sure now that it was a trollvein. And I am sure that Thaw found many such veins in the map of the basilisks. I think he was trying to tell us that there is a way to use the trollveins to reach Aether's Cross.'

Suddenly Vox froze, his head tilted at a wild angle, his eyes wide. His wings beat heavily; his body was locked in position. The charm which Thaw had unlocked spread out from the six sculptures to encase the map. Then the map began to tilt.

With a tremendous groan, like the groan of Aether himself, the far edge of the map juddered and started to descend into the tiled floor. At the same time the opposite edge lifted itself up, shaking dust and debris from the fallen ceiling out across the chamber. The walls vibrated, the very air vibrated as the enormous disc of stone started to rotate. Vox rose upwards, beckoning the others to follow him, but it soon became clear that the map was doing more than simply rotating – it was elevating too. Quickly they slipped sideways and descended to the floor, watching agog as the great circle of lands and seas rose from its pedestal and moved upward past them, tipping over on to its back as it did so until it was floating above their heads with ponderous, impossible ease. One more time it turned over until it rested the same way up as it had originally. Except now it was a full tree's height above them, a new ceiling resting on a bank of charm.

Cautiously, Vox climbed up on to the empty pedestal, acutely aware of the great mass which was poised above him. But he had to trust to the charm, though there was precious little of it left. He peered at the upturned surface, exploring the undersides of continents and the basins of the world's oceans. The view was strange, artificial, and little of it made any real sense, but one thing was instantly clear, so much so that before he could speak Velvet bounded on to the platform next to him and pointed excitedly with her wingtip.

'They're there!' she exclaimed. 'They're all over the place! That *is* them, isn't it, Vox? Those are the trollveins?' He nodded, and invited the others on to the platform.

The belly of the world was dark and sombre, but through the darkness was traced a network of light, a lacing of thin and insubstantial lines which looked to Fortune like a tiny fragment of the Maze of Covamere. *Who knows?* he wondered. *Perhaps that's just what it is – perhaps something did survive.* The trollveins were spread across the entire world like the roots of some colossal tree, knitting the bedrock and laying trails through the deepest fires. They twisted and divided, these giant fibres; in some places they were massed into great formations; in others they were sparse and ragged, cautious in corners of the world where their influence was for some reason unwelcome.

Vox swiftly relocated Aether's Cross: the tortured scar of the Cross was easy to spot. Every dragon took a sharp breath as they searched for and found their goal. The map allowed them insight into solid rock and there, running directly into the Great Chamber of the Cross, was a single thread of light. A trollvein.

PART THREE

THE GATHERING OF
THE DEATHLESS

CHAPTER 26

Division

Ocher and Tellere lingered in the air over the citadel for some time before striking out north. Ocher was eager to move on, to seek out the hiding place which the penultimate basilisk – Geiss – had chosen. Already it had resigned itself to the fact that they would not find Bacht.

. . . Six of the Deathless are the ideal, but five may succeed. And do not forget the dragons, Ocher – they have their part to play too.

Tellere's comments both inspired Ocher and filled it with dread. Ocher knew that they did not need Bacht to complete the ritual, but it was uneasy at the prospect of these flimsy dragons involving themselves with the Gathering. It was somehow . . . sordid. Greater than this reservation though was the vivid memory of its own brief symbiosis with Wraith – and the sure knowledge that between them they had so nearly created the abominable *bringer-of-shadow*, the world-eating monster which Ocher so feared to become. If the dragons entwined their lives again with those of the Deathless . . . was that danger a real possibility once more?

It looked up at the wavering river of charm and considered that it was too late to turn back. All the processes were in motion now and fate decreed that the Gathering would indeed take place, and soon. Very soon.

But will Ocher be a part of it? it thought.

Floating high above the mist, the two basilisks watched with penetrating senses the dragons as they cast the bodies of their friends into the waterfall, and perceived their manipulation of the map to reveal the existence of the trollveins.

. . . They are intelligent, these little dragons. Ocher, they have become a force in the world.

. . . Briefly, Tellere, yes. We should be wary.

'Please tell me who you are.'

Gossamer cowered beneath the overwhelming shadow of the cloud. Fortune was with her in her dream but he could not see what she could see. Where she looked up, he looked down, obsessed by a pattern in the ground. The cloud showed her things.

A divided river, two streams joining into one, and a dragon. The dragon splitting into two, each twin descending into the water and vanishing – one into one stream and one into the other. An ocean filled with bergs of ice. Cold and rain.

The cracking sound of an egg hatching, the first electrifying mew of the infant. The soaring of emotion, the tears.

White scales coiling and a face with no eyes.

And a direction. Like a bone directing flesh, like a trunk pressing skywards, like a shaft of lightning plunging inevitably to ground, a direction. North, of course, but so *imperative*.

'She's there, Fortune,' wept Gossamer, turning away from the cloud and its visions. But he did not reply, nor even turn himself. He simply stared into the ground, twisting his head as though trying to squeeze his gaze into the rock. She could not trouble herself with him, not yet. At least he was with her.

The cloud fragmented as an imperceptible wind broke through its body and the visions were gone. Only the direction remained. North.

The world was less flexible now that the storm had abated. The Turning had been a great wrench as the vulnerable planet was ripped free from the web of reality in which it had been held for so long. The Maze of Covamere, the network of force which had supported this and all other worlds for aeons, had crumbled away leaving . . . nothing. Through that nothing the world was tossed, searching for the new realities which would guide it into a new age. Lands twisted and laws changed. The storm worked out its anger.

Rain fell now, gentle and persistent, a balm which soothed the wounds made by the storm and softened the hard edges left by the jerking of the continents. For a time all that had once been solid had flowed like resin from the bark of a tree, but now the resin was hardening again, the shapes into which it had fallen strange and new but welcome if only for their sheer solidity.

Here and there remained the inevitable shreds of abandoned charm, slipping into the narrow spaces between the solidifying structures. They would continue to work their mischief for many aeons to come, making frost-cracks in the new reality and ever seeking out those few minds with the skill to unleash their power. But apart from these relics, and the mighty sky-river of charm currently flowing north towards the crest of the world, soon the world would be locked finally into its new, natural form and the future age would truly begin.

Thus was the world, for a short period of time, *between*. Ruled no longer by charm nor yet fully by nature it succumbed to a limbo, an emptiness damped by the constant rain yet full of potential. As the cosmos expanded and space began to curve round upon itself, the world was poised. In this limbo, perhaps, anything might happen.

The flight from the citadel was gruelling. The wind had freshened again, blowing the rain with them upon their journey and aiding them, for it too was travelling north; nevertheless the pace which Fortune set was punishing. None argued with the need to act quickly, and all endured the hard and constant flying without a murmur of protest, nor even more than the occasional word of conversation. It was for the most part a silent flight, and a grim one.

Such communication as there was mostly concerned itself with their route north. Tallow and Smoke led the way, although in truth their course was one which even the clumsiest of dragons might have followed for they were aided by two unmistakable and constant landmarks. The first – if landmark it could be called – was the river of charm. Faint, barely discernible as a watery texture in the sky above the clouds, it pressed north with undeniable authority and was their guide even at night, when it twisted the patterns of the stars. But beneath them a second river flowed, a natural river of water, and Smoke knew it.

'It's the Term,' she explained to Tallow early on in the journey when words were still welcome. 'The river which feeds the waterfall is the Term. I suspected it when I saw that map, but now I'm sure.'

Behind them the basilisk citadel, embraced by its curve of falling water, had all but vanished. As the dragons glanced back they saw it for the last time, a nugget of defiant stone set square in the path of this mighty stream, the dancing towers at its peak a misty blur of movement. Then it was gone.

'Thaw's land,' murmured Quill, who flew close in their wake and had heard Smoke speak. 'This must be Termanderel then, land of the flood plains. Thaw's home.'

She missed Thaw, for of all the dragons of Haven he had reminded her most of her beloved Covamere. They shared a heritage and though he had never returned her feelings, for a time she had fancied she loved him. Now he, like the place of the basilisks, was gone. *The sky is too big for any dragon to bear for long*, she thought wistfully. *How I long to find a place to be what I once was. An underground place, far from the troubles of the world.*

'We should be crossing the mountains of the Spine,' observed Smoke as they pressed on through the drizzle. 'But the land is flattening already. This realm has altered too.'

'We're rapidly becoming unnecessary, you and I,' commented Tallow. 'No place for pathfinders when all is change.'

'I think things are settling though,' frowned Smoke as she tried to peer ahead through the haze of raindrops. 'I feel that the world is slowing again. I think we've seen the worst of it.'

'Hmm.' Tallow was unconvinced.

The Spine slipped behind them, its alps mere echoes of their former selves, allowing the land to flatten out into a meandering river valley so broad that they could not see its extent to their left, and could discern only a thin band of pale grey which signalled far-off hills to their right. Smoke recognized the distinctive shape of the river however, for that had not changed since she had visited Termanderel many years before. After a series of languid turns it opened out into a long, wide lake across which were scattered countless tiny islands.

'This is Hundred Isle Lake. I came here once . . .' she said. 'After Wraith . . .'

As she stopped herself she noticed Vox shadowing her, flying above and behind and drawing gradually nearer as they soared. She glanced back just in time to see him snap his neck away again, as though embarrassed at having been caught listening.

'Well?' she snapped. 'What do you want?'

'I'm s-sorry,' stammered Vox. 'I d-didn't mean to s-spy.'

At once Smoke regretted her irrational anger.

'This is Termanderel all right,' she gabbled. *I wish I had never told Velvet and Ratchet about the Black Dragon*, she thought. *A hatched egg can never be put back together*. 'I'd know it anywhere. The river's the same, although it's in the wrong place and it's flowing north to south instead of east to west. What do you think, Tallow?'

'Indeed,' rumbled the big dragon, as puzzled as Vox by Smoke's odd change of mood.

Smoke's brief outburst marked the beginning of the silence which descended then over the company, although ultimately it was a silence not of tension but of sheer fatigue. As soon as it became clear that Tallow and Smoke were for the time being redundant, Fortune took the lead and accelerated the pace. None complained, not even Quill for whom flying was a chore most unwelcome at the best of times. All knew there were important tasks to be undertaken, with little time in which to complete them.

For three days they journeyed above the river as it wound its way back towards its source. The flood plain narrowed, growing steep sides and straightening as the waters became wilder. The land started to rise into barren foothills, scarcely protected by their thin skins of moor and moss and to their left the sound of the sea was a constant, distant hiss. Traces of salt infiltrated the fresh rain which fell still and the dragons, though exhausted, felt encouraged by the new surroundings; at last they seemed to be getting somewhere.

They spent the night of the third day resting in a large cave in the side of the river valley – which had by now assumed the proportions of a shallow gorge – then set off again on the morning of the fourth. The air had become cold and patches of ice were creeping on to the hilltops. Peak after peak rolled past, their contours growing sharper and frostier with each wingbeat the dragons took. Ice encrusted most of the slopes yet long after they might have expected snow to fall still it continued to rain, gently and insistently. A line of mountains appeared on the horizon; somewhere among them, the dragons guessed, was the source of the river.

It was now that Tallow and Smoke began to feel needed again, for they alone of the group had the capacity to retain all the shapes they had seen on the basilisk map. Smoke grew nervous, peering out into the rain to see what was ahead. Tallow simply stroked his way on through the air with calm, confident beats of his wings. Their companions eased back, allowing the two navigators to take the lead again. In the end however, the signal was plain enough for them all to see.

The gorge widened slightly, then split in two. The main gorge continued north but a major tributary joined the river here, pouring its own cargo of mountain water into the foaming torrent. At last it seemed there was a decision – or decisions – to be made.

The dragons gathered over the fork. The wider way was broad and, for all its ruggedness, inviting; the eastern route was narrow and twisted, the confines of its sheer canyon most unwelcoming. They had been expecting this, for the basilisk map had shown it to them, but now that they were here they felt anxious to be gone again. This was a place of uncertainty, a stark contradiction to the relentless mood which had driven them on so far. Most of all they knew that here their company would part.

'Look!' exclaimed Vox before any of them could speak.

They followed his gaze upwards, squinting into the rain, and gasped. The split in the natural river they had expected, but not the one in the sky: like its mirror below, the river of charm divided too. The primary stream forged its way ever northwards but here it sent forth a pale and shimmering band of charm which was more luminescent than its parent. This secondary magic looped behind the rainclouds and descended to the east to be swallowed by the distant haze. No clearer signal could have been given: this was indeed the place.

Their parting they had not actually discussed, but all had accepted that it would happen sooner or later. They loitered briefly, maintaining a loose, hovering formation in the damp air, until at last Gossamer spoke.

'Fortune and I must go on,' she announced, her voice strong and stern. Then her tone softened and her voice wavered a little. 'Aria is somewhere ahead, you see – we have no choice but to follow the river north.'

'But how do you know?' began Cumber, only to be waved to silence by Velvet.

'Shush,' she hissed. 'She knows, all right?'

'The way to Aether's Cross lies to the east,' said Brace, moving close to his sister. 'I don't want to leave you again. Won't you come with us? As soon as we've done our work we'll search for Aria, however long it takes.'

'That might be too long,' replied Gossamer, her eyes filmed with tears.

'I made a vow – I have to go.'

'So do I.'

They touched awkwardly, and then Brace turned to speak to Fortune. But Fortune's face was stiff and he said nothing, nor did he show any kind of emotion. Brace retreated into the group which was collecting behind him – Tallow, Volley, Quill and Vox, all of whom were gathering a little way from where Gossamer and Fortune hovered alone.

'We will finish what we started, Fortune,' rumbled Tallow as if by way of apology. 'Then we will meet again. Remember all that I have taught you.' If Fortune heard him he did not respond.

Brace was glad to have in his company both Quill the healer – they might have need of her skills if any Cross dragons were indeed alive to be rescued – and Vox, who had demonstrated such perception in his analysis of the basilisk map and the discovery of the trollveins. But it tore at his heart to see his sister and her mate floating in what seemed complete isolation over the divided river. They looked so lost and so afraid, and so in need of help; yet they begged for no help. He felt wretched, as though he were abandoning them, and he knew that although they felt wretched too they would have it no other way.

'Scoff, Smoke?' he called over the hiss of the water. 'Are you coming with us. Cumber? Velvet?' He felt a surge of love as Gossamer's eyes burned into him, recognizing his understanding of her needs. *They want to be alone now*, he acknowledged. *It is the only way they can beat the horror.*

Smoke came readily enough, but the other three were not convinced.

'Well, if you think I'm just going to abandon my friends while you lot all flap off on your own private adventure then you've got another think coming!' Cumber pounded the air indignantly. 'I mean to say, poor Fortune and Gossamer have got enough on their minds without having to worry about going on alone, and I for one don't plan to let them do it, whatever any of you lot may think.'

'Oh, Cumber.' Gossamer managed a weak but warm smile. 'Dear Cumber. You have to let us go now. We *are* alone, whatever you or any other dragon may wish, and we alone can put that right. We don't want to leave you, but we must. Can't you see that?'

'She's right,' butted in Velvet, her voice shaking. 'Remember when you left us on the mountain, Cumber? You said you felt you needed to be somewhere else, but you didn't know where. It's the same thing, only they *know* where they're going. Don't you, Gossamer?'

'Yes. And no. All I know is Aria is north. And that's where we must go.'

In the difficult silence which ensued Velvet and Gossamer nuzzled each other briefly before Velvet swung away to round up Cumber. He was hovering next to Fortune, who was regarding him with a blank stare.

'Remember this, old fellow,' whispered Cumber. 'There's always a way to cheat the magic. You discovered that long ago and it's saved you more than once, so don't forget it now. Take care, my friend.' Then he kissed him.

Emerging briefly from whatever interior world had claimed him, Fortune lifted his head slightly. His eyes cleared, focused, then flooded with tears. 'I'm lost, Cumber,' he murmured, too quietly for any but his old friend to hear. 'I don't know where to go.'

'Follow Gossamer. She knows.'

Only Scoff remained as Cumber and Velvet reluctantly joined Brace's party. He cycled his massive, rainbow wings in decisive fashion and systematically outstared his companions before announcing, 'Don't care what you think.' He looked at Gossamer. 'Or even you. I'm heading north. I'm all you're likely to need.' His words brooked no argument, and as he said them Gossamer felt a tiny fraction of the weight lift from across her heart. Of all the dragons who might have demanded their company Scoff was the most welcome – taciturn, kind and brave in turn when the occasion demanded; his decision to join them brought her comfort beyond all her hopes.

A few more tears flowed then but all that was needed had been said. In the end it was Fortune who turned first, opening his wings against the wind which blew from the south and accelerating into the distance without a single word. Grim-faced, flying close, Gossamer and Scoff followed him.

Brace watched his sister as she flew off down the gorge, thinking how much this place reminded him of the Cross, his home, which he so yearned to see again. *I will see it again*, he resolved, *if only in broken pieces. There are dragons alive there – it must be so, or else all this will have been in vain.*

'Well,' announced Cumber briskly. 'I don't know who's got the harder job – us or them!' Though his words were light he could not erase from his vision Fortune's face, hard and expressionless, and he remembered another flight they had shared, when he himself had retreated into the clutches of Realmshock. *Scoff helped me then*, he thought. *Perhaps he can help Fortune now.*

False though Cumber's good humour was it galvanized them into action, although it was a comment of Tallow's which finally broke the tension. As they made their way east up the narrow confines of the lesser canyon, the big dragon said,

'Gossamer knows what she's doing. Aria will be found, just as we will find Aether's Cross, and I hope for Archan's sake Gossamer's anger is spent when they finally catch up.'

The new mood of optimism infiltrated the group like a thaw, and it was with lighter strokes of the wing that they proceeded steadily higher into the chill realm of Trollstorr.

The rain lashed against Fortune's face. He looked down as he battled through the cooling air, turning with the river as it whipped its way north through the brownstone canyon. His mind, like the rapids beneath him, was turmoil.

What will I do if Aria dies? This was the thought which damped all others, crushing his heart and trapping him in limbo. In place of rational thought he had substituted physical action – hence the punishment he was inflicting upon himself and his companions by flying so hard and so fast. Neither complained however, for their motivation was as strong.

Back on Haven he had flown through a different kind of limbo, an emptiness in which – he knew now – he had simply been waiting for the storm. They had all been waiting, for on Haven time itself had stopped flowing, for a while at least. His restlessness had now become a passion, yet a passion which could not properly express itself. While the river thrashed below him, giving ample vent to its fury, his anger and fear were all internal. They burrowed inside him like paired parasites and would not be released.

I cannot go on! The thought was like a fresh claw-slash each time he beat his wings. *I cannot go on!* Yet he went on.

Though she knew much of what Fortune held trapped inside, it held little interest for Gossamer. Her intellect balked at the task of answering this, Fortune's silent shouting to her that he needed her, that they should share their terrors. And her own grief and worry were so great that they left no room in her heart for anything else, not even her beloved mate.

You are stronger than you think, Fortune, she thought with awful coldness, but that was all she could think on his behalf. Filling her inner vision was her daughter and the incalculable peril that had swallowed her. Already Aria had been violated by Archan – and, Gossamer was sure, in an even worse way by Thaw. But where obsession took Fortune into a bleak realm of silence it worked rather differently on Gossamer, firing her nerves and strengthening her confidence.

'I have never felt so strong,' she explained to Scoff, who flew easily at her side. 'I can't explain it but . . . I know I have the power to save Aria. If only I can find her.'

'Find her,' echoed Scoff gruffly. 'Tough job. Don't forget Fortune.'

'I must. For now.'

Scoff shook his head, for while he was old and wise enough to recognize much of what was passing between these two young dragons, still he grieved for their forgotten love. To him, as to many of the survivors of the Turning, Fortune and Gossamer were dragon talismans, the one couple who had brought new life into the world – perhaps the last dragons to do so. Yet their youth and innocence had been blighted and he feared that they might never recover. All depended on the manner of their reunion with Aria, for he had no doubt that they would find her, sooner or later. The look in Gossamer's eye alone told him that.

'Very sure, you are,' he commented to Gossamer as they rose higher to clear a steep and rock-filled cataract.

'I am,' she whispered. 'Because I have placed my trust.'

'Trust?'

'*From the horror will come salvation*. Those were its words. I have to believe them.'

Scoff shook his head, failing to understand. Ahead the gorge narrowed to a sliver, a wound in the burgeoning mountains which offered little enough salvation in his eyes. However, as they passed into the gloom he felt strangely content – Gossamer's faith comforted him, and it seemed to him that a faint light from her eyes softened the hard edges of the canyon walls. Melt water cascaded down into the torrent and ahead the peaks were losing their snow.

CHAPTER 27

Chaemen

The lesser gorge, though tortuous, led swiftly out on to a high plain of rock broken by thousands of fissures. The rain fed countless rivulets which gathered and poured down into the stream the dragons had left, the water seeming to hiss as it trickled into the darkness. Higher now, they could see behind them the rising western slopes of this realm which led, Smoke asserted, to sea cliffs and fjords, but their path lay still to the east. Next morning they made good progress and by midday their ultimate goal lifted over the horizon. The barren wastes of Trollstorr gave way to a land even less inviting, and as the low sun struggled to achieve the barest fraction of its zenith the dragons passed beneath the shadow of the great glacier of Chaemen.

'The graveyard of the trolls,' quavered Velvet as they skirted the huge wall of ice. Cumber flew close at her side, nervous beneath this monster, acutely aware of the slickness of its flank as the rain coursed down it, pulling with it melt water and chunks of ice. It dwarfed the dragons, this mountain of ice, and it was with reverence that they kept a respectful distance from it. High above floated the charm which had led them here, its journey ended, its power seeming to dissipate into the cloud and rain. On the basilisk map, the world beneath the surface had shown a thin line running from Aether's Cross directly to the northern tip of the glacier. There, they hoped, it finally broke the surface and allowed access to the world's interior. To the Cross. After a brief discussion, Tallow and Smoke struck out around the glacier, asserting that they knew where the mouth of the trollvein should be.

'That is if it's not buried beneath this beast,' murmured Volley to his old friend Tallow, not loudly enough for any of their companions to hear. 'Well, Tallow, we're seeing the world, just like we wanted to.' Breathing deep of the cold air which rolled off the glacier he started to sing a quiet, reflective melody which Velvet recognized. With an eager smile, she joined in. The song flew with them around the cliffs of ice, expressing their wonder at this awesome spectacle.

They flew low at first, as though reluctant to acknowledge the sheer height of the glacier. Here the ice was stained brown, spoiled by the sand and ash which it accumulated as it dragged its way inexorably across the plain. Angry spring water burst at intervals from this junction, erupting from cracks and faults and powered by pressure and internal distress. They could hear the pressure, an irregular heartbeat of hidden avalanche, a constant reminder that within the glacier were caverns and clefts and a thousand secret ways, opening and closing and occasionally throwing forth their contents. These explosions of ice and water proved increasingly hazardous and before long the dragons ascended the blue face of the beast. It was shortly after this that they saw their first troll.

Brace saw it first, but it was Cumber who identified it, for he had seen many bones of these once-mighty creatures in his time. It stared at them from behind the ice, its corpse preserved in frozen perfection, contorted by the movement of the glacier through the aeons but intact nonetheless. Its heavy-browed face was pressed up against the leading edge of the wall as though trying to escape, and the dragons guessed that before long it would indeed emerge, forced out by some unimaginable current in the solid ice behind it. Sharp quills framed its blunt head like a mane, many of them plaited into what they guessed to be a ceremonial crown. A burial ritual, no doubt. They shivered, not just from the cold.

More trolls became visible behind the ice. The further round the glacier they flew the more they discovered, some set deeper than others, their forms less distinct. In one place some catastrophe had fractured the ice wall and a huge abyss had opened up, a yawning gully which ran the full height of the glacier and ran back into its interior for tens of trees. Within the fault, half-exposed, was locked another troll, its body frozen solid but clearly visible. Its naked skin was pallid, the claws on its massive hands were strangely gentle. Had it clapped those hands when alive, it could have crushed twenty dragons between them.

The northern tip of the glacier was badly scarred. Here it met a line of low crags, and clearly the impact of the moving ice upon the rock had caused much damage to both. The glacier was a slow-moving giant, its incredible presence a reminder of the ancient world which was now melting away behind them, its inexorable motion a clue to the true nature of the flow of time. The dragons were enthralled by this evidence of movement so slow in contrast to the frenetic changes which had racked the world over recent times.

'What are you thinking, Cumber?' asked Velvet tenderly as they followed their comrades down towards a patch of clear ground some way distant from the threatening expanse of the huge ice wall. Her mate's expression was thoughtful, and when she glanced at him she thought he was frowning; a second look revealed the frown to be a half-smile.

'Oh, I was thinking about how things turn,' came Cumber's reply. 'It was not so long ago that I was flying blind like Fortune is now, and Scoff was helping me. You know, Velvet my dear, I think I do actually miss the charm now, despite all we've seen and been through – isn't that strange?'

'Not at all, my darling.'

'Fortune will find the light again, because you see things turn – everything turns – and the light always comes in the end.'

'And Aria?'

But Cumber did not get the opportunity to reply. A yelp came up from the other side of the group – it was Smoke, and as they looked across the loose pattern of wings they saw her jolted in the air as though struck by something. A brief flurry of motion followed, during which it became apparent that Vox was struggling with his half-Charmed companion. The dragons grouped, assembling themselves into a rough circle as they hovered defensively over the barren landscape.

'What happened?' demanded Quill, pushing Vox away in

order to examine Smoke. 'What did you do to her?' Vox began to stammer something, but the words caught in his throat and he could not speak them. Tallow and Volley loomed over him, their faces grim, looking to Quill for some signal. Vox was after all a convicted murderer and they would see none of their friends hurt by him.

But Smoke called out, 'No – Vox saved me. He pushed me out of the way just in time. I didn't even see it coming.'

'Didn't see what coming?' barked Quill suspiciously. As if in answer to her question a whistling sound slashed the air beside her face. A white blur lanced across her vision and she whipped her head around to see a pale arrow vanish into the distance. 'What was that?' she exclaimed.

'I see it,' answered Vox, pointing with a foreleg claw to a shadowy recess in one of the crags near the glacier. 'There's a d-dragon down there.'

'Leave it to us,' thundered Tallow, nodding once to Volley. Together the two big Naturals tucked in their wings and angled the protruding tips so as to bring them hurtling towards the ground. By unspoken agreement the long-time friends levelled out barely a wing's width above the stony soil and accelerated into the shadow of the glacier. There was sudden movement in the narrow cleft and a flurry of ice-shards was catapulted from the darkness, each projectile flying harmlessly over the heads of the speeding dragons. Tallow entered first, snapping his head sharply to the side as he did so, followed closely by Volley. There was a series of muffled impacts and then silence.

'Come on,' announced Quill. 'I haven't flown this far to be knocked from the sky by a few icicles!'

Tallow and Volley were already emerging from the cave. Between them they dragged a strange-looking dragon, all leg and tail with a plump body but hardly any wings to speak of. The dragon's dark green scales were well weathered. Wattles gyrated below his neck, another sign of considerable age, yet his eyes were bright and sharp as stars. As he was bundled out into the open air he wrested himself free of his captors' grip, shaking his flimsy wings and flexing his long, mobile claws as though trying to regain some dignity.

'And who might you be?' demanded Quill. Now that

Thaw and Fortune were no longer part of her company she felt obliged to take the lead. She still considered herself a councillor, despite all that had happened, with duties to perform and a role to fulfil. 'And what did you think you were doing trying to knock us from the sky?'

'I might ask your identity first,' retorted the dragon, regarding his captors with a supercilious air. 'And I might also ask what right you have to send your . . . thugs down into my private chamber.'

'Why you . . .' began Volley, quickly to be restrained by Tallow.

'Private chamber?' scoffed Quill, peering into the cave. 'I've seen better kept dung-pits.'

'Well!' The strange dragon pulled himself up to his full height – which was considerable – and started to pace backwards and forwards. 'Such outrageous presumption! You invade my territory, ignore my attempts to warn you down from a particularly dangerous patch of airspace and what do I receive? Abuse of the first order and the threat of physical violence. I have never encountered the like of it before in all my life. Well, really!'

'If you've finished?' sighed Quill impatiently. 'Would you please just tell us who you are?'

'I shall not!'

'I'll break your bones and feed them to you one by one,' growled Tallow pleasantly.

'Oh, very well then,' moaned the dragon after a moment's consideration, 'for I don't suppose a name can hurt. I am known as Scape, and before you ask the next question I tried to bring you down simply because you should not fly around here.'

'Why not?' inquired Brace, attempting to bring a more friendly note into the proceedings. He frowned at Quill, hoping to warn her off antagonizing this stranger too much. *He lives here*, he thought excitedly. *He might tell us things we need to know!*

'Ah, well, that's more like it, young fellow,' replied Scape. 'It's nice to find that at least one of you has a modicum of politeness.' Here he glowered at Quill and his two attackers. 'Your friends I will tolerate; you I shall inform.'

Taking three paces to the left, and in doing so forcing Volley to back away awkwardly, Scape opened his inadequate wings to the glacier. 'Behold Chaemen,' he proclaimed dramatically. 'Burial ground of the troll lords of old.'

'Yes, we know,' muttered Cumber.

'Be not scornful, young Charmed,' said Scape, wheeling round suddenly to face him. 'All that seems obvious may yet conceal a secret or two, and Chaemen is no exception. The ice is a great keeper of secrets, for while a dragon thinks he sees all that there is on the surface, underneath there is much, much more.'

'Yes, yes, the trollveins, we know all about those,' sighed Cumber, exasperated. 'Is there anything else we should know while you're pursuing the subject?'

'Hmm.' Scape was clearly disappointed that one of his major set-pieces had been undermined, but not to be deterred he went on, 'Well, since you seem to know so much about this place, perhaps you can tell me by what means I was launching ice into the sky?'

'By charm, I assume?' suggested Velvet when none of the others spoke. Scape rewarded her with a sympathetic smile.

'A valiant guess, dear, white dragon. But sadly misguided, for as we all know there is no magic left now in the world. Or little enough at least.'

Cumber looked suspiciously up into the sky as Scape said this, for had they not seen a trail of charm leading to this very place? Where had that charm been headed; why had it stopped here?

'No,' went on Scape, and as he spoke Quill looked anxiously around at the others, seeking support. The initiative had been stolen from her by this overweight, long-legged dragon and the longer he spoke the less hope she had of regaining it. She resigned herself to listening for the time being, watching him closely as she tried to assess whether he was friend or foe. 'No,' Scape repeated, 'it was by cunning artifice that my spines of ice were launched. Would you like to see my apparatus? It will take but a breath or two.'

His audience was hesitant, but in the end Velvet took the lead and followed Scape into his cave. Cumber followed her hurriedly, unwilling to let her out of his sight, and the others followed with varying degrees of reluctance. Quill was last to enter the gloom, casting a final glance as she did so back up at the glacier. *At least it's underground,* she thought philosophically. *I've had enough of sky and storm to last me a lifetime!*

Scape's cave was much bigger than it appeared from outside. From the narrow opening it expanded into a large, triangular living space littered with bones and scraps of moss. Darkness in both of the far corners promised hidden passages beyond. Some of the moss had been woven into lengths of rope and plaited to form screens. Against one wall was stacked a great line of grey timber, carefully felled trees and smaller branches arranged in no particular order and astonishing in their variation of length and circumference. Here was the home of a practical dragon – an untidy one to be sure but one who took great care with his constructions, of which there were many: in fact the entire chamber was filled with weird assemblages of timber and vine, some no bigger than a dragon's head, others reaching the full and not inconsiderable height of the cave. Their various functions none could guess.

'Behold,' announced Scape, puffing out his chest, 'my workshop!'

Cumber and Brace, the most inquisitive of Scape's visitors, walked up to the nearest of Scape's strange structures and regarded it with a mixture of amusement and curiosity; never had they seen such work before. Most dragon communities boasted at least one dragon skilled in the cutting and joining of timber – at Cumber's native South Point that dragon had been a Natural called Tongue – and the Charmed were renowned for their ability to shape their environment, but Scape's constructions were something else entirely.

The contraption by which Scape had hurled his ice missiles at the company was set into the wall. An out-reaching talon of ice actually connected the advancing glacier to the crag in which the cave was cut, and clearly one of the pressurized springs inside the ice wall had forced its way through a fault in the rock to break free again just inside the cave entrance.

'I devised a simple plug by which I can stop the flow of water just long enough for me to insert an appropriate projectile into the hole.' Scape demonstrated by snapping an icicle from the overhang and pressing it home into a round orifice just above his head. Then he looked at Velvet. 'Would you kindly press your wing against that wooden pole, please, dear,' he smiled.

Cautiously she did so. A mighty 'crack' shook the air and the splinter of ice was blasted skywards from the hole, followed closely by a fine jet of water. It vanished into the distance, a scintillating scratch on the misty sky. Scape reached across her and returned the pole to its original position. 'Of course,' he confided, 'I have diverted the main part of the stream. Otherwise it might be dangerous.'

'Of course,' she agreed weakly.

'What does this do?' inquired Brace, ducking his neck down to look into an odd, curled tube which ran the length of the thing he was examining. Spars of timber held the tube firmly in place; at the far end it flared out like a lily while near to Brace it was narrow and fluted. The whole artefact rested on a dome of bark scraps laid across some hidden internal structure like scales across a dragon's back. Rough though it was, crude in its joints and clearly unfinished, it had a beauty all its own; much care had gone into its making.

'Ah,' sighed Scape wistfully, 'if only it were perfect. This particular piece has no name – or at least, I should say it has no name a dragon can ever speak.'

'What do you mean?' asked Brace, intrigued.

'We should let it speak for itself,' answered Scape. 'Stand back.'

Flapping his feeble wings he ushered his audience back against the wall of the cave. Velvet yelped as she fetched up against a collection of wooden spikes set into a long trough; Cumber frowned at her, as eager as Brace to see Scape's demonstration. Squatting down in front of the bark dome, Scape bent his head and closed his jaws around the narrow end of the hollow tube. Taking a deep breath he exhaled into the tube.

A long, bellowing moan resounded about the chamber. It came from the wide end of the tube, but as they listened it seemed to thicken and grow louder, echoing off the rock wall behind them, a wordless voice which rolled through the air like a wave through the sea. Only slowly did it fade, and only slowly did the dragons emerge from the dream-like realm to which it had transported them. Volley especially was clearly moved by the experience and, as soon as the sound had finally stopped, he blurted,

'That was a song, or a piece of one. Wasn't it, Scape?'

'Indeed it was, dragon. Very perceptive of you, if I may say so. That was a troll song – or at least the nearest I can get to simulating a troll song. There were many words contained in that single sound, many different stories in fact. They were economical with their voices, trolls were.'

'What does the song mean?' asked Volley, captivated.

'The main part tells of a female troll called Dessen. She was stolen away from her true love by an evil tyrant and lived out her life in captivity in a desert of ice at the base of the world. Her lover killed himself when he found her gone, and where his body fell there grew a tree which touched the moon. When she too died their spirits climbed the tree and escaped this world forever.'

'That's beautiful,' sighed Velvet. Smoke too was entranced, and was about to ask Scape about the story when she spotted Vox staring at her from behind Quill. He looked quickly away when their eyes met, blushing furiously, and it was at that moment that Smoke realized he had fallen in love with her. *That story meant something to him too*, she pondered, the new knowledge infusing her with warmth. *What, I wonder?* Before she could even consider her own feelings towards this contradictory dragon Scape was talking again.

'Standard troll melodrama,' he commented, 'but a nice enough tale nonetheless. A bit gloomy, but then that's trolls for you.'

'And you would know all about trolls, I suppose,' said Quill sceptically.

'My dear, there is no dragon in the world who knows more about trolls than I,' replied Scape with a gracious bow and not a trace of sarcasm. Cumber and Brace exchanged a glance and chuckled – much to Quill's annoyance; they could not help but like this plump artificer.

'This is all very fascinating,' interjected Quill, 'but can we get back to business: why exactly did you fire on us? You did say you were going to explain.'

'Ah, yes, that. Well, as I said, it is very dangerous to fly too close to Chaemen. She is ever more unpredictable, now the days are getting warmer. There is no knowing what she might do; already her leading edge is beginning to break up. Never trust the ice, dragons – that is something you should always remember.'

'What do you mean: "the days are getting warmer"?' shivered Velvet. 'It doesn't feel very warm to me.'

Scape pointed out across the rocky terrain. 'Rain,' he said, 'or hadn't you noticed?'

The truth was that the dragons had not noticed. It had been raining constantly for so long now that they had grown used to it, but as soon as Scape pointed it out they realized that the air really was warmer than it had any right to be. And the rain was getting stronger.

'Don't tell me the storm is coming back again,' moaned Velvet.

'Storm?' responded Scape, eyeing the clouds. 'No, I think the storms are over for the time being. But I think the rain will just keep on coming; Chaemen won't like that, not one little bit. And if the thaw comes to Chaemen I fear the trolls will not be pleased either.'

Here Brace stepped forward, clearing his throat. Clearly this dragon was well placed to help them find the trollvein they sought, and he considered that the time had come to speak of their mission. 'Scape,' he began, 'we need to ask you . . .'

But a rumbling sound cut off his words and they all turned to see a massive chunk of ice fall to the ground from the very top of the glacier. A gaping slit raced from the top to the bottom of the great, blue-white wall and further groaning noises issued from within its flank. Shards of ice, many of them bigger even than the dragons who watched in awe, exploded across the ground and the air was filled with tiny fragments. Undammed, a once-concealed stream burst forth from the new fault and poured its icy water out over the plain.

'The life-blood of Chaemen,' sighed Scape. 'Ah, such changes in the world. Such changes. Now, what do you want with trolls? Quickly – there may not be much time.'

307

CHAPTER 28

Ways North

When the dragons departed, still the basilisks loitered at the citadel, for some reason unable to leave. Tellere at last turned to the north, but even then Ocher would not move.

... *I sense your conflict, Ocher. You wonder if death is the answer after all.*

... *The Gathering will take place, whatever my will.*

... *Perhaps. Once I was angry, Ocher, but then I simply yearned for sleep. My anger you reawakened when you reawakened me, but it has faded again, so swiftly. I am reminded of how tiresome the world is – how tiresome all worlds are, for we have seen most.*

... *New worlds come, Tellere. I have seen the cosmos growing large before my eyes. There are new wonders even we have not perceived.*

... *It is too late for us, Ocher. Come, let us go north. To the Gathering.*

As Tellere wheeled in the mist to follow the course of the river of charm, Ocher spotted a flash of charm sparkling at the base of the waterfall. Tellere flew on, buoyed on the vestiges of magic which it groped from the hidden corners of the atmosphere, but Ocher descended, plunging through the cloud and seeking out the stone plateau where the magic had flared.

The air was thick and white here and Ocher had to use strange and subtle visions to seek out the event it had detected from on high. The flat slab of stone receded through the cataract and into a deep recess, a cave behind the water. Passing through the torrent – a procedure which would have dashed any mortal creature to its death – it emerged into the gloom. Spray lashed the smooth sides of the recess but the air was otherwise clear and astonishingly fresh. Ocher breathed deep, savouring the taste.

Three bodies lay on the stone. Two were dragons, their wings broken but somehow elegant in death. Ocher was not interested in them; the glow of charm was emanating from the third body.

It did not recognize the chitraka either as an individual or as a species. Intrigued by its fur and the way its markings so closely mimicked those on the smaller of the two dragons, it drew closer, scenting and probing. Charm bubbled beneath the striped gold of the creature's flank and Ocher was reminded of its experience in the deep, of the birth of the leviathan . . .

Slowly the light grew bright, so that even basilisk eyes and senses shrank from its glare. Gold like the chitraka's fur, it filled the cave then receded, leaving emptiness where the body had lain.

Not emptiness, realized Ocher. Turning, it regarded the tunnel which led out through the back of the cave. Movement blurred the darkness within and it entered.

The tunnel was smooth-sided and grey. A trollvein. Ocher's knowledge of these passages was extensive and it analysed how this particular way divided over and over, leading out into distant places of the world through countless hidden exits. Before it divided however there was a junction, and this junction Ocher was now approaching.

It did not enter the arching space ahead, though. Crouched in the shadows before the opening, it observed the pale phosphorescence illuminating the chamber with a green and eerie softness. Its basilisk perception registered close on a thousand tunnel entrances glaring down at the curved floor, where there was movement. Air blew quickly through the system, eager to find its way to the surface.

For each tunnel eye which stared down there was a creature squirming on the floor. The light was dim, and the inherent charm of the trollvein damped even basilisk senses, but Ocher could see that they, like the great beast under the sea, were wholly new to the world. The offspring of the chitraka. They grew with unnatural speed, pink skin softening with fur, limbs becoming sleek and muscular. A thousand pairs of bright, green eyes opened in the gloom as these heirs prowled the chamber before making their escape. No two of them were the same in their markings: some bore stripes like their common parent while others were plain. Yellow and tawny rippled across their backs like waves in the sea, a family of gold. All were female. Ocher became aware that all were pregnant.

Some unspoken signal burned through the group and they fled, each one to a different exit route. Gold flickered across the silver mirrors of basilisk eyes as these virgins made for freedom and long after they had gone Ocher crouched there, its thoughts filled with the wonder of all it had seen since its awakening.

Magic like a vein through the body of the sky. Whether the charm was an integral part of the atmosphere, or merely passing through it, the two dragons could not determine. Not that they paid the question much attention. In a state of rapture they moved into its mystery.

The ruins of Haven dropped out of sight, but it was not by natural flight that Hesper and Ledra ascended; rather they were enclosed and swept along by the currents of charm unravelling their way north. Subtle hazes plaited themselves into delicate skeins which in turn connected into great, looping strands of magic, spiralling ever onwards in a relentless drive towards the world's crest.

It was Hesper who entered the river first, accelerating vertically into a wide and lacy channel of charm. The magic – pure and vital now that it had been distilled from its various places of abandonment – coated his scales with darting flames, burning points of light which moved across his back like a herd across the plain. He glowed, and as she looked upon him Ledra found that she adored him. The magic cloaked her too – less spectacularly because she had not been born Charmed but with sufficient energy to turn her every scale into a brilliant beacon. In her eyes the river swelled about Hesper's soaring form and transformed him into a creature of wonder.

Ever since he had given her the magic and changed her Natural's body to that of a Charmed she had been under his spell. Before, she, like most of the other dragons of Haven, had seen only Hesper the bitter, Hesper the ruffian, but now all her prejudice had been swept aside. He was Hesper the great wielder of the new charm, the returned charm. No matter that others cautioned the magic would not last – what did they know? She could feel the charm, she knew its might. And she thought she knew Hesper.

Love was something Ledra had never before experienced, so engrossed had she always been with herself. Now she was experiencing an emotion which she thought of as love, although in truth it was closer to adoration, or even obsession. Obsession with Hesper, her saviour. All her history, all the liaisons with the many dragons who had travelled so fleetingly, so superficially through her life, all these were instantly forgotten. Ahead was a new future for Ledra, a new spring to thaw the ice in her heart. This ice she recognized and regretted; the sooner it was all melted away the better.

Hesper's fantasies were more ambitious than those of his acolyte. He too was convinced that the charm had returned for good, and he planned to turn it to a very specific purpose. The magic would heal their sterility and he would sire a new dragon race. No longer would he be a lackey in some mighty dragon's army, nor even the chieftain of a petty-minded gang made up of dragons with little brain and even less ambition. Unlike Ledra he had not forgotten his past: for Hesper the past was a livid flame which he could not look on for long, so angry did it make him. Like Ledra, however, he yearned for that which he had never had, and which he believed he could buy: respect. Dragon father he would be and, in the absence of any other, Ledra would suffice as his mate.

So together these two misguided dragons entered the river of abandoned charm, and the physical union they enjoyed filled its flow with crackles of fire. Magic sparkled about them as they writhed upon currents of air and as time went on they grew less and less concerned with any notion of the world beyond the river. Time mattered little here and they had each other. The future would come, sooner or later, and they would enter it fully equipped to spread their wings wide across the sky and embrace all that they were to inherit.

At that instant, with Haven destroyed and the storm – for all they knew – still laying waste to continents, they felt as though they were the last dragons left alive in the world; this they planned to change.

The charm billowed around them. Perhaps it was oblivious to its living cargo.

It was not long before Gossamer too descended into the silence which had claimed Fortune. Scoff's occasional attempts at conversation were rebuffed or, more commonly, ignored, and in the end he fell back to the rear, his face a constant frown against the equally constant rain. *They must heal*, he thought sadly. *They will need each other very soon*.

On the third night Scoff managed to ensconce himself with Fortune. They lay easily together beneath a bulbous mat of moss and lichen which was suspended from an ice-covered overhang. The ice was melting, washing into the moss with the rain and hissing as it percolated through to the rock beneath. Water dripped steadily on to the ground beside the dragons, gathering into deepening pools; soon this whole valley where they had stopped to rest would be under water. Some distance away Gossamer lay alone, asleep it seemed, by the steady rhythm of her breathing.

'She copes so much better than I do,' blurted Fortune suddenly. Scoff wisely said nothing, simply folded his rainbow wings forward and rested his snout on their tips. If Fortune wanted to talk he would allow him to do so with no interruptions.

Fortune said nothing again for some considerable time, then he continued as though he had not even paused. 'Because,' he began, 'I should be the strong one. I was there at the Turning, Scoff. I should be able to deal with this – Aria's not dead after all, at least, not as long as we . . .' Here he stopped, his breath catching in his throat. 'I can't cry though,' he went on when he had recovered himself. 'It just feels like a great knot inside me. They say your love lives inside you – well, if this is my love for Aria that I'm feeling then it's like . . .' His voice trailed off as he struggled to express his emotions.

'Like indigestion? Worst you've ever had?' suggested Scoff, not looking round.

Fortune regarded his companion for a moment, his mouth working, his expression a ghastly muddle of grief and amusement. 'Well, yes, Scoff,' he replied at last, his voice on the verge of laughter. 'That's exactly what it feels like. How did you know?'

'In love once,' explained Scoff tersely. 'Pretty young thing. I was young too. Hard to believe, I know. True though.'

'What was her name?' asked Fortune, fascinated. Here was a side to Scoff he had not imagined.

'Gingle. Don't laugh. I liked it. Liked her too.'

'I'm not laughing,' smiled Fortune. 'What happened?'

'She got bored. I got boring. One or other. Or both. She left.'

'Oh, Scoff, I'm sorry. Was this while you were living at Aether's Cross?'

'Yes. I survived. Halcyon's ambassadors – now some of them were special . . .'

'I don't think I should enquire any further,' chuckled Fortune. Then he let out a long sigh, a weary sound sent into the murky night to be swallowed by the endless rain. 'Oh, what am I to do, Scoff? I feel like I'm forever being trapped. On Haven I felt trapped by responsibilities, then I was trapped as we all were, by the storm. Now I'm locked in by a terrible emptiness in my own heart. I can't find a way to deal with the fact that Archan has stolen away my daughter, let alone a way to talk to Gossamer. What's wrong with me – am I to remain a prisoner for the rest of my life?'

'You're trapped. But you're no prisoner.' Scoff looked across at Gossamer and sucked his teeth. 'Listen. I'm getting old, so I've learned things. I don't know what you're feeling, but I know your heart feels too big for your body.'

'It does.'

'You asked what you could do.'

'Do you know?'

'I do. Grow.'

'Grow?' Fortune lowered his brow. Miraculously, Scoff's

313

words were actually releasing the pressure he felt inside and a glimmer of understanding was beginning to illuminate his spirit.

'Don't fight it, Fortune. Grow with it. Or it *will* imprison you. Go to Gossamer now.' After surprising Fortune with this conclusion Scoff closed his eyes and would talk no more.

The rain was pounding now but Gossamer seemed oblivious to it in her slumber. Fortune edged close to her, and was about to speak when she raised her snout to his. Gently they touched, water coursing across their joined lips and spilling into their mouths. Breath passed between them but no words; when Fortune tried to speak again Gossamer's tender wings pressed him to silence. He huddled nearer, wrapping his tail across her back and entwining the delicate tips of his wings with hers.

Grow, he thought, and as Scoff's answer filled his head so he felt himself turning inward to face the turmoil. All that he had so far seen in his life he placed at the centre of his soul: his memories of infancy, the spectacle of his journey south from South Point to Covamere, and the horrors and triumphs of his experiences with Wraith and the Maze of Covamere; Haven and the storm; the dragons still imprisoned at the Cross; Aria, grown and lost. So much . . . too much! Terror of losing Aria

I must grow too, or I shall be lost.

CHAPTER 29

Breakthrough

Scape listened hard as his visitors explained their quest, his evergreen wings twitching thoughtfully as Brace spoke at length about the Cross, his story filled out with occasional details provided by Cumber and Smoke.

'The map showed us enough to find our way here,' concluded Brace, 'but now we need your help. If there is a trollvein somewhere near, can you take us there?'

'Hmm,' pondered Scape. 'Well, I might help you, but . . . ah.' He gave an exasperated sigh. 'You're in the right place sure enough, but . . . well, just follow me and I'll endeavour to explain.'

Dutifully the dragons trooped back into Scape's cave. The plump old dragon led them past his many contraptions to a narrow tunnel entrance hidden in shadow, into which he beckoned them follow him. The passage was short and descended at a steep angle, so steep that their claws had trouble maintaining a grip on the damp floor. A low overhang caught several of the party unawares and it was with grumbles and bruised heads that they emerged into a small cavern illuminated by a skylight, a perfectly circular hole, in the domed ceiling. Rain accompanied the light, creating a frosty column of water in the centre of the space; the floor sloped severely towards the far wall where the water gurgled out of sight down a variety of sinks and crevices.

The floor was covered with markings, daubs of red ochre in a complex pattern of dots and lines over which the dragons now walked. Many of the marks were faded and streaked by the recent passage of water across their cracked surfaces.

'It's a constant battle to keep it updated,' said Scape, his voice hard and metallic in the confined space. 'Especially with the rain.'

'What is it?' asked Brace, although he thought he knew.

'This is *my* map,' answered Scape, proudly circumnavigating his creation. 'This represents the glacier, Chaemen, as it was at sundown yesterday. Soon I shall have to update it yet again, for that task has become a daily one now that the ice is moving so much. Each mark is a troll – dead of course – but you'll be much more interested in these lines. Each line represents a known trollvein; all you have to do is find the one you need.'

Brace looked open-mouthed down at the floor. The dark red lines glared back at him. There were hundreds of them. They had not looked at the basilisk map in this much detail.

'But where do we start?' he moaned.

'Well,' replied Scape, 'that is a bit of a problem, I'll admit. I think the best thing is for you to tell me everything you know about this "Cross" of yours. That way I might hear something which jogs my memory, as it were.'

'But we've told you everything we know,' groaned Cumber.

'Then tell me again,' beamed Scape.

It was late afternoon before Scape called a halt. The discussions had broken down and now Tallow and Vox were poring over the map, one or other of them occasionally glancing up to ask, 'What about this one?' to which Scape would merely shrug and answer, 'Maybe. Any dragon's guess, really.' At last he called his visitors together.

'I really ought to do my survey now,' he announced. 'You're welcome to come with me over the glacier, if you think it will help your cause.'

'Can't do any harm, I suppose,' grumbled Brace. 'And there's no harm in stretching our wings.'

The afternoon light was low and steady; the day had seemed long and the orange sun dropped only slowly towards the rolling horizon of ice. Elongated dragon shadows rippled across the surface of the glacier, climbing slopes and delving chasms, touching trolls . . .

'Why the fascination with trolls?' asked Brace, amazed that Scape could fly so well with such disproportionately small wings.

'It's a very long story, young dragon, and one better suited to an evening filled with good food and a hot fire, but I'll tell you in brief, if you're interested.'

Scape had always been a solitary dragon. The broken plains below the Injured Mountains had been his home, a bowl-shaped valley that was known as the Valley of Skulls, a perfect description.

Troll skulls they were, of course, and the hillsides were littered with them. A few of the bolder dragons had even made their homes inside the cavernous bone structures, although most were superstitious and viewed the remains with a mixture of dread and awe. When a contingent from Wraith's army visited the valley, the community was ripe for change. Most of its dragons were fed up with living in barren terrain and readily joined up, journeying to Cova-mere with Wraith's lieutenant and eventually dying in the conflagration when the Plated Mountain erupted.

Scape and a clawful of charmed dragons remained. Scape alone still lived in caves beneath the cliffs at the north end of the valley; the others, only seven, inhabited a variety of troll relics. The killing madness which was decimating Charmed communities the world over claimed them one by one until only Scape was left.

The skulls had always fascinated Scape. He had never felt the urge to live among them, nor did he fear them – they simply interested him. He soaked up legends about the ancient, giant lords more eagerly than any stories about valiant dragons of old, and his dreams were filled with the migrations and battles of these fearful predecessors. He occupied himself with scavenging wood and building contraptions in his cave, with sculpting the soft, black rock of the region and assembling elaborate aqueducts, at his happiest when reshaping the environment in which he lived.

When the bones began to move, turning to stone and sinking back into the black rock until they could no longer be seen, the process interested Scape and he endeavoured to study it. But soon all the bones were gone. At last he was truly alone, and he found that he missed the relics.

Koan, Massel, Antyre – names of trolls echoed in his mind, calling him . . .

He set out north. Coincidentally, he left the Valley of Skulls the day the Plated Mountain erupted. The disaster filled his world with ash and fire: he struggled through choking fumes and blistering heat, an ordeal he did not expect to survive. But survive he did and on he journeyed, thinking briefly of the dragons who lived at Covamere and wondering if any of them had escaped. But dragons were of less concern to him now than trolls.

The days lengthened as he approached Chaemen, to which the great troll armies had in legend travelled at the end of their reign, trudging across the world to find final rest in the ice. A perfect end for the giants who were born of fire. In the graveyard of the trolls, ice and the remains of their charm had kept their bodies intact, so far at least. From behind the glacier they observed Scape with careless, blank eyes as he in turn studied them. He catalogued and mapped, learning and speculating as he fitted pieces of lore into the spaces between the frozen corpses. Was this Laos? Perhaps, but the legends spoke of her as being beautiful – still, a dragon's notion of beauty was necessarily different to that of a troll. And this couple – were they the fabled Urish and Napete? He had no way of knowing, but he hoped they were for their story of passion and unrequited love was a particular favourite of his.

The exploration of the glacier became an obsession, interrupted only by the creation of ever more outrageous sculptures and contraptions in the small cave system he had made his home. Not once did he ask himself what it was that drove him in his self-appointed task, nor did he tire of his endless roaming of the sky over the glacier, the cracks and caverns which marred its blue-white surface.

Not, at least, until now.

'I've never been a superstitious dragon,' he commented to Brace. 'Or I should say, I never *was*. But, having lived here for so many years, I can't help wondering . . .'

318

'Wait a moment,' interrupted Velvet, who had been listening too. 'Did you say *years*?'

'Oh yes,' answered Scape brightly. 'Over three thousand eight hundred days, if you want to be exact.'

'Oh dear,' sighed Cumber, 'I think we've just encountered another twist in the flow of time – the Turning has certainly shaken up the world good and proper.'

Scape shrugged, not understanding. 'That may be so, young dragon. I daresay you have a rather wider view of recent times than I, given my isolation. But just lately I've been restless; the rain hasn't helped, I suppose, and Chaemen – she's been on the move in a way I've never seen before. And now you lot arrive . . .'

Scape's reference to the rain reminded them all of the deteriorating weather. The constant shower of the preceding days had become a downpour and flying was misery. Wing membranes grew heavy and it was hard to predict the air currents as warm rain met the cold air which hugged the glacier surface. Even Tallow and Smoke, proficient fliers as they were, had to admit that they would prefer to turn back.

'Well,' sighed Scape. 'I suppose I've seen enough for today, although the map won't be complete tonight. Still,' and here he scanned his eyes across the rest of the glacier, 'I suspect it will never be complete again, not the way Chaemen is moving now. I'll never be able to keep up.'

With varying degrees of reluctance the dragons turned back towards Scape's caves, grateful to be staring no longer into the slow sun, however dull it was through the driving rain.

It was as they plodded their way heavily through the drenched air that Vox said, 'I wish I had been to Aether's Cross. It sounds a wonderful place.'

Abruptly Scape stopped, pounding his small wings against the rain in an unlikely hover. '*What* did you say?!' he exploded.

'I-I just said it sounded a wonderful place,' stammered Vox, glancing nervously at Smoke. He had intended the comment for her, knowing that she had once visited the Cross, and in doing so had hoped to spark a conversation. His recognition of her dazzling beauty – in his eyes at least

– had come as an overwhelming flood of hope and he was struggling to deal with the prospect that, outcast no more, he might yet live the life of a normal dragon. That he might put behind him the horror of Choliel's death and his thirst for a revenge he could never gain; that he might actually love again.

Scape approached the embarrassed, purple-scaled dragon and spluttered, 'I don't know what you did to merit those colours and I don't really care, but that wasn't what I meant. What did you call this place you're looking for?'

'Th-The Cross?'

'No, no, no. That's exactly what you've all been calling it up to now. The Cross, the Cross! You didn't tell me that wasn't its full name, did you? Call yourselves explorers? Don't you know that attention to detail is the most important part of . . .'

'Hold on,' soothed Brace, trying to calm his pounding heart. Suddenly he knew that they were near to finding his home. Very near! 'All right – the place we are looking for is called Aether's Cross. It was a pass through the Low Mountains in the northern part of the Heartland. Now, does that help you?'

'I don't know anything about any Low Mountains,' blustered Scape. 'It's *Aether*! *That's* what you should have told me. You should have told me that straight away. This changes everything! Dear me, I'm quite overwhelmed with it all. No wonder I've been restless lately – I must have known you were coming!'

'Then . . . you can help us after all?' hazarded Brace.

'Help you? Why, my dear dragon, I can take you straight to Aether himself!'

If Fortune could ever have isolated the moment in his life when he finally stepped over into adulthood then that night would have been it. That night, that place, nestled close beside his love and chilled by the rainstorm. He grew. For when he woke he found that though his troubles had not diminished, nor his grief subsided, his heart had expanded to embrace them. His new strength Gossamer perceived too, for though she still could not speak to him she touched him over and over, reassuring him with soundless affection that she flew still at his side.

And when Scoff saw a familiar ease to Fortune's gait – what the young dragon's mother had once called his 'economy' – he knew that his friend had entered a new airstream.

'Archan had better prepare,' he smiled grimly. 'With you two on her tail she should worry. I would.'

Resolve blazed from the eyes of Fortune and Gossamer as they led Scoff into the sky once more. Ahead the mountains looked insubstantial, as though they might flicker and fade beneath the lethal gaze of this dragon pair. North beckoned, strongly now.

The wind blew them on at a speed it was hard to judge and the mountains which had looked so insignificant rose like giants before them, their peaks reaching up to break the flow of the river of charm itself. Clouds jostled the summits, while the rainstorm they delivered coursed down slopes and foothills and swamped the ground beneath the dragons' wings. A world of water rolled past beneath them now, ever deepening.

'No land left at this rate,' remarked Scoff. 'Everywhere's flooded.'

'That's the least of our troubles,' answered Fortune. At his side Gossamer nodded mutely. Together they were watching the mountains, watching them closely for it seemed that they grew disproportionately higher as they approached nearer.

The dragons ascended through the cloud base, enduring the turbulent eddies within the rainstorm, breaking free again into brilliant sunshine. Here the air was cold and thin, but the sun was warm on their backs. Fortune found time to observe the way the light caught the scales of his companions: Scoff's garish wings and Gossamer's white. His own scales, as they had always been, were a dull, nutty brown. *Typical Natural colours*, he thought a little sadly. *Boring. Still, I did experience charm – that's more than most can say.*

Above them and closer now flowed the river of charm. It was clearly visible, more vibrant than it had appeared from lower altitude, tendrils of glowing magic coruscating back and forth within the main body of the stream and sparking off contacts with the broken spells trapped there. It moved like a wild animal, an endless chain of energy which divided into many pieces as it neared the mountain range, each piece selecting its own course through the treacherous alps, perhaps to rejoin its brethren on the opposite side, perhaps to journey on alone.

'Look!' barked Scoff.

Fortune and Gossamer looked behind them and for a breath or two could not work out what it was he had seen. Then they saw it too.

The tail of the river.

It was far behind but gaining on them, an agitated line low on the horizon of grey-white cloud. There the magic was pale and hard to see, but as it approached with blinding speed it grew thicker. Bars of light enfolded the river's end. Periodically claws of charm slashed outwards, cutting into the cloud and sparking lightning in its depths. The dragons watched in fear and amazement as a seething ball of charm sped towards them.

'Down!' barked Fortune once he had gathered his wits, but when he looked down he saw that they were trapped.

Already the mountains had risen through the cloud. The wind had driven them on while they had loitered and now there was nowhere for them to descend. Ahead icy peaks stretched gnarled claws towards them. Much higher and their wings would fail in the flimsy air.

'Up into the charm?' suggested Scoff. The river was close now, just within reach, but there was no telling what they might encounter there.

'I want to be as far as possible from *that*,' responded Fortune with feeling, waggling his wing at the river's angry tail. They could see it lashing from side to side; already it had halved the distance to them.

It was Gossamer who made the decision in the end, and characteristically it was a decision of instinct. She had been staring into the cloud during her companions' brief debate and though she did not hear the mysterious voice she fancied that the presence she had encountered in the tower was her companion too. White vapour coiled around ice-clad slope, thin and wispy, and it seemed to her that they should fly. *Fast!*

'Gossamer! What are you doing! You'll kill yourself!' Fortune's yell was followed at once by action, and no sooner had he jerked his wings into motion than Scoff copied him. Together they accelerated after Gossamer, pumping the thin air as though their lives depended on it, which they almost certainly did.

Gossamer remained as silent as she had through all the past days as she led Fortune and Scoff at ever-increasing speed into the mountains. Peaks began to block their way, rearing up from the cloud bank and turning their flight into a dance. More than once they rounded an impossibly high turn of rock only to be confronted by an impenetrable cliff. They cleared ridges they thought impossible and cut beneath precarious arches where the speed of their passage set off avalanches. And behind them all the time, growing steadily nearer, lashed the river's tail.

'Why don't we stop and hide?' was what Fortune wanted to shout but his breath was like cold fire in his throat and the words remained unsaid. On they sped and closer came the river's tail. Booming sounds reached their ears, the sounds of mountaintops falling beneath the wrath of abandoned charm, angry at having been dragged from its rest. The mountains reared yet higher, carving the river into its many separate paths; what would happen when the ball of energy reached this place of division they could not guess.

Aware of her companions' distress but increasingly sure of her decision, Gossamer flew in a kind of ecstasy. Their goal was near, she believed, nearer than they had realized; memory of the Cloud buoyed her wings, lifting her over each successive peak, pulling her round each bend, pushing her faster and faster despite the mounting peril. She was right – she knew it – she was right and when they came through this ordeal a part of the horror would be lifted. *The fog will be lifted from our eyes*, she thought deliriously.

Flight now an agonizing labour, they struggled through the thinnest air over a jagged ridge to find a massive cliff wall scant breaths away. Behind them the tail of the river bit into the air they had just escaped. Splinters of rock showered against their wings and a great cloud of ice exploded beneath them. Thunder wounded their ears and the air grew hazy, flickering. They dared not look back.

There was a sudden increase in pressure, as though they had descended too fast into denser air. Charm filled the sky on every side. The looming cliff crackled with red ribbons of magic and chunks of rock sheared away from its face. Fortune and Scoff closed their eyes: they were going much too fast to avoid the collision. Gossamer opened hers wider, anticipating the end.

With a crash the air cleared again and the lashing tail had passed them by. The pressure returned to its former thinness and they cried out with the pain of the sudden transition. Blood welled in Fortune's ears. The charm fled the cliff wall, leaving only solid rock. Fortune opened his mouth to scream.

Then there was silence. Complete silence but for the rush of wind across their wings. Their speed unchecked they flew on. Cautiously, Fortune opened his eyes.

The cliff had vanished. This fact was astonishing enough but when he threw a glance behind he saw something even more amazing – the whole mountain range had vanished! Rock had given way to water, for beneath them had opened an ocean. Flecks of white dotted its surface, merging in the far distance to form an endless expanse of ice. The cloud had gone, the rain had gone and the river of charm and its angry tail were no longer to be seen. Grunting his shock Fortune nearly folded his wings and fell from the sky, but one further surprise jolted him back to sensibility.

'It was an artifice,' said Gossamer, swooping in to fly close at his side. 'The mountains were an illusion put there to prevent our coming, or slow it at least.'

'But who put them there?' blurted Fortune before he could even think to ask Gossamer how she was feeling, how overjoyed he was to hear her voice again.

'Archan, I suppose,' she frowned, but then she saw Scoff shaking his head.

'Doubtful,' he determined. 'Possible, but ... doubtful. Tasted the charm at the end – didn't notice it at first, not like you. Didn't taste of dragon. Too big for Archan too.'

'So who?' repeated Fortune.

'Once would have said, "Don't know",' Scoff answered. 'But now I know. Basilisk charm, Fortune. The Deathless are here too.'

'*Are* here? You mean all of them?' Fortune shuddered, for his fear of the basilisks outweighed the fascination he held for their kind. 'You mean it's not just Archan we've got to deal with?' Scoff shook his head, his easy face for once quite devoid of humour.

'No knowing their minds,' he said. 'Archan we might predict. But the Deathless . . .' He let the words trail away while Gossamer and Fortune stared long and deep into each other's eyes.

Gossamer spoke at last. 'I think . . . I think the Turning is far from over, and I think this new world is far from complete.' When she saw Fortune's puzzled stare she went on, 'I can't explain it any better, I'm afraid, my love, but finding Aria is just the first part. I think there may be a few surprises left for us yet.'

They embraced with a strange, cold passion. Confused, but uplifted by the depth and radiance of Gossamer's smile, Fortune followed as she again took the lead. They swooped down into more buoyant air, heading for the icebergs.

CHAPTER 30

World's Crest

No longer did they have the river of charm to guide them – indeed they found its absence disturbing, for it had become a curious comfort – but they kept to their path, for Gossamer's instinct was strong and she still led the way.

A crystal sky observed the dragons' flight over the icebergs. The new clarity was a revelation after the glowering rain of the previous days and they forged enthusiastically ahead, the hiss of air across their wings accompanied by the growling of the bergs as they glanced and collided in the ocean below. The water was a deep and vibrant blue, the ice sheer white in the brilliant sunshine. Every contour of the floating mountains was finely delineated; iceberg bases were wave-worn smooth, while their backs were sculpted into astonishing forms, some plain and unadorned, others intricately textured. The dragons had never before seen the like of these leviathans.

'Not heard of this,' commented Scoff as they swooped down to take a closer look at a particularly spectacular formation. This berg had collapsed in its centre, leaving a soaring arch of ice supported by two massive pillars. They turned into its shadow and rushed beneath the arch, thrilled by the majesty of its construction. 'Thought the ice was solid.'

'The world has turned,' answered Fortune, uttering the phrase they all used to explain so much ... and so little. 'Something is causing the ice to break up. I wonder what.'

Towers of ice, like islands afloat in the dazzling immensity of the northern ocean, grew broader and larger as they flew on. The ice began to homogenize until the terrain beneath them was less a sea filled with bergs than a land broken by water-filled cracks and holes. The sun remained bright and high, refusing to set. Midday seemed to elongate into an endless, circling dance of sunlight.

They landed briefly on the fractured surface, as much to test its integrity as to rest, and they found it solid enough. Weird pressure ridges sprinted into the distance as ice-sheets ground together. One enormous berg groaned as its waist was crushed by two opposing floes, spilling dragon-sized chunks of ice on to its attackers. The dragons did not linger.

Hungry now, yet with no promise of food, they set off north again. Under their wings the ice grew more solid and ever more contorted, throwing up pillars and fins and rolling like a wallowing sea monster.

The exertion of flying cancelled conversation again, although this time the silence was good, even confident. But as they flew deeper into the endless noon the two males grew restless – the ice moved past unchanging but for the details and the rhythm of their wings began to hypnotize their senses.

'It's as though we're flying but not getting anywhere,' observed Fortune. 'And with all the strange things that have been happening lately, I wouldn't be surprised if that's just what we're doing.'

But they had proceeded only a few hundred wingbeats further when Gossamer opened her wings wide and halted before them. She spun round, maintaining an elegant hover, her wings afire in the glare of the sun. 'We're close now,' she breathed. 'Look there, ahead.'

Something disrupted the smooth line of ice against brilliant sky, a shallow curve of darkness which obliterated the horizon directly ahead. Fortune fancied he could detect movement there, but he could not be sure.

'What is it?' he murmured, fascinated. His heart was thumping fast – it knew they were nearly at their goal. *Whatever it may be*, he thought.

'I don't know,' replied Gossamer. 'But I know we're nearly there. We've nearly reached the crest of the world.'

Air seethed, the very fabric of the reality which held the air boiled as the river's tail erupted past Hesper and Ledra.

Briefly enclosed within the concentrated ball of charm which had pursued its parent river across much of the world, the two dragons were battered and stretched until it seemed they had no breath left. Fire of every colour they knew and many they did not jetted over their scales, although it did not burn them. Rips opened in the sky, brief glimpses into other worlds, other realms, but glimpses only, for the gateways were slammed shut as soon as they were made. The magic was strong but brief, its power unable to sustain itself; its grip was tenuous in this natural place.

The shock of the encounter knocked the two dragons from their dream-state and plunged them without warning into cold, empty sky. They floundered, falling many hundreds of trees before instinct opened their wings. Recovering, they swooped together, blinking and looking about them as though they had been doused in cold water. Ahead, the tail of the river dwindled, an angry point of motion against the sky. Then it was gone. Where it vanished was a shadow, a curve of dark mist laid across a land of ice.

Uncertain of where they were, dazed still and equally uncertain of where they should go now, Hesper and Ledra flew towards the shadow.

The curved shape appeared more solid the closer they approached. Soon it filled their vision, revealed now as a broad dome capping the ice for thousands of trees in every direction. What it was made of they could not guess, for its surface looked both smooth and slightly misted, as though a vapour were being exuded from hidden pores. Dark grey and mottled with deep blue, it squatted uncompromisingly before them, the illusion of hazy movement they had detected from afar quite gone. On the ground it was a barrier; flying higher to look down upon it they saw that it was a perfect circle, a dark scab over white ice, hiding . . . what? The sun remained high and stubborn; the dragons landed, devoid of a plan.

'Archan?' suggested Fortune, fully aware that it might not be just Archan and Aria who awaited them beyond this blockade. Scoff shook his head as though catching his companion's thoughts.

'No,' he replied. 'Like the mountains. Basilisk.'

Fortune nodded, fragments of a puzzle whirling through his head and failing to resolve themselves. Somehow they had involved themselves with some plan of the Deathless; what this meant to their own quest he did not dare to speculate. *No matter,* he thought coldly. *We are here for one reason alone. Aria.* The claws still bit every time he thought of his daughter but now the wounds they made were clean and welcome. No longer was he bound by the petty rigours which had overwhelmed him on Haven: now he was journeying again, his purpose clear as the sky, his heart strong. Glancing across at Gossamer he saw his own thoughts mirrored in her eyes. There was communion between them, and even with Scoff too, he realized.

We have the power to do this deed, he thought with a thrill, *whatever it may be.*

Gossamer smiled and nodded her acknowledgement, though when she looked up at the sky she shivered, for nowhere in its glaring emptiness could she see a single cloud.

'Aria is within,' she announced, her voice ringing loudly against the impenetrable surface of the dome. The statement went unchallenged for though they had no proof in fact they had all the proof they needed in their hearts. They had arrived at the crest of the world – and now the real task would begin. 'Now,' Gossamer went on, 'how do we get in?'

'Always a weakness,' suggested Scoff after a moment's deliberation. 'Any barrier. Never flawless. Suggest we search.'

'Where do we start?' sighed Fortune, suddenly daunted by the overwhelming size of the dome. How could they negotiate this impossibility? Was it not a basilisk fabrication after all – how could they challenge the charm of the Deathless?

'If I had made this,' said Gossamer slowly, 'I think I would put the entrance where no intruder would think to look.'

'Where's that?' demanded Fortune excitedly.

'In plain view. Right on top, in the middle!'

Gossamer's notion rang true in their ears and they lifted

off the ice to fly up over the rising curve of the blue-grey dome. Gossamer herself emptied her mind of all but a vision of Aria surrounded by charm, priming herself for the encounter which she knew to be imminent. In a few scant breaths she would see her daughter again. Anticipation of the joy she would feel undammed tears and she wept as she flew, half-blinded but leading the way as confidently as ever up towards the dome's peak. Until this deed was done her life was frozen like the ice here at the world's crest – only when Aria was rescued could she move on into the future. *Into the time of the Cloud*.

They had seen the top of the dome already when they had first surveyed the area, but now they were much closer and able to discern a mosaic structure within its piebald skin. Circling, they scanned the entire upper surface to no avail – no break, nor any hint at gap or closure was revealed to them. Fortune sighed heavily, disappointed.

'Perhaps we should land on it,' murmured Gossamer.

'Bad idea,' warned Scoff. But his words were too late for Gossamer had already dropped her wings and opened her claws to descend on to the basilisk dome. Before he or Fortune could rush to block her she had made contact with its skin.

Tiny ripples chased outwards from the points where her claws made contact with the mosaic . . . but that was all. The dome supported her weight without complaint and no defensive charm reached out to claim her. And still no gateway appeared to take them inside.

'Well,' said Fortune, 'what now . . . ?'

Two dragons rose into view, heading their way. Instinctively Fortune and Scoff took up station in the air to each side and slightly ahead of Gossamer, protecting their grounded female. She did not move, though to remain there made her vulnerable; she observed the newcomers with intense interest.

'Hesper,' she called as they grew near.

'Ledra!' muttered Fortune as he recognized the other.

The unexpected reunion began tensely, with Fortune and Hesper circling each other warily. Scoff and Ledra hung back, expecting the two males to come to blows, but in the end it was Gossamer who called a halt.

'All of you, stop fooling around and come down here,' she barked, adding to herself, *for the Cloud's sake!* 'It's perfectly safe.' Surprised by her directness but grateful for the chance to rest their wings, all four of her companions obeyed. Hesper and Ledra squatted a short distance from Gossamer's group, eyeing them suspiciously. 'Now,' Gossamer went on, 'what brings you two here?'

Before Hesper could speak Ledra was pouring out their story. Though she left out many details about the destruction of Haven she told enough for Gossamer to realize that she regretted much of what she had done. That Ledra actually appeared to possess a heart was a revelation – but it was from the heart that her tale emerged, not from the calculating mind for which she was better known. Hesper glared at her as she spoke, clearly displeased by her candour.

'The charm just swept us up,' concluded Ledra, 'and brought us here. Hesper has made me charmed, and I have seen such wonders, but . . . but I don't know who I am any more.' These last words she spoke in a whisper, her eyes pleading with Hesper to understand. She looked to Fortune for support but he would not meet her glance; he seemed embarrassed in her presence.

'Whatever my . . . *colleague* has said one fact remains,' growled Hesper, his unnaturally high voice ringing oddly against the mosaic. 'There *is* charm left in the world and there are still dragons who can wield it.'

'You for one, I suppose?' commented Fortune dryly.

'Of course. Now we are vulnerable in such small numbers, but five is stronger than two, or even three. Why not combine our forces and hunt down the charm? This appears to be its final destination after all.'

'Hesper in charge?' prompted Scoff.

'If you wish,' Hesper grinned broadly, quite aware of the animosity being directed at him.

'If we join together,' said Gossamer, not taking her eyes from Ledra, 'it must be for mutual benefit, do you not agree?' Hesper grunted as she went on, 'We believe our daughter, Aria, to be held captive beneath this fabrication of the basilisks. We too wish to gain entry but for our own reasons. We might help each other but when our various tasks are completed that would be the end of it. Is that satisfactory to you, Hesper? And to you, Ledra?'

Hesper grunted, his thug's mind working hard to interpret Gossamer's proposal. In the end however he found it straightforward and to his liking. *When I have reclaimed the charm*, he thought, *it will be up to me whether or not there is an end to anything.*

'Of course,' he beamed. 'Anything you say. Now, do you have any ideas?'

'We were rather hoping you might,' sighed Gossamer. 'We've run out.'

'Hmm.' Hesper paced to and fro, making a great show of deliberating. 'Well, most defensive places have a weakness.'

'I said that,' muttered Scoff.

'At Covamere for instance we always took pains to protect the corners and the edges.'

'The corners and the edges?' repeated Fortune, his curiosity aroused.

'Exactly!'

'It's round,' observed Scoff sarcastically, demonstrating the curve of the dome with one sweep of his extravagant wing.

'Yes . . . well, I was going on to say that it's really *junctions* that are weak. Where two walls meet, for example, or . . .'

'Or where a wall meets the ground?' barked Fortune. 'Come on!'

Thus enthused they hurried back down the flank of the dome to the ground again. The ice was smooth and packed hard where the mottled wall met it, the junction apparently seamless. Between them Hesper and Scoff searched for some shred of charm by which they might melt it, to see if they might excavate a way through from below, but there was no magic nearby. Both felt a faint hum of power from within the dome itself, confirming their suspicion that here was the earthing-point of the great river, but there was nothing that could be used.

'Let's circle it,' suggested Fortune. 'We might find a weak spot somewhere on the perimeter.'

Off they trudged, soon passing into thin, blue shadow. Fortune was surprised when Hesper joined him to walk at his side; Ledra remained at the tail of the group a tree or two behind the others, and smiled when eventually Gossamer dropped back to join her. Fortune noted the glare which Hesper threw at her, and also the way Ledra seemed almost to want to cling to Gossamer.

'We've had our differences, you and I,' said Hesper suddenly. 'Strange that we're working together now, isn't it?'

'Not for long,' replied Fortune acidly.

'Now is that any way to go on?' answered Hesper, feigning hurt. 'Look, Fortune. We don't like each other, I'll grant, but we can help each other. Afterwards you don't ever need to see me again.'

Fortune paused to look across at the big, grey dragon. Spikes and splinters of scale projected from his hide at all angles – he still looked like the warring dragon he had always been. 'Do you still want power?' he asked.

'I want the charm,' grinned Hesper. Fortune shrugged and they moved on through the shadows. The dome was unchanging; no hint of an opening marred its surface and it looked as though this search too would prove in vain.

'All right,' sighed Fortune at length, genuinely keen to accept this dragon's company. 'Let us just be honest with each other, Hesper, and we'll get along fine.'

'Agreed! Now, tell me what you know about this thing. Did you say the basilisks made it?'

Before Fortune could reply they were interrupted by Scoff. 'Found something!' he cried. They hurried forward to where he was brushing carefully at a small drift of snow. A gentle wind blew on this side of the dome, bringing in the fine powder from distant dunes and collecting against the wall. Apparently a projection of some kind had collected more snow than usual.

'What is it?' demanded Fortune as Scoff cautiously dug into the dragon-sized drift. Scoff ducked his head down to look closer, then took several hasty steps back.

'It's a basilisk!' he hissed.

Silver eyes without pupils glared at them from beneath the snow, frost-lined and featureless. Charm shimmered at their lids and crackled across their surfaces and Fortune remembered the legend that the Deathless could kill with a single look, a single breath. Motionless it stayed, the precise direction of its gaze impossible to determine, the aura of its presence paralysing the dragons.

'This is a different one,' whispered Fortune. He knew the creature would hear his every word but still he kept his voice hushed. 'We should leave it be – move on.'

Neither of his companions argued, and as they backed away they signalled to Gossamer and Ledra to join them at a safe distance. A nearby ridge seemed to offer the protection they all agreed might be necessary and here they conferred. After some debate Scoff made the casual observation that the positioning of the basilisk seemed odd. Then Gossamer put her claw on precisely what was wrong.

'It's too close to the wall,' she announced suddenly, interrupting a muttered discussion between Fortune and Hesper. 'Unless its back is broken it must be lying *through* the wall! I think we've just found the way in!'

'And the sentry,' observed Hesper unhelpfully.

'Hesper's right,' agreed Fortune sadly. 'Unless we can get past this basilisk we've got no chance of getting in at all. It's obviously guarding the place, and it's my guess this is the only entrance.'

They lingered disconsolately for a while before Ledra finally spoke up.

'We could always go and ask it,' she suggested brightly.

CHAPTER 31

Into the Ice

An immense crater in the glacier yawned below them, its depths immeasurable and darkening swiftly to midnight blue within a tree's height from its lip. The dragons hovered nervously over its maw, sculling the cold air which wafted across their wings. The sun finally descended below the icy horizon and the blue of the sky hurried to meet the deepening blackness of the chasm depths. A less inviting place none of them could imagine.

'Is this it?' asked Velvet tremulously. 'Is this the trollvein?'

'This the trollvein?' laughed Scape. 'Oh, my dear, no, no, no, indeed no. This is just the way in. Aether's buried deep, you see, too deep to be seen from the surface. First you have to reach Aether – then you'll find trollvein.'

'Then what are we waiting for?' urged Brace, impatient now that their goal was apparently so near. His wings twitched and tucked, ready to take him down.

'Now hold on there, young dragon!' Scape swooped beneath Brace, preventing his descent. 'Now's not a good time of day to be entering Chaemen. Best that we wait until morning, if you ask me.'

'Why's that?' inquired Velvet.

Scape shuddered, but he would say no more. Velvet observed the wideness of his eyes and the tightening of the skin around his mouth as he prowled the air over the crater and realized that he was horribly afraid of this place. His fear bothered her, for up to now he had seemed so in love with the glacier. The crater gaped at her, a hungry mouth.

'Let's go back,' she whispered to Cumber. 'There's something bad here. Let's come back tomorrow, when it's light.'

Cumber shrugged, and was about to reply when he saw that Brace had overheard Velvet's words.

'I won't ask any of you to come in with me,' Brace announced, his voice strong and calm. 'But I don't believe we can afford to waste time now. Scape – I would be grateful if you would tell me all you know about this place.'

As Scape had shivered so the whole group seemed to shiver, an involuntary reflex which ran through them all as though they were a single entity. A breath of frigid air was exhaled from the crater and they bunched together uncertainly.

'I see you are determined,' said Scape slowly after a moment's consideration. 'Though I would counsel against it, young dragon, I really would. I will not go in tonight, but I will tell you a little of what you might expect. I shall return tomorrow to help you – if you are still in need of help.'

The ambiguity of this last phrase was lost on none of the dragons and several nervous glances were exchanged as Scape and Brace muttered to each other in the failing light. Meanwhile the group fragmented, breaking into two halves: those who would accompany Brace and those who would wait until morning. Of these latter it was Quill who was most vociferous.

'I can't see that another night will make much difference one way or another,' she proclaimed, eyeing the crater with distrust. 'Not even to the poor dragons of Aether's Cross. I shall take Scape's advice. Will any of you join me?'

The rest were less willing. Tallow and Volley, perhaps the most seasoned adventurers of the party, at once flew to Brace's side, thus signalling their loyalty. Vox was just turning to join Quill when he found himself face to face with Smoke. She smiled at him.

'I'm not sure what to do, Vox,' she said pleasantly. 'What would you advise?'

'W-well,' he stammered, hardly able to believe that she was actually asking his opinion. 'I've been in a trollvein before – as has Quill for that matter, and it was all right, I suppose. But I could feel that there was something behind its skin, something evil. I think that if you go in expecting trouble then you'll find it. And I think it could be very bad trouble.'

'Then I'll wait for daylight with you, Vox,' replied Smoke sweetly. 'I agree with Quill – one night will make little difference.'

Behind them another conversation was taking place, this one more heated. 'Of course I understand his impatience,' Velvet was saying to Cumber in exasperated tones, 'but I also think we should listen to what Scape has to say. He does know this place rather better than we do, don't forget, and if he's warning us off then I think we should take heed.'

'But we can't just abandon them,' protested Cumber. 'We promised to find the Cross, and anyway I, at least, should go since I was there when the disaster occurred. I might be of quite some use as it happens – and I'm ex-Charmed; they'll have charm to deal with down there, you can be sure of that.'

'Well, go then!' snapped Velvet. 'Leave me if you want to, Cumber. I'm not going down there to have my wings chewed off by some monstrous magic that I've been warned against!' Her anger was genuine enough but it was merely the coating on a core of fear. The crater simply terrified her; she was convinced that if she entered it she would die and even her desire not to be parted from Cumber could not take her into its depths, not until morning at least and perhaps not even then. 'Can't you feel it?' she went on, her voice quieter now and trembling. 'Can't you see the evil coming out of it?' And as she looked she *could* see it, a palpable smoke which drifted lazily from the blue-black abyss and climbed towards them like searching ivy. She blinked and it was gone.

'I can't see anything,' snapped Cumber, his own anger also a mask. He wanted desperately to play his part, and genuinely believed that he was a vital member of the expedition. But could he leave Velvet again as he had once left her on the Plated Mountain? He did not want to, but . . . 'Come with me,' he offered bravely, 'I'll look after you, I promise.'

'But who'll look after you, Cumber?' answered Velvet sadly. She searched her heart and found there the depth of her love for this absurd dragon, but she knew that the chasm into which he and her friends were about to descend was deeper still and that even her generous heart could not compete. It would swallow her and her love as she might snap at a bug. 'Must you go?' she whispered, nuzzling him as tears sprang to her eyes.

'You know I must.' Cumber cried too as they embraced clumsily and for an instant she thought she had found the resolve to go with him. *What of Scape's warning?* she thought. *Might he not be wrong? I haven't heard what he's told Brace, and what you don't know can't hurt you.* But then she saw the midnight glare of the crater, the creeping tendrils of smoke which were there and yet were not, and she knew she could not go. 'Not yet,' she murmured, too quiet even for Cumber to hear. 'Not yet.'

Their separation was the final decision, and as they parted so too did Scape and Brace, allowing Cumber to complete the band of four. Their companions watched them, wings lifted in salute as they dropped into the darkness, then turned towards the last remnant of light in the near-night sky and stroked their way through the air towards Scape's home.

'Were the trolls evil then?' asked Velvet quietly when they finally passed into the sanctuary of the small cave. She felt weak and useless, already regretting her decision. But the crater had felt so *bad*.

'Evil? The trolls?' responded Scape, surprised. 'By the skies, no. They were magnificent beings, lords of the earth for as long as they lived. They had their wars, to be sure, but then so do dragons. Evil? No, no, no. Not evil, not at all.'

'Then what was it I sensed down there?'

Scape frowned, pausing as he settled himself against the back wall of the cave. Dim starlight glinted off his evergreen scales; his eyes were invisible. 'Whatever you saw, or think you saw, is best kept to yourself, young dragon. We will go back at dawn, when a dragon may more safely seek the route to Aether. Then you may understand.'

'And the others? Cumber, Brace?'

Another pause, longer this time.

'The evil of the place comes not from the trolls,' he said at length. 'So long as they understand that they will come to no harm.'

'And if they don't?' Velvet's voice was as a breath of wind through reeds. But Scape did not reply.

The crater was even larger than it had appeared from the air, large enough in fact to accept all four dragons flying side by side with their wings at full stretch, and with sufficient space left for four more. The scored ice walls glowed pale blue; they seemed to suck the faint sound of their wingbeats and swallow it without echo. The descent was less like being consumed than being . . . absorbed.

Total darkness swiftly conquered the inadequate starlight and they were flying on instinct alone. Cumber found he was very glad Tallow was here, for the big Natural could fly through blizzard and fog and still reach his destination as efficiently as if he were in the clearest air. He listened to the steady, powerful rhythm of the air as it moved past Tallow's wings and wished that he too possessed such control.

Of course, he thought, *no charmed dragon ever needed such control. We had the magic.* And he found again that he was grieving for charm. He, who had ever mistrusted the Realm, who had always claimed to be unmoved by the departure of the magic from the world – yes, he missed it terribly. At last he could admit it to himself. *I want the magic back*, he mourned. *But what would be the cost?*

The chasm turned about them, bending to the horizontal. The change was accompanied by a flare of light far ahead in the blackness. A rich, blue glow sprang from some distant, invisible source and illuminated the winding tunnel, filtering through thousands of tongues and strings of ice which criss-crossed the way ahead; it looked as though some enormous spider had been hard at work spinning webs of frost across the passage.

'Tricky flying now,' commented Volley dryly.

'I've seen worse,' offered Tallow. 'Come on.'

The flying was indeed tricky, but not impossible. The two big Naturals led the way, picking the safest course through and around the myriad growths which extended in all directions across their path. Logs of ice barred their way; upreaching stalagmites which had fused with descending stalactites formed pillared halls through which they had to weave; many of the icy fingers had broken beneath their own weight, leaving sharp spikes which the dragons avoided. All the time they flew they were staring into the blue light, now seeing it clear, now watching its refracted ghost through a net of rime. It grew steadily nearer.

Brace felt confident. He was free of Archan's dungeon and back in the company of dragons he knew and trusted. They were close to the end of their quest, and what Scape had told him of this tunnel had not scared him. There seemed no great danger, not to him.

'Before you go down there,' Scape had said, 'clear your mind. Clear it of everything, do you understand? Everything! Whatever's down there – and it's not troll, you can be sure of that – will know your thoughts and play with them.'

'Play with them?'

'I choose my words carefully, young dragon. It is less evil than ... restless. But it is nocturnal. During the day it is asleep, oblivious to anything you or I may care to undertake – that is why I urge you to wait until dawn.'

'I can't wait. Now tell me what it is that's down there.'

But Scape did not know, or chose not to say. 'If evil comes of tonight it will be your own, dragon,' he concluded enigmatically.

Brace considered Scape's words without fear. *I have no reason to flee the dark*, he decided. *I have come through worse torments than anything this Chaemen can throw at me. Let it try – I'm ready for it.*

And now, in the generous confines of the huge tunnel, he felt his confidence magnified to fill the space through which he flew. Nothing would go wrong now that Aether's Cross was within their reach. Nothing.

The webbing fell behind them and they were back in clear air. The light was blinding now and painful to look at, but just as they were about to halt it faded almost to nothing. A weak glow remained, dim blue defining a sharp turn ahead: the source of the light was just around the corner.

Cautiously they advanced, Tallow at the head, Cumber at the tail. The sound of running water overwhelmed the gentle flap of their wings and they saw that the tunnel walls were glistening, moving. Rivulets were speeding down its translucent surface to join the stream which flooded the curved floor. Spray danced in the dim light and there was a crashing sound.

They reached the corner and turned.

Tallow, normally so difficult to shock, gasped and reeled back, bumping Brace with his cycling wings. They flurried together briefly before separating and moving forward into the chamber, followed at once by their two companions. None of them spoke – there seemed no words to express their wonder.

The chamber was bigger than any they had seen in ice or rock, world or Realm. It expanded across their vision as though in motion, a massive bubble trapped in the heart of the glacier. Bigger than any Great Chamber made by dragon, bigger even than Shatter's fortress, it defied all natural laws as it basked in its own, inflated glory. No columns supported its centre, nor did any structures mar its pearlescent walls; it simply *was*, and it was grander than any hall they had seen before.

Long and oval, it stretched into blue haze to either side; they had entered about half-way along its length and could barely see the far ends. Its ceiling climbed outrageously into the mist which filled this particular part of the chamber, and looking up they saw the origin of the spray. A jet of water exploded from a crack several trees above their heads, launching its icy load out across the chamber where it struck the floor in a great eruption of water droplets and ice crystals; the floor itself was awash.

But all this was as nothing to what the chamber contained. Ice-covered, shelved and sloping, something huge occupied the main part of the cavern like an outlandish sculpture, and the dragons thought for a crazy moment that Scape had been down here, and had carved some mighty block of ice into this weird form.

Then Cumber recognized an angle, a curve. He flew higher, dodging the water jet as he struggled to gain the right perspective on the monolithic thing. He saw a string of frozen quills, and a great, yawning socket, and he knew that this was a troll. *But not just any troll*, he thought breathlessly. *Aether!*

Awe became celebration as he told the others. Brace cried openly as he circled the bones, greatly moved by this encounter. They clung together, the four dragons, for they felt minuscule beneath the troll's shadow, even more so when they realized that this cliff, this *mountain* which filled the chamber and loomed over them like the Plated Mountain itself was merely Aether's skull, that the rest of him was buried in the ice behind the chamber wall.

'How can anything so huge have *lived*?' exclaimed Brace when he had finally caught his breath.

'The world was very different then,' shrugged Cumber. Then his voice grew strangely distant. 'It was charmed, and so were the trolls. Charm ruled. Charm was lord of all.'

'Where's the trollvein then, do you think? Is it literally that? A vein? Do we have to go into Aether's body to find it?' Brace shuddered at this unwelcome prospect. Until now the word 'trollvein' had been just that: a word. But now that he was confronted by this astonishing corpse he felt uneasy, revolted even. Majestic though the noble skull undoubtedly was, Brace was acutely conscious that over those bones had once been spread meat, that within the cavity of its skull had pulsed a brain and vessels filled with blood. Veins! He turned away, pressing down the gorge in his throat.

'I don't know,' answered Cumber shortly. Brace's change in mood reflected a change in the whole group, a surge of irrational suspicion. They drew apart, eyeing each other warily and flicking nervous glances about the chamber itself. *This place is a grave*, thought Brace suddenly. *Are there ghosts here?*

A tremendous groaning sound filled the cavern, its source unidentifiable, and they bunched together again, their mood crystallizing into stark fear. The groaning swelled then slowly faded – very slowly, as though it were teasing them. The silence it left was worse.

Indeed the silence was very bad, for the dragons realized that *all* sound had ceased. The water still exploded from its bolt-hole and splashed to the floor . . . but there was no sound. A sudden chunk of ice fell from the far wall and crashed against the troll skull. Silently. Then the groaning came again and with it returned normal sounds, slapped back into existence from wherever they had been banished.

Again the groaning ceased, and Brace heard the echo of Scape's voice: *Whatever's down there will know your thoughts and play with them.*

'It's nothing,' he announced bravely, his voice ringing false in the vault. 'Come on, we have a job to do.'

Scarcely reassured, his companions raised their brows. It was Tallow however who initiated the discussion, for he had already had an idea. 'I was looking closely at this skull,' he said slowly, 'and I thought it looked particularly dark inside.'

'Well, that's not really a big surprise, is it, Tallow?' babbled Cumber. 'I mean to say, it would be dark inside a troll's skull, don't you think, especially when it's buried underground, and especially when it's fair odds we'll have to fly inside it, after all, wouldn't you think it rather odd if . . .'

'Steady on, Cumber,' interrupted Volley in his rich baritone. 'Let's just calm down and let old Tallow speak, eh?'

Tallow went on as Cumber tried to calm himself. 'In fact, I believe that of the two eye sockets, one is even darker than the other.'

'So you think that's where we should look first?' prompted Brace excitedly, his fear temporarily forgotten. 'For the trollvein, I mean?'

'Unless there are any other suggestions.'

There were none. Tallow led the way through the cold to the very brink of the colossal eye socket. It gaped before them like no cave they had ever seen, blacker than it had any right to be. Icicles hung like great incisors from its upper edge, poised as though to drop on them as soon as they passed the threshold. Brace felt his wing brush Cumber's and they shared an agonized glance, their nerves seemed to tinkle audibly like ice crystals.

'Well,' said Brace, 'here we go.'

'Wait!' cried Tallow suddenly. Without further word he turned smartly around and retraced the path they had taken to approach the eye socket. Then he rose vertically into the haze and out of sight. Long moments passed; the breath moved slowly, laboriously through the throats of his companions. Where had he gone? What had he seen?

'Tallow?' called Brace, but softly. Then more loudly, 'Tallow?!'

Cumber found the shaking in his wings too much to bear and landed on the craggy lip of the eye socket, its rough surface scratching against his flank. Behind him the shadows loomed.

Just when the terror began to creep into their hearts Tallow reappeared, his face grim. 'Something was casting a shadow on the far wall. I saw it when we came in and thought it wasn't right, but I couldn't see why. Then it came to me; come and see for yourselves.'

Brace's head thumped as he followed Tallow up over the skull. The anticipation of entering the blackness had generated such tension that he did not know what was worse: actually going in or experiencing this unexpected reprieve. At his side Cumber flew expressionless, his own thoughts unreadable. Brace watched him closely, for he was beginning to think that Cumber was not himself. Not himself at all.

Flying over the top of the skull was like flying over a range of hills. Ribs of bone unrolled like mountain ridges, the valleys filled with the stiff quills which adorned the heads of most of the troll corpses they had seen earlier in the glacier. It grew darker as they proceeded for here the blue light did not penetrate so well. The sound of the water behind them became muffled, then faded altogether.

Presently they cleared the skull's crest and started to descend again, but they did not have to descend far before they saw what it was that Tallow had called them here to see. Volley gasped and Brace groaned. Cumber said nothing, then began slowly to laugh.

'I saw the shadow of a skull on the back wall of the cavern,' explained Tallow, 'and I assumed it was the shadow cast by the skull we could see. But then I realized it couldn't have been: the angle of the light was all wrong. So I came to check my suspicion, and found this.'

The gesture of his wing was wholly unnecessary, for his discovery was monumental enough to be plain to all his companions. Here in the shadows was a second skull, almost identical to the first. Its shadow bounced up the curved ice wall, a flat echo of its dark majesty. They were hovering in the space between the skulls, a space like a canyon of bone, and looking down towards where Aether's body disappeared into the wall they saw the reason for the twins. Two skulls, two sets of vertebrae defining necks capable of supporting a small island. One body.

Aether, troll-lord of old, had possessed two heads.

Two more eye sockets glowered at them, one filled with fallen ice but the other open and even darker than the one into which they had been about to enter, and they knew without investigating that here was the entrance to a second trollvein.

'But which one is the right one?' cried Brace incredulously.

Before his words had stopped ringing off the bone and ice the groaning noise came again. It too was twinned now, and there was no mistaking whence it issued. It came equally from the two trollveins, from the twin eyes of Aether, challenging them to enter. Challenging them to choose.

Cumber's laugh went on.

CHAPTER 32

Choices

Velvet had no idea how long she had been pacing when a voice intruded into her reverie. 'I could see how worried you were, but I didn't say anything – it's not an easy subject to talk about – and now I'm regretting it.' It was Scape, emerging from his inner sanctum.

Velvet had found it impossible to sleep. She paced the cave, picking her way repetitively through Scape's many contraptions and glancing continually out through the entrance into the long, northern night. An age seemed to pass and still there was no sign of the sun rising; was there no end to the darkness in this remote part of the world?

'You saw the shadow,' Scape suggested gently.

'Shadow?' But although she queried his remark Velvet nodded all the same. Yes, it was a shadow she had seen, a stain on the ice, in the air around the ice.

'Well, whatever it is I don't think it will harm your friends, not if they stick to the correct path. It may scare them a little – probably will, in fact, and maybe more than a little if I'm honest with you – but I don't think they'll come to much harm. Any harm,' he stammered hastily when he saw her eyes grow wide. 'No, really, they'll be fine, so long as they go quickly into the trollvein.'

'Oh, they'll do that all right,' confirmed Velvet, thinking of the importance of the quest to them all, especially to Brace, for whom it was so much more personal. But Scape's exaggerated attempts to make light of the issue had put her ill at ease; he seemed unconvinced, and so she remained unconvinced too. 'Will they find it all right? The trollvein, I mean? Will they really be safe?'

'Oh yes, no mistaking the trollvein, my dear. Clear as your eye, you might say. Only one route to choose, really.'

Velvet sighed, only partly reassured. Suddenly she found herself yearning for the feel of fire, for the coldness of this northern place had invaded her bones and would not leave. She realized that she, like Cumber, was missing the charm, missing the way things used to be. 'How do you know so much about the past?' she inquired presently. 'About trolls especially. I mean, they died out years ago.'

'Ah well, now that's an interesting question.' Scape's eyes sparkled in the faint starlight as he settled down next to Velvet. He appeared relieved that she had changed the topic. 'You should be careful about getting me started on trolls, young dragon, or you may find me difficult to stop!'

'I'll take the chance.' Velvet smiled despite herself, surprised to find that Scape reminded her a little of her beloved Cumber.

'Trolls. Yes, they lived a long, long time ago, and they are extinct – although I fancy a few may still lie near to death but still quick, perhaps taking a single breath every thousand years. But they too will die soon, of that I am certain. They were fiery creatures, dragon – Velvet, is it? – and they stood tall on the earth. If you've seen an earth giant you'll have some idea what a troll looked like, although they were hairier and had manes of long, sharp quills and, of course, they were much, much bigger.

'But you know all that, I suppose. You've even seen some of their bodies on your way around Chaemen. You asked me how I know so much about them. Well, I'll tell you. There was a time, many, many years ago, when dragons and trolls co-existed. Charmed dragons, naturally, if you'll excuse the pun.' Here Scape chortled, clearly impressed at his own wit.

'And so there are stories from those times, passed down through generations of charmed dragons?' guessed Velvet.

'Of course, and they helped me greatly, to begin with. Many of the dragons I met knew stories about trolls – Aether included – and if ever there was a dragon who liked gathering information it's me, but that was not all, Velvet, indeed no. You see, once I came here to Chaemen, to the graveyard of the trolls, I found that dragons had been here too. Listen.

'When the trolls began to feel the fire dying inside them, when they began to feel what was in reality the first itching which would eventually lead to the turning of the world, many of them journeyed here. What brought them to Chaemen I do not know, and probably never will. Perhaps it was a special place for them, perhaps it was chosen at random. Their minds were strange. It does not really matter though, for they came and that was enough. And dragons came with them. Or rather, *a* dragon came with them.'

'*A* dragon? Just the one? What was he, some sort of mascot?'

'In a way – she had certainly been adopted by the trolls. And she travelled in their company as though she were one of them. Her name was Perior. But she was more an observer than a mascot. In fact, she was a record-keeper. And a mapmaker.'

'Just like you,' said Velvet slowly as she began to realize just what it was that Scape had been doing here.

'Indeed. She recorded the demise of the trolls, their final movements, their final resting places. Every detail. And when she died another came to continue her work, learning from the information she had embedded into charmed niches in this very cave, and when he died another came, then another, and so on through the aeons.'

'And now you're here.'

'And now I'm here,' agreed Scape. 'Although I've been a bit slack lately.'

'But why bother?' asked Velvet, genuinely puzzled.

'In case any one needs to know,' offered Scape lamely, discomfited now and shifting uneasily from one claw to the other. Up to now he had never questioned his purpose in charting the movement of the glacier – he had simply done it. Records needed to be kept and he was the dragon for the job. But now . . . 'Now you have come,' he whispered.

'And we need to know,' agreed Velvet.

Scape sighed and turned to one of his contraptions. He fiddled with a set of bellows attached loosely to its flank and then it too sighed. 'A talking machine,' he explained limply. 'Never worked. I should have doubled up on the . . .'

He stopped and frowned, then he breathed. 'Aether . . .'

'What?' prompted Velvet, acutely sensitive to her host's sudden change of mood. The shadows seemed to shift above her head, leaning down to listen more closely to their words. Their conversation had been too pleasant, too safe, and now they were going to pay – now *she* was going to pay! 'What's wrong?' she blurted, irrationally and horribly frightened. Scape's frown had deepened and that creeping dread had started again to insinuate itself into Velvet's spine.

'Well . . . I was just thinking about Brace, I mean, of course I told him everything I know,' answered Scape, a little flustered now, 'except . . . oh, it may be nothing.'

'And just what was it you *didn't* tell him? Are there dangers you didn't warn him about? Answer me, Scape, and quickly, please!' Velvet heard her voice become shrill, almost hysterical.

'It's nothing,' flustered Scape.

'We'll be the judges of that,' came Quill's voice suddenly. The matronly dragon marched resolutely up to Scape from the corner where she had been sitting, listening. Now she and Velvet had blocked his retreat, forcing the crumpled, evergreen dragon back against the entrance pillar; he fidgeted there uncertainly. 'Are you all right, Velvet?' Quill asked.

'I will be as soon as this crazy inventor tells us exactly what it is he's forgotten to tell anyone else,' replied Velvet curtly, addressing herself to Scape as much as to Quill.

'Well,' stammered Scape, quite overwhelmed now but trying desperately to retain his inadequate grasp on the initiative, 'if it's forgetting things you want to talk about you might remember that you wholly forgot to tell me it was *Aether's* Cross you were searching for, and not just any old Cross. I mean, you could have been talking about anywhere. "The Cross", indeed! I've never heard the . . .'

'Just shut up, Scape,' butted in Quill, not unkindly, 'and tell us what you know – or what you suspect.'

'Oh, very well,' muttered Scape. 'It's just this: did I tell you that Aether was a Troll Without Lineage?' The two dragons regarded him blankly. 'No? Well, it's true, so you see . . . oh, I don't suppose you know what that means do you? All right, apart from the fact that he was one of the very first trolls to be formed from the fires beneath the earth, and apart from the fact that he was therefore a ruling troll, one of their wisest and one of the inventors – yes, *inventors* of charm, or at least of the spells which charm makes possible – apart from all that what most concerns us here is his physical appearance.'

'You've lost me completely,' intoned Quill. 'Get to the point, please, Scape.'

'The point? Ah, yes, the point. Well, the point is this: Aether, as a Troll Without Lineage, possessed two hearts and two heads. Now, his body, up until now at least, has always lain – in a particularly spectacular cavern within Chaemen herself, I might add – in such a way that only one of his skulls is exposed. The trollvein you need runs directly from one of the eye sockets in the exposed skull.'

'Up until now?' prompted Velvet, not liking where this was leading.

'Yes,' squirmed Scape, 'and you must understand that this is all speculation, but it occurred to me just now that if the glacier is indeed moving and melting then that situation may have changed – the other skull may be exposed, too.'

'So?' demanded Velvet, although she already knew.

'I have every reason to believe that a second trollvein exits from the second skull. Your friends will have no way of knowing which is the correct way.'

'And what lies down the second trollvein?'

'The shadow.'

'Is there no way of knowing?' moaned Brace. His body was twitching; every muscle, every sinew in his body was ready to carry him into one of these strange veins, to face whatever terrors might lie within. All discussion was past – now it was action that was called for, the decisive action he had so long awaited. And yet doubt remained, choices remained. Which was the right path? To choose wrong might prove bad for them but – and here the crushing threat of elapsing time pressed hard – how long could the dragons of Aether's Cross endure, if they even lived still?

'No way to be sure, that's for sure,' chuckled Cumber,

recovering from his bout of hysterics and gawping at his unimpressed companions. Tallow and Volley looked at each other meaningfully: they were worried about Cumber.

'Unfortunately that is so,' agreed Tallow at length, though he still eyed the young ex-Charmed dragon warily. 'However, a little logical thought might prove our ally.'

'Think away!' beamed Cumber, closing his wings and settling against the rough brow of the second skull. Flakes of ice and shards of bone splintered beneath his weight, dropping into the very eye socket they were contemplating entering.

'Very well,' persisted Tallow. 'We are faced with two possible routes: one obvious – we saw it almost as soon as we entered the cavern – and one hidden, this one.'

'Hidden ways often lead deeper,' suggested Volley.

'But we don't necessarily want to go deeper,' blurted Brace, growing increasingly frustrated by the lack of action. 'We just want to go the right way.'

'Or the left way,' suggested Cumber unhelpfully. The others ignored him; his strange behaviour they would address once they had solved this more pressing riddle.

'I think what Volley means,' said Tallow slowly, 'is that treasures are more often hidden than left in the open. Aether's Cross is a treasure – perhaps it lies down this more concealed way.'

'Or perhaps it's a bluff and it *is* down the obvious way,' replied Brace impatiently. 'Or more likely the two trollveins are in their respective places by pure chance and we might as well close eyes and point a wing as try to deduce which is the right one.'

'We could split up,' suggested Volley darkly, clearly unenthusiastic about the idea.

'No,' answered Tallow in a firm voice. 'Whatever we do we do together.'

'But what *are* we going to do?' moaned Brace. 'Oh, why didn't Scape tell us about this?'

They dropped from the air one by one and took up station with Cumber on the horny skull. Aether's massive quills soared behind them like tree trunks, a forest bed in which a dragon might lose himself in a matter of breaths. Brace shuddered, suddenly overwhelmed by the sheer size of this monster and horrified at the thought that he was actually considering entering its corpse.

But then he thought of the Cross, his home, of the hundreds of wretched dragons trapped in the rock, among them his own parents, Aria's grandparents. He could not go back, not now, whatever perils may lie ahead. He would go on. *But which way?*

'You know, I think I might have a solution,' said Cumber brightly. 'Does anyone want to hear it?'

Vox and Smoke had woken and joined the debate. Velvet felt cold and wretched in the icy grip of the northern night, but when she saw them make their way over from the far corner of the cave she was warmed, if only briefly. Vox was infatuated with Smoke, that much was clear, and Smoke, though remaining aloof, did not seem displeased with the attention. *Even here*, she thought, *even now, love fights through.* She thought again of her Cumber and decided that the fear was not so powerful after all, that her love for him was stronger, and she knew that she would return to the crater that very night. *Shadow or no shadow.*

'W-what's wrong?' asked Vox, casting a nervous glance at Smoke as he did so. He was keen to impress her, Velvet observed with amusement.

'Scape was about to explain precisely what danger our friends are in,' replied Quill, her eyes not leaving their host. Her voice was hard and menacing and demanded a response. For a moment Scape stood erect before her, then he wilted.

'Oh, I'm sorry,' he sighed, exasperated, perhaps with himself. 'I was only trying to protect you the best way I knew how. I'm a solitary old dragon, you know – I've never been much good at being in company.'

'Then start practising,' responded Quill at once, the ghost of a smile turning the scales at the corners of her mouth.

'If your friends go down the correct trollvein,' began Scape, his manner suddenly much more relaxed and open, 'they should have little trouble. I have not gone down it myself but I understand that it proceeds south-west with the minimum of contortions and, as far as I know from the information at my disposal, leads in the direction you need it to.'

'Listen,' said Smoke, 'don't keep qualifying everything. Does it or doesn't it lead to Aether's Cross?'

'Well, as I say, I've never actually . . .'

'Scape!' warned Quill.

'Yes, it does. I'm sure of it, though what you'll find when you get there I really cannot say.'

'We'll tackle that when we do get there,' answered Velvet. 'Thank you. Now – the shadow? And this other trollvein?'

'Yes, that. Well, as I said, this second way has been buried for as long as I have been here, but I remember consulting one of Perior's early records which actually chronicled the death of Aether. Nothing particularly dramatic, you understand – he simply died of old age – and when he did finally lie down and close his eyes he was swiftly engulfed by the glacier, as were most of his contemporaries. Over the years the trollveins formed from their bodies; trolls had fire charm in their veins, you see, not blood, and when a troll died the charm had to go somewhere. So the charm took their blood vessels and wove them into new shapes, underground passages which tunnelled of their own accord right across the world, dispersing the charm out into the rock. That's one of the reasons charm has always worked better below ground than above: it's nearer the network of trollveins.

'Anyway, Aether's veins were changed in the same way, and because he had two heads his body spawned two trollveins (most trolls only produced one, you see). Both trollveins made their way back to the place he had most loved: Aether's Cross.'

'They both lead the same way!' blurted Velvet in astonishment. 'So what's the problem?'

'The problem is, my dear, that while the first trollvein found an easy route through to Aether's Cross, the second took a more difficult way. It bored through deeper rock, harder rock, older rock. It got to its destination in the end, but not before it had disturbed something along the way, something which would have been better left undisturbed.'

'The shadow,' breathed Velvet. 'But how do you

know this if you've never been down either of these veins?'

'Perior explored both,' explained Scape, his eyes distant now. 'And she barely escaped the second with her life. She recorded her experiences in crystals of charm, and I have consulted them all.'

'So what did she find down there?' asked Vox bravely, though he could not disguise the shake in his voice.

'A monster,' replied Scape reasonably. 'A monster that waits and eats. It likes to eat things, you see.'

Velvet watched the shudder move through the group but she felt strangely liberated. A monster? Well, they had dealt with monsters before, not least the monstrous dragons who had brought their kind to the brink of extinction. Monsters were terrible to be sure, but they could be defeated.

'We're going back,' she announced without preamble. 'If they've chosen the right way we can catch up with them and help free the dragons of Aether's Cross. If they've chosen the wrong way . . . we can rescue them.'

The initial, incredulous glances changed one by one. Quill's look of surprise melted into one of knowing compassion, the look of a mother who has seen her offspring finally take to the air; Smoke swiftly adopted the look of concentrated resolve with which she had battled through much of her life and Vox, at her side, looked nervous but bright-eyed and ready for flight. Scape simply narrowed his eyes and regarded Velvet closely.

'You're serious, aren't you?' he said. Velvet nodded. He shrugged, and surprised them all with an embarrassed smile. 'Well, I've let it all slip so badly here that I don't suppose it will make much difference now whether I stay or go. I think I'll join you, if only to show you the way.'

'Showing the way is no small task,' commented path-finder Smoke. 'We'll be glad of your assistance, Scape.'

'And your company,' added Quill, her eyes searching Scape's.

Outside the night moved slowly and their wings felt muffled by the darkness. *We must hurry*, thought Velvet as they stroked their way up over the leading edge of the glacier, but for all her enthusiasm the ice rolled by too slowly for her liking. Urgency flew at her side but it did not help. The crater seemed far away.

'It's a stupid idea!' exclaimed Volley, but Brace hushed him.

'No it isn't,' the young Natural said determinedly. 'It's the only idea we've got. Tallow?'

The big dragon sniffed and thought for a moment before rumbling, 'Cumber is right.'

'Excellent!' proclaimed Cumber, his strange energy disturbing. His eyes were wide and wild, and his wings twitched as though being controlled by some outside force. Without further ceremony he sped up through the air to the overhanging brow of Aether's skull and broke off a small icicle. Upon his return he placed it on its side on a slightly raised part of the lip of the eye socket where they had been debating. Then he looked at his companions one by one, and for an instant the old Cumber was there. 'Shall I do it?' he asked nervously. Tallow nodded.

Cumber bent down and nudged the sharp end of the icicle with his snout. It spun round on the bone's convex surface, spilling shards of ice down the precipice of Aether's cheek as it did so. Presently it slowed, turning once, twice, until it teetered to a halt. They all looked in the direction it was pointing. Straight ahead, into the skull which had been hidden.

'There!' cried Cumber, wild and exuberant again. He reminded Brace of a dragon who has flown too far without rest, hyperactive through lack of sleep. *Dragons like that usually reach a point where they simply crash,* he thought uneasily. *When will you crash, Cumber, and what is doing this to you?*

'In we go then!' shouted Cumber, his voice cracking, and he launched himself into the darkness. His companions had no reason to delay and so they followed him, anxious not to become separated in the black emptiness within. Into the shadows they flew, into the trollvein which Scape, had he been there, would have counselled them not to enter.

CHAPTER 33

Bacht

The walls of the trollvein, woven as they were from pure fire charm, were like a huge antenna probing the undersides of the world. Signals filtered through from the surface, dispersing information into the vast underground network. But the signals were distorted, the news was malformed, for the charm had grown weak and the earth and rock were dense and unforgiving. Former clarity had given way to a staccato pulsing and those few who listened to the increasingly random noise could not tell if it was the world itself breaking down or simply the system.

There was a bulge here, a deep, subterranean blister where those weak and listening walls swelled to accommodate a living space. The monster pacing to and fro within the confines of its chosen cell knew this space only too well, for it had resided here for many aeons. It was, of course, a basilisk. Its name was Bacht.

Silver claws tapped on the mesh of the trollvein and hard skin slithered behind. Bacht's body was long, mostly tail; two muscular limbs dragged it across the curved floor, back and forth, back and forth in endless repetition. It was not mad, though its self-imposed exile here would surely have driven any other creature mad long before, but it was hungry. And restless, for it knew that food was on its way.

When the Deathless had parted again, abandoning the citadel and dispersing across the world – or in the case of Veil fleeing to another world altogether – Bacht had journeyed at once to Chaemen. Of all the mortal creatures which had come and gone, wandering the skin of the world for the duration of their brief lives, it was the trolls which interested

Bacht the most. Their massive presence and considerable longevity – at least by mortal standards – had made them more real to the basilisk than most and now it felt the need to be near them during their time of decline, as though by association it too might find a way to dwindle.

Bacht, the closest thing the six Deathless had ever had to a leader, shared their common desire for dissolution. But more recently – ever since it had buried itself here in fact – it had discovered that simple suicide, if ever it were possible, was not enough. If the Deathless were ever to die Bacht would have to be the last of them to do so. It felt compelled to outlive its peers, if only for the merest blink of an eye, in order to confirm its position of superiority within the clan. An unreasonable obsession this urge became, and when Bacht began to sense Ocher moving through the world above, plotting and recruiting, when it understood that the time of the Gathering was fast approaching, that was when it began to believe that its final wish might actually come true. Soon, at the end of everything it had ever known, it would consume its brethren before finally being consumed itself. The Gathering would eat them all, but Bacht would eat the others first.

Bacht had spent little time with the trolls in the end. Mighty though they had been, the basilisk soon tired of their petty, mortal concerns. More interesting to it were the trollveins, durable tendons of charm laced beneath the hide of the world, and it was into these that it soon ventured, hiding away like the others of its kind as the Deathless once more entered a phase of retreat and, for all but Bacht, sleep.

Bacht did not sleep. Bacht had never slept, not once during all eternity. Unique among its kind, it alone had found the key to the survival of the mind under the onslaught of an impossible weight of memories, and so it had never felt the need to slumber: Bacht had learned to forget.

It was a false technique really, as much an artifice as the mountain range Veil constructed near the crest of the world, or the dome of charm which concealed and contained the final throes of the Gathering, for nothing was ever truly forgotten. But Bacht found a place deep within itself where old memories, unwanted memories could be stored, locked away where they might trouble it no more. It was a deep and track-less place and what was hidden there was hard to recover – for it *could* be recovered, with no little expenditure of effort – but it worked. It was a pit in Bacht's mind, simply, a well into which the basilisk threw every unnecessary thought, every useless recollection. And however much it threw down there, the pit never grew full: it remained open, gaping. Hungry.

As the pit remained hungry so Bacht remained hungry. The retreat it formed within the confines of the trollvein served its purpose admirably: deep, remote, shielded by finely-tuned charm from the probings of its fellow basilisks and even, while it lasted, of the all-knowing Maze of Cova-mere, it was the perfect haven for Bacht to prowl and con-template. But Bacht grew hungry, and hungrier still, and the more memories it banished the hungrier it grew until the hunger became an ache and finally a gnawing agony which ruled its life.

When the pain became unbearable – and basilisks could bear a lot – Bacht would break for the surface, or more frequently tempt some unsuspecting and mortal beast down into the trollvein by way of a false entrance and a luring charm. As the years passed it ventured outside less and less, relying instead upon its skill as a waiting hunter, an immor-tal spider working patiently in a web of charm. Soon it would not leave its sanctuary at all, relying wholly on what it learned from the listening trollvein for its knowledge of what was happening both in and to the world above.

But lately, of course, the signals had been growing weaker ...

Soon it would be time to leave. The trollvein had lost much of its former integrity and it was hard to have confidence in the news it brought. Still, none of that would matter when the Gathering finally took place for by that time Bacht would be returned to the open air and reunited, if only briefly, with its fellow basilisks. Reunited for the Gathering or, as Bacht preferred to think of it, the last supper.

Before then, however, there were intruders to deal with. They would make a suitable appetizer, Bacht contemplated. Once it had eaten them it would emerge from its cocoon, recreating itself for the final time, doomed at last and hungry for death. But first the dragons: there was a charmed mind among them, or at least an ex-Charmed mind, for that was how things were in this turned world. That was where it would begin. That was where Bacht would start to eat.

Since entering the great chamber inside the glacier Cumber had not felt in control of himself. It was as though some creeping parasite had infiltrated his mind and body and was working it as he might work his own wings. His mind remained lucid but his body – including his mouth and therefore his words – were not his own. He had been taken over.

The control was not total. He felt as though he could break through if he really tried, and the few times he did try proved moderately successful, but whatever had violated him seemed to have suppressed his urge to retaliate. Helpless in the grip of motivations not his own, Cumber simply allowed this alien presence to play with him as a young dragon might play with an insect.

I know what happens to those insects, he thought powerlessly. *They get their legs pulled off one by one.*

Muscles not his own worked wings not his own and the pale, woven tube of the trollvein slipped past with effortless grace, its milky walls shedding light in the form of a dim, shadowless glow. Aware that the others were concerned about him but unable to articulate his own fears, Cumber floated through the strange tunnel like a seed blown on the wind.

So the journey proceeded, drab and featureless, and as it proceeded Cumber felt a new sensation join his weird detachment, a gnawing in the depths of his stomach. The image of a parasite sprung again to his mind and all at once he was convinced that something, some alien organism, had actually entered his body and was feeding off his internal organs, feeding and growing and emptying his body of its vital stuff as it did so. Expanding to fill the cavity it was creating inside him, this creature would sooner or later burst out through his hide, sending skin and scale cascading all around and leaving nothing of dragon Cumber but a few white flakes. *Consumed from within*, he thought frantically, wishing he could rouse his stubborn lips to shout his terror. But they would not respond and so he flew blindly on, weak now and horribly afraid.

This section of the trollvein was featureless, with nothing to mark off distance or to affirm direction. Unbroken and quite undecorated, it twisted and rolled through the earth with no clue as to where or how far it might lead. Even more disorientating was the curious fact that the trollvein seemed to carry its own gravity with it, for no matter which way it turned – up, down, left or right – 'down' remained constantly beneath the dragons' wings. Even when the tunnel described a sharp loop-the-loop, gravity denied the truth which their other senses were affirming and the effect on them all was distressing, especially Tallow who had learned to trust his senses in everything.

Eventually their surroundings began to change; the trollvein widened and grew darker. Cumber felt himself pulled unceremoniously to the head of the group and heard the whispers exchanged by his companions as he thumped his wings hard against the still, warm air.

'If only we knew what had happened to him . . .' That was Brace, his voice tight and concerned.

'No getting through to him . . .' Volley too sounded troubled, his normally rich baritone hesitant.

'He's in trouble,' said Tallow suddenly. 'Serious trouble.'

Tallow's voice rumbled from one side of the darkened trollvein to the other, then expanded and echoed as though his words had been snatched by some flying presence and whipped up into a huge, vaulting space. Simultaneously the walls opened up and they rounded a tight corner which had stolen up on them without warning. Everything came loose then, the sound of Tallow's voice, the rounded walls, the air itself. Their whole environment exploded outwards in a silent concussion and they entered a cavernous arena even mightier than the glacial chamber in which they had discovered Aether's frozen corpse.

Haze filtered distant arches into surreal, leaping wings of light. Circular apertures receded from both floor and ceiling, bringing in livid, yellow light from unseen fires. White pillars, twined about each other like sapless vines, soared up to the ceiling where they flared into huge buttresses; their sister structures sped from one side of the chamber to the other, horizontal echoes which turned the entire space into an organic lacework of line and curve. Construction of this kind the dragons had seen in only one place before, and they knew instantly what it was they were about to meet here in this wide place in the trollvein.

'Basilisk place,' breathed Tallow, preparing himself for the encounter they all knew was imminent.

But nothing could have prepared them for Bacht.

'It's incredible!' exclaimed Velvet as they swept into Aether's burial chamber. None of the oppression which Brace's group had felt was present here any longer and now the chamber was simply mighty, blue-white and elegant despite its macabre content. Aether seemed calm and benevolent, prostrate beneath a skin of ice and lovingly decorated by millions of icicles, although his surroundings were anything but peaceful: the arching waterfall had become a torrent and ominous cracking noises filled the immense space. The floor was flooded, waves lapping at the base of Aether's skull; the water level rose even as they watched.

'Chaemen is breaking up,' observed Scape, frowning at the eddies chasing through the lake beneath them. 'It's definitely getting warmer, you see. Since the Turning, the world is getting warmer; the ice is melting.'

'Good thing too, if you ask me,' shivered Quill. 'Now, where do we start?'

Scape led them briskly over the mountain of Aether's visible skull and stopped short as they rounded the last ridge of bone. An eloquent gesture was all he required to indicate the second skull gleaming from the wall of ice, staring back at them as though defying them to take the same choice as their companions. 'But which way did they choose?' he wondered out loud, as much to himself as to the others.

They searched the half-exposed skull for any sign of dragon and found none. Velvet found herself watching Vox closely as they hunted, for of the five of them he seemed most at ease here. Eventually she questioned him about this.

'It's j-just that . . . when we went through the trollvein before – the one between Sharp and Haven that is – I felt that I knew which way to go. The charm seemed to fit my mind, if you know what I mean . . .' he trailed off, his eyes bright and hopeful. Velvet shook her head – she didn't understand.

'I'm a Natural,' she sighed, 'but I trust your judgement. It seems to me that you know a lot more about these trollveins than any of us, even if your knowledge is unconscious. You must lead the way.'

'Pathfinder now?' smiled Smoke, surprising Vox by swooping up behind him. 'You won't be needing me at this rate.'

'I – that is, w-we'll always n-need you,' stuttered Vox. 'I wouldn't presume to . . .'

'That's all right,' replied Smoke warmly. 'But it's you we need now, Vox, and I think you know that, don't you.' He nodded his head, his scales glinting in the strange, underground light. 'There's a lot I want to talk to you about,' she added in a whisper, her face close to his.

'Me too,' he replied, his head swimming with the near-contact. *Oh, Choliel*, he thought. *Can I really let you go at last?*

'Let's try the first skull,' announced Quill suddenly. 'We didn't look there properly. Maybe we'll find a clue.'

And so they returned to the first skull, where it was Smoke who eventually found the scale. She called Velvet over at once and it was as much as the young Natural could do not to burst into tears there and then. She turned it over in her claws, a broad, white flake which Smoke had found caught on a knob of bone low on the open eye socket. White like her own, except it was not her own – it was Cumber's.

'They must have gone in this way!' she cried happily. 'Scape – that's good, isn't it? I mean, this is the way that leads directly to Aether's Cross, not to the . . . the shadow!'

'Indeed it is, young dragon,' beamed Scape.

'Then let's go,' Velvet urged, flinging herself into the dark cavity without further ado. Her companions followed one by one, for the evidence seemed plain enough, false though it was. Smoke and Vox paused at the rim however, and exchanged a meaningful glance, for both suspected that the clue was misleading, that Cumber might indeed have landed here, but that he had not entered here. Pathfinders both, they feared that this was the wrong decision, but what could they do?

'Which way?' whispered Smoke, ready to yield to whatever decision Vox might make.

'We came to save the Cross,' he replied, the words burning like fire in his throat. 'And time is short.'

'How do you know that? What's going to happen?'

'I don't know. The trollveins tell me, I think.' Vox looked down into the chamber apprehensively. 'And this water's rising all the time. Soon the trollveins will start to flood. We have to go this way. Now.'

'And the others? Brace? Cumber?'

Vox did not reply for several breaths. It seemed to Smoke that he was listening to something, something deep within the trollvein.

'Time is short for them too, but there may be enough for all of us. Just barely.'

Smoke shook her head, not understanding. The buzz of charm from the trollvein was beginning to tug at her nerves, bringing on the familiar, hated pain, but she would endure it, if only to stay at the side of this intriguing dragon who was so much more than he seemed. 'Come on then,' she sighed, 'before we lose the others.'

They entered the trollvein.

Bacht lurched from its hiding place with a great exhalation. The connections it had made with the trollvein's structure pulled free from its glistening hide, leaving patches of raw and weeping skin which healed themselves busily as it clambered across the interlacing network of supporting spars and beams. Its mind was seething with the dragon now, seething with *Cumber*, for that was the name of this feeble creature, but it was not filled by him. Another presence had entered Bacht's mind as the dragons had entered its lair, a ghostly, half-formed thing which called to the basilisk from some near-future time. *A potential future*, it decided, narrowing its greedy mind down on to the elusive yet powerful intruder.

This potential future unleashed upon Bacht an image of a black dragon contorted by an alien presence, a basilisk presence, a white and deathless tail protruding from the dragon's flank. *Ocher*, thought Bacht, recognizing its sibling. Then, as Ocher's tail had jutted from the dragon, it saw a dragon's tail jutting from its own flank: Bacht and Cumber united to make something greater, something which might fill even eternity itself.

Bringer-of-shadow! The monster!

Bacht had experienced this thrill before – each time it had lured a dragon down here in fact – and it knew well the symbiosis into which it might enter with one of these curious flying creatures. Basilisk and dragon joined to make *bringer-of-shadow*, and the entire cosmos at its mercy thereafter. Here was a means by which Bacht's hunger might at last be satisfied; here was a mind into which the infinite burden of memory might finally be emptied.

Each time in the past it had stopped short. Each time, as Bacht had loomed over its dragon prey, silver teeth dripping in anticipation, it had not joined but simply bitten down, killing and devouring not as host but as predator. Each time the dragon had not been the right dragon. But this time . . .

. . . *Cumber. You, dragon, have seen much. You have seen the turning of the world; you have seen the Maze of Covamere, or a fragment of it at least. You have seen the Seed of Charm sent outwards into the stars. You have seen more than most mortals might hope to see in a lifetime. You of all dragons might have a glimmer of understanding about all that I have seen. You alone might grow to learn the power of eternity. You alone might be, with me, bringer-of-shadow.*

Bacht's thoughts sliced through the warm atmosphere of its lair like ravening claws, seeking their target and striking with unerring accuracy. The instant they struck Cumber folded his wings and fell to the floor with a heavy thud, not moving.

'Cumber!' bellowed Tallow, dropping to his aid. The others froze, watching the monster emerge from its den.

Its shape was the same as that of its siblings, a shape with which the watching dragons were piercingly familiar after observing the fight between Ocher and Tellere at the citadel. A blunt head topped a pallid, neckless body; a pair of gauntly muscular arms were the only limbs, the rest of the body narrowing swiftly into a scaly tail. Silver eyes glared expressionless from an unreadable face, the direction of their gaze impossible to determine.

What was different about Bacht was its size. Where its five siblings were small, each less than half the size of an average dragon, Bacht was huge. It loomed over the cowering dragons as they themselves might loom over a cornered rat, but where a rat might leap for its attacker's throat they found no incentive to do likewise. Vapour scintillated about the basilisk's gaping jaws and they knew that with a single exhalation it could kill them where they flew; its breath, like its vision – when it chose at least – was lethal.

Bacht's body seemed to expand to fill the cavernous space into which they had been swallowed, its pale flesh squeezing between pillar and bar until it was virtually upon them, its odour rancid, the sound of its breathing hoarse and fast – excited. It leered, fangs like metal spikes in its deadly maw; they were dwarfs in its presence.

'We took the wrong tunnel,' murmured Volley. 'We're lost.' The enormous basilisk tipped its ugly, oversized head down and despite the blankness in its eyes they knew exactly where it was looking: straight down to where Cumber lay unconscious on the chamber floor. Its jaws gaped wide and strings of bubbling fluid showered down across the limp dragon form, hissing as they struck Cumber's white scales.

'I've never been lost in my life,' answered Tallow, his head empty of all plans but his spirit undaunted. 'Brace? Are you all right? We haven't much time.'

'I'm with you, Tallow!' responded Brace at once. 'Beyond this place lies whatever is left of my family and my home. Nothing is going to stand in my way. I made a promise. I plan to keep it!'

Bacht tilted its head at the sounds of their tiny voices. It sensed their bravery and found it amusing. Perhaps it would be more amusing if it consumed them first before joining with this . . . Cumber. Before creating an entirely new life form the like of which the world – even the cosmos – had never before seen.

Bringer-of-shadow! it thought hungrily as it turned away from Cumber and advanced upon his three companions. *But first, Bacht will eat!*

CHAPTER 34

Openings

The trollvein took Ocher due north and would, it swiftly calculated, bring it out on to the surface again only a short distance from where Geiss, the last but one of the basilisks it sought, was sleeping. Behind it, the chamber where the chitraka's strange heirs had gathered and then fled receded into gloom, leaving only the twisting reliability of the trollvein to guide it onwards. Ahead lay the world's crest, and the Gathering of the Deathless.

Ice splintered as Ocher broke through the thick crust and emerged into a dwarf forest. Trees filled its vision but all were shrunken, their growth stunted by the severe temperatures of this extreme northern clime, their needles small and gripped protectively by tiny growths at the roots as though their parent branches were reluctant ever to let them fall. This was the last forest before the ice floes and Ocher felt a surge of excitement as it exploded into clear air and was rid of the cloying troll charm which oozed from every pore of the tunnel it had just negotiated. Clean basilisk magic scented the air now, the charm leaking from the site of the Gathering, from the crest of the world.

Ocher will be there soon, it thought. *And eternity will find its end at last.*

The trees were very beautiful.

The retreat which Geiss had chosen was perhaps the strangest of all the basilisks' hiding places, for it had neither buried itself nor fled to some remote world – though this forest was certainly in a remote part of this world. Unlike its siblings, Geiss had relied wholly upon charm to construct its retreat, even though to another basilisk this made it the easiest of them all to spot. Ocher could sense the charm now as it approached the clearing, filling the cold air with invisible light and sparks of pure magic.

Extravagant, it considered, *especially now that the world has turned. Such expenditure of energy cannot be renewed. Geiss abandons charm where there is only abandoned charm left to use. Even the Deathless should be hoarding, not squandering.*

But Geiss had ever been the reckless one. This was largely why Ocher believed it would be the easiest of the six to recruit. The wild use of charm had always appealed to Geiss and it would not think twice about being party to the greatest wielding of charm this incarnation of the world had ever seen. And, Ocher suspected, it would not be sorry to find its own life ended at last as a result.

Slipping its mind aside and re-entering the clearing from a strange, *sideways* direction, Ocher easily unlocked the outer shell of Geiss's invisible cocoon and entered to find its sibling wide-eyed and ready for the visit. Silver reflected silver, an infinite succession of mirrors within which it was impossible to find an end. Their breaths mingled, a lethal brew.

. . . My answer is yes. Geiss came straight to the point.

. . . You will join us? You know our intent?

. . . You thought you would have to convince me? Surely you know me better than that, Ocher.

. . . This is the last time so much charm will be gathered on this world. You could not miss the event.

. . . Indeed. And I will participate, Ocher. But you must promise me one thing.

. . . Name it, Geiss. If it is within my power I will grant it.

. . . Bacht must be there. If we are to die, Bacht must die too.

Ocher held its breath, hoping that Geiss would not detect its hesitation. More impulsive and hence less perceptive than the others, Geiss was the easiest of the six to deceive. Nevertheless, deceiving a basilisk was a dangerous game and it was with trepidation that Ocher lied.

. . . Bacht awaits us now at the crest of the world. It remains only for you to join the circle.

. . . Then I will come now. We must hurry, already I sense the charm is building.

Trembling with relief, Ocher led the way out of the cocoon

of charm, which was already disintegrating as Geiss turned its attention to more pressing matters. Ocher wondered how long it could maintain the deceit, and if it would be long enough.

The fight between Bacht and Geiss had come at the end of their long habitation of the citadel, and had in part led to the exodus. Bacht had grown greedy and lazy, preferring to loiter in the citadel's halls, eating and eating and eating . . . Geiss taunted Bacht continually, accusing it of wasting time when it might be exercising its many skills. A discussion of philosophy became an argument of principle and finally a violent and unwinnable contest of strength. Unwinnable because neither opponent could possibly have achieved its objective: to kill the other.

Basilisk bodies were shredded and burned over and over again, each death an agony, each resurrection worse. Eventually it was Bacht who fled, unable to bear the constant renewal of tissue, the mindless regeneration which symbolized so graphically their immortality. Then Geiss too departed and the time of the citadel was over; the time for sleep had come again.

But now that time was past and a new era was dawning, an era which would begin and end with the Gathering.

Yet I do not know where Bacht is, mused Ocher as it led its sibling towards the dome. *Will Geiss stay when it discovers the truth?*

Despite all its insights, all its myriad senses, Ocher could not determine the answer to that question. The doubt was a reminder that to be immortal was not to be omnipotent. Increasingly now, Ocher found this knowledge thrilling.

'I've been evil,' said Ledra, with one shining eye on the basilisk. With increasing urgency, she whispered, 'because until now I never knew how strong love was.' Gossamer half-frowned, half-smiled, unable to speak in her apprehension of what was about to happen. Ledra went on earnestly, 'I have never truly loved, or been loved. I thought Hesper and I were in love . . . but now I know what he really is.' She saw Hesper through new eyes now, saw him as the calculating and cowardly thug he really was; how she had ever thought she loved him she could not imagine. She gazed at Gossamer. 'I used to think charm was everything, but you, and your love for your daughter, that seems to me . . . so wonderful . . .' She broke off, quite unable to articulate the complex transformation she was undergoing.

Gossamer saw Ledra trembling and thought she was about to weep, until she realized the trembling was in the air all around them. The sky growled. Ledra looked round sharply, ready to act; she felt liberated here at the world's crest, suddenly respectful of dragons she had for too long despised – suddenly despising the dragon she had once been. And she would almost certainly have taken up the very challenge she herself had laid down, namely to walk across the ice and parley with the basilisk sentry, had not Ocher and Geiss descended from the sky.

The basilisks swooped in on their hard-won cushions of charm. The magic splintered erratically beneath their smooth, streamlined bodies, but they controlled its outburst with casual flair. They landed softly, raising tiny puffs of ice from the flat, white plain, then immediately made their way up to their fellow immortal, presumably to enter the dome. They looked small to the dragons, yet they crackled with suppressed power. Their presence was almost overwhelming.

'Well, Ledra,' murmured Hesper sarcastically, 'do you still want to go and have a chat?'

Ledra ignored him, turning instead to Gossamer and whispering, 'Now is our only chance. But what can we do?' Gossamer shook her head – she did not know. Hesper leered at Ledra, his contempt undisguised, and the two females turned their backs on him.

Meanwhile, Fortune and Scoff had been exchanging terse sentences. Now they looked across to their companions and opened their wings together.

'What are you doing?' called Hesper hoarsely. 'They'll see us.'

'Exactly,' answered Fortune, and he and Scoff took to the sky.

The others watched with pounding hearts as the two dragons rose slowly and powerfully upwards until they hovered together at a point in the air roughly halfway to the dome. Then Fortune shouted, 'We wish to gain access to this place! Will you help us?'

'What's he doing?' blurted Hesper frantically. 'He'll get us all killed.'

'You know a lot about basilisks then?' inquired Gossamer acidly.

'I know enough to stay well clear of them,' Hesper snapped. 'There's got to be a better way than this.'

'Such as?' Ledra's voice was cool and unimpressed. She looked across at her new friend and smiled. 'Will it work, Gossamer?' she asked.

Gossamer said, 'We must have faith.'

There was no movement amid the knot of basilisks. A wind brought powdery snow from the east and Fortune shivered, then for the first time wondered that he was not frozen to the core. Glancing across at his wing membranes he saw only the merest glint of ice upon their labouring surfaces.

'It should be much colder here,' he said to Scoff. 'Is it the charm, do you think?'

'No doubt,' answered Scoff at once. 'Much charm here now. Abandoned charm. No longer abandoned though. Gathered. Very powerful. Very dangerous.'

'But what are they going to do with it all?'

The sedentary basilisk pulled itself clear of the dome. Green fire filled the hole it left and ice vaporized in a great gout of steam. Through the cloud Fortune saw a widening darkness, the fire becoming a hole growing behind the basilisk's squat form, and as the air cleared again he saw that an aperture had appeared in the dome, an opening barely bigger than the basilisk itself but big enough – just big enough – to admit a dragon. He held his breath; there would be little time.

Just as he was about to call down to Gossamer he felt the air swell beneath him. Wind rushed past and he was forced to flatten his wings, flicking stall-reducing blades of cartilage from their leading edges to stop him dropping from the sky. *You taught me well, Tallow*, he thought distractedly. What was happening?

Another buffet of air, and this time a long, groaning sound and a crash like an earthquake. The dragons and the basilisks all turned to look south (and it was at this moment that Fortune realized *every* direction was south here) to where a great ridge of ice was lurching upwards. Far in the distance they could see an enormous iceberg turning over, breaking practically in half as it wallowed in the warming ocean. Pressures in the ice changed and a long-restrained current dragged an island of frozen water out into the fragmenting floes. The crest of the world was breaking up.

'The world is getting warmer,' realized Fortune as the dome itself shook with the concussion. Then he looked back to where Scoff was pointing.

Behind the ridge where Gossamer, Ledra and Hesper crouched, still hidden, a mighty split had appeared. The world's crest was now a ragged island of ice surrounded by a berg-dotted ocean; even here the water was breaking through as the ice succumbed to the rising temperature. Much of it was a local effect, caused by the leaking charm from the basilisk dome but Fortune's observation was true nonetheless, for these moments signalled the end of the winter of the Turning and the beginning of nature's spring. The ice of the crest would resolidify but only after much of it had been released into the world's oceans. In observing the melting of the ice cap, Fortune and his companions witnessed the engine of the final reshaping of the continents. Lands would be carved back by swelling seas, glaciers would retreat and a new, temperate climate would descend upon the world. And here was where it all began.

Some of this Fortune realized, or at least he sensed its form if not its detail, but he could not dwell long on such planetary concerns for the splitting ice had revealed something extraordinary. The nearest opening took the shape of a circular cavity, a pale tunnel mouth into which Fortune found himself looking directly ... and he saw that it stretched away to infinity!

He blinked, that first impression resolving itself into the sight of a round and milky-walled passage receding beneath the ice until its furthest end was lost in haze. It was enormous – easily broad enough to have accepted ten dragons flying abreast – and he knew at once that it was a trollvein. But what did it mean?

Suddenly the basilisks were busy.

Tallow broke first, cutting down and then up towards a thick web of trollvein weave supporting the end of the chamber. It was impossible to judge the direction of the basilisk's gaze but it seemed to him that those blank, silver eyes flickered in his direction. He hoped his diversion would give the others sufficient time.

'Fly!' he bellowed and to his relief they did.

Volley, so used to his long-time companion's behaviour that he could almost predict his actions, fired his wings into motion the instant Tallow peeled away, nudging Brace forcibly with his long snout. 'Cumber first!' he barked, 'then the way out!'

'But Tallow . . .' blurted Brace, only to be half-winded by Volley's insistent blows.

'No time!'

They plunged together through the tangle of criss-crossing struts into which Cumber had fallen, their course bringing them perilously near the enormous basilisk's twitching claws. Each claw was the size of Brace's head; each muscular arm longer than his body at full stretch. This was clearly no ordinary basilisk.

Tallow's gambit seemed to have worked, for the pale-coloured monster lurched up over the weave and snapped at the air with its forest of silver teeth. Tallow's tail slipped through two of those teeth with only a scale's width to spare and Volley, catching the incident in the corner of his eye, grunted in horror. Again the basilisk lunged and again Tallow managed – somehow – to avoid its crashing jaws. Thunder echoed about the chamber as the basilisk leaped and landed, shaking its web with great, concussive slaps from its broad tail.

Tallow flew higher, dodging in and out of the treacherous supporting structures in an effort to gain the height he needed. His wings slipped through the air with flawless grace, precise and powerful in their manoeuvring as they thumped against the cloying breath of the monster. He did not look it in the eye nor did he inhale the stinking miasma which clung to the basilisk's mouth, for he knew both gaze and breath to be potentially lethal. His heart laboured and his eyes bulged as he kept his own mouth and nostrils clamped tight shut, desperate to reach clear air and take a fresh breath.

Suddenly the basilisk seemed to change its mind. It dropped abruptly through three levels of the web and lowered its head towards Volley and Brace, who were closing in on Cumber. Without warning it slashed its tail forward and cracked several vertical members. Fragments of the strange, woven material showered around the dragons as they tried to swing left on to the only course open to them: directly between the basilisk's great arms and down through a narrow channel which would lead them straight beneath its pulsing body. Now it had chosen to ignore Tallow they would have to be the bait.

The tail whipped again and struck Volley, knocking him sideways into Brace and crushing the two dragons against a pair of supports. More of the material shattered and they were flying without effort now, wings awry, bodies turning and tumbling as they fought to draw breath into their winded lungs. Brace saw clearly the basilisk's intent as he skidded through the air – the monster was already leaning close to Cumber and opening its tremendous jaws wider than he cared to contemplate – but there was nothing he could do. Something hard and unyielding thumped him in the back and tiny points of light showered across his vision before everything went dark.

Vox and Smoke agreed wordlessly that they would take charge. Velvet, Quill and Scape were all too confident, they considered, and despite what Scape had told them about this safest of trollveins they were dubious. Vox sensed the presence of other trollveins nearby, twisting and tunnelling through the deep rock and Smoke felt a new kind of pain here – the pain of troll magic, an unpredictable ache which made her wary.

Here at last was the elusive network Vox had sensed

beneath the Plated Mountain when he had wandered there mourning his lost Choliel. Though he had not known it at the time he had recognized the trollvein complex, winding and threading through the underworld. No dragon had ever spoken to him of it – perhaps his sharply-honed charm sense, the result of his punishment, had made him sufficiently observant to detect what few others could. Whatever the reason, he *knew* this place, and felt untroubled here.

Untroubled, he thought, and he realized that for the first time since Wraith had murdered Choliel he flew without pressure on his wings. And when he thought of Smoke, bringing up the rear of the party, he actually felt a warm current of air buoying him up.

The journey was short, surprisingly so. The trollvein turned a few times, and they experienced the same, constant gravity which had disorientated their friends. Then, just as they were settling down for what would surely be a long flight, the walls of the tunnel opened out and admitted them into a wide, rock cavern which Smoke recognized at once.

'It's the Great Chamber!' she exclaimed. 'I came here once, many years ago. I wouldn't forget it. It's the Great Chamber of Aether's Cross!'

They soared in the welcoming space, so reassuringly *dragon* after the strange paleness of the trollvein, quite unable to believe the ease with which they had found it. Two tunnel entrances beckoned from opposite sides of the huge and deserted cave. One was dark and foreboding – apparently the main entrance from the dragon system beyond; the second was aglow, another trollvein by the light of which were they seeing the Great Chamber.

Sounds came from the trollvein as well as light. Screams.

At the crest of the world the eternal midday sun cast short basilisk shadows against the ice. The dragons soared, Fortune and Scoff having now been joined by their three comrades, anxious to take advantage of the opening in the dome but reluctant to approach too close to the Deathless.

'What are they doing?' whispered Gossamer to Fortune, but he shook his head.

'I don't know,' he replied. 'But you can bet there'll be some charm involved sooner or later.'

It turned out to be sooner.

While the sentry remained stubborn before its gateway, the other two basilisks drew close and bent their heads together. Their tails lashed erratically, cutting broad swathes in the ice and powdery snow. Light glimmered in their eyes. One of them Fortune recognized: the rhythm of Ocher's tail stirred memories of Wraith, that same tail bulging from the black dragon flank. It was like hearing a familiar song, hypnotic . . .

Suddenly the light in the basilisks' eyes flared and the dragons blinked and looked away. When they looked back they saw the basilisks aglow, bright red fire connecting their eyes in two slender beams. Slowly they turned towards the gaping trollvein, the fire bulging outwards until it formed an arc of light whose source was silver eyes reflecting its flames into infinity. Out towards the trollvein the fire sped, its edges sharp and well-controlled despite the weakness of the charm from which it was made. It passed into the milky tunnel, lighting the walls livid red as it receded, still connected to its source and lengthening with every breath the dragons took.

'What are they doing?' repeated Gossamer, and this time Fortune thought he knew.

'They're fishing,' he said, almost able to smile.

CHAPTER 35

The Call of Eternity

Despite Vox's protests Velvet was first into the illuminated trollvein, raw instinct responding without question to the screams she heard echoing from the light. This tunnel too was short, laughably so, and she had scarcely drawn a single breath before she burst into the biggest underground space she had ever seen, a massive chamber filled with shadowless light and countless spars of trollvein weave. Bacht's lair.

At the far end of the cavern the basilisk was clearly visible and for a moment the emerging dragons were deceived, unable to judge the scale of what they were seeing. Its back was wrinkled yet strangely infantile, its spine a ridge of knobs like the coils of a serpent breaching some pallid lake of flesh. It seemed near yet . . . far. Then they saw the tiny dragon shapes flying low beneath the monster and they realized that this basilisk was different. This basilisk was big.

They saw the monster's tail raise itself and sweep through the air, then after a short delay they heard the dreadful thumping sound as it made contact with dragon bodies. The attack spurred them into action. As one they opened their wings wide and thundered through the intervening strut-work towards their common enemy.

There is nothing we can do against this thing! thought Vox frantically and then Tallow was at their side.

'We cannot defeat this beast!' shouted the big dragon, his certainty echoing Vox's thoughts precisely. 'We must rescue and retreat! Velvet – with me. You others, pick up Brace and Volley. Stay hidden. We'll see to Cumber.'

Tallow's orders were delivered so confidently and unarguably that the dragons obeyed without question. Vox led

Smoke, Quill and Scape down through the network to where Volley was crouched over Brace's unconscious form in the relative safety of the niche where they had both fallen. Velvet and Tallow flew close together, their wings working in unison.

'Fancy flying is what's needed here,' explained Tallow. 'You and I might do it together.'

Velvet nodded, grimly pleased that the great Tallow considered her capable of what he called 'fancy flying', though she was unsure of what exactly it might entail. No matter – Cumber was down there, prey to the monstrous basilisk; she would do whatever was necessary to save him, even if it meant sacrificing her own life. Quickly Tallow explained his plan.

Cumber drifted. Around him the web of trollveins glowed with unearthly light, filling his mind with their pattern. The air was thick as water, the channels of the veins busied themselves like the pores of a reef; the world was as an ocean. No, not an ocean: a river, for a current was flowing.

Now almost nothing felt his own. Only a tiny flame remained which was Cumber, a spark of individuality which struggled to remain afire in the fluid which surrounded it, pressed in on it. Many times it guttered, many times it appeared to die altogether – but each time it faltered back to life, spitting and fighting. Surviving. The body which it had once operated was now limp and disowned, the mind which had been its protection was lost to the overwhelming current, sweeping it out towards . . . towards the intruder. Pale and ill-focused, this thing wafted at the limits of Cumber's perception, nearer than the complex trollvein network yet dimmer somehow, less well-defined. Indistinct though the intruder was however, of one thing Cumber was certain: it was huge.

Battling to keep a clawhold on what was left of his soul, Cumber reached out into the river and managed to steal information from the water. In doing so he realized that the current was actually flowing two ways at once, carrying parts of himself towards the intruder and likewise bringing alien pieces from it into his own vicinity. Exchanging information; merging identities; creating a hybrid. Creating the *bringer-of-shadow*.

Some remote part of him realized what was going on. Fortune's assessment of what had so nearly happened between Wraith and Ocher, together with half-remembered fragments of legends which Ordinal had told him, oh, so long ago, conspired to show him the horror which was about to consume both him and the intruder basilisk. *Bringer-of-shadow*, the monstrous symbiote, half-dragon, half-basilisk yet so much more than both. Immortal, insatiable eater-of-worlds. Its image – all fang and swollen belly, dripping with sweat and caked in blood and gore – filled what remained of his awareness, expanding to swallow him, poised at last to extinguish once and for all the flame which was Cumber.

Yet still the flame burned; still Cumber found a way to hold on. Somehow he fought, somehow he resisted. *Velvet*. The thought might have been his own, or it might not. It too struggled to stay alive in the relentless swell of the unreal water, swimming out into the void, searching . . . *Velvet . . . it is vulnerable now, like me . . . there is still time to bring it back . . .*

Velvet and Tallow pulled out of a steep dive just in time to avoid Bacht's gyrating forelimbs. The monster seemed intoxicated, out of control even, and they worked to bring this to their advantage. The unpredictability of its movements made it difficult however, perhaps made Tallow's plan unworkable.

'I'll explain quickly,' he barked as they closed the distance to the spot where Cumber's body lay. 'The beast must break those spars to reach Cumber. That will slow it. You must distract it while I pick up Cumber. I'm big, but I'm smaller than it is, and faster. There will only be one chance.'

Velvet nodded, though Tallow could not see her. He was leading the way, halving the gap between them and the basilisk's lurching back, quartering it . . .

At first it seemed that it would work. Giving herself no time to doubt, Velvet turned from Tallow's slipstream and climbed into the basilisk's gaze. Silver eyes gleamed as she crossed their line of sight and circled the creature's massive, bony head. Bacht twitched to the side, clearly struggling to track her rapid movements as she darted to and fro in the air, dodging and spiralling as she fought to keep clear of its crashing jaws. Steaming spittle hissed beneath her wings and she climbed high only to turn and dive again, the sight of Cumber's limp form giving her all the courage she needed.

Metal teeth thundered behind her, splintering the very air through which she flew. Several scales tumbled down towards the floor of the chamber and she felt a sharp pain at the tip of her tail. *Too close!* she decided, not daring to turn and look, then the angry motion stopped and the air was clear again.

Risking a glance behind, Velvet winced as she observed the thin spray of blood staining her long, white tail, then saw a sight far more dreadful: the basilisk had decided to ignore her and was biting instead through the criss-crossing beams. A veritable forest of spars and supports crumbled into its maw and saliva rained down upon Cumber's body. In a single bite the basilisk had destroyed most of the cage which had up to now protected Cumber. Now only a clawful of thin struts lay between it and its prey. Velvet howled her agony and entered a bone-wrenching spin, her wings cutting fine lines of vapour from the air.

Tallow was directly in the basilisk's path when it bore down upon the structure it had itself made. Shock waves hurled him beyond the immediate danger of the basilisk's fangs and into the dubious safety of the hail of broken struts which were being scattered by the monster's explosive descent. Muscles tearing at his breastbone, he cycled his great wings against the downdraught and forged a way through the airborne debris, picking his safe course instinctively and all the time making his way towards Cumber. Moist basilisk breath rained down upon him and he closed his lungs against it, aware that in such a rage the beast would surely exhale its most lethal poisons.

Weaving and diving – always diving – Tallow snapped his neck to the side, swinging wide to avoid a lance of trollvein fabric which sliced across his flightpath. At once he was forced to lift sharply to the right as the pale spear impacted beneath him and shattered, spraying angry shards up towards his vulnerable belly. Then all was clear and he was flying suddenly free, speeding down towards the slight rise – now littered with the remains of the web and dripping with rank basilisk spittle – where Cumber's unconscious form awaited.

It was then that all breath was knocked from him and the world turned red and silver with pain. Punched as though by a bolt of lightning, he felt the strength leave his wings in a single breath and then Cumber was taken away, dropping still motionless as Tallow was lifted high. Twisting his neck violently backwards he saw the nearby glint of metal and realized that he was in the basilisk's jaws.

'Velvet!' he tried to bellow, but the sound was a mere whisper between his clenched teeth. 'Now!'

She saw Tallow pick his way through the debris, saw him arrow towards Cumber, felt her heart lift in her breast as his claws extended to snatch her love from the jaws of the basilisk – then Tallow himself was snatched. She bleated, just once, before she found that all fear, all sense of horror or grief had left her and that her heart was as cold as the ice through which she had flown to reach this abominable place. All she saw now was the space she needed, the gap into which she must fly if Cumber were to be saved.

They did not at first see what it was that saved Tallow's life, what it was that finally distracted the monster where they had failed. All they knew was that the basilisk suddenly spasmed and gaped, flinging Tallow free of the foam which was beginning to gather about its jaws and thrusting its head up into the clear air of the chamber. It groaned, a rich and curiously sonorous wail like the song of some great sea beast yet obviously a cry of pain. Then the red light blossomed about its body . . .

Tallow heaved his damaged ribs into action, dragging breath into his lungs and forcing his heart to pump blood through his flailing wings. Red rain fell in his wake but he paid it no heed, desiring only to be further clear of the beast which had so nearly consumed him, and which might consume him yet. The pain became an agony as he took himself higher and for the first time in what seemed an aeon he flew without counting his wingbeats; for once in his life, Tallow flew simply to live.

Though his eyes were misted he managed to look down and his struggling heart leaped when he saw the white spear which was Velvet crash into Cumber, scarcely slowing as she collected the limp dragon form in her claws and thumped her way up and out of the pit which had so nearly claimed them all. Despite the tremendous bolts of pain which were shooting across his chest and flanks, he flipped forward, intending to relieve her of the burden, for though Cumber was small and light and Velvet surprisingly strong, an adult dragon was too great a load for another to bear for any length of time. But he found he did not need to, for in his ringing ears echoed a familiar voice.

'Stay there, Tallow, my friend! Let Volley do the fancy flying for a change!'

And Tallow, usually so backward in showing his emotion, wept as Volley and Brace sprang into view. Tears of pain and relief filtered into the blood which showered still from his side, seeming to cleanse his wounds until clots formed and the air grew clear again. He watched as Brace steered the struggling Velvet towards Volley, whereupon the genial mountain dragon took Cumber delicately from her grasp, prising her claws open tenderly despite the ferocity of her clutch upon her loved one. After an initial and half-hearted protest Velvet relented, recognizing how badly she was shaking now and glad to be able to pass over at least some of the responsibility for Cumber's safety.

'Quickly,' she begged, 'let's get out of here! We have to land – I must see if he's all right.' Her concern was shared by them all, for as yet Cumber showed no signs of coming round, despite his turbulent rescue and subsequent ride. His neck, wings and tail drooped lifelessly and Volley was only too aware that this dragon was dead weight. 'He must be all right,' she added desperately, her eyes red and filled with tears.

They turned to find the exit and turned into fire.

A fierce, red glow had surrounded the basilisk, licking around it like a great tongue hungry to seize the beast and carry it away. And this indeed seemed to be what was about to happen, for the end of the tongue of fire had located itself in a great slash in the basilisk's neck, burying itself in its flesh like some barb which would not work free while the main body of the flame appeared to be stretching, tugging even. The dragons watched, too overwhelmed by the closeness of their escape to wonder as to what was happening, simply observing.

Brace was about to speak when the basilisk opened its mouth again, and this time an intelligible sound emerged, though it meant nothing to the dragons. *'OCHER!'* it bellowed, and then the flame hauled it away.

The motion was as sudden as it was irresistible. Now the fire was dancing, writhing against the basilisk's pale flesh; now it was pulled taut, clearly defined against the maze of the supporting structure. A hole opened at the far end of the chamber, then a sound like the slap of a dragon's wing resounded through the massive vault and the basilisk was yanked away through it with a speed which left air popping into vacuum like an earthquake. More spars exploded and more bellows echoed, fainter now and growing quiet. Then there was a tremendous silence, broken only by the steady rush of air against the dragons' wings.

Then Brace did speak, and what he said made Velvet snap her head round in an instant. 'Look,' he said, 'it's still here. The chitraka!'

The instant the trollvein entrance was uncovered by the breaking iceberg, Ocher knew that Bacht lay at the other end. *Here* was the way the last of the six had found to shut itself away more completely than any of its siblings: it had surrounded itself with troll charm! As the lair's web had detected so it had protected, jamming any attempts to infiltrate its core. But now Ocher could see, could see all the way through to the centre. All the way through to Bacht.

Geiss saw the secret an instant after Ocher and together they drew threads of abandoned charm clear of the dome in which it had been trapped. It was a calculated risk: to diminish their hard-won store of magic in an effort to reclaim the sixth of their kind – and thereby provide the preferred complement for the Gathering. Ocher had already determined that the ritual could succeed with only five – just barely – but the inclusion of Bacht would make its success assured. Once Bacht entered the circle the Gathering could begin with the surety that at its end the way to oblivion would at last be opened.

They sent the fire speeding down the trollvein, a red line of light with a single target: Bacht. The charm was rough and difficult to control, and it took all of Ocher's and Geiss's failing skills to prevent it from cutting into the trollvein itself and spilling out into the ice and rock beyond. Then, when it finally reached Bacht's chamber they struggled to fix it on to their prey. It was only when the chitraka intervened that their magic found a way to latch itself about Bacht's mighty heart. Made fast, it retreated, dragging its victim sharply from whatever encounter it was about to enter.

Information sped back along the approaching fire and Ocher reeled with the news: Bacht had been attacked at the very instant it was about to enter into the state of being Ocher most feared: *bringer-of-shadow*. Bacht had been about to join with a dragon, as Wraith had so nearly joined with Ocher.

Horrified, terrified even, Ocher frantically bound the charm around and around Bacht, transforming it from a mere snagging line into a tight and practically unbreakable cocoon of magic. Geiss regarded its companion coolly as it did this, relinquishing its own grip on the charm and allowing Ocher to take full control. It too feared the *bringer-of-shadow*, but it found Ocher's fanaticism intriguing. *Such passion in one which has lived so long*, it thought. *And I will not forget, Ocher – you lied to me when you said Bacht was already recruited.*

Ice and snow were hurled aside as Bacht, wrapped now in a skin of impregnable fire, burst clear of the trollvein and was hauled right up to the dome's perimeter, huge furrows opening up in its wake. The ground shook as it rolled over, its back thumping against the dome, red sparks making steaming craters in the powdery snow. From deep within the cocoon came an angry rumble, the sound of a caged beast, then an ominous silence.

Aware that time was short now, Ocher turned to Tellere, the sentry basilisk which had waited patiently – if a basilisk knew anything it was patience – maintaining the single entrance fault by which they might enter to join the others. To join the Gathering. No communication was necessary: Tellere simply expanded the portal to create an opening broad enough for Bacht's swollen body to be propelled through. Steam billowed from within, grey and liquid. Having pushed Bacht inside, Tellere, Ocher and Geiss disappeared through the entrance and into darkness. Scant dragon breaths later the portal snapped shut, sealing the dome from the outside world.

It was the chitraka ... and yet it was not. Velvet's heart lumbered halfway towards her throat before she realized that this sleek, golden form was not Mokishi but something else, something related perhaps.

'Mokishi's daughter?' she wondered. 'Or perhaps her son?'

It prowled the girder as Mokishi might have done, muscles oily beneath a sleek, yellow pelt, eyes glinting green despite the red fire which lingered still in the chamber. Yet its fur was not marked as Mokishi's had been, bearing neither stripe nor mottle and displaying only a slight paling across its belly. It carried a thick mane across the back of its neck and its head was broad and intelligent. A pair of enormous tusks erupted from its upper jaw, straddling the lower like claws. Silver blood dripped from them both.

'It attacked the basilisk,' explained Brace haltingly. He, like his companions, was unable to take his eyes from the great, golden creature. 'It was hiding on that ledge up there, and just when that monster had Tallow in its jaws it sprang. It took a great bite out of its neck, and then the fire came and buried itself in the wound. I don't think the chitra ... whatever it is ... expected the fire – I think it was trying to save you, Tallow. I think it was trying to save us all.'

'Thank you,' called Velvet in a carrying whisper which she hoped the elegant creature would hear. It contemplated them for a moment, then turned with silky grace and bounded down the girder and into shadow. A few breaths later they saw it retreating speedily into the chamber, glancing back just once to regard them. They seemed to see the green of its eyes long after it had gone. 'Thank you,' repeated Velvet.

Then Volley yelped, and Cumber's voice said groggily, 'Well, I have to admit that was one of the least pleasurable experiences of my entire life to date, and in that I include both my first trip into the Realm and the time I overcooked an entire warren of rabbits because Ordinal insisted I stay to the end of a particularly uninteresting lecture. Now, Volley, while I appreciate your efforts, this position is a mite uncomfortable and I really would appreciate it if you would put me down somewhere, if you could manage it that is, old fellow.'

'CUMBER!' screamed Velvet, and the rest was a flurry of wings and a clumsy descent to the ground where Cumber was deposited – a little unceremoniously, he later protested – amid broken struts and splatters of blood both red and silver. The others emerged then – Smoke and Vox, Quill and Scape – adding their respective weights to the pile of dragons which had formed itself in the midst of the rubble and laughing with relief that such a dreadful enemy had been vanquished, albeit by some means beyond their comprehension.

'I'm sorry!' gasped Smoke. 'We were about to help you get Cumber but the whole place seemed to fall in front of us.'

'It blocked off our attack route in fact,' added Scape with considerable relish. His eyes were shining and it appeared that this long-time recluse had actually enjoyed the heat of battle. 'So we had to force a way through. I was even trying to get a little charm ready, just in case it was needed, you understand.'

Cumber groaned and shrugged off all but Velvet, pulling her close to him in a tight embrace. 'Well,' he grunted, shaking his head as though to dislodge some unwelcome insect, 'it was charm that came to our rescue in the end, that's for certain. Basilisk charm, unless I'm very much mistaken – what do you think, Vox?'

'No doubt about it,' Vox concurred. Unconsciously

mimicking Cumber's pose he put his own wing around Smoke and drew her near, the action suddenly quite natural. 'And now,' he went on, grinning at them all, 'I think it's time our pathfinder here really got to work.'

Though he did not know exactly what the basilisks were doing, Fortune guessed correctly that their one chance to enter the dome was fast approaching. He saw in Gossamer's eyes the single imperative which had brought them across half the world to this place of ice: *Aria is within!* While the basilisks' attention was distracted by whatever they had discovered in the trollvein he quickly marshalled his companions in the air.

'On my word!' he called. Hesper grunted sarcastically and was about to make some gibe when Fortune interrupted. 'Just do it, Hesper!'

Ledra chuckled, a light, icy sound which surprised Fortune and irritated Hesper, but before he could retort the moment came. The red light swelled in the distant trollvein entrance and something – some huge, pulsating sac of charm – broke free. The three basilisks heaved the sac through the entrance to the dome. The instant they had entered, while the torn edges of the gap in the wall of charm – and it was only now that Fortune realized that the dome was *made* from charm, pure abandoned charm – were still rippling in and out of existence, Fortune barked his command and led them at high speed down to the ground. Levelling out just above the ice, scattering white powder in their combined wake, they accelerated towards the steam-filled opening.

The hole contracted with blinding speed, its rough perimeter sharp with teeth yet strangely fluid in the way it glided shut. There was an instant when Fortune was convinced that he would be sliced in two by the shrinking gap but then he was through, and the close, rushing wingbeats behind him reassured him that his companions had made it too. Opening wing membranes again they braked, unnerved by the darkness into which they had sprinted and reluctant to fly blind into this new fortress of the Deathless.

All was hot, damp and black. Neither light nor shade offered any description of the space into which they had flown, but something in the feel of the air told them it was some tremendous chamber, presumably the void within the dome. The sound of their wingbeats escaped into the gloom, echoless.

Then a furnace erupted in front of them and where they had been blinded by darkness now they were blinded by light. Slowly they began to see again.

CHAPTER 36

Coils

Archan wondered if Thaw had killed himself yet. The charm she had burned into him at the last would almost certainly have driven him to do so, although it was also designed to prevent him from joining – or even aiding – his former companions. She simply could not afford to have the dragon she had rejected turn against her. Yes, he had to be dead.

But what a legacy he had left! She hoped that the egg which Aria bore was fertile, and when it hatched it would bring forth Archan's long-awaited mate, the magnificent male dragon who would share eternity with her. It was this hope which sustained Archan through those last crucial breaths when she finally rejected Thaw and elected to turn north with Aria. Then as she finally entered the great river of charm, she found a searching spell for her inner senses. With it she probed Aria's mind and body, infiltrating her in a way far more intimate than Thaw's crude violation. Leaving behind her earthly shell she entered the familiar travelling world of the dragon spirit – a world she knew well from the global link she had shared with Halcyon and the others of the Ten – and by slipping her mind into Aria's found confirmation of all her hopes: Aria did indeed carry an egg and yes, it was fertile, and yes – it already bore a male dragon embryo, Thaw's son. And as Archan probed deeper into the unformed consciousness of the infant dragon-to-be she uncovered the final miracle, the final proof that her impossible dream would be fulfilled.

Aria's son would inherit his mother's unnatural disorder; he too would age too fast, reaching maturity almost in the blink of an eye.

Archan calculated. Instead of growing in the egg for months, the infant would be born within five days, maybe less. *Soon enough to join me at the Gathering?* Archan could not be certain but she thought so. More than that – she *believed* so. She had to, for her sanity depended upon it.

More and more she believed that while she craved eternity she feared the solitude in which she had once revelled. A mate was now a vital part of her plan and she doubted she would be able to go through with the rest of it if this strange infant dragon were not hatched in time. *If it looks to come late,* she decided as she and Aria approached the crest of the world, *I will break the shell and drag it into the world! I shall live forever, and Thaw's son shall be at my side, whatever the cost!*

When they reached the polar cap the river of charm was still flowing into the half-finished basilisk dome. Archan was thrilled to see basilisk magic so alive, so vibrant. The river poured into the pliable cap of the smooth-surfaced dome like a liquid rainbow, passing through the translucent membrane with subtle ease and filling the chamber within with multi-hued light. Even as she watched though the skin of the dome was hardening, growing opaque; soon the river's tail would arrive and the new citadel of the Deathless would be ready, a perfect sphere of concentrated magic, only the tip of which protruded from the ice.

It is like an egg, mused Archan as she eased herself and Aria through the still-soft membrane. *A shell of power, a shell of life. Forever.*

As the outside was cold so the interior was hot. Moisture was thick in the air, making breathing a clammy and uncomfortable experience. The light was confused by magic but since Archan had no eyes this did not bother her unduly. Richer senses than mere sight showed her the way down to one of the few safe landing places in this tropical enclosure; Aria followed close and meek at her tail, utterly reliant upon her guide.

In this way Archan led them to a flat outcrop of ice projecting a full tree's height from the chamber floor, a floor which she had fully expected to be simple ice but which the tremendous heat of the gathering charm had reduced to mirror-perfect water, leaving only this and one other iceberg afloat, but melting swiftly. Their touchdown generated a shock of concentric ripples which Archan observed with her charmed senses as they chased away the motionless surface.

Aria wrapped her wings over her elder's smooth flanks and hugged her close. In turn, Archan enfolded Aria in her coils, twining her tail around and around the young dragon until she had no means of escape even had she wanted to break free. Aria had grown introverted during their journey north and now she seemed to be retreating further. Not that this mattered to Archan, for the youngster was only a vessel in which a greater prize was contained. A vessel she would shatter, if she needed to, in order to retrieve the contents.

Near the centre of the dome were six hexagonal pillars arranged in a ring. These stood even higher from the water, fully twice the height of the iceberg on which Archan had chosen to land, perfect, metallic prisms with flat summits. Two of them were occupied by hunched beasts; the other four were not.

The beasts were basilisks, of course, and Archan breathed in sharply when she scented them. The sweet stink of death permeated the moist dome air and here was its source: the breath of the Deathless, or one third of their number at least. Would the rest come? Archan assumed so, although she understood from Ocher's records that only five would be necessary to effect a successful Gathering.

They will be distracted at the last, she predicted. *It will be easy for me to steal away that which they wish to abandon. I shall be the world's greatest thief: the stealer of everlasting life!*

Ocher's records had also revealed that the Gathering was in many ways a straightforward procedure. Theoretically. During the ritual, each of the Deathless would be responsible for channelling one of six strands of charm from the dome and weaving it into a column of pure magic. There were four main strands – fire, earth air and water – but these were qualified by the two directional forces of north and south. While these were not strictly speaking charms, and while their influence on charm in the normal course of events was so weak as to be negligible (hence the fact that, if necessary, a single basilisk could manipulate them both, reducing the required number of participants from six to five), nevertheless during the Gathering their role would be vital.

Every act of charm generates a flow of energy which must be allowed to drain away. This normally happens without fuss and generally without effect, and the magic either flows north or south, earthing itself at either the northern crest of the world or its blunt and rounded southern tail. But during the Gathering, charm would be focused in such colossal concentrations that the paths of every individual spell would need to be controlled for, left to its own devices, the magic would tear itself, and large portions of the world, to pieces. Calling the Gathering at the crest of the world simplified matters, for there was no need to use the pull of the south; all the magic would earth itself right here, at the northernmost point on the planet. But still it was dangerous.

All this Archan knew, for she had laboured long to decipher the bubbles of charm which Ocher had left inside its many museums of knowledge, painstakingly translating the strange combinations of picture and sigil until she had found the solutions to most of the basilisk codes. She knew almost as much about the mechanics of the Gathering as Ocher did, but above all she knew what its end result would be.

The abandoned charm, gathered and amassed in a dome of pure magic at the world's crest, would be separated into six strands and then aligned and focused into a single point, a dimensionless star which would burn hotter than any fire charm had ever burned before, and more briefly than the merest fraction of a breath. And in burning, it would destroy anything which came into contact with it: flesh, bone, mind, matter. Even time itself. And even the state of eternity.

Then it would wink out and be gone, and the pools of abandoned charm left after the Turning would have dried indeed, leaving the merest scattering of magical dew across the world.

At that instant however, before the basilisks' immortality was consumed by the claw-point of fire, it would be released. It would be free of the basilisk bodies which had trapped it for so long, free to burn ... or to find another host. *This* was the point where Archan planned to work her miracle. By stepping in at this critical juncture she – and her mate – would steal the immortality from the fire. That they themselves might very easily be burned in the process was a risk she was prepared to take; indeed, she had spent her entire life preparing herself, it seemed to her now.

The Deathless at last would die, while Archan and Thaw's son would live forever, the last dragon heirs of a turned world. The last forever.

These thoughts and more Archan was contemplating when a blaze of fire mushroomed from the centre of the ring of platforms, throwing six wavering shadows out through the moist air and doubling the already unbearable heat. Within her coils Aria flinched, and Archan drew her tail round tighter. Her captive's belly was swollen: the egg would soon be laid.

How long then until it hatches? thought Archan. But there was no way of knowing.

The layout of the dome's interior imprinted itself upon Fortune's mind as soon as the fire burst forth at its centre. Directly ahead, surrounding the sudden flames, he saw six, tall, hexagonal towers. As he watched, the four basilisks they had followed in – one huge and still cocooned in red magic – alighted, each on its own individual column. Two of the dreadful creatures were here already; there were six then. A full complement, it seemed.

The fire diminished swiftly to a small, quiet glow, looking now like a pile of coals planted in the air in the middle of the ring of basilisks. A second fire burned below: its reflection in the water's immaculate mirror. Everything was doubled by the water. The pillars had no bases – they simply met their reflections to create floating, elongated columns suspended in nothing. Looking beyond the fire, Fortune scanned the middle distance, then hitched his breath as he spotted Archan. Gossamer saw her at exactly the same time. Her wingtip brushed Fortune's as they both faltered in mid-hover and a spark of electricity seemed to chase between them.

Archan was poised on a small iceberg at the far side of the dome, a great, white snake. Her wings they could not see – they must have been tightly furled behind her coiled body – and it seemed that they looked upon the featureless sketch of a dragon, a dragon which was not yet fully formed in the mind of its creator. Though she was eyeless, they knew that she was watching them. Her long and sinuous tail was curled tightly in upon itself, forming a fleshy platform on which the rest of her body lay. Just visible in its folds was a brown arrow, a dragon's head. Aria.

'There she is,' breathed Gossamer.

Scoff was at their side. They watched with trepidation as Archan slowly began to uncoil herself. Fold after fold dropped away until her tail hung down, its tip nearly reaching the surface of the water. Aria lay revealed, motionless but for the steady swell of her breathing. Gossamer caught her breath but Fortune was more astonished still, for he had not yet seen his daughter grown. His heart swelled.

Her face was so like that of his mother that he could not take his eyes from it. She was hornless like Clarion, and her scales were dull brown like his own. In her eyes, distant though she was, he thought he could see confusion and pain but beneath, and slowly coming to the surface, a look that belonged to Gossamer – an indomitable spirit. She seemed to be coming awake as he watched, and she was searching, searching until she found . . . him! Their gazes met and she recognized him, recognized her father, and his eyes filled with tears.

'Aria,' he whispered. 'Come to me.'

Fortune surged forward and Aria half-opened her wings. But then she fell back, clutching at her belly.

'Oh no,' murmured Gossamer.

'What?' cried Fortune, wheeling in the air and cycling his wings frantically. 'Come on – we must go to her.'

'Look, Fortune,' came Gossamer's weak reply. 'Look at what has happened to your daughter.'

He turned and looked, and saw that Aria was doubled over. Her body writhed, just once, then lay still. Archan bent her head and for a breath or two their view was obscured. Then, when the great white dragon looked up again they saw the glint of firelight on a familiar shape. An egg.

Fortune was speechless. He turned again to Gossamer, who was shaking her head sadly. 'Thaw's,' she said, and that was all the explanation Fortune needed. Comprehension dawned and with it came terrible, blind rage. That Archan had taken his daughter and worked her shameful magic on her was one thing, but to learn of this second violation was more dreadful yet. A great, bubbling cry erupted from his mouth and he thumped his wings against the unyielding air. The speed at which he took off surprised even Scoff, who called after him – but in vain.

'Let him go,' chuckled Hesper. 'You know how emotional he gets.'

'Shut it!' warned Scoff dangerously, and if his words were not threat enough then the look on his face was darker than any Hesper had seen on any dragon before. Hesper shut his mouth with a slap.

'Go after him, Scoff!' barked Gossamer. 'It's too soon.'

Scoff did not question her, accelerating into Fortune's wake. He was older and slower than Fortune, but the young dragon's flight was erratic and he was barely halfway across the dome before Scoff caught up with him. Folding rainbow wings about him, Scoff forced the struggling dragon into his claws and gripped him tight, though Fortune squirmed and protested. Scoff managed to turn them both back away from Archan's pedestal. By the time they regained the airspace where their companions hovered still Fortune had given up and was weeping uncontrollably, though whether from sorrow or anger it was hard to tell. Gossamer flew straight up to him and cuffed him hard across the face.

'Shape up, dragon!' she ordered. 'What's done is done. Now, do you want to save your daughter and her unborn infant?'

The effect was instantaneous: Fortune stopped crying and burst free of Scoff's grasp with a single shrug of his wings. Fury darkened his brow and he opened his mouth to speak . . . then thought better of it.

'Grow . . .' murmured Scoff in his ear, and the anger drained away from Fortune like melt water. He saw in

Gossamer's eyes the same anger, the same grief he had allowed to boil over from within himself, but he saw something else too, a kind of control. *No, not control*, he thought. *Faith*.

'We can do this thing, can't we?' he whispered. She nodded.

'Come,' she said. 'Let us land for a moment. There is work to be done and it won't do for us to wear ourselves out.'

Brace began to give up hope that they would find any dragons alive. The monster was gone from the Great Chamber of Aether's Cross but it had all the atmosphere of a grave site. Water coursed through the rockfalls, and Scape cursed. Beyond was the tunnel system which had once been home to hundreds of Charmed dragons. Latterly Wraith had made it a gaol in which all the Naturals of the Cross had been imprisoned, taken from their nests on the west wall.

As they passed through the Great Chamber water poured in from the first trollvein entrance – clearly Aether's burial cavern had flooded at last. The glacier had finally given way and emptied its contents down into the trollvein network. The dragons hurried through, anxious not to be trapped down here as the flood level rose.

The pale limestone tunnels beyond the Great Chamber had been almost completely crushed. At first Cumber thought he recognized part of the passageway through which mighty Brutace had flown, his great wings carving swathes of rock from the walls, but all the tunnel walls had been disrupted down here and it was impossible to be sure which was which. Corridors once high and proud had been squashed down by the force both of Mantle's earthquake and the subsequent restructuring of the surrounding mountains. It was with the greatest difficulty that the dragons managed to squeeze through some of the gaps and as they proceeded the way became narrower and narrower until they could barely crawl through.

'It's a mess, all right,' commented Scape unhappily as they came to a halt before a low and uninviting overhang. Shattered boulders were piled high on all sides and the tunnel floor sloped down at an alarming angle. These tunnels led higher than the Great Chamber but already water was lapping at their claws; they could not afford to delay. But Cumber did not share Scape's concern, for the very fact that they could *see* the devastation gave him hope.

'But don't you see?' he announced. 'Beads of charm in the walls, giving us light just like thousands of little stars. Wraith's charm is still alive down here – I knew it would be. Wraith did nothing by halves!'

At the mention of the Black Dragon's name both Vox and Smoke gave an involuntary shudder. They shared a glance, each detecting in the other no small measure of their mutual hatred of the dragon who had ravaged the world – and their own lives along the way. Vox frowned as Smoke's eyes searched his own. He had not yet revealed to her the identity of Choliel's killer, though he wanted to very much, and he in turn knew little about her past. But as they looked at each other that name seemed to fly between them, forging links which had not been there before. *Wraith . . .*

'There's light, sure enough,' agreed Quill, 'but are there dragons?'

Cumber shrugged. 'We'll soon see,' he said.

Bending low and tucking vulnerable wing membranes against their flanks as best they could, the dragons clambered through this latest, tightest hole. It was worst for Tallow, and it seemed at one point as though he were stuck fast in a critical bend. But then Volley thumped his backside and he splashed free again. 'Thank you,' Tallow grunted, clearly unimpressed. 'Did I ever tell you your singing stinks?'

Presently they emerged into an expansive cave, one which Cumber did at last recognize. 'This is the Switchcave,' he proclaimed, ' – or at least, that's what I called it when I was here last, though it was rather drier then. Do you remember, Brace?'

At last Cumber's continued optimism broke through Brace's melancholy, helping him to think. And now that they seemed to have negotiated the worst of the damaged areas he started to feel excited. This was the same cave all right and there, looking exactly as he remembered it, was the entrance to the prison corridor. The other tunnels – those leading to guardrooms and living areas – were blocked.

Here at least they seemed to be in luck. He scented the air, twisting his neck as he tried to see further down the waiting tunnel.

'Air's fresh,' he said. 'It's not just the light – something else is still working down here too.'

Cumber nodded. 'I tried to shut everything down while I was stopping the cells from flooding, because the whole system was running out of power, if truth be told, but I don't think I managed to stop the charm flow altogether. In fact, I think I may have done the prisoners a favour, because slowing it as much as I did will have conserved the energy much more efficiently. And the earthquake itself could have done the rest.'

'You said it might have created a stasis,' prompted Brace hopefully.

'Possibly, because you see when charmed materials are subjected to change they are unable to sustain their dual integrity, that is to say they have a choice: either they keep the charm together or they keep the nature together.'

'You've lost me,' grinned Volley. He was little concerned with this philosophizing – there was a rescue operation to be undertaken here.

'Well, all I'm saying,' concluded Cumber, 'is that either the material itself has to collapse or the charm does. But occasionally – very occasionally, mind you – if the change is sudden and violent enough . . .'

'Like an earthquake,' prompted Vox.

'. . . exactly, the charm has no time to decide which structure to maintain – its own or that of the natural material which it has infiltrated. So it freezes.'

'Freezes?' yawned Volley.

'Yes, freezes,' butted in Velvet impatiently. 'Let's get on with it, Cumber. All we need to know is that the dragons of Aether's Cross are probably frozen in time down here and if we don't get them out soon all the charm will melt away anyway and they'll be dead for certain. Am I right?'

Cumber looked at her amazed, then confused, then resigned. 'Well, if you want to put it so simply . . .' he began haltingly.

'Yes, I do. Now come on, we've wasted enough time already.'

They entered the prison tunnel, Brace leading the way through the flood. Vox and Smoke brought up the rear, lagging a little behind the others and walking close enough for their wings to brush frequently. After a tremendous internal struggle Vox said to Smoke, 'I saw the Black Dragon once.'

She nodded, wordlessly inviting him to go on.

'The s-stories about me – they're not t-true. I d-didn't kill her. I could never k-kill any dragon.'

'I believe you,' she said softly.

'He killed her.'

'I know.'

And that was enough for now. As they hurried on through deepening water Smoke thought about Wraith – whom for a short time she had believed she loved – and how he had spared her alone of all the lovers he had taken. She thought about Choliel, who had not been spared. And she thought about Vox, and the place he might occupy in her life.

'Come on, you two!' called Cumber from up ahead. 'We've found something interesting!'

'There's dragons to be saved,' said Smoke to Vox. 'Care to help me?'

'I'd like nothing better,' came the outcast's eager reply.

The air was damp and thundery; the sense of anticipation was overwhelming. On their own island beyond the circle of pillars, Archan and Aria remained motionless – and the six basilisks were equally still. The other dragons had found a second iceberg reaching up from the lake, though there was room only for three of them on the narrow perch. The steady dripping of the ice melting beneath their claws beat a tattoo on the water below. Scoff and Hesper held station impatiently in the air, their faces hot and strained with the effort of sustaining a hover under the tropical conditions of the dome.

In a voice full of urgency Ledra leaned over to Fortune and whispered, 'I'm sorry for everything I've said to you. I hope you can forgive me.'

'Of course I can, Ledra,' he replied warmly. 'I'm glad you're here.'

The glowing, floating coals in the centre of the dome flared suddenly, filling the space with orange light, then the fire subsided once more. A pulse of energy moved through the air, like a deep and unheard sound which the dragons felt in their chests, through their bones. Tiny sparks jumped across the dome's internal skin, making star-sharp reflections in the lake.

Breaths were agonizingly drawn out in the stillness. The basilisks might have been sculpted for all the signs of life they displayed; even the shell of fire surrounding Bacht had ceased its shimmering. Only the very tip of Archan's tail moved, back and forth, back and forth in relentless rhythm. Over the dripping of water they could hear only the distant crackle of the airborne embers . . . until a new sound floated across the water. It was a faint tapping, scarcely audible but plain enough once it was caught by an attentive ear. And no ears were more attentive than those of Fortune and Gossamer. Cocking their heads and sharing a glance they turned their attention to their daughter, and to the egg she cradled between her claws. It was from there that the tapping sound was coming, from the egg. Their grandchild was ready to be born.

Ledra gasped as she too realized what the noise was, but her voice was drowned by Hesper's.

'That's the way to the charm!' he cried suddenly, and then he was off, flying straight towards the glow of the coals without heed for his own safety or that of his companions. Ledra hissed at him to stop but he ignored her, slapping his wings against her face as he passed.

'Stop him!' called Gossamer, turning to Fortune as though to push him bodily from the perch, but Ledra forced her way between them and spread her wings.

'Let me!' she announced and then she launched herself into the air in pursuit of Hesper. Fortune looked across at Scoff who was staring past Hesper's fleeing form.

'It's started,' said the ex-Charmed dragon curtly, and Fortune saw that it had.

The basilisks had turned on their hexagonal columns until

they were facing outwards, away from the fire. Even the blank cocoon which was Bacht had rotated, presumably under the control of one of its siblings. As one they raised their claws upwards and outwards, then jerked them in towards their pale breasts as though to disembowel themselves. Lightning flashed from the innocuous coals at their backs and chased across the outer wall of the dome, spreading over its skin and locking on to it. Then the lightning pulled.

Just as Bacht had been dragged from its lair so the dome itself was dragged from its comfortable circumference and in towards the centre of the arena. Fortune watched with mounting fear as the walls contracted, bearing down upon them with hypnotic speed. As the dome shrank, the glow of the coals increased, turning brighter orange, then yellow, then searing towards white as bright as sunlight. In a mere breath from now the dome would strike the dragons from their perch as it grew too small to embrace the lake. It was too late to take any kind of avoiding action; Fortune simply clutched at Gossamer and closed his eyes against the unimaginable impact.

It did not come. Instead there was a sickly gliding sensation as the curved wall of charm somehow passed *through* their bodies . . . then it was past. Opening his eyes Fortune found that they were now outside the dome again. He squinted into the sudden glare of the noon sun reflected off a landscape of ice. He was about to protest, half-lifting himself from the berg when Gossamer held him back.

'Don't worry,' she said urgently. 'It's not over yet. Just wait.'

Hesper and Ledra were hidden now inside the still-shrinking dome along with the basilisks, but Archan was just visible, a crown of white beyond the reduced arc of the charmed walls. Her wings were spread, her neck tilted forward in eager anticipation.

Fortune noticed that the dome itself had started to glow. Now a tearing sound accompanied its motion, which was becoming jerky and asymmetrical. The lower parts of the dome emerged from the waters of the lake, revealing the true sphere of this gathered charm, and as it lurched ever smaller, pulsing and bulging, it became a second sun, flaring too bright to look at. At last it broke free of the lake altogether and floated free like the coals it still contained. Then with a sudden spasm it diminished yet further and the basilisks on their six pillars reappeared as the walls slipped past them. Whether the charm was shrinking still was impossible to tell, so brilliant was the star it had become, but Fortune suspected that it was slowing now, not yet completing its ultimate journey to . . . nothing?

The waters of the lake, broken by the passage of the sphere through their mirror, settled only slowly, their edges crackling against the ice which was already trying to dominate them. But now the lake, the pillars and all the creatures – basilisk and dragon – who had entered the dome were exposed again to the sky. The dome had become a burning focus of magical energy suspended in the very centre of the ring of pillars. And approaching that focus were three dragons.

Hesper would reach it first, and already the light was flaring round his wings as he grew near. Ledra was on his tail and closing the gap but it seemed unlikely that she would catch him.

But Archan was there too and she was flying more swiftly than either of them. Her white wings flashed in the rediscovered sun like wings of ice and her long tail was tucked tight against her sinuous belly. In its coils was Aria's egg.

CHAPTER 37

Sunburst

Cumber knew a few of the tricks powerful charm could play on the passage of time – and had indeed experienced some of them directly – but he was quite unprepared for the sight which met him as he rounded the last, waterlogged bend before the run of cells. Smooth limestone was suddenly disrupted by explosions of ice . . . yet it was not ice. Cumber stared long at the phenomenon, until gradually it dawned on him what he was seeing.

Wraith had personally overseen the creation of this new prison tunnel, a long, spiralling corridor behind one wall of which were concealed hundreds of cells, each an individual bubble in the rock of the mountain. Each cell was accessible only from this corridor and only by means of a particular breaching charm which would create a temporary gateway through the solid rock. The perfect prison for the natural dragons whom Wraith had once hoped to rule.

When Cumber had freed Fortune and Gossamer from this prison some moons before, the charmed systems which had up until then maintained a flow of air and water through the cell complex had already been breaking down. All charm had been breaking down by then, a result of the build-up to the Turning. Part of the collapse caused the cells to fill with water and it was this flooding which Cumber had tried to prevent, ultimately closing down the whole charm system and punching tiny airholes in the rock to permit breathing. A desperate act and one in which he had little confidence. But then the earthquake struck and the effect of Cumber's actions were academic, for the entire mountain collapsed and the prison was buried.

But Cumber had often wondered since then – what really happened when the caverns of Aether's Cross closed their seven eyes? Now he saw.

The corridor had been split wide by great faults which opened chasms in the floor and zigzag cracks in the ceiling. Beads of light still glared from the walls but their illumination was fitful, sparking like damp firewood. Floodwater from the glacier washed across the broken floor. But the incredible thing was the dragons.

The cells had burst open, spilling their occupants out into the tunnel . . . and then, at the critical point they had frozen. Fountains of water had erupted from along the entire length of the tunnel's right-side wall, but their sudden motion had been arrested almost immediately by the charmed stasis which Cumber had anticipated. The pressure of the earthquake upon Wraith's control system had indeed overloaded the network of charm to such an extent that it had locked itself in place, literally halting the passage of time in the cells and freezing the drama of the moment of release for the dragons of Aether's Cross. For free they were, though they were still trapped: each frozen fountain contained a natural dragon, perfectly captured in the throes of escape and perfectly visible through the crystal sculptures which these explosions of water had become.

'It was the water that did it,' breathed Cumber. 'It's a marvel – time is running properly everywhere but in the water. These fountains look like ice but they're not: they're water in stasis. And that's where the charm is still locked away, waiting for some dragon to release it again.'

'Can we do that?' said Velvet, the loudness of her voice jolting him free of his contemplation.

'Oh, er, well yes, at least, I think so. It's just a matter of working out how.'

'Incredible,' Brace was saying as he weaved his way down the tunnel. Each one of the frozen fountains was a work of art, a delicately modelled snatch of time. Individual droplets floated free of the main structures like rogue crystals, suspended impossibly before the eyes of the astonished dragons. Thousands of tiny light charms threw brilliant blue highlights across the translucent sculptures. They all agreed they had never seen anything like it in their lives.

'They were so close to freedom,' exclaimed Quill, shivering as she examined the face of one of the dragons trapped in the static water. Its eyes were wide and hopeful.

'*Are* close,' corrected Velvet. Then she added proudly, 'Cumber knows how to get time moving here again, don't you, Cumber?'

'Well, I . . . that is to say . . .'

Brace returned then, grim-faced. He had been conducting a brief search for two particular dragons he knew to be here somewhere – his parents – but in vain. Still there was a lot more tunnel he had not yet explored. 'Let's get on with it,' he said briskly. 'I can't bear to see these poor dragons trapped like this for a single breath longer than I have to.'

'Oh, it's quite all right,' breezed Cumber, 'time will have stopped in their heads as well – they're not aware of anything at the moment, nothing at all!'

'That's even worse,' shuddered Quill. 'Come on, let's get this place moving again. I don't like it one bit.'

'Well, Cumber?' prompted Velvet kindly.

Cumber did not reply at once, instead making a great show of circling the nearest of the fountains and tapping it with his wing. He hummed and hawed, looked expectantly at his colleagues for a moment, then his shoulders slumped.

'Oh dear,' he began unhappily. 'I'm rather afraid I'm going to let you down, and on two counts as well.'

'What's the matter?' demanded Brace, clearly unimpressed with Cumber's delaying tactics.

'Well, it's just that . . . well, first of all, as far as these wretched dragons are concerned the Turning hasn't taken place. They don't know what we know because they're still stuck behind us in time, so when we release them we'll have a lot of explaining to do.'

'So we'll explain,' retorted Brace. 'Really, Cumber, I don't . . .'

'Yes, but you're not Charmed, are you? Or ex-Charmed, I should say. And I am, and Quill and Scape and Vox are too.'

'So?'

'As far as these dragons are concerned,' sighed Cumber,

'charmed dragons are still the enemy. They were ravaged, Brace, as you yourself know only too well – remember how you felt towards me when we first met in this very tunnel? If we suddenly release a hundred or more Naturals into this tunnel, we four ex-Charmed won't stand a chance – they'll be on us before you can blink. They'll tear us to pieces, Brace.'

Brace's eyes softened. 'Of course, Cumber,' he sighed. 'You're right – I wasn't thinking. But surely we can get you to a safe distance, or even hide you away somewhere. You don't need to be right here to work your magic, do you?'

'Ah, well, no, you're right, but you're leading me on to the second problem now.'

'Which is?'

Cumber fidgeted apologetically. 'I, um, I don't actually know how to get them free, I'm afraid. I'm most dreadfully sorry.'

Brace stared at Cumber, then back down the tunnel. The trapped dragons stared back, mute and uncomprehending. The silence was devastating. The water continued to rise.

Two suns blazed at the crest of the world. The new star outshone its skyborne rival, its pure white fire unbearable to look at. Fortune's eyes wept uncontrollably, shedding water into the lake more rapidly even than the melting ice. He squinted, narrowing his lids until they were mere slits, desperate to see what drama was unfolding among the basilisk pillars. He saw dragons flying into the light, and he saw the basilisks writhing in agony. The charm tore at their bodies, beginning to pull the bones out through their skins, emptying their minds of a billion hated memories, sucking away at their immortal souls. Soon only shells would remain, quite mortal and ready to be destroyed in the final conflagration. But not yet, not quite yet . . .

Hesper was approaching the Gathering Light, drawn here by pure greed. The sight of so much charm – the charm he believed to have returned to the world for good – was too much for him and he thought that to take control of it would be to become master of the world. It might even have been true, if the charm was controllable by any one dragon. It was not, of course.

Ledra flew in close pursuit of Hesper but she would not catch him, and whether she was driven by concern for his safety or desire to see him consumed by the fire was impossible to tell. Archan too would reach the light a mere breath behind Hesper, and what her plans entailed neither Fortune nor even the trembling basilisks knew.

Suddenly there was a flash of red as Bacht's cocoon disintegrated under the pull of the Gathering Light; Ocher had lost control. Never had so much charm been focused in a single place and the results were unpredictable even for the Deathless. The gyrating hulk which was Ocher seemed to flinch, perhaps expecting to be attacked, but where huge, deformed Bacht might have fled the circle or even turned berserk upon its captors, it simply bowed its head along with its siblings and began to chant.

The song was a guttural series of drones punctuated by staccato outbursts. It contained no meaningful words, serving instead to release a complex sequence of sounds which both contained and manipulated the floating Gathering Light. It was the means by which the basilisks would instruct the gathered charm to destroy the web of eternity which kept them in its mesh; it was their last song. The basilisks had swiftly assessed the merits of Hesper and found him adequate for he was physically strong and mentally weak: a perfect combination. His role in the Gathering was ultimately one of sacrifice, for the strands of eternity, once separated from their basilisk hosts, would be exposed for a brief instant before they were destroyed. In other words, for a breath or two, the basilisks' immortality would exist as a tangible force which, unless it were contained, would flee before the abandoned charm could be unleashed upon it. Before it could be destroyed.

Hesper was the vessel in which the immortality would be contained. He was the factor which the basilisks had never before thought of using. For the merest fraction of time he instead of them would be deathless. Then he – and the immortality itself – would be slaughtered.

The unearthly song grew louder and louder until Fortune

could bear it no longer and neither, it seemed, could Gossamer. 'Stay here, Scoff!' Fortune barked as he and Gossamer launched themselves after Ledra. 'We might need a dragon to pull us back.'

Their wings cut fine lines of vapour from the cool air as they dipped from the iceberg and accelerated low across the lake. Their reflections pressed up against them as though trying to escape their watery prison and the air rushed clean past their faces. The speed was good, the freshness of the challenge a revelation, the lack of surety like an extra heart beating the blood through their veins.

'You get Aria,' commanded Fortune but already Gossamer was peeling away from his side and arrowing towards the pillar on which Aria, forlorn and sick, now lay alone. Gossamer's white wings shimmered in the sunlight and he gulped in deep draughts of air as he looked away from her and back at the basilisk ring. The light seemed brighter, if that were possible. Hesper had all but disappeared and Ledra was merely a vague dragon blur embraced by a cloak of white. Archan loitered in the pulsating aura, her long tail curled tight against her belly with its precious cargo.

The egg alone must be saved, if nothing else, determined Fortune. Hesper had gone altogether, and Ledra and Archan were hovering directly above the moaning basilisks. The basilisks for their part seemed oblivious to the movement of the dragons, but Fortune knew that they were not, just as he knew that Hesper was destined for a terrible fate. But he could not help him now – he had to save those dragons whom he loved. Especially the dragon who had not yet been born.

'Ledra!' he cried over the swell of the basilisks' voices. 'Get back there and help Gossamer.'

'I can't do that, Fortune,' she replied calmly. 'My help is needed here.'

Before Fortune could interrogate her he felt a rush of air as Archan swept past, circling the light with growing impatience. He flung his wings back and hurried after her, catching up on the opposite side of the ring, out of sight of both Ledra and Gossamer. Archan halted, swivelling to face him with her bland, eyeless glare. She laughed long and loud, then she unwrapped her tail from around its precious burden and held the egg tantalizingly over the lake. Fortune could clearly hear the faint tapping sounds coming from inside. Archan twitched, pretending to drop it but Fortune did not flinch, keeping his gaze fixed on the blank spaces on her face where her eyes should have been.

'You will not let it fall, Archan,' he said confidently. 'But you do not need it. Give it to me, then finish whatever it is you have come here to do.'

Archan's face was unreadable but Fortune fancied she scowled as she coiled her tail around the egg once more. If he thought she was ready to parley then he was quite mistaken. Instead she slashed her right wing down towards his face, lurching upwards and backwards as she did so. He reeled at the unexpected blow, the side of his head humming with the sudden pain. Three dull, brown scales fluttered down towards the water and blood welled in his left ear. The basilisks' chant was a screeching blade of sound which hurt Fortune's throbbing head. He floundered in the air as Archan turned coolly away. Then the Gathering Light turned brilliant red.

The light transformed itself into a bloody tidal wave, exploding into six distinct spears of fire which extended out and down towards the waiting basilisks. Revealed again at the heart of the detonation was Hesper, a horribly changed husk of a dragon with black, unseeing eyes and a charred body which hung limp as though suspended from some giant, invisible claw. Through the glare of the flames Fortune saw Ledra reappear, saw her dart forward then fall back again, unable to approach for the heat. Incredibly, she seemed to want to rescue Hesper, the dragon who had done her such wrong, and it was then that Fortune realized how much she had changed, how much compassion she had found within herself.

But there was no time to dwell on such thoughts for already the fire was changing, each spear swelling tenfold as it sucked essential powers from the basilisks and drew them back into the centre of the circle. Massive shocks of charm pumped their way along the fiery vessels and jarred their way into Hesper's waiting body, which was tossed and jerked like a limp plaything as the energy poured in. Fortune prayed for Hesper's sake that he was already dead. He realized that the song of the Deathless had stopped.

Archan folded her wings away, floating now on some charm she had conserved for this very moment, her attention directed wholly at Hesper.

Then the basilisks screamed.

Vox took charge as soon as Cumber had made his confession. 'Come on now,' he urged. 'The only way we'll know is to try. So, Cumber, let's start with the control system. Where is that?' Cumber led him meekly back in the direction of the Switchcave until they came to a shallow depression in the corridor wall. 'Here?'

Cumber shook his head. 'No, because the control centre itself is actually near to the guardroom but that's all blocked up and we'd never reach it, but this is one of the thin points on the network so we should be able to access it all from here.'

Vox nodded gravely, then bent his head until it touched the wall. At once he jerked back, hissing as though he had been burned.

'What is it?' cried Smoke, touching his trembling wing with some concern. She had hurried after them while the others had lingered near the trapped dragons and now the three of them stood huddled together, staring at the wall as the water sluiced around their claws.

'It's all right,' replied Vox slowly, fighting to keep his voice under control. 'I'd just forgotten who set up this system in the first place.'

'Wraith,' breathed Smoke.

'I can taste him here,' confirmed Vox. 'It reeks of him.'

'Can you do anything?'

'I'll try.'

The wait was agonizing as Vox touched his head against various spots on the wall. While he was working their companions traipsed up, generally disconsolate.

'Any luck?' asked Scape with forced optimism but Smoke shushed him, requesting that he let Vox work in peace. Brace hung back, inspecting his claws and struggling to conceal his deep unhappiness. To have come so far for nothing!

'Can I help?' whispered Smoke in Vox's ear. He waved her silent, then paused and cocked his head as though listening.

'I might have found something,' he announced suddenly, pulling back from the wall and facing the others. His eyes looked red and puffy, as though he had been awake for many days. 'The magic is hard and cruel, but logical, too – it seems that Wraith thought of everything.'

'What do you mean?' demanded Brace, his face hard. Clearly he was reluctant now to allow himself any hope.

'He obviously built in allowances for catastrophes such as this. That's why Cumber found it impossible to shut the system down altogether: Wraith put in so many safeguards. The dragons *are* still alive, and they *are* frozen in time, just as we suspected. The charm is entirely contained in the water, you see.'

'Yes, but like you say, we know all this,' protested Quill. 'What's the . . .'

'I'm getting to the point,' Vox interrupted. 'Above and beyond all the safeguards there is a single trigger, an emergency release if you like. When it is activated it will open ways for the charm simply to drain away. It will unlock the stasis; the dragons will be free.'

'Then let's do it,' rumbled Tallow. Volley nodded enthusiastically at his side.

But Vox could only give Cumber a wry smile and say, 'But I'm afraid I can't operate the trigger either. Only Wraith would have known how to. He left no clues.'

He looked at each of the group in turn, seeing on their faces varying degrees of distress. Velvet hugged close against Cumber, who murmured to her gently, his tenderness surprising to Vox. Brace looked as though he had been struck and struck hard; the others were simply sad. Except Smoke. She was frowning intensely, her eyes glistening.

'Wraith must have personalized the command,' she said hesitantly, 'so if we had some insight into Wraith's mind then we might be able to work out what the trigger command is, yes?'

'Well, yes . . .' agreed Vox uncertainly. Smoke sighed and smiled a sad, trembling smile.

'I think I might be able to help,' she said quietly.

The basilisks screamed and Fortune was blown clear as though he were but an autumn leaf tossed on a gale. Ledra too was hurled outwards but Hesper and Archan both remained at their respective stations, Hesper because he was trapped in the light and Archan because she had the presence of mind to work ferocious charm, spending a great shower of sparkling magic as she fought to keep her place in the sky. The Gathering Light continued to glow and pulsate livid red, the tendrils of charm pulling the life force from the basilisks on their six hexagonal pillars. A noise was swelling above the howling of the Deathless, a tremendous storm of sound which started the ice shaking at the perimeter of the lake. Looking back over his shoulder, suddenly reminded of the vastness of the landscape in which this drama was unfolding, Fortune saw icebergs ripping up through the ice plate, carving the floes and opening great wounds in the false land. The air vibrated, both with the massive humming and the shock of the surrounding destruction.

Then he saw events he did not understand.

First the Gathering Light grew dim and the six tendrils wavered, then winked out of existence. The basilisks were bowed low now, each presenting its armoured back to the waning glare of the Light. Then, as Fortune watched, the basilisks seemed to turn themselves inside out.

Their pale skins folded outwards as though some bizarre internal pressure had inflated them beyond the limits of their elasticity. It was not a gruesome sight, for the transformation occurred in some vague dimension where *inside* and *outside* had no real meaning; no guts were released on to the flat pillar summits, only luminous bars of light which cycled through all the colours of the rainbow before joining to form six new connections between the Deathless and the Gathering Light itself. The unfolding continued, doubling round upon itself until the basilisks were reformed.

But they seemed different, they seemed . . . *less* somehow.

411

Fortune's head ached as much from the effort of fathoming what it was he was observing as from the after-effects of Archan's substantial blow. Then it came to him: those bars of light were what made the basilisks deathless. He was witness to nothing less than the surrendering by the Deathless of their very immortality.

It was only a guess of course, but the instant the thought struck him he knew it to be true. Archan's talk of eternity took on new relevance now and in a staggering blast of insight he believed he knew why she wanted the egg so badly.

Wraith was terrified of being alone, he thought, *and Archan is just the same. She has stolen Aria's youth and now she wants to steal the whole future. She is a thief of time, this monstrous dragon, and she must be stopped!*

There was no time to act before the bars of light were suddenly absorbed by the Gathering Light. There was an ominous pause as the red glow swelled and the six, drained basilisks lay motionless on their pedestals. Then the Light fell in upon itself, tearing huge gouts of air from its surroundings as it did so. It folded and rolled like a series of ocean waves turning endlessly inwards and Fortune could feel the wind of its throes even from here. The shrinking light vibrated frantically, faster and faster as it grew tiny, then became a mote of dust held in one of Hesper's blackened and empty eye sockets. As Hesper's body was revealed more clearly again so it shook and expanded, scales and skin bulging until it had taken the form of a grotesquely distended sac, barely recognizable as a dragon any more. Its tail twitched and Fortune realized with heart-wrenching horror that Hesper was still alive.

An uneasy peace descended. The basilisks remained unmoving; Hesper's bloated body bobbed uncertainly in their midst, occasional arcs of magic lancing between his shattered scales and the basilisk pillars. Overhead the sun, no longer subordinate to the fierce glow of the Gathering Light, reasserted itself, casting short and angry shadows across the trembling ice plain. A pressure ridge raced towards the arena from the middle distance, striking the shore of the lake and disrupting the perfect waters as it divided the shaking land in two. Far out at sea bergs groaned and clashed. Behind Fortune the mouth of the distant trollvein gaped.

Archan lifted up into the sky from behind Hesper's broken body. Aria's egg glinted in the rediscovered sunlight, its perfect ovoid balanced casually on the coiled tip of the white dragon's snaking tail. Archan's jaws gaped wide, fangs like icicles reaching out towards Hesper. Then three things happened.

Ledra screamed and leaped forward, blocking Archan's way.

Two of the basilisks – Bacht and Geiss – launched themselves from their respective pillars and landed one on each side of Ocher, heavy jaws bared upon their sibling.

The Gathering Light expanded for the last time from beneath Hesper's scales, ready at last to take the immortality it had sucked from the Deathless and scatter it into the waiting void. Ready to exterminate the now-mortal basilisks . . . and any other creatures unfortunate to be caught with them here at the crest of the world.

Fortune hurled a glance across the lake to where Gossamer and Aria were just lifting off from the iceberg. Gossamer's eyes were ablaze, her wings made red by the fire erupting from amid the pillars. He wanted nothing more than to gather them both up in his wings and carry them off away from this dreadful place, to leave these dragons, these basilisks to their petty concerns and reconstruct his family in some distant haven.

But Archan still held the egg.

CHAPTER 38

The Gathering of the Deathless

Ocher felt . . . Ocher felt as it had never felt before. Through all eternity it had survived an infinity of disasters, died uncountable deaths, experienced the endings of worlds more times than its clotted memory could determine. But now . . . now it felt different. It felt *vulnerable*.

The myriad senses which had formed its barrier skin were all but gone, sucked away by the Gathering Light; now it could see and hear, taste and touch and scent, but that was all, apart from a few vague flashes from its inherent charm sense. Its bones felt weak, as though they might splinter inside its flesh at any breath. *Breath*. It exhaled, and it knew that it could no longer kill in that way. At last it was fragile, at last it was poised on the edge of oblivion. At last it was mortal.

Ocher had little time to come to terms with its new state for no sooner had the last vestiges of immortality been drained from its system and into Hesper's waiting body than the fire reached out for the last time. But the explosion of red was not the only attacker, for at the very same instant Bacht and Geiss pounced. Both were larger than Ocher – Bacht considerably more so – and there was nowhere for Ocher to turn. *How will I die then?* it thought with a stab of disappointment. *Consumed by the fire or at the claws of my angry siblings?* Yet it opened its arms and bared its tender breast to both flame and basilisk, for however death might come it could only be a mercy.

The basilisks moved fast, faster even than the speeding fire, but they did not attack: they spoke. For the first time in aeons basilisk throats and mouths articulated audible speech. The red light stretched out from Hesper's shattered remains like an opening flower, seeming to move so slowly . . .

'You deceived me,' growled Geiss. 'I believed Bacht already to have been recruited. Instead you were prepared to risk all without Bacht's presence.'

'Five would have been enough,' countered Ocher defiantly. 'I needed only you and I took you the best way I knew.'

'So you would have ignored me,' murmured Bacht, its massive brow low and full of threat. Its face grew redder as the fire bore down upon them all. 'You would have taken your siblings into oblivion and left me alone, the last immortal in the world.'

'You could always have become *bringer-of-shadow*,' sneered Ocher. 'Or did that scare you at the last?'

'Do not taunt me, Ocher,' warned Bacht, lurching forwards. 'I might still be tempted.'

But Ocher shook its head. 'You know that cannot be, Bacht. You are mortal now, like the rest of us. This dragon –' and here it indicated wretched Hesper, scarcely recognizable behind the swollen red flame '– holds eternity now; already the fire reaches out to destroy us once and for all. Your ambitions are over, Bacht, as are all of our desires. Be grateful, for these dragons have helped to bring about the final end we never thought possible.'

Bacht thought for a moment, then slumped on to the flat surface of the pillar. Geiss sped forward then, glancing uneasily at the looming fire and cursing its one-time companion. The heat began to blister their weakened skins.

'Still there is a punishment to be exacted,' it intoned. 'Your deceit is not forgivable, Ocher, not considering the magnitude of the ritual of the Gathering . . .'

'I am fully aware of the magnitude of the ceremony,' interrupted Ocher angrily. 'I told you only what you wanted to hear.'

'Nevertheless,' Geiss continued with increasing menace, 'you will be punished.'

Ocher looked on in fury as Geiss loomed over it with claws outstretched, then it laughed, a dry, cracking sound which stopped its sibling in its tracks. 'Then kill me, Geiss,' it chuckled. 'And believe me when I say I shall be grateful.'

But even as it spoke it felt a new rage swell in its mortal heart. Suddenly, minutely aware of its surroundings, Ocher drank in all the tiny details of the world – the contrast of hot sun and cold ice, the gentle ticking sound of melt water, the lazy flapping of dragons' wings, the scent of charm and the taste of fire. Especially the fire, which was so close now that they could practically touch it. Death was a mere claw's breadth away. *What is this new anger?* Ocher wondered, confused.

Then Geiss and Bacht descended upon their victim, cutting great slashes down both of its flanks and hurling it out over the lake. Instinctively Ocher flailed outwards with flight charm . . . but there was none to be found. It catapulted clear of the pillar and struck the icy water with a mighty explosion of spray, disappearing instantly from view. Bubbles streamed up through the waves. Presently they stopped. Geiss and Bacht looked down uncertainly – that had surely been too easy.

'You shall not share our oblivion!' cried Geiss in a hoarse, broken voice, but it wondered all the same. Then it turned with Bacht into the fire.

Smoke cried out with the pain of the ordeal, but when Vox reached towards her she shrugged off his wing angrily, pressing her head more firmly against the depression in the limestone.

'Leave me,' she hissed. 'This is what I must do, for myself as well as for these dragons.'

The glacial floodwater had reached their breasts now and all the dragons were growing increasingly restless. In an effort to ease the tension, Cumber asserted confidently that there must still be a way out, for the water seemed to be flowing steadily through the tunnel and not flooding it as quickly as it should have done. 'There'll be a crack leading out some way we haven't found yet,' he blustered. 'I'm sure there's an escape route waiting, somewhere or other.'

'Yes,' muttered Volley to Tallow, 'but only for a dragon the size of a sprite.'

Smoke groaned again and they all turned sympathetically toward her. All now knew that she was half-charmed, and all were aware of the terrible pain which this desperate effort was causing her. For Smoke, a dragon who had never actually wielded charm in her life, was delving deep into the Black Dragon's network of magic to find the one trigger which would release the stasis and set the prisoners free. And her companions could do nothing but watch and wait.

Vox remained close to Smoke as she hugged the wall, feeling with his own lingering charm sense the agony she was experiencing. Then he gradually began to realize that the agony was not simply a physical pain but also one of the heart. Somehow, as she probed nearer and nearer to Wraith's primary spells, she was opening some long-closed wound which had never properly healed. Feeling like an intruder in her soul, he could not stop himself sharing as much of the journey with her as he could; as she dug deeper and deeper so he fought to join her in the labyrinth of charm, if only to help show her the way. He focused in, concentrating . . .

White light buzzed inside his eyes, even though they were shut. Smoke was a moaning presence some distance before him, a dragon shadow afloat on a sea of limestone milk. Pressing down on them both were the sharp angles of ancient charms, while ahead was the ordered system of magic which had once controlled the prison but which was now locked in stasis. Already Smoke had reached this towering wall of charm, already she was probing the guiles and glamours, the controls and commands, searching for the one trigger. The wall was alive with magic, coated with hundreds of tiny images, each one a trigger for a particular function in the labyrinth of Aether's Cross.

Smoke, Vox called, reaching out with all his heart and mind. She responded at once, turning into his presence and wailing her agony.

It is too much for me, Vox, she howled. *I cannot bear the pain. I cannot bear the memories.*

You don't have to bear them, my dear, Vox countered at once. *You can share them. Tell me, Smoke – tell me everything.*

And so she did. There, at the dark heart of Wraith's

atrocity, she told Vox how once she had loved the Black Dragon and, for a time, believed that he had loved her. She related every detail of their brief passion, and of the soulless destruction of the settlement she had adopted for her own. And finally she told of how Wraith had abandoned her.

You cannot know how lost I was, she wept. Then she paused, her shadow-self regarding Vox's presence with a ferocity he found unsettling. *But then . . . perhaps you can, Vox. Yes, I think of all dragons, you are the one who can understand me.*

He took my love too, replied Vox, and that was all he needed to say.

They lingered there briefly, as remote from time as the dragons trapped in the frozen water, then Smoke's heart suddenly opened wide, filling the dark labyrinth with light.

He has left so much of himself here! she shouted into the unreal space. Then she launched her shadow back towards her waiting body. *Come on, Vox! We don't have much time left!*

He followed, confused and excited, speeding back across the milky sea to the reality which waited beyond the charm. As one they broke free of the interior world of magic and re-entered their trembling bodies. The magic sucked at their backs, hungry to reclaim their vitality. Vox snapped his head round as Smoke lurched away from the wall, a dazzling smile breaking across her face. He thought he had never seen anything so beautiful in his life. He knew for certain that he loved her.

'It's so simple!' Smoke cried to the astonished dragons, dancing to and fro in the water. 'Wraith was obsessed with bringing back the past, so much so that he built his obsession into almost every spell he wove. He hated death, that was the point. Despite everything he did, he hated death.'

'Had a funny way of showing it,' murmured Volley.

'Yes, he did,' agreed Smoke with conviction, 'but all Wraith ever wanted to do was rule, and he needed dragons alive so that he could do that. But more than that, he wanted to rule *everything*, even those creatures which had long since left the world.'

'I'm sorry, Smoke,' began Brace, glancing nervously at the rising water level, 'but where is all this leading us?'

'To the answer,' she cried triumphantly. 'I knew Wraith, and I knew what was dear to his heart.' Her companions, with the exception of Vox and Velvet, both of whom knew her secret, gasped in surprise, but already she was going on. 'He left many triggers here – they are like tiny pictures, images of reality frozen into charms. It's no wonder Vox couldn't tell which was which.

'But I can. Wraith told me once that he wanted nothing more than to fly across the world and see all the creatures which had ever lived roaming its surface, and to see them bow beneath him as his shadow passed over them. And there was one creature – an extinct animal – which symbolized that whole dream for him.'

Carefully, delicately, Smoke raised a wingtip and sketched a shape in the air. Charm sprang from the wall behind her, falling into the tracery which her claw made and creating a bright, glowing form floating before her wide eyes. The creature she drew was tall and elegant, with an impossibly long neck and long, slender legs. It was a zirafa.

'Wraith loved them,' she whispered. 'And he wanted nothing more than to resurrect them, to bring them back from the prison of extinction. They were the symbol for his new golden age, before it all went wrong. Before dragons began to die.'

Here her voice broke, and a single tear rolled down her cheek. Tenderly, Vox wiped it away, then turned to the ghostly image of the zirafa. 'Brace,' he whispered. 'I think you should be the one to do this.'

Driven by some instinct he did not stop to question, Brace took three determined paces forward and sent his wing crashing through the zirafa's wavering image. The illusory creature shattered into a thousand splinters of light and from around the bend in the corridor came a tremendous rumbling sound. Lightning jerked across the corridor, winding its way out from the depression in the rock wall and chasing down towards the countless crevices made in the floor by the earthquake. The water hissed as the magic pierced it and tendrils of steam danced across its surface. A blue haze hovered where the zirafa's image had been held suspended, then that too evaporated leaving clear air. There was a distant groan, a drawn-out, gasping bellow which died away slowly, like the last gasp of a fallen giant.

Then, from the prison corridor came a series of detonations and a rising clamour of water and falling rock and . . . and the voices of dragons! Shouts and screams, whoops of joy and howls of agony, all these sounds tumbled round the corner and crashed into the ears of the rescue party, spurring them into action as they surged forward to see the miracle of the release of the dragons of Aether's Cross. A neck-high tidal wave of crystal water – the water which had until scant breaths before been held captive by Wraith's frozen charm – broke across them as they floundered down the tunnel but even that could not slow them, so desperate were they to see their quest achieved.

As the tails of their companions disappeared down the tunnel, Vox and Smoke lingered, their wings wrapped together in a tight embrace.

'We might still die here,' whispered Vox, nuzzling her with his snout.

'I wouldn't mind,' answered Smoke, 'not now I've found you.'

Vox looked back the way they had entered. Fresh water gushed in, a new wave bearing down on them with terrifying speed and breaking against its twin springing from the cells. 'Maybe not,' he gasped, floundering as the water reached up towards his mouth, 'but I'm not ready quite yet. How about you?'

Smoke rewarded him with that same, sun-bright smile. 'There's life in this dragon yet!' she cried, and together they leaped into the torrent of water, half-flying, half-swimming towards the confusion and the reunion of the great release.

Ledra threw herself into Archan's path as the great, white dragon bore down upon Hesper. Her back crashed against Archan's breast, knocking her bodily up into the sky at the very instant the red flames ripped out from inside Hesper's body. Metal and skin exploded into the air; a shower of Hesper's spiked scales sliced across Ledra's flank and she bent double with the pain. The light filled the entire world of these two warring dragons and it seemed for an instant that the heat would consume them before they had a chance either to flee or fight.

But they were not the fire's target. Outwards it reached, not upwards, its movement slowed by ribs of charm which held it captive. Ledra recovered swiftly, her thoughts speeding through her mind as they had never moved before as she looked down upon the awesome spectacle.

The ghost of Hesper remained, a dragon skeleton painted red by the fire which emanated from within it. The transparent bones were stretching with the flames, as though reluctant to let them go. As Ledra watched with horror and fascination she realized that Hesper had somehow controlled the magic, or contained it at least, and that without his presence the fire would simply have shot towards the heavens, spreading out across the world like a tremendous volcanic eruption, unfocused. What primal dragon essence it was that enabled him to wield this astonishing power she had no idea, but its effect was quite plain to see.

A disc of red light was expanding gradually from the very centre of the pillars, from the region of Hesper's heart in fact. Its edges were disordered but its essential circular form was pure and undisturbed. It grew and grew until it reached halfway towards the six basilisks, and that was when Ledra saw that two of the Deathless had confronted a third. She saw them grow bright, their pale hides dyed in the face of the approaching fire and then, just before the light consumed them, she saw one strike the other bodily from the pillar. It dropped beneath the disc, out of sight.

Then the fire ate the basilisks.

Their immortality gone, they died instantly, although their remains seemed to linger. Bones and meat and strange, fluctuating shapes like tiny shreds of charm were dragged back into the disc of light, which was fading now, its vital work done. In her belly Ledra felt a tremendous impact and a shockwave pumped her up into the sky before her ears caught any sound of the explosion. Opening her wings, wincing at the pain from the wounds in her flank, she dropped slowly back towards Hesper's remains, wondering what had happened to all the magic.

* * *

421

Archan knew. She too had watched the Gathering closely and she understood rather better than Ledra what had occurred, and what was about to occur. Now that the basilisks and Hesper were dead, the immortality which the charm had extracted from the Deathless existed in fabulous isolation. She could see it now, a skeleton-shape of magic which held all the powers of eternity within its seemingly fragile form. Her whole life had been directed towards this moment. All she had to do was reach out and take it for herself; the basilisks' unexpected use of Hesper as their sacrificial vessel had been a revelation, for it had moulded the immortality into an appropriate shape – a dragon shape into which she might slip with the minimum of effort. *All I need to do is exchange my bones for these*, she thought ecstatically, *and I will live forever!*

She folded her wings, hugged the hatching egg close to her breast and dropped into the dwindling fire.

Fortune started when he heard a voice at his side, but it was only Scoff.

'Not waiting back there,' the bright-winged dragon said. 'Got an idea.'

'You have?' asked Fortune, hardly able to take his eyes from the dazzling red flames which were already receding back into the space between the pillars. The basilisks were gone; he could not say he was sorry.

'Help Ledra,' was all Scoff added before he soared high above the lake and arrowed towards Archan, who was moving into the glowing heart of the fire. Fortune thought he could see bones twisting there. Was that what was left of Hesper?

Help Ledra? he wondered, then he saw her. She was floundering in the air in distress. Blood sprayed out from her side and Fortune realized that she had been badly wounded. Without thinking he thrust his wings backwards and sprinted towards her. Out of the corner of his eye he saw Archan folding her wings into the dissipating glow of the red fire. The bones stood out clearly, shrinking now and losing their strange, distorted quality. They appeared to be retreating into Archan's flesh. *The egg!* he thought frantically, but already he was upon Ledra.

'The egg!' she cried as he clutched her with his claws, and then her wings folded and she fainted. Grunting with the effort, Fortune struggled to carry her weight before dropping like a flightless juvenile. He jerked his wings in the unsympathetic air, turning his descent into a barely-controlled glide aimed towards Archan.

I might not have a plan, he decided, *but I do have a target.*

Her white wings filled his vision, though they seemed transparent, their skeleton clearly visible beneath the skin. Archan's pointed head lifted up towards him like a spike on to which he might impale himself. Then the spike broke in two as her mouth opened, revealing wicked fangs and a throat hot with flame. He pumped his wings hopelessly; Ledra was dead weight, unconscious and heavy in his claws. More wings, colourful and fast.

Scoff shot in front of Fortune, dragging Archan's gaze away from him and Ledra so that she twisted her neck right round upon itself. The nearest of the six pillars rose up at Fortune's side and he poured all his energy into a final effort. His wings throbbing, he managed to lift Ledra up to the top of the tower and deposit her gently on its flat peak. To his surprise a dragon was sitting there, as though waiting for his arrival. At first he did not recognize her, then he did.

'Aria!' he whispered.

'Save my son,' she answered, her voice light and shatteringly *adult*. Reaching out a wing she turned her attention to the fallen Ledra, pulling her close and murmuring to her. Fortune gave himself no time to think: flicking his wings wide and turning on the spot he overbalanced into a screaming dive which brought him down to the level of the water where he fanned the air and switched directions. Climbing now, eyes narrowed, head clear, he aimed himself square at Archan. Her wings were wide, her neck and tail outstretched, a white cross against the lingering red of the fire.

He was convinced she would sense his approach and unleash some dire charm upon him, but he had not reckoned on Scoff. He buzzed around her head, tugging and gnawing at the airspace around her until she began to twist and fight. As Fortune drew near he saw that Archan was growing tired; her energies were being drawn off somehow. Beneath her skin and scales her new skeleton pulsated with sickly red light and occasionally her neck writhed not in retaliation but with pain. But he cared little for her trials; he wanted only the egg.

She had transferred it from her tail as soon as she had uncoiled herself and it was held firmly now in her foreclaws. Fortune could see it bulging and cracking, but worse – he could see the red fire inside Archan's bones reaching down into her claws and opening out into the air. Even as he watched he saw tiny flickers of lightning stretch themselves from the bones of her legs and draw a filigree of charm across the shell of Aria's egg. Then it too began to glow. Fortune judged that he was not flying anywhere near fast enough to reach it before it was entirely consumed.

I'm too late! he thought desperately. *She will take the infant into eternity with her. She will steal even my grandchild from me!*

Archan's new skeleton of fire pumped its energies into Aria's egg and it seemed that here, at the last, the white dragon would win.

The scene which met the eyes of Vox and Smoke was one of utter chaos. Water filled half of the winding tunnel and atop the waves there splashed dragons, hundreds of them. Wings whipped foam and necks coiled high against the ceiling; dragon eyes blinked into the stabbing light charms and dragon mouths cried greetings and howled fears amid the confusion. The sense of relief was overwhelming, but so too was the growing awareness of greater peril. The gaping cavities of the breached cells appeared only sporadically above the water level, and rising along with the water now was an irresistible panic, for the escapees had emerged from flooding cells into flooding corridor and there seemed no way of escape. Cumber's fear that former prisoners would turn on ex-Charmed saviours had proven unfounded, but only by virtue of the fact that the pandemonium was so great no dragon seemed to know what was going on. Then a single voice rang out through the uproar.

'This way, dragons!' It was Quill. Having busied herself

with ushering the more frightened of the Naturals out of their liquid cocoons she was now forging her way through the flood-water towards the far end of the prison tunnel, her wings flapping against the waves as though they were air. Through the mayhem Vox caught sight of Cumber and Brace, grappling together to keep a frail old dragon above the water level, and forced his way over to them.

'What's she doing?' he bellowed.

'Scape thinks there's a way out,' answered Cumber. 'He's seen a light under the water; we're trying to get them all to follow.'

'It's impossible,' cried Brace, clearly beside himself. All around them dragons were thrashing and moaning, many of them slipping below the surface and coming up again only with the greatest of difficulty. 'I never thought it would be like this!'

'Light, did you say?' demanded Vox, pressing forward to where Quill was.

And there was a light. There, beneath the water, a great crack ran the full width of the corridor. From behind it there came a tremendous glow, a brilliant, blue-white incandescence which Vox knew at once. Judging the situation with reckless speed he came to a decision.

'Trollvein!' he shouted, and plunged straight down into the maelstrom. The limestone floor rushed to meet him and his horns struck the edges of the crack with a dull thud. Air exploded from his lungs as his body was jarred by the impact, and then claws grabbed at the spines on his back and he was hauled unceremoniously back up to the surface. It was Quill, dragging him bodily clear of the whirlpool which was beginning to form itself in the middle of the flood.

'Well done!' she announced with a voice like thunder. 'For a breath or two there I wasn't sure I was doing the right thing, but now you've done it!'

'What is it?' cried Brace, joining them at the edge of the spinning cone of water.

'It's Aether!' gurgled Vox, spitting out a mouthful of the icy water.

'He wasn't quite dead!' added Scape, joining them suddenly. 'Or his magic wasn't, at least. There must have been the tiniest thread of charm still alive in his body, and when Chaemen collapsed . . .'

'The glacier?' Brace was confused. His heart was thumping and his head felt dizzy. The quest was achieved, but the danger was still too great to contemplate, and here was Scape telling stories of charm while the ground opened up beneath his claws. And still he had not found his parents . . .

'Of course. That's where all this water's coming from. The whole interior of the glacier must have melted long ago – only a fragile skeleton of ice was left holding the whole thing together.'

'That's where the new trollvein came from,' Vox went on. 'The one which that basilisk monster vanished down, not that we realized it at the time. From the last of Aether's charm. And it cuts through here, directly below us!'

'Aether's legacy,' murmured Brace.

'It's the way out,' concluded Cumber softly, nudging Brace with his wing and offering him a dazzling smile. 'Do you want to lead the way?'

Brace looked down into the widening crevasse into which the water was thundering. Then he looked up and around to find all his friends poised on the edge of salvation with him. Cumber and Velvet were already teetering over the edge, laughing and clutching at each other as they fought to hold their balance; they had never looked more like the young lovers they were. And there were the others – Vox and Smoke, Quill and Scape, Tallow and Volley, all looking to him to make the critical move. He blinked back tears and glanced behind him. All movement but the rolling of the waves had ceased: dragons stared back at him, suddenly aware that their final destination was awaiting them.

'Dragons of Aether's Cross!' he bellowed. 'Follow me!'

Archan grew cloudy in Fortune's vision, then he realized that a cloud had in fact enveloped her. Scoff continued to buzz her, snapping and darting with outstretched claws and teeth, but she no longer appeared to be aware of his presence. Billowing white, as white as Archan's scales, the cloud rolled in from nowhere and wrapped itself around her wings and tail, tying them into immobility. She struggled in its grip, grunting and spitting with the effort. Then came Gossamer.

The cloud reached out welcoming tendrils towards her, defining a clear route through the red glow still surrounding Archan. Though he did not lower his speed, Fortune felt his thoughts checked by the sudden and strange manifestation, and he found himself recalling Gossamer's curious comments from the previous days : *We must trust in the Cloud* . . . *if the Cloud is willing* . . . Was this the Cloud?

Sounds were muffled by the swirling vapour – except the relentless cracking which was coming from the egg. As he neared Archan, Fortune became increasingly aware of the colossal power which had stored itself up inside her body, making her adopted skeleton glow with such ferocity. He prayed that it had not infiltrated the egg yet, that it only skated across its surface without violating its precious content. The power of immortality, locked beneath Archan's scales – would she truly live forever?

So Gossamer brought the Cloud to Archan, and Archan brought the egg to the brink of eternity, then everything froze. The water vapour which comprised the Cloud crystallized, locking the three dragons – Archan, Gossamer and Scoff – into a tableau of conflicting energies. Their positions were etched into Fortune's mind as he approached: Archan coiled backwards, arching her back in an effort to throw off the intruding presence; Scoff reaching out with his rainbow wings, trying to deflect Archan from her sustained hover; Gossamer, his own, dear Gossamer, white wings casting a great shadow across the monstrous dragon who had stolen their daughter's youth. Yet Gossamer's face was strangely serene.

Fortune's vision was filled with white now, the white of the cloud, of the scales of Archan and Gossamer. The white of the egg pushing through from behind the red.

Tipping on to his back, Fortune reached up with his claws and felt the slippery curve of Archan's soft underbelly skate across their sharp tips. Resisting the urge to extend them fully and rake her yielding flesh, he tucked his legs close instead then jabbed them out at the last moment. Fresh curves met his claws, the smooth, warm curves of his daughter's egg, and with the most delicate of touches he plucked the fragile thing from Archan's grasp. At once the veins of red light which had encased it winked out and it settled into his grip. Turning his back on the frozen dragons he wheeled in the air and descended swiftly to the top of the pillar where Aria lay waiting with Ledra, who had recovered from her swoon.

Aria accepted the egg with open wings, eagerly sweeping it beneath her body where it lay, twitching now as the infant within began to tap in earnest at the shell. As Fortune watched, it began to hatch.

Behind him the Cloud dissipated, wafted away into transparency by some unseen force and releasing the three captives. Scoff shook his head, dazed, while Gossamer ushered him swiftly away from Archan's side and down to the pillar where their loved ones awaited them. As they alighted, the energies pent up inside Archan's body finally released themselves.

With a soundless rush of wind the red skeleton of charm turned dazzling white and for an instant the watching dragons were blinded. Gradually their normal sight returned, and against the afterglow they saw an astonishing sight: thousands of glittering scales fluttering down from the place where Archan had been hovering, dancing and twisting on their way down to the water, to float at first then slowly sink, until all that remained of Archan's presence was a single white scale, resting on the snow at the very edge of the lake.

Archan was gone, and whether or not she had entered eternity the dragons could not say, nor did they care, for before them now the greatest miracle of all was occurring. Having emerged from a storm during which they believed their race to be at an end, they now found themselves witness to the hatching of the first of a new generation of dragons. And as Aria's son was born, the sky behind them grew dark. From the new trollvein, the gaping cave of white from which the last basilisk had been drawn, there surged a huge cloud of flying shapes. Dragons. The dragons of Aether's Cross, free at last and filling the sky with their long-restrained wings. At their head flew Brace, head held

proud and high, eyes sparkling with joy and gratitude and
suddenly with overwhelming emotion as he spied his sister
and the new-born infant nestled on the pillar below him.
He turned down, leading his fellow dragons on a flight of
victory across the lake.

'Gossamer!' he bellowed. 'We're back!'

CHAPTER 39

Mortal

The sensation of mortality was all-consuming. Ocher crashed against the icy bed of the lake, blowing out a great cloud of bubbles as its changed and vulnerable hide was dealt a massive blow. Pain it had long known, but not this . . . *fragility*. Crimson light blossomed behind its silver eyes and for an instant it believed that it was already dead. But not quite yet; even though by simply inhaling ice water it could have completed that ultimate transformation, still it paused, still it wondered.

It thought. It thought of the new natural world and of its unexpected beauty. It thought of mighty sea beasts and a thousand golden chitrakae, of the countless newborn denizens of these burgeoning lands. It thought of its own vulnerability now that both charm and immortality had abandoned its bones. *I can no longer fly*, it mused. *The Deathless cheated even in the skies. Only dragons have true flight*. The dragons; it thought of them too.

Freezing water pressed against its bony temples, its own silver blood pushing back until it felt trapped between the two opposing forces. The thump of its age-old heart had never been so loud. Five more beats and it would surely give out. Death had never been so close. Four, three . . .

The taste of mortality was like copper in Ocher's mouth. It faced death now, outstaring it as it surveyed the monster's every contour, tested its insatiable hunger. Its smell was sour and Ocher searched around, seeking something sweeter. It found something, the very thing which it had fled and which lay hidden now beneath its claws, much as the world itself had been hidden . . . it seemed so long ago now.

Never again will I leave this world, the basilisk thought ecstatically. *Except once, when I face this monster again.*

It chose the only remaining option. Life.

The sun beat on the back of Ocher's head as it emerged triumphant from the lake which had so nearly been its grave. Noon light sparkled off the drifts and ice crystals reaching down to the water's edge. All was blue-white and clean as creation. The charm was gone, the dome was gone, and the crest of the world seemed pure and open, inviting journey and discovery. Ocher crawled forth, revelling in the pull of muscle against flesh, fascinated by the beating of its own heart.

Each beat brings this body nearer to its end, it pondered. *How do mortal creatures come to terms with this knowledge?*

But for the moment the question was academic, so overjoyed was the basilisk to have bettered its siblings. It alone of the Deathless would experience the joy and horror of mortality; it alone would savour the anticipation of the final blow, from wherever it might come. The thrill was immeasurable; now it truly understood the precious nature of life.

The basilisk detected movement high on one of the six pillars, then noticed the great swarm of dragons wheeling in the sky over the place of the Gathering. Voices buzzed and wings whirred. The signs of celebration were unmistakable. Fascinated, aware that it in some way owed these dragons a tremendous debt, Ocher dragged itself over to the base of the hexagonal column and began to climb.

Halfway up the tower it was struck with a new and dreadful fear, for it suddenly realized that if it fell it would die. Paralysed by this unanticipated revelation, it clung to the craggy sides of the column, claws locked in an almost unbreakable grip. By degrees it forced itself to relax, and even found a place for its recently acquired sense of wonder in this predicament. Here again was a new experience, a new sensation. The basilisk who had thought itself to have seen every possible event many times over was suddenly confronted with something hitherto unseen. The thrill was unparalleled.

Eventually it reached the top, although not before several of the circling dragons had nosed in to inspect it. Each time it froze, locking its claws again and closing its blank, silver eyes. Though Ocher's breath had lost its powers, an insistent itching at the corners of its eyes informed it that its gaze might still be lethal, the legacy of some internal charm still reluctant to abandon its host. Though the power was controllable, it had no desire to knock any of these creatures from the air by some accidental glare. The interest continued until it pulled itself up over the sharp lip of the tower and on to the six-sided plateau which was its crown. Here a small group of dragons lay gathered around one of their number, and as Ocher approached their eyes tracked it with unguarded suspicion.

Keeping its head low and trying to move in as unthreatening a manner as it could, the basilisk cautiously approached the group. Though it knew their language it considered words to be inappropriate; instead it sought out the one dragon it remembered well. *Fortune*. The dragon from the Maze, the dragon who had helped the world to turn true.

The young dragon regarded Ocher mildly as the squat creature crawled up to him. Clearly he felt safe in the basilisk's presence and this made Ocher feel strangely humble. It resolved anew to do nothing to harm any one of these noble creatures. In seeing Fortune again it felt a great peace descend, and a sense of circularity, but it was more excited by the presence here of the dragon it had detected from afar when it had flown for the last time to the citadel: Fortune's daughter. And her son.

Here indeed is the future for these beasts of the air, it thought, *though not in any way they will expect*. It drew nearer, inspecting the scene so that it might remember it vividly in the years to come.

Aria lay curled around the remains of her egg. Broken shell and strings of mucus lay strewn across her tail but she showed no concern, so enraptured was she by the tiny form which she held close to her breast.

The infant dragon was small and dark, its tightly bound scales nearly black. Dark eyes gleamed beneath a soft brow and it seemed to pant rather than breathe; its gaze was wide and alert. Its wings must have been tucked behind it, for Ocher could see nothing but the smooth curve of its back, unmarred by spine or ridge. Minute teeth shone brilliant white against the shadow of its smile and it seemed to nod at Ocher as the basilisk leaned close . . . then backed slowly away.

The moment was sufficient, and already the dragons were closing round, understandably protective of their new heir. Ocher watched as they turned their attention away from the basilisk again and in towards their own, small cosmos. Words exploded from the group.

'I've seen his face before, I'm telling you.' That was a white-winged male talking, his movements nervous and skittish. Ocher identified him as the dragon with whom Bacht had tried to join. A white female hugged him close, her smile tired but full of conviction. 'I can't remember where though. I mean, it might have been somewhere in that cursed citadel . . . but no, it can't have been, can it . . . ?'

'Well I think he looks like Brace,' said Fortune's mate happily. She too was white, but her radiance fairly exploded from her scales and Ocher was struck with a sudden premonition. *The sky alive with fire. The last of the night dragons and the coming of creation.* An incomprehensible vision sped across its inner eye and was gone, leaving trails of white light dancing before it. The trails coalesced around the female's head, appearing to form a protective cloud. She glanced briefly at Ocher and her look was one of majesty.

Shaken, wondering at the surprises these strange mortals continued to hurl at it, Ocher looked up at the dragon to whom Fortune's mate was looking, a young Natural with the fire of triumph in his eyes. Brace then, this one, and he was about to speak when behind him approached two others. They were older dragons, one male and one female, and Ocher could see at once a shared look, a common twist of the wing. It saw the female's eyes widen further and her mouth drop open, then it saw Brace turn and nearly fall from the sky with shock.

As Brace and Gossamer were reunited with their parents, Ocher discovered a sorrow it had never known. Sexless, birthless, a true eternal, it had neither sire nor heir. Awareness of the continuity which these mortal creatures enjoyed came as a vicious, low blow, and it recalled one of Wraith's final terrors, a rogue thought Ocher had snatched from the dying dragon's mind as the basilisk had coasted through the crumbling Maze in search of oblivion. It concerned Welkin, Fortune's father: Wraith had for an instant believed that Welkin's spirit permeated all natural dragons, and that he would never be rid of the one who had shamed him. So now did Ocher find wonder in the dragon spirit which all these creatures of the sky shared, and it hoped that its belief in their future was founded in fact and not some misguided instinct.

There seemed no more to see or to do, and certainly nothing to say, and as the flying dragons closed in on the seated group Ocher turned fully away and reached its claws over the edge of the tower's peak. Just before it began its descent it stopped, for the voices behind it had grown hushed and it could not help but wonder what was about to be said. After a few moments of whispering, it was Fortune's voice which rang out.

'Welcome back, all of you,' he said, his words strong and confident. 'I know there is much you want to ask, and there are many stories we are all anxious to share, but first there is a duty to be done. The world has turned, and in doing so it has twisted itself badly out of shape. But the storm is passing now, or so I pray, and we must look forward rather than back. Many things have been reshaped, not least the flow and even the meaning of time itself, as a result of which Gossamer and I find ourselves present at the birth of our daughter's son, when we ourselves are barely adults. This is not the way things should be, but it is the way things are and we must accept that.

'So take heart, dragons, for here we find the hope we have searched for. Above me fly Rarch and Jevell, the parents of my own dear Gossamer, the grandparents of my daughter Aria and the great-grandparents of her son. Their coming is symbolic, I believe, for our greatest fear in recent times has been for our future. Dragons may still be sterile – or they may not, only time will tell – but one thing is certain: here today we can see together four generations of dragon pushing the flow of the river of time forward into another land. Aria's son is born into that river; let us hope he will one day lead us to the new haven we all yearn for.'

There was some whispering which Ocher did not hear, then a clear, female voice spoke out. Ocher deduced at once that it was Aria and as she spoke, though her words were few, the basilisk found itself transported back to the instant of revelation it had experienced when first it had embarked on its final quest, when it had remembered the one thing which had catalysed the entire sequence of events leading up to the gathering of the Deathless.

'This is my son,' said Aria, her voice like crystal, 'and I name him. He shall be called Wyrm.'

His name! thought Ocher, hot tears welling in its silver eyes.

One final cry echoed in Ocher's head as it lowered itself cautiously down the tower. A dragon – it was not certain which – asked a question of one of its fellows.

'She was a nasty one, all right. I wonder what really happened to her?'

Ocher nodded. It had its suspicions as to what had happened to Archan, but it would not speak them, not to these innocent dragons at least. Perhaps one day it might seek the answer to the riddle . . . or perhaps not. There were many things it wanted to do now that the Gathering was achieved. Many things indeed.

It dropped the last half-tree to the soft snow and began the long journey south. There was no other direction to go, of course, but it had a good idea of some of the places it wished to visit first. Crawling clear of the short shadow of the tower it wondered how long it would take it to travel the great distances it had once conquered in the blink of an eye. Such things had never mattered before; they mattered now, and the basilisk had no desire to waste any time.

After all, life was too short.

EPILOGUE

THE LAKE FROZE SWIFTLY. Although the general global heating proceeded unabated the local temperature at the polar cap, raised temporarily by the events of the Gathering, fell once more and ice reclaimed the crest of the world. The sun did not set however, and would not for some time; midday lingered here, and so did dragons.

Fortune and Cumber lay together on the shore of the lake. Powdery snow was blowing in, covering the fresh ice. Though vanishing slowly beneath the drifts, this blue-white surface remained visible for the time being, a polished plate in which the sun was reflected with maddening intensity. The two dragons searched its depths, seeking the answers to riddles.

'We'll have to go soon,' said Fortune. 'It's getting colder again.'

'I suppose so,' sighed Cumber. The thought of yet another exodus weighed heavily upon his young shoulders. Behind them the massed dragons of Aether's Cross – and their own friends and lovers – were beginning to stir restlessly. Where would they find the energy for yet another great journey?

'Wherever we go must be safe,' added Fortune, interrupting Cumber's wandering thoughts. 'It's protection we need now, protection for Aria. And Wyrm. Especially for Wyrm.'

Cumber nodded. 'An infant dragon needs a great deal of looking after,' he said. Then he added carefully, 'Especially one born without wings.'

Fortune did not reply, simply gazed into the depths of the crystallized lake. 'We're all vulnerable now,' he whispered.

More snow blew in front of them, and the whistle of the

wind was sharp in their ears. Both shivered – it was time to leave.

'I wonder what happened to Archan,' blurted Fortune suddenly. 'There are so many questions buzzing in my head but of them all that's the one I want most to know the answer to. Isn't that strange?'

'Archan,' mused Cumber, brushing at the snow with his white-scaled tail. 'Well, I have a theory, if you want to hear it, that is.'

'Put me out of my misery,' answered Fortune, his smile suddenly dazzling in the sunlight.

'Come here,' said Cumber, and he ushered Fortune down to the lakeside. 'What do you see?'

Fortune peered into the deep. He saw shapes abstracted from the ice: weird flaws of air and water; bubbles trapped beneath fractured layers; great blue slabs vanishing into darkness. 'I see ice,' he ventured.

'Look closer.'

Fortune looked deeper. As he focused, the lake seemed to expand, absorbing him into its boundaries as though he were but a part of the landscape. Further down into the very heart of the lake he looked, until he began to see something else, something entirely lacking the blue frigidity of the ice, something red and riblike, something . . . moving? He squinted, dropping to his belly and craning his neck out in an effort to see more clearly.

'What is it?' he asked.

Cumber paused, then responded, 'I noticed it when we first came down here, and I wasn't sure what it was. But then I started thinking about your account of the Gathering and something didn't quite add up.'

'Go on.'

'Well, what I mean is, the basilisks gave up their immortality, and in doing so they made it solid – that was the red form you said you saw, the thing that looked like a skeleton – and then Archan actually absorbed it and so she must have become immortal.'

'But we saw her destroyed. There was nothing left of her but a few scales.'

'Exactly. Remember the fight we saw – the two basilisks

at the citadel? When one was blown to pieces we saw it reassembled before our eyes, but the charm that took must have been phenomenal. Well, the same thing obviously happened to Archan – some final discharge of magic from the Gathering, I suspect – *but there wasn't nearly enough charm left around to recreate her body!'*

Fortune was aghast. 'But where is she then? How can she still be alive if her body is gone forever?'

'I don't know *what* she might be now,' pondered Cumber, 'but I think I know *where* she is.'

All through this exchange Fortune had been staring at Cumber, his attention diverted from the lake. But now he followed his friend's gaze as it swivelled down again on to the ice. Into the ice. Down, down *through* the ice, to where pale bones of red swam hopelessly in their cold and impenetrable prison. He stared long, watching the endless, circling motion of the faint and blurred shape, trying to imagine the prospect of an eternity without freedom. He could not, but inside his head he fancied he could hear the thinnest of screams, an endless string of sound which cut tiny lines across the surface of the ice, lines which quickly filled with snow and were gone.

For a long time neither dragon spoke, then as one they turned to find their friends waiting behind them. At the head of their group was Aria, her head high and proud, a dark bundle of scales bunched on her back.

'Well, father,' she asked, 'which way do we go?'

Fortune thought for a breath or two, then shrugged. 'South, I suppose.'